W9-CTX-303

Praise for *Beyond the Red*

"Ava Jae's *Beyond the Red* is a sand-swept fantasy of court politics, rebel attacks, and forbidden romance. While reading, I had flashes of *Star Wars*—a new planet, a fascinating culture, a fresh look on a ruler struggling to keep her power—and I had to know what happened next. Dangerous, exciting, and fast-paced, *Beyond the Red* is a story not to be missed."

—Francesca Zappia, author of *Made You Up*

"Packed with political intrigue and smoldering romance, *Beyond the Red* left me craving more of Kora's and Eros's story and the unique, fascinating universe that Ava Jae has created."

—Sarah Harian, author of *The Wicked We Have Done*

"*Beyond the Red* is a sweeping, compelling romance in a complicated and gritty world. Intrigue and heart on every page—I couldn't put it down. I'll be following Ava Jae to see what comes next!"

—Kate Brauning, author of *How We Fall*

"I loved this book! I couldn't put it down! What a fantastic debut, perfect for fans of *Firefly* and *Star Wars*. Ava Jae's *Beyond the Red* packs a punch, a total thrill ride that will keep readers turning the pages. I stayed up all night reading it. From page one, I was sucked in. Jae's writing style is a perfect mix of stop and go, and her world comes to life within the first few pages. The action was power-packed, and the star-crossed romance had me begging for more by the end."

—Lindsay Cummings, author of The Murder Complex series

BEYOND THE RED

AVA JAE

WITHDRAWN

Sky Pony Press

NEW YORK

Sky Pony Press books may be purchased in bulk at special discounts for sales promotion, corporate gifts, fund-raising, or educational purposes. Special editions can also be created to specifications. For details, contact the Special Sales Department, Sky Pony Press, 307 West 36th Street, 11th Floor, New York, NY 10018 or info@skyhorsepublishing.com.

Sky Pony is a registered trademark of Skyhorse Publishing, Inc., a Delaware corporation.

Visit our website at www.skyponypress.com.

10 9 8 7 6 5 4 3 2 1

Library of Congress Cataloging-in-Publication Data is available on file.

Cover design by Sarah Brody
Map design by Kerri Frail

Print ISBN: 978-1-63450-644-1
Ebook ISBN: 978-1-63450-645-8

Printed in the United States of America

To my maker, with all the love You've given me.

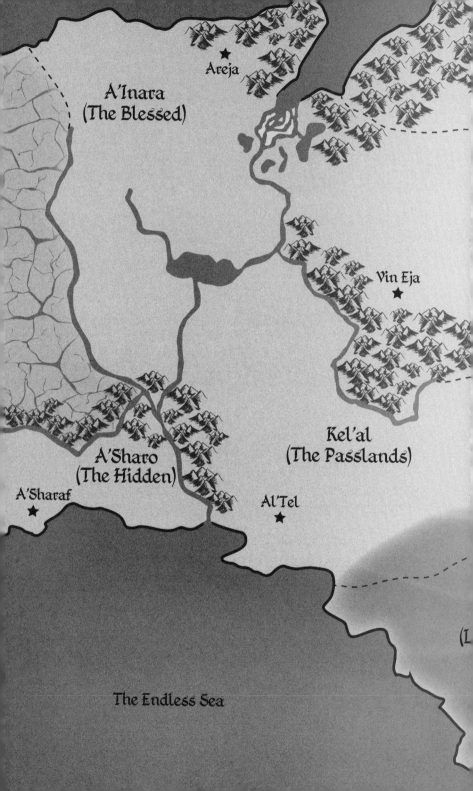

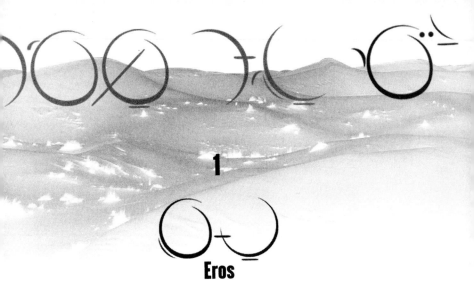

Eros

My brother just killed me. Again. I know, because I wake with a knife to my throat and the cool barrel of a phaser pressed against my forehead. Good morning to you, too.

"Blazing suns, Day," I murmur, rubbing the grogginess from my eyes. "If a Sepharon soldier manages to find camp while I'm sleeping, I accept I'm dead, okay? Now let me rest."

I'm ready for some kinduv snappy comment about how I'm dead twice now—when I'm too tired for Day's drills, he sometimes mock-kills me in six or seven different ways before launching into his *the aliens won't let you rest* spiel—but it doesn't come. Maybe I should apologize for not taking him seriously, but it's hard to be amped up all the time over such a distant threat. Most of us haven't even *seen* a Sepharon, let alone come close enough to have to fight one, even if Day insists we'll eventually have to.

Still, the quiet is unlike him.

I lower my hands and peer into the darkness of the tent. It must be earlier than I thought, because the suns haven't risen yet. A shadowy figure cloaked in black stands over me. Silence twists through my chest. The hiss of shifting sand nearby sets my pulse racing. There are others here. And since when does Day wear a cloak?

"Sit up, boy," the figure says, and his light voice surprises me—he's a kid, can't be older than fourteen—and he's calling *me* boy? He nudges the phaser. "Scream for help and I'll cook your brain."

I sit up. Carefully. No sudden movements. My fingers are cold and my heart's about to explode, but I force a slow exhale and swallow a bout of nausea. If this is some kinduv training exercise, Day's gone *way* too far. As head of security, my brother's obligated to be paranoid about raids from the Eljan Guard, but if they ever find us, they won't sneak into my tent and hold me at phaserpoint—they'll just raze the place to the ground.

A thought worms into my mind and a shot of ice hits me in the stomach. *What if this isn't a drill?*

My eyes adjust, and I can make out the others—three figures cloaked in dark colors, curved black phasers in hand, standing near the entrance of my tent. They shift nervously, and one is digging the toes of his left foot into the red sand. Definitely not trained soldiers. Judging by their lack of height and use of English, they're human, which means they're probably from camp. So what do they think they're doing?

If they weren't armed, I could take them out easily, but I'm not willing to risk a lucky shot to the chest with a phaser blast. The only way for me to escape this would be to turn their weapons against them. There's no way I'd do that to a bunch of kids.

"We should hurry," one of the companions whispers, and the boy holding the phaser and knife outstretched nods and steps back.

"Get up."

I slip off my bedroll and reach for my pants folded at my feet, but the hum of a charging phaser and the telltale red glow stops me in mid-reach. Red, not white. It's actually set to kill, the little star-cursed idiots.

"What are you reaching for?" the boy's voice is high and tight. "I'll kill you, I swear I'll—"

"I'm putting on pants," I say calmly. "Unless you plan to parade me around camp naked?"

A long pause. "Just hurry up."

I've barely thrown on a pair of shorts when the warm barrel of the phaser nudges my spine. "That's enough," he says. "Put these on."

He passes me two smooth metal cuffs.

"Where are you taking me?" I ask.

"We don't answer to half-blood bastards," one of them says. It's meant to be an insult, but the words roll harmlessly off my shoulders.

"Put them on," the boy behind me demands, pressing closer to me. I could refuse, but the heat of the charged phaser on my skin makes me think better of it, so I slide them on. They shrink to mold to my wrists, their edges glowing blue as the magnet activates. The boy pulls my hands behind my back and the cuffs snap together.

"Move."

I duck out of the tent. A blast of warm wind slaps my face with chalky scarlet sand. Powder coats my tongue and absorbs the moisture in my throat, turning cold and muddy in my mouth. My foot catches on one of the tent supports, and without my hands to break the fall, I slam into sand, my tent crumpling behind me. Something hard presses into my thigh—the metal handle of the switchblade in my left pocket. One of them grabs my shoulder and yanks me to my feet—or tries, anyway, but he's barely gone through his voice drop and I'm not exactly a small guy. I shift onto my knees, then stand. They prod me forward through the maze of sleeping tents, each marked with a circular family crest of varying designs and colors. I spit cool, bland sludge.

I can see my captors more clearly under the light of the quadruple moon-dotted sky. The tallest is nearly a foot shorter than me. They wear matching black hoods with scarves covering their mouths and noses and long dark clothing to conceal their skin. Each of them carries several weapons—knives, phasers, and a club. Their movements are swift and silent, their heads ducked, as though they're afraid of being seen as they keep me between them. They move with a synchronization that twists my stomach—I'm not the first person they've taken.

As we move through camp, the hum of the phaser at my back keeps my mouth shut. I don't doubt they'd use any opportunity to roast my organs with a well-placed pulse.

It's not long before camp is a circle of tents in a valley of crimson sand way behind us. Our destination—a sleek capsule-shaped transport with a flat base and trunk—rests on a dune up ahead. It's camo'd, the color of the dark purple night sky, the paint shimmering slightly as it adjusts to its surroundings. Even the mirror-glass making up the front half of the port is ultra-reflective to help it blend. Camo'd ports are practically invisible when hovering a foot off the ground—and not exactly cheap transport considering the intensely expensive exterior and near-silent engine that lets it race over the sands with little noise.

I arch an eyebrow. "Where'd you get the port?"

"Shut up," the boy at my back says. His voice I recognize. I can't for the life of me remember his name, but I work with his sister, Aryana.

She hates me. Like most people. Though for her it has to do more with too much brew and a messy lay in the sand she won't talk about than it does my blood. Still.

"It's not like anyone will hear us out here," I say. "And it sure as sand didn't come from camp." After a long silence, I add, "Do your mothers know what you're doing?"

"Shut up."

We reach the back of the port and one of the boys presses his palm against the horizontal seam between the doors. It opens with a hiss as the bottom door digs into the sand. The boy beside me gestures inside.

"You still haven't told me where you're taking—"

Sand explodes at my feet just as I register the screech of a phaser pulse. I gasp and stumble back, crashing into someone. The kid at my back gives me a hard shove as the trigger-happy boy soldier levels the phaser over my heart.

"Shut your mouth and get inside. I'm not giving you a second warning."

I climb in with my heart in my throat and sand stinging my eyes. The doors come together like a closing eye and hum as the seal locks. The compartment goes black. Their footsteps whisper in the sand and thump as they climb into the front seat.

I wait for my eyes to adjust. Someone to my right is sniffling, and the metal floor is cold on my bare feet. Breathing fills the empty silence, and I make out the whimpering form in the shadows.

A kid. They've taken a kid.

"Hey," I sigh. "Are you okay?"

The walls shudder as the engine hums to life and the port rises off the sand. The sniffling in the corner breaks into outright sobbing. I crouch and move near the huddled figure in the corner. My eyes have fully adjusted now; his cropped blond hair and shivering form emerge through the dark. He's thin and small—maybe four or five years old.

"My name is Eros," I whisper. "What's yours?"

He quiets and peers up at me from between his arms. The shadows obscure most of his face, but—

"Uncle Eros?"

I tense as a flash of heat races through me, and for a split second I wish I'd beaten the stars out of those kids. Then his wide, terrified eyes fill with fresh tears, and I bury those emotions where he can't see them.

"Aren," I breathe, scooting next to him. "Are you okay? Did they hurt you?"

He hugs me tightly. His little arms are covered in a fine layer of sand, and despite the heat, he shivers against me. "I'm scared," he whispers.

I lean forward and kiss the top of his head. "Don't worry, buddy. I'll protect you."

We sit like that in near silence, with only the hum of the transport and the occasional gust of wind against the walls. Heat prickles the back of my neck. In a couple hours, my family will wake to find Aren and me missing. Will they be relieved to know Aren isn't alone, because I was taken too? Will they think us dead? I knocked over my tent so they'd see there was a struggle. If we're lucky, Day will be able to follow our tracks to wherever they take us.

I just hope he won't be too late.

The seconds drip into minutes slower than the setting suns during the season of endless days—but eventually we come to a stop, and the port lowers into the sand. Aren hugs me tighter as I shift in front of him, pressing his little body into the corner. He doesn't protest, but his fingers dig into my skin.

"Aren," I say softly. "I need you to be brave for me, okay?"

He shakes his head and whimpers into my side.

I bite my lip. My heart races and sweat slips down my temple, but I try to sound calm. "Let's play a game. I know you like games."

His grip loosens a smidge and he glances up at me. "A game?"

"It's called soldier, like your dad and me. Doesn't that sound fun?" He hesitates and I continue before he can say no. "We're going to pretend you're a soldier tonight, so you're going to have to be extra brave to win. Think you can do that?"

Aren pauses, then nods. "Okay," he whispers.

"Good. There's a special soldier tool in my pocket right next to your leg. I need you to take it out of my pocket and hide it in yours, then when I say so, slide it into my hand without letting the others see. Think you can do that?"

His breath shivers as he exhales. "Yes. I think so."

"Okay. Take it out of my pocket."

Aren unseals my pocket and pulls the switchblade out. He looks at it for a mo, then drops it into his pants pocket and smiles at me. "I did it."

"That's good. Now, when I say—"

The doors pull apart and bright light floods the compartment. I squint away, unable to shield my face with my arms.

All I see is the burning white shining into the van, and then a hand grabs my shoulder and rips me away from Aren. He screams and I twist back to face him.

"It's okay!" I shout. "Aren, don't—"

Another tug—the port's floor disappears beneath me and the night topples sideways. Sand fills my mouth and nose, turning cold on my tongue. Heat and the salty taste of rust drips down my face as I spit saliva, muddy sand, and blood, and someone grabs a fistful of my hair and yanks me to my feet. I squint through the tears washing the sand from my eyes and the blinding light from their torches. Seven shadowy figures. Four of them I expected—the boys that pulled Aren and me from the camp—but the other three tower over the boys, the tallest standing a foot and a half over the shortest kid. Dark hair trimmed to military perfection. Skin suns-bronzed like ours, but darker, with paths of lighter skin filled with black circle-like text, marking their bodies like elaborate maps. Towering forms stronger, faster, and born with better senses than any human. Trim white and red uniforms of the Eljan Guard.

Fuck. They're Sepharon soldiers.

I guess Day was right about those drills after all.

One of the boys places Aren next to me, and he clings to my side again, his cheeks stained with tears. No one pulls him away. I'm just relieved they didn't cuff him.

A quick glance around rewards me with nothing but endless sands. I'm not sure how far they took us from camp, but the cluster of tents, fire pit, livestock pen, and parked ports aren't visible from here.

"We brought two," the tallest of the boys says in broken Sephari, hesitantly stepping toward the soldiers. "Like we agreed."

The center soldier snorts and steps toward us. "These are hardly quality workers." He circles us, and his dark skin gleams in the light of the moons. The soldier glares with multi-toned eyes—rings of color after color. Aren shrinks into my side, but I meet the soldier's eyes when he leers down at me. The corner of his lip quirks and he steps in front of me.

"This one may do," he says. "What is his age?"

The boys glance at each other, so I speak for myself. "Eighteen."

He arches an eyebrow and nods at one of the other soldiers. The shortest one tosses him a light, and he shines it in my face. I grimace and try my best to keep eye contact. My eyes burn and tear up.

But it's not my eyes he's looking at.

The soldier brushes my shaggy dark hair out of the way and grabs my ear. I scowl but I don't dare pull away—if he didn't let go, I might lose an ear. It doesn't last long, though—it only takes seconds to recognize my misshapen ears. Not quite long, pointed and notched like the alien Sepharon, nor short, smooth and round like the humans. The light moves to my chest, illuminating the faint maze-like lines of slightly lighter skin winding around my body. Not as prominent as the ones the Sepharon are born with, but definitely still there.

Definitely not human.

He shoves me away and turns on the boys. "A half-blood? You try to sell me a baby and a half-blood? How dare you insult us?"

The boy stammers and stumbles back. I nudge Aren and nod. He stares at me blankly and my stomach plummets—he's forgotten our game. But then he slides the smooth handle into my fingers and cool relief surges through me. I conceal the knife in my fists and pull my shoulders back.

"He's strong!" The smallest boy jumps in. "And faster than the rest of us. He—we thought—"

The soldier pulls out a phaser. The boys scream, but it's too late. I push Aren into the sand with my shoulder as the screech of the pulse shatters the night.

"Run!" I hiss, jumping to my feet. Aren scrambles up and races toward the port as three more pulses stop hearts just ten feet ahead of me. Nausea roils inside me. Their mothers will be devastated in the morning—I can already see the somber cremations and ashes floating through the quiet wind, releasing their souls to the stars. The kids were fucken morons, thinking they could make an equal trade with Sepharon soldiers—and with people from camp, no less—but they didn't deserve to die.

Then the soldiers face me.

I could turn and run, but then they'd probably shoot me in the back. And even if they didn't, they'd see I'm armed. And I'd lead them right to Aren.

So I don't move. I stand as tall and straight as I can manage and look them right in the eye as they step toward me. With any luck, their sense of honor will keep them from shooting me outright. They respect bravery and strength, and it's all I have to bargain with.

But it won't be enough. Not when most of my kind are killed at birth.

The soldiers are half a head taller than me, but they don't tower over me like they did my human captors.

"You don't run," the tallest says, a man with swirling, sharp markings, like the contour of sand dunes.

There are many things I'd like to say, but I go with the answer most likely to keep my head on my shoulders: "I'm not a coward."

They smirk at me and I fight the twisting of my stomach. The switchblade slips in my sweaty fingers and I readjust my grip.

"You should not be here," the leader says—the darkest of the three, the one who nearly ripped my ear off. He doesn't mean the desert—he means alive.

I take a risk. "*Kala* has wished it so, or I wouldn't be."

Their eyes widen. A fist slams into my cheek. I stagger sideways, but manage to stay on my feet. The leader grabs my throat and pulls me onto the tips of my toes. Stars speckle my vision and it's all I can do not to drop the useless knife. I struggle against the cuffs, but the magnet is too strong. Spots of darkness blot out the night and my lungs are burning. My head is pounding. My eyes fail and pain shoots down my neck and I can't do anything. I can't even struggle.

Then the magnet turns off and my wrists separate. I'm blind, but my hands are free.

My hands. The knife.

I squeeze the hilt, releasing the blade like I've done a thousand times, and slash it across the leader's throat. Though I can't see, my aim is true—hot, sticky liquid slaps my face and he drops me. I gasp in a mouthful of desert and spit blood, spit sand, swallow air, taste sickly sweet rust. My face is sticky, my lips are sticky, the sand is turning dark and cold next to my head.

Someone screams and I've got seconds before they execute me like a rabid animal, but I'm so heavy. I still need air.

I need to move, but all I can do is lie in the sand and shake like a terrified child.

Like Aren. I can't leave Aren. I have to get up and protect him before it's too late, before—

Two screeching phaser pulses rip through the air, and I should be dead. But my vision is clearing, and the burning in my chest is fading, and I can move, slowly, carefully, muscle by muscle. I push onto my knees. Squeeze the slippery knife.

There are seven bloody bodies in the sand.

Someone grabs my shoulder and I lash out with the knife. A hand catches my wrist and twists hard. My fingers release the weapon, and I pivot into a punch, but then I see him.

Day catches my fist, then releases my hands and clasps my head. "Breathe," my brother says, staring hard into me with familiar blue eyes. "It's me. You're safe."

His words crumble my defenses like a phaser cannon to a decrepit wall. There are so many things I want to say, so many *thank yous* and *how am I alives* and *how are you heres*, but instead I say, "Is Aren okay? Did he see what happened?"

"He's fine, thanks to you." Day runs a hand through his short blonde hair as he glances around the blood-soaked sand. "A little shaken up, but fine. I told him to cover his eyes and wait behind the port."

I nod. Exhale. Wipe my sticky palms on my pants. "He can't see me like this," I say. "I'll terrify him."

Day pulls a cloth out of his pocket and wets it with his flask. I wipe off my face until the rag turns dark purple from the soldier's blood, but my skin still feels stiff and tacky. It'll have to do though, because we don't have water to waste. I stand and he passes me my knife.

"Are you sure you're all right? I was worried I didn't unlock the cuffs in time."

"I'll be fine. How'd you find us?"

Day grimaces. "Mal woke me up to say Aren was missing, and when I saw your tent knocked over . . ."

I nod and glance around. "You came out here alone?"

"You think I'd waste time gathering backup when my son and kid brother were missing?" I force a stiff smile and he shoves my shoulder. "Besides, I wouldn't deserve my position if I couldn't handle a couple alien assholes on my own."

He helps me to my feet and I nod at the transport parked in the sand. "Any idea where they got the port?"

"I was hoping you knew."

After relieving the dead of their weapons, we step around to the driver's side and Aren leaps up and attaches himself to his father's leg. Day pulls him into his arms as I press my palm against the sealed mirror-glass door. It doesn't open.

"We could break it," Day suggests with a shrug.

"With what? You know not even phasers can get through this stuff."

"Hmm." Day looks over the sleek, reflective exterior, shifts Aren to his back, and peers inside, cupping his hands around his eyes. I don't need to try to know he can't see a blazing thing.

He leans back, running his thumb over the small patch of hair below his lip. He nods at the bloody knife in my hand. "Hack off a soldier's hand, then. I'll cover Aren's eyes."

I grimace. "Right, because sawing through reinforced Sepharon bone with a dagger is as easy as making sand mud."

"True." He shifts Aren higher and squints at the port. "Well, the kids were driving it, weren't they?"

I glance at Day. Back to the bodies in the sand. My stomach churns. "You think the door's coded to their palm prints?"

"I'll cover Aren's eyes."

I sigh and step around the port, clutching the knife in my slippery fist. "Give me a few mos. Don't let him peek, Day."

He says something, but I can't focus on his words—my gaze is caught on the smallest boy with trim black hair and olive skin. The boy sprawled face-first in the sand with a singed hole the size of a curled-up lizardmouse in the center of his cloak.

I shouldn't turn him around. I shouldn't look at his face. I shouldn't try to recognize him when it doesn't matter, not anymore.

I do it anyway.

He's staring right at me and my breath freezes in my lungs. Wide hazel eyes and thick dark lashes, exactly like his sister. Aryana despises me already—what will she think when we return her little brother's body to her family? Why do I care?

I crouch beside him and close his eyes. Glance at his hand. The knife is shaking in my grip, but I can't bear to do it, so I slip it into my pocket and grunt as I hoist the kid over my shoulder. He's heavier than I expected, but it's not too much.

"Toma," Day sighs as I step around the port. His name is a boulder in my stomach—the name I couldn't remember. Toma, Aryana's brother, now deadweight on my shoulder. "Did he and the others . . . abduct you?"

I shift Toma's body into my arms. "It doesn't matter."

"How did a bunch of kids—"

"It doesn't matter!" I snap. Close my eyes. Inhale. Open again.

Day shakes his head. "You're too soft, Eros." He places a hand on my shoulder. "It's going to get you killed if you're not careful."

I ignore him and press Toma's hand against the glass. The door hisses, then pops open.

Resting the body in the sand, I peer around the long front bench. It was obviously built for Sepharon adults, who are way taller than most humans—the bench and backrest are much larger than anything a human would need. The kids were small enough that the four of them were probably able to easily cram in.

I climb in and glance around the compartment. I'm not sure what I'm looking for; it just seems odd that they would've had easy access to a port. Nomads never use ports this large—they're too conspicuous. Most of us have sand bikes and we share four beat-up half-dead junkers to put the heaviest equipment and animals—but a camo'd port? You only ever see those in the cities—the cities humans aren't permitted to enter. Not without tracking nanites clouding their eyes and masters' names tattooed to their arms.

I run my fingers over the wide steering unit. The handgrips are cool to the touch and coated with some kinduv flexible, slightly sticky material. The unit is shaped like a sideways X with closed off ends. My fingers stop at the symbol in the center where the handgrips meet: eight stars forming a circle with the Eljan moniker scrawled in the center. The insignia of the Eljan Guard—the Sepharon military sect for this territory.

"Day, I think I know where this came from."

He looks up at me and peers inside. "Find something?"

I point to the moniker. "It's got to be from one of the cities, maybe Vejla. But why would the Guard give a group of human boys a port?"

Day shrugs. "Easier than transporting slaves on sand bikes."

"Maybe," I say, but something's not right. The Sepharon don't make trades with humans—not even greedy human kids selling slaves. I trace the circle around the symbol, then slide off the bench. There's something going on here, but I'm not sure what. "We should get back to camp. Have you commed someone to collect the bodies?"

Day grimaces. "I forgot to grab one when I was running over to save your ass. And besides, we're way out of the two-league radius."

I frown. "How far did they take us?"

"More than twice that. But if we hurry, we can get back and send some guys to collect the corpses before sunrise."

"You mean before Nol and Esta see we're missing."

He smiles grimly and sets Aren onto his bike, steadying him as its scratched red body hums to life and rises off the sand, shining bright white light below. Aren giggles and clings to Day's arm. I start to comment on the scuffed up paintjob—Day is usually pretty obsessive about keeping the old thing as polished as a new phaser—but I close my mouth. Better not. Last thing I need is another lecture about how if we could just sneak into Vejla and steal a decent coat of paint, she'd be back to her "former aerodynamic glory." Right.

I turn back to the transport—and that's when I see it: a blinking blue light just below the steering unit. I crouch, peering closer at the little light, and curse under my breath.

Day ducks beside me. "What is it?"

I point to the light. Bite my lip. "Isn't their gear usually tracked?"

He whirls to me, paler than Safara's largest moon. "Did they bring—"

"A tracked port to the camp," I finish. "What if they—"

Day swears and jumps onto the bike in front of Aren. "We have to go. Now."

I climb on back, reaching over Aren's little body to grab Day's waist. It's awkward and I'm barely half-seated, but there isn't a blazing chance I'm about to bring that tracked port back to camp.

My brother doesn't waste any time. He kicks the bike forward and we speed across the sand.

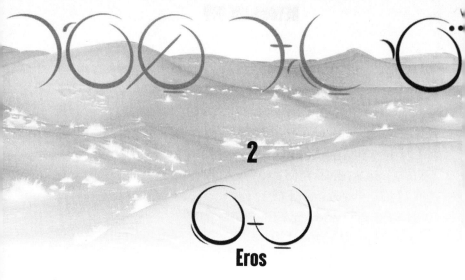

2

Eros

We ride in silence, past patches of glowing blue tube-like prickleplants and zig-zagging between scattered lizardmice burrows until the skies shift from deep, blackish purple to a striking red, stained by the rising suns. The orange glare from the larger of the two is directly in our eyes, and it's so bright I almost miss the smoke on the horizon.

Almost.

"Day," I gasp. "Is that . . .?"

It is. He leans forward, and we shoot faster across the red desert sea. My eyes are trained on the black line reaching into the sky, but it isn't until we crest the highest peak of the sandy mountains that we see camp. Burning.

Every tent is a ball of flame—well over a hundred bonfires spitting black into the stars. The livestock pen is a crimson blanket of severed pink and once-white hodge heads and bloody, curled up fetchers. Our people are screaming, on fire, fighting soldiers dressed in white and red.

No, not fighting, not really—the sand is stained dark with slaughter.

Day stops the bike and jumps into the sand. "Eros, stay here with Aren."

I scoff. "Right, because I'm just going to let you waltz in there alone."

"I need someone to protect him while I get everyone out. I'll catch up with you, but stay here with the bike."

Wait. He's not serious. He can't really expect me to stand here while he dives into that bloodbath, can he? "Day—"

He spins back and glares at me. "I swear to the suns, if you follow me and leave my son out here alone, I'll paint the sand with your blood. Got it?"

I scowl and glance at Aren. He's staring at camp, oblivious to our conversation. "Go," I grumble. "He'll be safe with me."

Day nods once, turns on his heel, and races down the dune.

I watch until he plummets into the smoke, and that's when Aren starts crying. Pulling him off the humming bike, I turn him away from the massacre. He clings to my bruised neck and buries his face in my shoulder. The added pressure stings, but I don't try to stop him.

The fires spread across the sand, and my people are gunned down fleeing from the blaze. The blend of horrified screams, crackling flames, and the high-pitched whine of phaser pulse after pulse rips down my spine and sucks the warmth from my blood. Through the smoke, a soldier yanks a man away from his wife and teenage son. I recognize the husband's short, dark ponytail—Bram is the only man in camp besides myself who doesn't keep his hair cropped. Heat twists around my lungs. Bram is one of Day's closest friends, and one of the few who doesn't look at me like a dirty half-blood.

And there's no one around to help him.

Bram rips out of the guard's grip and spins around, curved knife in hand, screaming. The soldier shoots him in the face with a red blast and he crumples silently in the sand. His son, Zeyn, breaks away from his mother and races toward him, shouting as he lunges. He takes three steps before a phaser burst rams into his chest.

I want to close my eyes, but I can't. I won't. The soldier nears Bram's wife, Lia, who is sobbing on her knees. He grabs her hair and she slams a dagger into his arm.

The blast of a phaser silences her, too.

I don't even realize I'm shaking until my grip on Aren slips and he squeezes tighter around me, digging into my bruise. I'm glad for the burst of pain blossoming over my shoulder— I need something to remind me I'm here. Something to tell me not to move because Aren isn't safe here alone.

But my family. My people. They're screaming.

Small groups break from the smoke and race for the hills, scattering in all directions. No one chases them—they're too busy with the massacre in the center of camp. I search for Day's muscular frame, for Nol's slight limp, Esta's tied-back hair, or Aren's pregnant mother and young siblings. Two bloody teenagers crest the dune and collapse beside me, retching black from their lungs and shivering despite the furnace-like heat radiating from camp. Aren has quieted, and I keep my hand on the top of his head, more to make sure he doesn't turn to look than to comfort him. I count thirty-two escapees, only a fraction of our two hundred thirty-six. I don't see my brother.

I'm about to tell Aren to wait with the teens—we're far enough away that he won't be seen if I leave for a couple minutes—when three faces I recognize break from the smoke—

Day's wife, Jessa, and her two older children, Nia and Mal. They stumble up the sand dune and wrap their arms around me. The kids are in tears and Jessa is crying, too. Day isn't with them.

I put Aren down and take Jessa's shoulders. I don't have to ask—she grabs my wrists and bores into me with piercing gray eyes. "Some soldiers attacked Nol. You have to help them—"

My feet start moving before I've registered her words—I tear down the dune, grab a dead guard's phaser, and race into the smoke. My eyes and lungs burn—I forgot to grab a scarf from Jessa in my rush—and I steal one from a body at my feet. It smells like blood and ash, but it filters the air well enough.

The western edge of the camp grows eerily quiet—only the crackle of flames touches this side, while phaser blasts and shouts echo from the other end. Every breath tastes like soot and smoke. My heart slams in my ears and my eyes water as I crouch, jogging around the edge of camp, the sleek black and red phaser held up to my face. The Kit's tents are on the far west edge—where Day and our parents should be. A five-minute jog—less if I push harder. I move quickly and silently, trying not to think about what's happening—what may have already happened.

I'm not too late. I can't be too late.

Nearly there. I race around the half-burnt orange tent bearing our neighbors' white family crest—my foot catches on something heavy and I tumble into the sand. There's movement just ahead—just around the row of tents—and I know what I've tripped over, but I don't look back to see who it is. I grab the phaser and whirl around the tents and aim.

I register three things at once:

One: There are two bodies in the scarlet-stained sand. I recognize my father's close-cropped gray hair and my mother's soft tanned hands, her fingers interlaced with Nol's.

Two: Day is on his knees with a phaser pressed to his skull. There are four soldiers around him, including the injured one who murdered Bram's family. Day's face is bloody and bruised and his eyes widen as I step around the corner to face them.

Three: My phaser isn't shooting.

I pull again and again, but the blazing thing is fucken fingerprint-locked and it's useless to me. Thank the suns the soldiers are facing Day and haven't noticed me. I grab my knife instead and run toward the nearest of the four as Day closes his eyes. There's a sound like a muted screech and Day jerks sideways, crumpling into the sand.

Something inside me breaks.

A scream rips from my throat, but by the time the soldier turns and sees me, it's too late—I slam my dagger into his neck. He drops, gurgling as I rip the blade away, whirling on the second soldier and catching him in the throat.

Lightning cracks across my eyes—

I'm on my knees. Someone has a fistful of my hair and is yanking my head so far back that my spine might snap. My vision returns in a slow fade, and a second dark-skinned soldier with sharp, angled markings who's more muscle than a man-eating wildcat towers over me, my knife in his hand. Blood drips down my face and neck, soaking the scarf tied around my head, but I'm not sure whose it is. The soldier's white uniform is soaked in red.

"How dare you?" he hisses in Sephari, leaning over me so closely that the trim beard around his lips and chin nearly touches my nose. "How dare you take the life of a warrior?"

He straightens and his boot slams into my gut. I gasp and jerk forward, but whoever has my hair yanks me back again. My stomach burns, my head is throbbing, but I don't care. I keep seeing Day collapse, over and over; I keep seeing my mother and father tossed in the sand like trash.

My home is burning. I don't care what they do to me.

The soldier brings my knife to my neck. There's some irony to this—dying by my own blade when they're each armed with phasers—but it's no accident. Killing me with my own knife is their idea of punishment, like it matters to me whether my blade gets my blood on it, too.

I guess it matters to them.

The blade bites into my neck, and a shock of pain floods me with understanding. He didn't just choose my knife out of some twisted sense of justice—he's going to do this slowly. I could throw myself onto the blade—heave my shoulders forward and end it. But now that the choice is in front of me, I don't want to die. Not like this, and not now.

The knife slices deeper, wedging behind my jawbone. The agony is unlike anything I've felt before. It spreads across my face and down my spine. It clenches the space around my heart. My whole body shakes. I can't breathe. I squeeze my eyes shut and bite back a scream.

"Stop," someone says.

The metal slides out of my neck and I gasp. Hot blood spills down my skin and drips over my chest. The soldier spits at me and spins on his heels, the knife clenched tightly at his side, his shoulders pulled back. All the soldiers have gone stiff, and together they drop to one knee, pound their left fists against their right shoulders, and hold them there.

Then I see her.

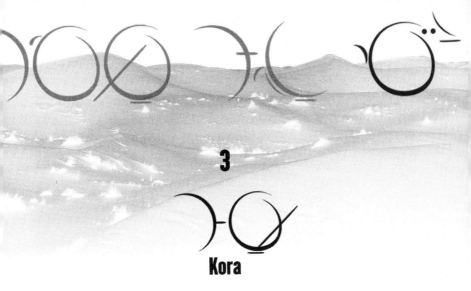

3

Kora

He is clearly not one of them—one of the redbloods. The faded paths of *Kala*'s mark on his light brown suns-ready skin, his tall, sculpted physique, and the dark purple-tinted blood spilling out of his neck make the truth clear enough. I don't doubt he hides misshapen ears beneath his shaggy brown hair.

Truth be told, he shouldn't be alive. Half-bloods are an impurity, a dilution of our blood, and must be eliminated at birth to preserve our race. And yet, here he is, living among the rebels like one of them.

Jarek's uniform is drenched in deep red, but the knife in his dark, dripping fingers isn't stained scarlet. I turn the full force of my gaze on him and cross my arms. "I don't recall sanctioning torture."

Jarek keeps his eyes trained over my head. "He killed two of our men, *el Avra*."

I nod, but the soldiers' bodies aren't the only corpses in the near vicinity—a woman and two men are dead beside the half-blood, and judging by the way his eyes drift toward them, they were dear to him. My heart sinks and the heat of the nearby flames sends my mind to a different place, a different time. I lost my own mother and father to fires not so different from these—fires that left me to rule as *Avra* alone and ultimately brought me here. I should not have come. The blood, the screams, the fire and smoke and death—these are truths that I must accept as *Avra*. And yet the twist of my gut and the ever-present taste of bile and ash tell me I don't belong.

But I must not allow them to see my weakness. I accompanied the men to prove that I could, to show them I am not the inept ruler they believe me to be. I need to be here. I resist the urge to touch my earring or tug on the black wrapping covering my left arm and shoulder, and swallow the grief clinging to the back of my throat. The men are an unfortunate casualty of this campaign, but I specifically ordered women and children be spared.

I nod at the mother. "And her?"

Jarek glances back, then looks over me again. "She attacked a warrior as well, *el Avra*."

"I see. And she managed to kill your men, did she?"

A pause. "*Naï, el Avra*."

"So you explicitly disobeyed my orders because a grieving woman attacked one of your warriors? Was she too much to handle, Jarek?"

His lips go thin and tight. "*Naï, el Avra*. It was an oversight. An error in judgment."

An error in judgment. How many other "errors" have there been? I've already seen far too many small bodies twisted in the sand, far too many blood-drenched mothers and innocent dead. Men deliberately disobeying my orders, killing people I never meant to—

My eyes sting and the back of my throat goes tight. I'm losing control of this campaign. Worse—I'm losing control of myself. This is my responsibility. I have to assert my authority before this gets any more out of hand.

Strength and power. Demand respect.

I clear my throat and level my most cutting gaze on Jarek. "That it was. Which one of you killed her?"

Jarek hesitates, but the others glance at the warriors in the sand. Answer enough. "I see," I say. "Then he carried out the same punishment I would have ordered." No one answers, but I didn't ask a question, so they won't.

I step toward the half-blood to survey him more closely. His eyes are human enough—one solid shade of deep green—and he wears his title-free skin with a sort of pride I will never understand. But more interesting is the way he looks at me—not over me. His gaze meets mine and he doesn't blink or flinch away. He holds and I hold and his posture is firm despite the blood spilling from his neck and the way Jarek's man holds his head back, ready for slaughter.

He's strong—in body and spirit.

I need him.

I turn away and face Jarek again. "Move him with the other servants. I want him cleaned up and assimilated with the rest."

Jarek's eyes widen. "*Avra?*"

"That's an order."

"But *el Avra*, the boy murdered two—"

"Are you questioning me?" I step toward him and stare up into his face, though he will never look directly at mine. He may stand a full head and a half over me, but my word is what keeps the air in his lungs and his blood off the sand.

He presses his lips into a line. "*Naï, el Avra.*"

"I didn't think so." I turn away with the half-blood's glare cutting into me like shards of broken glass, and for a moment, I nearly regret this entire campaign. But I straighten my shoulders and walk confidently past the smoke and flame.

I am *Avra*, and an *Avra* never bends.

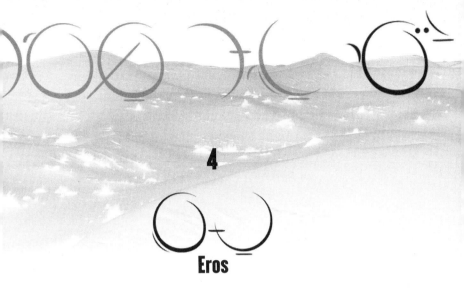

4

Eros

I'm in a camo'd dark port again, hands cuffed behind my back. Fancy high-tech paintjob on the outside, stripped metal walls, ceiling, and floor on the inside. No windows. Warm air pumped in through a thin vent against my heel. But this time, it isn't my four-year-old nephew and me in the shadows of the stifling compartment—there are at least two-dozen people crammed in here with me. And everyone is doing their very best not to touch me.

That's saying a lot, considering there's barely enough room for everyone to stand, let alone leave extra space between people. But even though these are my people—even though I recognize the faces of the women and children huddled in the darkness around me—they won't come near me. I'm not one of them. Not really.

As far as they're concerned, I am, and always will be, one of *them*. An alien. Because as long as I have Sepharon blood running through my veins, as long as I'm taller and stronger and faster than a human, as long as my senses are heightened and my body better equipped for this planet, how can my allegiance ever truly lie with the humans?

It doesn't matter that I grew up with them. It doesn't matter that I was raised by humans. It doesn't matter that the Sepharon just came through and destroyed my home, my family, and my life, too.

I'm not human, and I never will be.

To be fair, it probably doesn't help that I'm covered in purplish blood. One of the guards tied a scarf around my neck to help stem the bleeding, but the cloth is soaked and my face is stained with purple and red. But despite everything, I got lucky. I don't have any broken bones or fatal injuries. Unlike most of the men cut down in the sand, I'll live.

I'm the only guy here.

That might be yet another reason they so carefully avoid me. Most of these people have seen their husbands, sons, and brothers butchered tonight. They're probably wondering why their loved ones died and I lived.

I'm wondering that, too.

I lean against the corner and close my eyes. The air reeks of soot, sweat, blood, urine, and vomit. In my mind, Day collapses, empty, dripping in scarlet. My mother and father lie motionless, their fingers intertwined forever. The family who took me in when no one else would, when not even my birth mother could bear to keep me—gone. Biting my lip, I force my eyes open and stare at the ceiling. I can't think of them now—I can't break here in the back of a port with twenty sniffling women. I will not break. I will not break.

I'll be strong. For Day, who taught me the importance of masking my emotions from my enemies. For my people trapped with me, who may not see me as their own, but will be affected if I lose control now. Even for Esta and Nol, who said it was okay to break in the comfort of the people who love you. I may never see what's left of my family again, but until I do, I'll be strong—even if it means for the rest of my life.

My eyes sting and the back of my throat goes tight. I take a breath despite the stench. Clench my fists and exhale.

A part of me always wondered if I'd get the chance to leave camp and venture out on my own. If I'd want to, even if I had the opportunity. Maybe I'd go out to the coast one day to see the Endless Ocean, or go up north to the mountains, or just wander aimlessly and see the rest of Safara for myself. Or maybe not—I was fine with the life I had. I didn't mind living my days in the desert surrounded by the people I loved. Sure, I'd probably never have a family of my own, but it didn't matter because I was perfectly happy living with the Kits. But now the choice has been taken from me, from all of us. I doubt I'll ever see home again.

I doubt there'll be a home to go back to, even if I somehow manage to escape. How many of us survived the slaughter? We've never been attacked like that before—the Sepharon have never been able to find us. But now all I can think of is blood, screaming, and fire, and it's hard to imagine many of us managed to get away.

Whispers whisk past my ears as glances are thrown in my direction, then ripped away. A little girl with long dark hair asks her mother if we're going to die. Her mother hushes her and pulls her close.

We're not going to die, at least not right away. But this is worse. This is so much worse, because I'd rather be dead than serve the queen who ordered the slaughter of my camp.

Who looked at my family's corpses like sacks of grain. She may expect my loyalty, but she'll never get it.

I've been in this port for too blazing long.

Esta, Nol, and Day won't have funerals. That's the reality pounding in my skull, echoing in my ears, pumping through my veins as I watch the women sniffle into their hands or children's shoulders. Their bodies might burn with the rest of camp, but it won't be complete and no one will be there to witness the release of their spirits to the stars.

Or at least, I won't be there.

I'm not sure if I even believe the whole spirit thing—that by cremating the dead we're doing anything more than turning their bodies to ash. But Nol and Esta sure did, and Day used to say it was a nice sentiment—that we were releasing our loved ones so they could watch over us from the unending expanse of night. *We'll be with you wherever the stars reach,* Esta told me once with the softest of smiles.

More than anything, I want to see the stars tonight and wish them well, but I doubt we'll get out of this port before the suns rise.

Leaning my head against the cool wall, I fight the lump in my throat as I picture their faces. I see Esta's smile, the laughing lines on Nol's tan face, and the mischievous glint of Day's eyes as I breathe their names to the ceiling.

"Go to the stars," I whisper through the pain in my throat and the burning ache in my chest.

Go to the stars. I love you all.

It's hard to sleep standing up, but eventually exhaustion wins over and I nod off. It's not exactly a sound sleep—every turn and whisper startles me awake—but I do manage maybe an hour. Maybe less.

Regardless of how much sleep I actually get, all it manages to do is confuse my sense of time. I'm not sure how long we've been standing in this blazing port, but my legs ache and my head feels light and the pain constricting my neck is a vice of red-hot agony. It almost hurts worse than the actual strangling.

Eventually the port stops and the cabin falls quiet. One of the mothers starts sobbing and squeezes her young son tight to her chest, but otherwise the darkness is eerily silent. The murmur of voices slips through the walls, but their words are impossible to distinguish, especially as they're speaking rapid Sephari. Most of the women and children here don't speak Sephari. I learned it during my military training, all of our soldiers do, but otherwise it's not a common tongue among our people. As useful as it is, it's a dirty language. No one wants to be anything like a Sepharon. But now they'll have to learn, and learn quickly.

The doors open and sunlight floods the cabin. My eyes water and adjust all too slowly, but thankfully I'm in the back. It'll take time to get everyone out, and hopefully by the time it's my turn, I'll be able to see.

The soldiers are shouting and more people are crying now. Screams begin outside and I don't have to see to know what's happening—they're separating mothers from their children. My stomach twists. I wish I could do something, I wish I could stop this somehow. But standing here cuffed in the back of a port—I've never been so powerless. Thank the stars Aren isn't here.

These children will probably never see their mothers again, but at least Aren is safe with his.

When my turn comes, I step out of the port before someone can grab me, and a soldier beside me mutters, "*Vejla ora'jeve.*" Vejla greets you.

We're in Vejla, the Eljan capital.

My moment of independence doesn't last—I've barely stepped foot in the sand before a hand grips my arm and yanks me away from the rest of the crowd.

I recognize the dark, bearded soldier the queen called Jarek.

He doesn't say a word, but he jerks me forward. My guess is he'd like me to fall so he'll have an excuse to drag me, but I keep up despite my dizziness. The shouting dies away behind me as he pulls me onto the gleaming white street, then past the gate of the impossibly tall imported white sandstone wall surrounding the palace grounds.

Everything here is white and red. Endless red sands stretch far into the horizon. Strong, smooth white walls reach to the stars. Glistening white stone buildings shimmer different colors under the heat of the suns, all draped in red flags and banners with the Eljan insignia. Eljan citizens of all ages walk quickly down the streets, doing whatever they voiding do in the city, every adult marked with varying degrees of black unreadable text on their bodies. All the buildings have darkened windows and closed doors—the people here are just *so* friendly. Reflective black spheres the size of my fist zip in and out of the crowd, ducking around buildings and between heads. Paved white pathways wind between the buildings, around the wall, and into the palace complex, where I'm sure it's even more disgustingly elaborate, but we're not headed there.

Jarek pulls me behind a small building just out of earshot from the port. There's no one here, and there aren't any windows on the back of the building that someone might peer out of.

It's just me and a soldier who stands head and shoulders above me—a mountain of ridiculous, dark, tanned muscle that the Sepharon soldiers are so well known for. And I'm handcuffed.

It's obvious why I'm here, but at least I won't go down quietly.

"I take it these aren't part of your orders," I say in Sephari.

If he's surprised I can speak their language, he doesn't show it. Instead he shoves his forearm into my throat and slams me against the building. Pain ricochets into my skull and heat gushes out of the side of my neck where the knife was earlier this morning. I blink back tears and take short breaths through my nose—he hasn't cut off my airway. At least not yet.

"*Ken Avra* may have ordered you alive, boy, but in the name of *Kala,* I will make sure you pay for the lives of my men," he hisses. His breath rolls hot over my face and smells like meat and some kinduv fruity brew. "Starting now."

"Do you require assistance?"

Jarek freezes. My mouth has been known to get me in trouble, but the question definitely didn't come from me. A low whirring noise fills the air as a black orb hovers over Jarek's left shoulder, spinning slowly in the air.

"Do you require assistance?" it chirps again. Not sure if it's talking to him or me, but I don't dare answer—any "assistance" would probably involve more Sepharon soldiers and major retribution from a fuming Jarek. I almost want to laugh, but somehow I don't think it'd improve his mood. Plus it'd probably hurt like prickleplant venom.

"*Naï*," Jarek snaps, swatting at the thing. "Get away from here."

It dodges his hand and races away.

Jarek releases me and I try to duck out of the way, but his hand grabs my shoulder and his other fist finds my jaw, then stomach, then nose. I drop to my knees, gasping for air, but he yanks me to my feet again and shoves me back toward the port. "You should be more careful," he mutters to my back. "Another fall like that may very well kill you."

My stomach is aching, my head is pounding, my face is burning, and my lips are sticky and salty. But there's little I can do like this, so I walk in silence back to the line of weeping, cuffed women. The kids are gone now.

Jarek shoves me to the back of the line and nods to his soldiers, who lead us forward onto palace grounds.

Those who aren't crying stare in awe at the grounds—at the fountains glistening with jewels, the thin white trees with glimmering silver leaves reaching toward the clear purple sky, the stark white pathways cutting through the crimson sand. In another situation, when I didn't feel lightheaded and vaguely like throwing up, and I didn't have blood pouring down my face, I may have appreciated the landscape. I mean, most of us have never seen anything but waves of endless sand, so the complex is impressive.

But as the red gates close off the walls behind us, I can't help but think we're walking through an elaborate prison.

They lead us around the side of the main building—a glittering white palace with tall, twisting spires and nearly as many windows as there are white bricks—and past several smaller, but equally extravagant buildings. We stop before a long squat building bordering the far end of the wall. There aren't any windows.

The women go quiet as we're led inside. Cold tile nips the pads of my feet and frigid air blasts around us—they have a cooling system, I guess, except it's on way too high. The building itself looks like an enormous tiled hallway with rows of metal doors. A person stands beside each door, still and silent as stone. Their silence isn't what sends a chill over my skin—it's their appearance. Their heads are shaved, their eyes are a clouded gray, and their skin is so white, I'm sure it must be painted or powdered over with something.

Then there are the tattoos. They all wear the same matching black bands of illegible, circle-like text on their arms. Signs of slavery.

They wear the same white knee-length skirt and the women have their chests wrapped in some sortuv white silk cloth. Are they clones? No, there are differences in their facial features and slight variations in height and build. They aren't clones, but they're made to look like them.

This is what we will become. This is what they will turn us into—hollow, nameless copies. We lose more than our families, our homes, our freedom.

We lose our individuality. We lose ourselves.

I linger in front of the room for just a mo, making eye contact with the servant across the way. His stare is expressionless. Have the nanites that clouded his eyes made him blind, too?

Then a soldier gives me a shove and I stumble inside.

The door slams shut behind me. The lights are brighter in here, and the artificial whiteness makes us all look two shades too pale. There are three chairs at the front of the room with three metal bins of some sort beside them. A larger container is in the center of the room, and on the west wall is another door.

The cuffs demagnetize as Jarek steps to the front of the room—I'm not sure if he deactivated them or if someone else did, but I guess it doesn't matter. Most of the women have stopped crying now, so he doesn't need to do anything to make sure he's the center of attention—no one utters a sound.

"Take off all of your clothing, handcuffs included, and place it in the bin in the center of the room." He points to the bin. "After you have undressed, stand against the walls. Anyone who disobeys will be punished severely." No one moves, and he scowls. "Begin."

Still, no one makes any immediate movements. The women glance at each other and a couple whisper, but no one is undressing.

And then it hits me—they don't understand him.

Jarek pulls out a red-barreled phaser and shoots the woman nearest him in the forehead. She drops like a rock and the women all scream. "Silence!" he shouts, but his voice is lost in the hysteria. He points the phaser at another woman and I shove my way to the front of the room.

"WAIT!"

Jarek's eyes narrow as I step in front of the targeted woman. "If you think I won't shoot you, half-blood, just because—"

"They don't understand you," I say. "They don't speak Sephari."

"You speak it well enough."

"I was taught, but I'm an exception. Most of my people are not."

He scowls. "Then they'll learn quickly enough."

"Just let me translate. No one else has to die—I'll explain."

He hesitates, then nods and lowers the phaser. "Instruct them incorrectly and you won't be the only one to suffer." He gestures toward the dead woman with the phaser.

I grimace and face the women. I don't like standing up here, like their spokesperson. I don't like the dirty looks and the glares—if they didn't see me as a traitor before, they do now.

I take a breath. "We have to obey him, or he'll kill us."

Silence. How can I put this delicately? There's really no safe way to tell a room full of women to strip naked, so I point to the bin in the center of the room. "He says we need to put our clothes and handcuffs in there."

Uncomfortable understanding passes through them like a rolling sandstorm. I half expect them to resist or argue— our women are not known for being docile—but after more than a couple of glances at the dead woman on the floor, the first few begin to pull off their clothes. Then others follow.

I glance at Jarek, and he nods once. Then he gives me a pointed stare and nods to the bin and—oh. Right.

I'm not exempt from this order.

I'm already shirtless, so I start with the cold cuffs around my wrists. They pop off at my touch and clatter on the tile. Then I move on to the scarf tied tightly around my neck. It's stiff in some places and so soaked in others that my fingers come off a deep purple-red just brushing past it. My muscles ache as I gingerly unwrap the scarf and bundle it into a ball, but I don't feel a rush of warmth down the side of my neck, so at least I won't bleed to death. I slip out of my pants and toss the clothes into the bin in the center of the room, trying not to feel self conscious.

Of course, when you're the only naked guy in a room of naked women and clothed Sepharon soldiers, it's a little hard not to feel every glance. And I do get glances—from the women, mostly. One stares at me openly, which is awkward, but most turn away—though whether in disgust, modesty, or embarrassment, I'm not sure. Some of the guards give me disgusted looks, but that probably has more to do with the faded light lines mapping my body than my stuff. I think.

I stand at the front and face Jarek with my shoulders pulled back and my eyes boring into his. He smirks and I keep my face expressionless. This may be uncomfortable, but I won't let him see just how much I'd like to reach into that bin and put my pants back on.

A blast of cold air whisks through the room and I suppress a shiver. Maybe the frigid cooling system isn't an accident. They want us to feel cold, naked, vulnerable.

They want us to know we're at their mercy.

When the last of the women have abandoned their clothes, Jarek nods and points at the four seats. "Four at a time," he says. "Sit."

I go ahead and move first, and a couple nervous women follow suit. The chair is metal and a shock of ice stabs my skin as I sit down. I shudder and fold my arms over my chest, then rub my palms on my thighs. Nothing helps—my skin is a field of bumps and frozen hairs.

A soldier steps behind me, grabs a fistful of my hair, and pulls my head back. Heat and pain sears my neck and slice down my spine as my heart jerks against my ribcage— they're going to kill us? But then a low humming noise starts up behind me and something warm buzzes over my skull. A clump of dark hair falls to the tile.

Oh.

I close my eyes. Try to ignore the gazes burning my skin. The hair sliding off my shoulders. The endless buzzing and hum of the hot razor-thing against my scalp. The sniffling of a woman beside me, the chill of the never-ending frozen air, the stubborn pain prickling my neck.

Everyone's going to see my ears now. It'll be even more impossible to hide what I am.

Not that they didn't already know.

The humming stops and the soldier shoves me forward. I stumble and resist the impulse to run my hand over my skull. I don't want to feel it. I don't want to notice how my head feels light, how the chilly air blows directly on my scalp, how I have nothing to protect my neck, nothing to hide my ears.

One by one, the women sit in the chairs. One by one their hair falls around their feet, swept up into bins. One by one we stand against the wall.

We already look more like the servants standing outside the room. We're already becoming them.

When the last woman is shaved, Jarek opens the door on the west wall and gestures inside. I don't need to translate this time—they move inside with their eyes low.

This next room is identical to the last—tile floors and white walls, bathed in light—except this room is four times as large and has row upon row of long metal tub-looking things. Beside each tub is a pale, bald, gray-eyed servant.

"One per bath," Jarek says, but no one really needs the instruction. We line up beside the tubs, which I can now see are filled with what looks like purple water pumped with miniature bubbles. The servant at my station doesn't react to my gender or ears or light markings. She barely looks at me at all as Jarek instructs us to climb in.

I step inside and gasp—the water is ice-cold and fizzes around my skin. I submerge myself before I can change my mind—and regret it. Whatever this is isn't water and it sets my neck on fire. I surface, gasping, spitting the salty liquid, pressing down on the wound in my neck, but the pain doesn't stop and the agony reaches up into the side of my face and down into my shoulder. The servant takes my hand and pulls it away from my neck. I almost protest, but then she takes a wet cloth and starts to clean the gash. It hurts worse than the fizzy water, but I grit my teeth and stare at the bright white ceiling and bear it. As much as it hurts, I need this. At least I won't die of infection.

When she finishes wiping around my neck, she pushes my head under again. The bubbles gather around the wound and it stings, but not as badly as the first time. My skin burns from the frigid water as I resurface and my teeth chatter loudly, but she works fast, cleaning the blood off my face, chest, neck, and hands. Soon she nods and I can climb out. She passes me a towel and I dry myself as quickly as I can manage. I do my head last, and even though I'm expecting it, the fabric on my scalp sends a cold shock blossoming through my gut.

We enter another room. This one is just as large as the last one, except instead of tubs there are chairs, and before the chairs is a long row of glass floor-to-ceiling tubes with an opening in the front and back. Jarek instructs us to step into the tubes, then proceed to one of the chairs, and the women look at me to lead as example.

So I step into a tube. The openings in front and behind me close, and bright blue light shines over me. My skin tingles like there's an invisible energy in the air prickling my skin, then the light disappears and cold water dumps over me followed by a jet of frigid air. I'm shivering when the tube opens up again and I step onto the tile. I rub my arms and oh—I know what the tube did—the hair on my arms is gone. I'm entirely hairless.

Frowning, I try not to imagine what I must look like—stars know completely hairless isn't exactly attractive—as I step toward a chair. There are two Sepharon men at each station. They're not dressed like soldiers, but they wear a similar white and red high-collar shirt and long pant uniform that seems so popular here. I sit and bite my lip as the cool metal warms under my naked, half-frozen ass and back.

The men move without a word. The guy to my left slides a dark metal cuff over my upper arm and holds it there. The inner ring glows bright red, then my breath catches as the skin beneath the cuff burns. Before I can ask what the cuff is, the man to my right turns my head and pushes my cheek against the chair, then plunges a needle into my neck, just below the gash. I shout, then clamp down on my tongue. I've felt worse pain today, but the bite of the needle is deep and my neck is already badly bruised. He releases me and his partner slides the cuff off my arm, and I understand what the cuff was for.

I'm marked.

I don't need to read the tattoo to know what it says—I'm forever branded a servant of Elja. A slave.

I slide off the chair and wait on the far end of the room as women make their way over after being tattooed. Their eyes are numb and they don't look at me.

Even now, after all we've been through, I'm still something to be avoided. I'll always be a dirty half-blood.

The next room has tubs again, this time filled with a liquid similar to milk or thick candle wax. This is actually the most pleasant procedure, because the liquid is warm. I hold my breath and stay under until my lungs begin to burn. Climbing out again is even more uncomfortable, though, because as warm as the baths are, the room itself is still freezing. I cross my arms and that's when I get a glimpse of my skin— my hands, arms, legs, and chest are a pasty, sickly white. I rub my fingers together. My skin is ridiculously soft, and as best I can tell the liquid dries into some kinduv white powder that sticks. The weird milk baths will probably be a regular thing if they intend to keep us ghosts.

At least it covers the light trails on my skin. Mostly, anyway.

Finally, the soldiers bring us clothes. Everyone dresses quickly, and I'd be lying if I said I wasn't relieved to be covered up again. Although I wish it didn't involve wearing a skirt. I guess it's better than nothing.

When everyone is dressed, I dare a glance around the room. Our eyes aren't the same color—at least, not yet—but my stomach churns as I look over the crowd. Thirty minutes ago, I knew these faces. Now, with their identical pasty skin tone, identical clothes, and identical baldness, I can barely tell them apart.

I still stand out, being a guy and at least a foot taller than most of them. But I probably don't look out of place among them, either.

I resist the urge to scrape my skin clean as the soldiers separate us. No one protests anymore. They split the crowd into six smaller groups with ease, then Jarek steps next to me and takes my arm.

"You have a separate assignment," he says, pulling me away from the crowd.

And though I have a vague feeling I'm not going to like this separate assignment, I'm too drained to fight him.

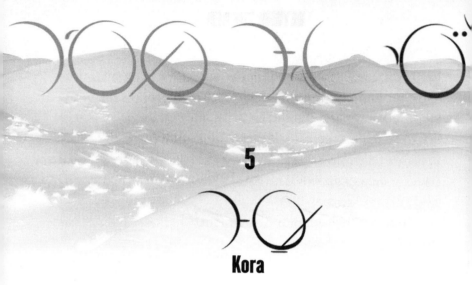

5

Kora

Anja has just finished maneuvering my silky black hair into a swirling, braided bun when my door slams open. In most circumstances, my guards would be on the intruder in an instant—no one bursts into my room without permission, or with permission, for that matter.

But my guards are partial to my brother, Dima, and they let him in without a word.

"Good morning," I say pleasantly, watching him approach in the mirror. "What upsets you today? Are the suns too bright for your liking? I can make a special request to *Kala*, if it pleases you."

Dima scowls at the wall to his left and crosses his thick golden brown arms over his chest. *Kala*'s mark entwines around his arms and chest in stiff straight lines and cornered angles, so unlike the smooth curves I inherited from our mother. The light markings on his arms are filled in entirely with text—everything from his many decorated statuses, to "a life without greatness is a life unlived" (our family creed), to excerpts from the ancient texts about strength and honor. "*Orenjo*" is shaved into the side of his cropped black hair and I resist the urge to roll my eyes. My brother doesn't know a thing about honor.

"You know very well what upsets me, dear sister," Dima says through his teeth.

Anja holds up a mirror behind my head to show me the bun. I nod my approval and spin around to face my childish brother. We may be the same age with nearly the same coloring—though his skin is a touch lighter than mine and his sharp jaw and severe glare make him appear older than me—but the fact that he still comes in here throwing his petty rages proves just how little he has matured over the cycles. "I'm not a mind reader, Dima. I haven't the faintest idea what you're going to wail about."

There are many things he would like to say to me in this moment, I'm sure, but sister or not, I'm still his superior—a fact he knows all too well. His lips form a thin line and he drops his arms to his sides and faces me. "There is a half-blood in my training room, Kora. And Jarek tells me he has been ordered to keep him alive—by none other than *ken Avra* herself."

There's an accusation in there, somewhere, but I refuse to be upset by it. Instead I stand and step toward the window at my bedside, looking out into the sandy gardens. Curved, beautiful rows of the most precious desert flowers trimmed into elongated crescents. Blue-leafed moonflowers that open and glow under the light of the moons. Tiny temperleaf blossoms that change colors when you stroke their white petals, supposedly predicting your mood. Striped bright pink kazipetals, shimmering silver morningbushes, and of course, the luscious deep purple angled petals of the bloodflower. They were Mamae's favorite.

My fingers long to reach out and stroke the soft fuzzy blue buds of the closed moonflowers just outside my window, but something warm and soft rubs against my side—Iro, the family *kazim*. Though really, Iro is mine—he's always been most attached to me, ever since Mamae presented him to us as a tiny cub. I run my fingers through the thick sand-colored fur between his ears. "If I'm not mistaken, you did mention to me not five sunsets back how you needed more servants in the training rooms to attend to your men."

Although I don't look at him, I hear the scowl in his words. "Servants, *sha*. Not trash."

I face him again. "If you prefer, I can move him elsewhere. I wasn't aware he was such an eyesore."

"He doesn't need to be moved—he needs to be executed. He shouldn't be alive, Kora, you know that. Half-bloods are terminated at birth for a reason—you let a couple live and you risk others following suit and weakening our *species*. Do you want to be responsible for that?"

He's right, of course. It's incredible that the half-blood has lived this long—how he escaped execution is beyond me—but now that he's here, I won't throw away his potential.

I keep my face expressionless. "He's one half-blood, and he's not exactly attempting a genetic overhaul. Unless you're suggesting he's contagious and will somehow contaminate your men."

Dima steps toward me. His height intimidates most, but it's difficult to intimidate someone who's seen you run around the palace naked with a scarf wrapped around your head as a child. "You find this amusing," he says.

"I wouldn't be giving you the credit you deserve if I didn't admit you entertain me."

He shakes his head. "I don't understand. Why do you keep him alive? And on palace grounds, no less."

"I have my reasons." I sit on my desk and lean back on my arms as Iro curls up at the floor beneath my feet, his tail swishing slowly over the stone. Dima scowls at the animal and I keep my voice firm. "You will respect my decision."

His pale-to-dark eyes flash for just a moment, but then he drops to one knee, his arm pulled across his chest. "As you wish, *el Avra*."

I roll my eyes. "*Kala*, Dima. I'm asking you as your sister, not your ruler."

"I wouldn't do that," he says stiffly. "Not if you wish him to live."

I frown, hop off the desk, and put my hand on his broad shoulder. "You need to trust me. I have good reasons for keeping him here. He will prove useful, you'll see."

"You ask me to trust you, and yet you do not extend me the same courtesy." He looks up at me. "Or will you tell me why you insist on keeping him alive?"

There was a time when I confided everything in Dima. As children we were secluded, kept away from others our age, so having a twin was the greatest kind of blessing—a dear friend I wouldn't have had otherwise. But that was before I took the throne. Before I began to question just how wise it was to trust him.

Because the truth is, my brother is the reason I need the half-blood. Because I would be stupid to ignore the swaying allegiance of my guard and the whispered half-conversations that cease abruptly when I enter a room. It's no secret that most believe a strong male warrior would be better suited on the throne, and eventually I may need someone to help protect me from the very people who have sworn their lives to me. If I want to keep the throne and survive, it is my responsibility, and mine alone, to keep myself safe so that I may.

But I can't say that to Dima, and my hesitation is all the answer he needs.

He stands and turns away from me. "He'll live, Kora, but only as long as he respects his place."

I start to answer, but then someone raps on my door and Dima pulls it open before I give the order. A guard steps inside and drops to his knee as my brother slips out into the hallway. It's not the way I wanted this conversation to end, but it'll have to do.

"*El Avra*," the guard says, his head bowed low.

I sit at my desk and try not to sound as irritated as I am. "*Sha*, what is it?"

"The priestess is ready for you, *el Avra*. She requested I summon you at once, before the suns reach their full height."

The priestess! I'd forgotten all about the Cleansing today—a ritual every Eljan *Avra* must perform every eighty-eight sets to refocus on *Kala*. Truth be told, my focus has been stretched thin this past term and a half, and none of it in places that would make the priestess—or, more importantly, *Kala*—happy.

"Of course." I stand. "Let's go at once."

We walk to the High Temple with guards flanking me on either side. Soldiers and servants alike bow as I walk past them, their eyes low as they murmur *Avra* in my wake. I keep my gaze focused forward, my shoulders back, and my head high as we move past them. *Strength,* I remind myself with every step. *Strength and power. Demand respect.*

The hard white pathways are warm against my feet as the suns wrap me in their stiflingly hot embrace. We pass glistening white fountains filled with colorful gems, and rows of white and silver *unaï* trees bordering the pathways. A warm breeze blows powdery red sand over my toes and a thin crimson layer sticks to my skin.

After moving beyond the main palace complex, the barracks, and servants' quarters, we are greeted by eight tall white and glass spires topped with floating golden spheres. Like most of the buildings on the complex, the temple is primarily white, built with *aska*—a white stone from Denae d'Invino, the mountains of the northern lands, that reflects subtle colors in the sunlight. Unlike most of the buildings, however, the intricately carved stone is coated in glass, which magnifies the multicolored sheen of the stone, making the whole building glisten brilliantly. The temple is the most beautiful building on the palace grounds, as it should be.

When we near the enormous golden doors, the guards stop. Only an *Avra* or a priest or priestess is permitted to touch the sacred double doors, which are blessed every morning with the rising of the suns. I take a moment to admire the beautiful designs carved into the gleaming doors—identical swirls with twisting paths and tight lines folding in on themselves on both doors, one the mirror image of the other. The high priests of Inara carved the doors by hand many generations ago when the temple was first built.

Breathing a soft prayer of blessing, I dismiss my guards with a nod. No one may enter the temple when the doors are closed without express permission, or in my case, an invitation, from a priest or priestess. I enter, and the heavy doors swing closed behind me with a resounding thud that echoes in the small reception room.

It takes a moment for my eyes to adjust to the darkness of the room. Closed off to the sanctuary and any windows, the reception room is lit only by golden candles—more out of tradition than lack of a more effective lighting system. The floors are cool, rough sandstone and the walls are draped in a matte dark red cloth, obscuring the archways leading to other rooms.

A section of cloth to my left ripples and shifts as the priestess steps into the room. Her beautiful near-black skin is lined with startling white markings that fill *Kala*'s mark across her body. The markings swirl around her face, intricately lining her cheeks, forehead, chin, and lips with small, tight letters. Dark, braided hair wraps around her skull and pours over her shoulders, reaching nearly her knees.

But most striking—and chilling—are her eyes. All of the priests and priestesses inject themselves with some kind of nanite serum during rituals and prayers that supposedly opens them to *Kala*'s messages. It also turns their eyes permanently pale and almost colorless, save for the pupils. Hers are a light pink, purple, and yellow, but the tint is so light that it looks nearly white.

"*El Avra*," she says softly, bowing low. Her loose robes scrape quietly against the floor as she moves toward me and gestures toward the wall she came in through. "It is time, *Kala*'s Blessed."

She turns away and steps through the curtained archway. I follow in silence.

Like the entry room, the outer hallways bordering the sanctuary have low ceilings and are candlelit only. We step through the dimly lit hallway, careful to remain as quiet as possible so as not to disturb the sanctuary. The priestess's long braided hair swishes softly side to side as she walks, not unlike Iro's tail. I smile slightly, then press my lips firmly together—I'm supposed to be focusing on *Kala*, not wake-dreaming about my pet.

I have to take this seriously. I'm *Avra*. The people expect me to remain spiritual so I may receive wisdom from our Maker—though it's unclear to me whether anyone other than the priests or priestesses ever receive some sort of divine counsel. It's certainly never happened to me, not that I've admitted as much to anyone.

Last thing I need is to give anyone more reason to doubt my ability to rule.

My father's words echo through my mind. *Strength and power, Kora. Demand respect and it is yours.*

After stepping through another curtained archway, we enter the first of the cleansing rooms, where two young apprentice priests and an apprentice priestess waits. Their eyes have not yet lightened, and they wear the unadorned, itchy gray robes of ones in training. In the center of the candlelit room is a small pool embedded in the floor, filled to the brim with steaming water. I step to the edge of the pool and wait as the apprentices come forward and slip off my wrapped top and skirt.

This is a part of the process I wish I could do myself—it feels rather juvenile to have to stand here uselessly while *actual* juveniles remove my clothing—but it's supposed to represent the divine stripping away the layers that mask my spirit. Or something like that. I haven't read the texts in probably too long.

The tight wrapping on my arm and shoulder comes off last. I look away as they unravel the black cloth hiding the ugly pink flesh of my scarred skin. Looking at it fills me with a cold emptiness that never completely thaws.

Lowering myself into the hot water, I relish the warmth against my skin. The priestess presses a circular black injection pad into the crook of her elbow, and her eyelids flutter as the serum takes hold. As she enters beside me, her robes spill out like ink on the surface of the pool. I watch them float serenely across the water, mingling with her braids as she dribbles warm oil over my head and recites from the ancient texts.

I should be paying attention, repeating her words in my mind, taking them in and meditating on their meaning. I should be emptying my thoughts and emotions and focusing solely on the texts and the divine. Instead, my mind drifts back to my conversation with Dima, to the anger in his eyes and his clipped tone as he marched out of my room. I saw that very same anger in the half-blood when Jarek yanked him to his feet and shoved him toward the other new servants.

Naï, stronger than anger. Hatred.

Oil drips slowly down my face like warm tears. Like the blood slipping off Jarek's fingers and knife. The tears spilling over the half-blood's cheeks. The screams and smoke and so many bodies, so many dead, because of my order. Because of me.

"*Avra.*"

The priestess's voice rips me out of my thoughts. She watches me with her cold, piercing gaze, and I suppress a shiver. I missed a queue. I'm supposed to say something. What did she just say? My face warms and silence drips past us and everyone's eyes settle on me. Expecting. Waiting.

I open my mouth and a low, distant boom echoes through the building. The priestess's gaze snaps to somewhere behind me, a deep frown settling over her features. Did someone just enter the temple without permission? I turn around, eyeing the entryway.

Footsteps snap quickly down the hall, growing louder until someone emerges through the curtain and drops to a kneel, his left fist on his opposite shoulder and his eyes low.

But I don't need to see his face to recognize my brother's closest friend, and the third in command—Jarek.

"You do not belong here," the priestess snaps, scowling deeply. "You're interrupting a sacred ceremony and have entered the temple without—"

"Truly, I apologize," Jarek says, cutting off the priestess. Her nostrils flare and she opens her mouth, but he beats her to it. "I would never have interrupted if it wasn't such an urgent matter, but *ken Avra* must be escorted back to the palace immediately."

The priestess starts to speak, but I lift a hand and she quiets. "What has happened?"

"It's the people," Jarek says grimly. "They're rioting."

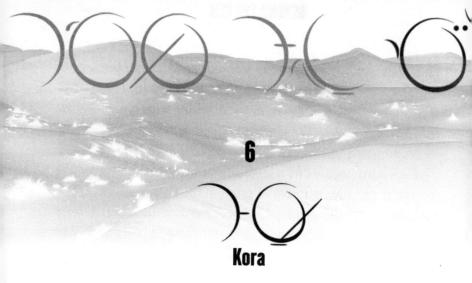

6

Kora

After dressing again, I've taken all of three steps from the temple when the first earsplitting crack echoes through the air, momentarily splitting the sky with sickly green light. I stumble, and Jarek catches me, realizes his error, then quickly releases me and bows. In different circumstances, I might care about him touching me, but in this moment it's the last thing on my mind.

My ears ring, and with it is an echo of something else—the low roar of angry voices carried through the air. Plumes of gray and greenish smoke rise high into the clear violet sky, turning it the ugly shade of an old bruise.

"We must keep moving, *el Avra*," Jarek says stiffly. "I have strict orders to bring you indoors, where it's safe."

I almost start walking, but Jarek's words stop me in midstep. He looks physically pained when I come to a halt, but I ignore it. "Orders?" I say. "Whose orders? My brother's?"

"I—*sha, el Avra*, but—"

"Am I not safe on my own grounds? You haven't told me anything—how bad is this riot?"

Another crack rips through the air and with it comes a burst of hot air and sand. I turn away just in time to avoid a blast of dirt to my eyes. The crowd must be closer than I thought for the aftermath of a burst bomb to reach here.

Jarek coughs and spits sand mud—evidently he wasn't as fortunate as I was. "They're storming the gate," he croaks. "They won't breach it, not with the nanite coating, but the Commander believes it's safest for you indoors."

To be fair, Dima's probably right—it *would* be safest for me away from the crowd and the violence. And yet, I hesitate—just because it's the safest option doesn't mean it's the right one.

Strength isn't cowering away in a protected room. Power isn't letting my little brother order me around. Respect isn't being escorted away in the middle of a ritual under somebody else's orders.

I straighten my shoulders. "I want to speak to them."

Jarek's eyes widen. "*Avra,* I'm not sure that's wise."

"I don't remember asking for your counsel," I answer crisply. "*I* am their ruler. I should be the one addressing them, not my brother."

Jarek opens his mouth to answer, but Dima's voice calls out instead. "What is she still doing out here?"

I turn to face my brother and answer, but Dima stalks right up to Jarek without even glancing at me. My face floods with heat—how dare he ignore me?

"I told you to bring her indoors." He grabs my arm. "I made it very clear she's not safe out here."

"I'm not going anywhere," I say loudly, wedging between them. "And release me immediately. You've no right to touch me."

But Dima just shakes his head and motions to four guards standing sentry nearby. "You four, bring *ken Avra* inside immediately and make sure she doesn't venture outside until I say otherwise."

I gape. Who in *Kala*'s name does he think he is, touching me, ordering my guards around, and flat out attempting to *overrule* me? And in public, no less?

The guards step forward and my stomach sinks. They're actually listening to him.

"Dima," I snap, trying to yank out of his grip—and failing. "I'm not going indoors—I want to speak to them. In case you've forgotten, *I'm* their ruler, not you."

"*Sha*," my brother says stiffly. "That does seem to be the problem."

Angry heat attacks my skin. "Excuse me?"

"You're not going to speak to them."

The heat prickles across my chest and sets a tremor to my hands. "I don't take orders from you," I say, barely controlling my tone. "*I am Avra*. My orders overrule—"

"They want you *dead*, Kora. If they see you, it'll incite more anger, not less. I'm going to take my men out there before it gets any worse."

His words are a kick to the gut and leave me breathless. They want me *dead*? "How can you be so sure?" My voice sounds weak. I hate it. "How do you know that's what they want?"

"I don't have time for this." Dima nods at the guards. "Bring her inside immediately. I'm not going to tell you again."

The guards nod and step forward. I should argue. I should demand to see my people, to try to reason with them, to see what I can do to help.

But I don't. I let them bring me inside with shame tattooed to my shoulders and stones gathering in my stomach.

I wish I could say otherwise, but Dima and Jarek weren't exaggerating about the riot, or its cause.

I sit in the dining hall with Anja and Iro at my side before a hovering stone table piled high with untouched food.

We sit in silence as my city descends into chaos on six glass screens floating over the opposite wall, each with a different view of the riot. Men, women, and even some younger than me throw stones and angry words, their faces covered with cloths, helmets, or masks. Smoke obscures the screens and I dig my fingers into my knees as the audio rings loud and clear around me, echoing throughout the hall.

They're chanting Dima's name.

Everything is falling apart. My heart aches and my stomach churns as they press against the gates, throwing burst bombs and screaming obscenities at the armored guards just beyond the gate. My fingers tremble as they set buildings on fire and break glass storefronts.

Dima says they want me dead, and the more I watch, the more I'm starting to believe him.

7

Eros

Pain builds behind my eyes like an impending storm. A head-ache magnifying to full-out brainblaze levels, that in normal circumstances would leave me seeking darkness.

Unfortunately, I'll never have normal circumstances again.

The soldiers watch me with undisguised disgust as I fill the water canteens. Jarek brought me here, to a large open room with mirrors on the walls, a deep red matted floor, and a row of long staffs on the far side of the wall—some sortuv training facility from the looks of it—and asked if I thought I could handle filling water bottles without causing trouble. I told him I'd do my very best, but we half-bloods have trouble comprehending more than the simplest tasks.

I expected him to punish me for my mouth, but he just turned and stalked away.

It's not difficult labor, which is surprising. Consider-ing how much everyone seems to hate me, I thought for sure I'd be given the hardest, most back-breaking work they could manage. Instead I've been told to sit and press my thumb against a silver, fist-sized cube sitting on a large, crescent-shaped floating slab of white stone until the cube spits out enough purple water to fill each clear, fabric-y bottle. I've never seen clear fabric before; the bottles feel like they're made of some kinduv canvas, but it's hard as bone and the water doesn't soak through—definitely not a material we had access to in the desert. I'd expected the water to run out quickly, but the mystery cube never seems to empty, so I guess it must be generated inside or something. All in all, it's boring, mind-numbing work, but not exactly challenging.

I've just filled up and stoppered the one hundred eighty-eighth bottle when a soldier comes over to the station and leers down at me. I ignore him and keep filling in silence as he drinks from the bottle, eyes focused on me.

Warm water squirts at the side of my face and drips down my shoulder. The men laugh as I glance up at the soldier and wipe the slightly slimy water off my face. He just spit at me.

There's a small crowd of soldiers now, all watching to see what I'll do. Or what he'll do. They want me to react; there's a hunger in their eyes I know all too well. They want a fight—no, they want a slaughter. They want an excuse to beat me to a whimpering mass of flesh and bone.

My head throbs. I keep filling bottles.

"You've got a lot of nerve to show your face here, half-blood," the spitting soldier says.

Yes, I want to say. *How crazy of me, to walk in here, dress up as a slave, and serve you water. I don't know what I was thinking.*

I plug the bottle with a black stopper and move on to the next one.

"How have you even survived this long, hmm? In fact, why would anyone even conceive you?" He turns to his friends and laughs. "Can you imagine—sleeping with desert trash? He must've been very drunk to consent to such a thing."

The men snicker and I begin filling the one hundred and ninetieth bottle. It's not the first time someone's tried to get me angry by insulting my genetic parents—something that'd maybe have more effect on me if I knew who my genetic parents were. To be honest, I'm probably a product of rape, like most of my kind. A servant and a drunk or power-hungry master.

I'm just not sure why I was kept alive.

I reach for another stopper and the soldier slaps the bottle out of my hand. It clatters on the tile, spilling water over the textured white stone floor. This is supposed to set me off, I guess, but it's not my water they're throwing on the floor. I take the bottle and begin filling it again. Just as the water reaches the rim, the soldier kicks the bottle from my hand again. Water splashes and this time the bottle skids out of reach.

"You should get that," the soldier says.

I ignore him and reach for another bottle instead, but he slaps that out of my hand, too.

"Didn't you hear me, half-blood? Go pick up your mess."

Something is building inside me, somewhere behind my eyes and in the pit of my stomach. I know what this is, what they're doing, what they want. I've dealt with people like this before. I've ignored the jibes and avoided fights with silence. Nol used to tell me they just want a reaction, and if you ignore them long enough, they'll get bored and find their entertainment elsewhere.

I know that. And yet this energy building in my core and bubbling in my blood—it's tired of taking abuse. It's tired of keeping quiet and waiting for them to get bored. But now more than ever, I need to keep my temper in check. An outburst here could mean the end.

I take another bottle. He kicks at it and I dodge his boot and start filling. I ignore the eyes on my back, the eyes on my ears, the eyes on my almost-not-really-markings, the chuckles and the whispers behind me. They'll get bored. They always get bored. Eventually.

The soldier grabs the edge of the table and heaves it onto its side, sending a cascade of bottles and stoppers scattered across the floor as the table spins and whirs, bobbing violently in the air. The cube hits the floor beside my foot with a *thunk*. I hope it isn't broken. I'm dead if it's broken.

I guess I might be dead anyway.

The soldier yanks the half-filled bottle out of my hand, dumps the water on my head, and throws the bottle at me. It bounces off the top of my head with a slight pang and lands somewhere in the mess of containers off to the side.

I blink water from my eyelashes. Lick some off my lips. Glance up at the soldier.

He crosses his arms. "Clean up this mess." A thin smirk twists his lips and the pain behind my eyes pulses and morphs into a steady burn. I already know what'll happen if I do as he says. I also know what'll happen if I ignore him. He has me trapped, and he knows it.

I stand and he shoves me to the floor. I was expecting it, though, so I don't hit the ground too hard. Bottles roll and rattle around me.

He steps toward me. "Get up." I do as he says, but when he reaches out to shove me again, I duck under his arm and step around the table, putting it between us. It serves a double purpose—I need to steady it in order to put the bottles back anyway, but it also adds an extra obstacle between us. He glares and starts toward me, but then the door slams open behind us and the soldiers snap to attention in unison, their left fists held against their right shoulders.

Someone important has just stepped in behind me. I grab the edge of the table until it stops spinning and tilting and try to clean up the bottles as quickly as I can.

Not quickly enough, though.

"What is this?" The voice cuts through me like a knife. This must be the one in charge. I keep my eyes low and start replacing the bottles on the table, but then he steps beside me and when I stand, his face is inches from mine. He's several inches taller than me, so I have to look up at him. I hate it. "I asked you a question, half-blood."

I haven't seen this guy before, but even though he doesn't look any older than me, he holds himself like someone used to power and respect. There's a Sephari word shaved into his short black hair, just above his right ear, and his uniform is nearly the same as the other soldiers, but has gold trim around the red decals. He also wears a red sash across his chest. I have no idea what any of it means. Not even Jarek—who stands beside him with a sharp glint in his eyes reflecting his earlier promise—has gold on his uniform or a red sash. Or a sash of any kind, for that matter.

I glance at the spitting soldier. Back to the guy with the sash. I could tell the truth, but he'd never believe me. He'd ask his soldiers if it was true, and they'd all deny it, and I'd be in deeper trouble for supposedly lying—which the Sepharon take as a personal affront.

"I slipped and knocked into the table," I say.

"You slipped."

I nod. "*Sha.*"

"*Sha, ve.*"

Sir. I have to call him "sir." I bite the inside of my cheek. Take a deep breath. "*Sha, ve.*"

Something sparks in his pale blue-to-nearly-black eyes. "Tell me, half-blood. How did you manage to slip while sitting?"

Jarek smirks, but I ignore him. "I dropped a bottle and it spilled. When I stood to retrieve it, I slipped in the puddle."

"Are you normally that uncoordinated, half-blood?"

My fingers tighten to fists. Relax. "*Naï, ve.*"

"Then get yourself in order." He slaps the side of my head and I stagger sideways. A slap doesn't sound like much, but it sets my face stinging and my ear ringing. "Clean up this disaster before I decide you deserve further punishment."

My face is burning, but not from pain. I clench my teeth and continue cleaning up the bottles and stoppers as the commander and Jarek step toward the other men.

"Well," the commander says, "you may have already heard what's happening beyond the gates. When I dismiss you, you'll put on your armor, retrieve your weapons, and wait in the barracks for further instructions."

I allow myself a small smile. I have no idea what's happening in the city, but if they need to gear up and go out there, it must be something bad.

Good.

"If I may, *ve*. Before we begin."

I glance back. The spitting solider is speaking.

"You may."

The soldier steps forward. "The slave was lying, *ve*."

I freeze in mid-reach. Exhale and pick up a bottle. Place it on the table and force myself not to stare.

"Oh?"

"He didn't slip, *ve*. He became angry and threw over the table on purpose. We tried to stop him, but he would not listen to reason, *ve*."

A long pause. I abandon the pretense of cleaning and make eye contact with the soldier. He keeps his face blank and his eyes flicker to mine for only a moment.

"Is this true?" the commander asks his men.

They nod in unison; not a single one of them hesitates. The commander turns back to me. "Come here, half-blood."

I place two bottles back onto the table, then step onto the mats. All eyes are on me now, and with the commander distracted, the spitting soldier shoots me a pleasant smile. It takes every ounce of my self-control not to step in front of him and knock his teeth out.

"It would appear you have lied to me," the commander says.

I don't answer. Neither denying nor confirming his accusation will help me.

"Had you confessed your error in judgment, I would have been more inclined to be lenient with your punishment, but as it is, you leave me little choice. I do not tolerate disrespect, and deception is a great form of disrespect, as I'm sure you are well aware."

Eye contact. Air in. Air out.

"To the center of the mat."

I obey and, as I do, the soldiers form a circle around the commander and me. Punishment, apparently, is a public spectacle.

The commander comes toward me, then swings for my face. I should take it. I should close my eyes, block out the brainblaze, stand still, and wait for it to end. It'd be the easy, smart thing to do. But while I brace myself for the hit, when his fist nears my nose, instincts kick in and I duck out of the way. The following silence and the glare from the commander sends a cold chill through my veins.

He nods to Jarek, who all too happily steps behind me and pulls my arms back, bracing me.

"Looks like I won't have to try very hard to keep my promise, half-blood," Jarek whispers.

I know three different ways to break out of this kinduv brace, and everything inside me screams that I use one of them. But escaping the blow will only make this worse. I have to take the punishment, whatever it may be, then go back to work and hope they leave me alone. All I have to do is stand still.

But when the commander swings again, I can't help it—I duck and twist hard, sending Jarek flying over me and into the commander. I'm in trouble. I should have stood still and let them beat me, but tell that to seven years of training. I turn on my heel, slam through the wall of shocked soldiers, and run. I don't know where I'm going—I've been on the palace grounds for less than a day and I hardly know the way down the hall, let alone how to get back out into the desert, but if I stay in this room of infuriated soldiers, I'm dead. They'll beat me into darkness and no amount of training will save me from an army.

"Take him!" the commander roars behind me. I slam through the metal doors and race down the hall. My bare feet slap the cold stone tile and the thunder of boots rages behind me. I take a left, throw the door open, and race into—

A dining hall. With six enormous floating glass screens hovering on either side of the doorway, showing some kinduv feed of people protesting at the gates and, I'm guessing, throughout the city; a floating crescent-shaped red and white stone table; and two occupied ridiculously elaborate cushions at the apex of the curve. The table is topped with enough polished red bowls of untouched steaming colorful broths, ripe fruits, and meats to feed a whole camp, and two women are kneeling on their pillows.

The queen, rubbing her temples, and a young woman with long braided hair and rich dark skin, leaning toward her and speaking quietly.

I skid to a stop. The queen stares at me with a shocked, wide gaze, her hands frozen on her temples and her painted bronze lips slightly parted. There's a huge, furry red lump next to them. I step toward them and the door slams open behind me. Something hard and heavy crashes into my back, slamming me into the ground. My cheek smashes into the rough tile. My head throbs and someone grabs my shoulder and yanks me onto my back.

Jarek is straddling me. I throw my arms up over my face just in time—his fist slams into my forearms, my stomach. I try to rock him off, but he's too heavy. He grabs my left arm with his free hand—his fist connects with my jaw, my nose, my neck. My head is roaring. My neck is hot and sticky and someone might be screaming, but my blood is thundering so loudly in my ears that I can't hear anything above the drumming of my pulse.

Then there's a pause in the onslaught of his fists, and I throw myself forward, crashing on top of Jarek. He shoves me off, but I manage to spit a good amount of blood onto his pristine uniform, and that's enough for me. At least for now.

I'm on the ground again, but no one pushed me. I'm not sure how I got here, but my head—the pins and needles behind my eyes have become hot agony. I squeeze my eyes shut. Press my palms against my face. Try to breathe. Red-hot pokers are stabbing the backs of my eyeballs and it's too much to bear. Every pound of my pulse is a hammer on my skull.

Someone is shouting the word for doctor. Then several people are yelling and I need to tell them to shut up, I need to tell them my eyes might be melting out of my skull. I need to tell them they can shoot me now if they'd like—in fact, I'd prefer it.

A sound like a dying animal rips through the air and the shouting gets louder and the noise is horrific—it grates against my throat and sets my skull hotter. It needs to stop; it's making it worse, that horrible, piercing noise.

Is it me?

I clamp my mouth shut and the noise becomes a muffled groan and somehow my knees got up by my chest and I'm on my side and my face is wet with blood and tears.

Someone takes my shoulder and pulls me onto my back. Hands hold down my arms and the pressure off my eyes makes it worse—it's like my hands were holding back the flood of flames. Without their pressure on my eyelids, the pain rushes forward, soaking my eyeballs in acid. I'm not sure if I'm screaming or crying or dying. I'm not sure if it's blood on my lips or tears on my cheeks or saliva on my chin.

Someone peels back the eyelid on my right eye and bright light pours into half my brain and the fire—it's an explosion.

I jerk my head away and someone mutters something and hands grip both sides of my skull, holding my head still.

I can't move and the white sun is igniting my eye and the explosion is going to consume me, the pain is going to kill me. I'm dying. I must be. I don't know what I did to deserve this kinduv death, this kinduv agony, but it needs to end. It needs to stop because I can't handle it much longer. I can't hold on like this.

Then someone says "phaser" and the sun shuts off and hands release my head, release my arms. It'll be over soon. They'll end the torture.

Something hot slams my chest—races through my veins—reaches my skull and—

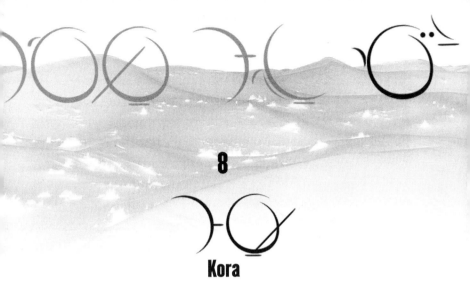

8

Kora

There is blood on the textured white floor of the dining hall and the doctor just shot the half-blood in the chest.

I whirl around and snatch the phaser out of her hand. "What in *Kala*'s name was that? I tell you to help him and you *kill* him?"

Her eyes widen, stretching the black text marked beside her left eye. "*N-Naï, el Avra*! He's not dead—I stunned him. Or, I should say, I stunned the nanites. He's having a reaction to the tracking nanites we injected him with. I-it's rare, but we can flush them from his system and—"

"Just take care of him," I say, and she nods and works with her apprentices to slide a floating board beneath him and rush him to the infirmary. Long after the doors slam shut behind them, the half-blood's screams echo in the room. In my ears, compounded by the angry chorus flooding the hall from the guide coverage of the riot outside.

I pinch the bridge of my nose and inhale deeply. Anja whispers something about bringing Iro to my room and finding someone to clean the mess. I nod. Her footsteps pad quietly across the cool stone, followed by the whoosh of a closing door.

I open my eyes and grimace at the blood smeared on the floor. I hope he'll be all right.

I turn on Dima and his men. "Everyone out except for my brother." For a breath, no one moves, and I step forward and clap at them. "Now!"

Jarek pulls his bloody fists behind his back and grimaces at Dima. The two exchange a look I don't understand—Jarek almost seems reluctant to leave—but before I can question it, he turns away and files out with the others.

Dima turns to me with an unapologetic glare, with a simmering behind his eyes that makes me want to slap him and strip him of his title. If he wasn't my brother, I would do just that.

I break the silence first. "You have yet to explain to me what in *Kala*'s name happened."

He pauses, then tightly crosses his arms. "He showed me disrespect."

"Oh? And how is that?"

"He made a mess in the training room, lied about it, then attacked one of my men." There was more—I can see it in the way he glares at the puddle of red-tinted blood on the floor—and the blossoming bruise on his left cheek might have something to do with it.

I almost hope the half-blood hit him. It's about time someone stood up to my *sko* of a brother.

"I assume all of this was unprovoked," I say. "And he began tearing apart the training room and attacking your men without cause."

Silence. That's what I thought.

"I must also assume, then, that your men were not aptly trained to handle a threat from a half-blood slave."

He scowls and steps toward me. "My men were handling the situation."

"Oh, that I can see. *Sha,* they handled it exquisitely well, didn't they?"

"You disrespect my—"

"*Naï,* Dima, I'm stating fact. Had your men handled the situation well, I would not have witnessed what I did. He never would have made it to the dining hall, and there wouldn't be blood on the floor at your feet."

He glares at the reddish-purple smear again.

"You went too far, brother. I don't know what you did to him, but clearly—"

"We did nothing. The only punishment administered was what you saw."

I find that a little difficult to believe. Even if it's true, Jarek seemed intent on beating the half-blood to death, and yet my brother defends his violence. "And if I had not stepped in, what then? Your man would have killed him."

A long pause. Dima looks up at me and steels his face. "He would have received the punishment he deserved."

Sometimes I don't know how it's possible I shared a womb with this boy. "I can't believe you. Was Jarek even injured?"

"That hardly—"

"It was disproportionate, don't you think? Beating a boy to death for—for what?"

"He attacked my men!" Dima roars. "He showed me a great deal of disrespect. I would never tolerate such an act from one of my own—let alone a half-blood slave who shouldn't be here in the first place."

It's moments like these I am most certain that despite what the guard and the people think, despite the rioters outside demanding he replace me, Dima does not belong on the throne. His first response is always the same: immediate and devastating punishment. He doesn't reason, he doesn't think, he speaks with violence and bloodshed.

Some interpret that as strength, but I know the truth. My brother would be the ruin of Elja.

I drill him with my most cutting glare. "I told you I have a reason for keeping him, but evidently that isn't reason enough for you to exercise some self-control. Fine. I'll handle him from here."

Dima opens his mouth to argue, but I cut him off.

"Don't you have a riot to put down? I'd expected you and your men to be out there handling the situation already."

He scowls, but then the door opens again and a thin young man wearing a high-collared red apprentice's cloak enters the room and bows low.

"*El Avra*, Chief Medic Neja requests your presence immediately. There's something you must see."

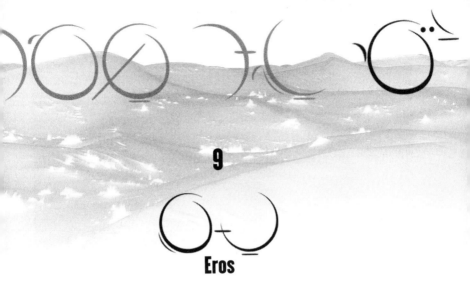

9

Eros

I dream I'm standing in the middle of the desert, surrounded by a ring of fire. The smoke is so thick that I can't see my hands in front of my face, and my eyes, nose, and lungs crackle and sting. I try to cover my mouth and nose with my hands, but it does little to filter the poisonous smog. Screams fill my ears and rain over me, attacking me from all sides. I stumble in circles, searching for the source, but the smoke is overwhelming and my head is fuzzy. My feet are heavy, dragging in the sand, impossible to lift.

A hand bursts out of the sand and grabs my ankle. The fingers are bloody and squeeze hard. A figure emerges from the ground, covered in gore and ash.

Day stares at me with clouded eyes, crying tears of blood.

My eyes flash open and I'm blinded by too-bright light. I squeeze my eyes closed and take a breath—my whole body is numb. Heavy.

Drugged.

There's something cold and sticky on my left temple and right wrist, but my arms don't cooperate when I try to move them to see what it is. I slowly open my eyes, this time prepared for the light. It takes some adjusting, but I can soon make out the white walls draped in red, the flat stone disc—table?—hovering at my bedside with a clear octagonal screen laying on it. I've never seen one before, but I think it's called a . . . glass? I close my eyes for a moment and try to clear my head—my thoughts are sluggish, memories coming back to me slowly, but I remember. Day once mentioned everyone in the cities has those glass-things, and they can get news and read on them and stars know what else.

I open my eyes again. Blink through the haze and inhale deeply as the drug fog fades and my eyes adjust. Rows of empty floating beds hum softly on either side and in front of me, covered in alternating red and white wrinkle-free sheets. White stone floors, though they're smooth here, unlike everywhere else. The far right side of the room is blurry—there's some kinduv semi-transparent wall that makes it impossible to make out any sortuv detail beyond it besides blobs of gray, white, and red, and fuzzy tall things that are maybe people walking around.

And next to me, the queen. Kneeling on an embroidered pillow beside my bed, wearing some kinduv tight bright pink top with silvery-white threaded swirling designs sewn into it. It's cut at a diagonal that starts just under her right breast and leads down to the narrowest point of the left side of her body, meeting the purple fabric of her waist-high skirt. It's sleeveless, but she's got some kinduv black wrapping pulled tightly across her left shoulder and down her arm, almost to her fingertips.

The light markings swirling on her stomach aren't tattooed, but the ones on her right ribs disappearing into the shirt are. More circular text with dashes, dots, slashes, and crescents. What does it say? Why'd she choose to have it written there, leading from the bottom of her ribcage, up to her smooth, round breast? Is her breast tattooed, too? My face warms and I force my eyes away from her chest.

She's watching me. Is that normal? I may not know a whole lot about Sepharon royalty, but it seems unlikely she'd care enough about a slave to wait in the infirmary with me. Unless I'm in trouble. Maybe this is bad news.

For a long moment she doesn't say anything, and I catch myself staring at her green to blue to purple eyes. Bordered by long black lashes and a stripe of some kinduv dark liner, I have to admit they're striking. Especially against her deep golden brown skin and long black hair.

I mean, if cold-blooded murderous alien bitch queen is your type.

"Who are you?" she says.

I hesitate and try to sit up, but my body doesn't cooperate and I slide lower instead. I guess even though my head feels clearer, whatever they gave me is still working out of my system. I settle for slipping my arms out from beneath the red sheets. There's a clear gel disc about an inch across on my wrist, but I leave it alone. "My name is Eros," I answer in Sephari.

"I didn't ask you your name. I asked you who you are."

I frown. "I don't . . . what are you asking?"

She sighs and drums her fingers on her lap. "My name is Kora Mikale Nel d'Elja, but I am not Kora. I am *ken Avra*. My brother's name is Dima Kuru Orolen d'Elja, and he is *ken Avra-kaï* and my second, as well as Commander of the Eljan Guard." She gestures toward me. "And you are?"

I shake my head. Glance at my hands. Who am I?

Before being dragged here, I was one of the top soldiers of the Nomad Defense. Brother of the Head of Defense, adopted son of Nol Kit—one of camp's most respected men, as the descendant of one of the original founders of our colony. Sure, most people didn't see past my ears and skin, and not even Gray, our leader, knew just how involved I was. But as far as Day was concerned, when it came to defense, I was second in command. It was a title I held proudly.

A title she has no business knowing.

"I don't know," I say.

She bites the corner of her lip, then stands. "Do you know who *Sira* Roma is?"

"The ruler of all of the territories. He's who you and the seven other territory regents answer to."

She nods. "And do you know what all *Sirae* have in common?"

This seems like a pretty pointless conversation, but I humor her anyway. Shrug. "They're all part of the same family."

"Besides that."

"I don't know."

She rolls her eyes. "Please. You must know this. Everyone knows—"

"The politics of the Sepharon aren't exactly a top priority to my people," I say. "Nor are the inner workings of the High Royal family."

She kneels again. Pulls her shoulders back and arches an eyebrow at me. "Well perhaps they should be."

"I don't see what this has to do with anything. Or why you're here, for that matter."

The queen—no, her name is Kora—pauses. "Okay. Answer me this—how could you tell a *Sirae* direct descendant from anyone else?"

"I don't know," I say. "And I don't care."

"You truly don't—"

"This conversation is getting boring." I should probably keep my mouth shut, but she didn't come here to chat about politics and, to be honest, I'm getting tired of this pointless interrogation. I glance around the empty room. "Shouldn't I have a doctor here or something? Or a soldier trying to beat me to death? Where is everyone?"

Kora watches me, drumming her fingers on her knee until I shut up, then says, "Gold eyes."

I glance back at her. "What?"

"They all have gold in their eyes—that's how you can tell a *Sirae* descendant. Only the sons, daughters, and grandchildren of the *Sirae* line have it."

"Great. Still irrelevant."

She squints at me. Leans forward. "You truly don't know."

I'm not sure what it is that I supposedly don't know, so I just shake my head. "Guess not."

Kora passes me a mirror, and I try to turn it away but she shoves it into my hands. "Look at it."

So I do. And I'm not sure what I'm supposed to be looking at. I mean, I don't look anything like myself—with my head shaved, my skin unnaturally pale, and my eyes—

My eyes.

"What the . . . what did you do to me?" I blink hard. Still there. Close my eyes and rub hard with my palms. It doesn't change.

"We didn't do anything to you. At least, nothing that would have—"

"Well you obviously did something, because that's not . . . my eyes are green. I have green eyes, not . . ." The more I stare at my reflection, the lower my stomach sinks. My palms go slick and a rush of cold rolls over me.

"During your initiation, you were injected with tracking nanites. It's a solution we inject in every one of our servants, and it allows us to track their location and vitals at all times. As a side effect, it turns their eyes cloudy, which makes identification easy. When we injected you, however, you had a reaction to the nanites, because they interfered with the ones already in your system. The ones making your eyes appear green."

I tear my gaze away from the mirror. "I didn't have nanites in my system until I came here. There must be a mistake or something—my people don't even have access to that kind of technology."

"The nanites couldn't coexist, and they attacked your eyes, which is what caused you to pass out. Our doctor says if we had waited much longer to stun the nanites, they would have blinded you."

I close my eyes. "Nothing you're saying makes sense. If I supposedly have nanites in my system, then my eyes should still be green or clouded or something."

"They would be," Kora says. "Except in order to preserve your sight, the nanites were flushed from your system. All of them. You are now completely clean."

I look at my reflection again. Bite my lip.

My eyes are still gold.

Kora straightens her shoulders and crosses her arms over her breasts. "So I ask again. Who are you?"

I keep waiting for my eyes to go back to normal. Or for me to wake up to Jarek dragging me out of bed by my ears. Or maybe this whole thing is some sick, prolonged nightmare and Day will wake me up with a slap to the side of my head and ask me what I think I'm fucken doin', sleeping past sunrise.

But it's all wishful thinking, I guess, because my eyes aren't changing and the queen is still waiting for an answer.

"I don't know," I mumble. "None of this makes sense."

"Who are your biological parents?"

"I don't know."

"You've never met them?"

I shake my head.

She slides the mirror out of my hands and sets it on the bedside table. "You're sure."

"I think I would know if I'd met my biological parents."

"And the family who raised you? Did they know your biological mother or father?"

"*Nai*," I say, but that's not entirely true. Nol met my mother, briefly, when she handed me over just days after I was born. I shake my head. "Maybe. They didn't talk about it much."

"And you never asked?"

A pause. How much is safe to tell her? "I did."

"And?"

My chest tightens as my fingers dig into my palms. Maybe I shouldn't worry about telling her something that she can use against me, because there's nothing to tell. It's embarrassing how little I know about where I came from, and now I'll never know. I grit my teeth. "And all I was told was my human mother left me with them. I don't know anything about her or who my biological father was."

Kora stands and starts toward the door. "Then we'll find your family and ask them."

"You can't."

She stops and turns. Arches an eyebrow at me. "And why is that?"

Heat washes over me, starting from my gut and spreading over my heart. My eyes sting and my stomach twists with echoes of screaming, crackling flame, and bloodstained sand—and she just stands there with this haughty air that sets my blood boiling.

"Because," I say, careful to keep my voice from shaking. "You killed them."

She stares at me for what feels like a long time, then nods once and steps toward me again. "Get up."

"What?"

"You've rested long enough. Get up."

I consider arguing, but to be honest, I don't really want to lie here anyway. And chances are I won't like the next person to come through that door for me. So I stand, slowly, grimacing as pins and needles prickle the pads of my feet. But whatever they gave me must be wearing off, because my limbs are a bit more cooperative.

Kora walks right up to me, leaving inches between us. Being Sepharon, she's taller than most girls I've come across—only a couple inches shorter than me—and she stares directly into my eyes. The warmth of her breath rolls against my lips and my whole body goes hot—what is she voiding—

Her knee flashes out and nearly strikes me in the groin—nearly, because I jump back just in time. "What the—"

Her foot swings toward my face and I duck out of the way and raise my fists. I can't hit her—I'd be executed on the spot if I so much as touched her—but she keeps coming at me with flashing fists and tight spinning kicks and jabbing elbows and it's all I can do to keep out of the way and avoid the blows.

Then my back hits the wall and I've nowhere left to run and her heel whips toward my face. I catch it and lift up—not enough to knock her over, but enough to throw her off balance. Hopefully.

Except she doesn't look unbalanced. She just watches me with an arched eyebrow and an expression like boredom.

Fabric slips off her skin—the skirt. She's fighting me in a skirt. A long skirt made of many layers of light colorful fabric, with long slits that reach her upper thigh. Which means, holding her foot like this, I've got a full view of her whole golden brown leg. And if I lift any higher . . .

My mouth goes dry. I clear my throat. Force my eyes to her face. "What are you doing? I'm not going to hit you."

She twists her foot out of my grip. "Who trained you?"

"Excuse me?"

She smooths down her skirt. Wipes black hair out of her eyes. "You're obviously trained. Who trained you?"

I hesitate, but I can't think of anything she could do with the information. "My brother."

"And he is dead as well, I presume?"

I wince. Nod.

"Hm." She crosses her arms and her gaze rolls over me, from head to toe. I'm not sure I like the way she's looking at me—like a slab of meat in need of inspection. "My brother thinks I should report you to the *Sirae* family." I don't answer, and she steps right up to me again. Her eyes run over my face, the wound on my neck, my pale shoulders and chest. I resist the urge to shift away from her; the way she inspects me so closely feels like an invasion of privacy.

"And what do you think?" I say carefully.

"I think they would come, execute you, and bury the ashes to hide the scandal. In fact, I know they would."

I scowl. "Scandal?"

"Well, you're obviously a son of one of the children of the throne, and relations between the Sepharon and the red-bloods are not exactly encouraged. And to have a child with one, no less—" She shakes her head. "I don't know what he was thinking."

Suns if I know. Who would deliberately have a half-blood kid? Stars, I'd like to meet the blazing genius who first decided to try inter-species breeding so I could do us all a favor and punch him in the stones. Besides, what was the point of *trying* to make a half-blood if they were just going to slaughter us all in the name of genetic *purity*? I shut the thought away and shake my head.

"It was an accident."

She arches an eyebrow at me. "What was?"

"Me. They probably didn't intend to, uh, get pregnant."

Her brow wrinkles and she tilts her head slightly to the side. "It wasn't an accident."

"You don't know that. People get pregnant accidentally all the time."

Kora blinks once. Stares at me, brows raised. "*Naï*, they don't. Sepharon men control pregnancy down to the sex of the child. There aren't any accidental pregnancies. Surely you know that."

They do? I frown and think back to Day and Jessa. The only kid they had planned was Aren, and I know of several women who became pregnant accidentally. Suns, after the whole drunk disaster with Aryana, she was throwing sand over a potential pregnancy—which never happened, thank the stars. It'd never even occurred to me that it might be different for the Sepharon.

"Oh."

"Oh? Is it not the same with the redbloods?"

I reach up to run a hand through my hair—wait, I don't have hair—and drop my hand awkwardly at my side. "Forget it."

She nods, then turns away and steps toward the door. "Follow me."

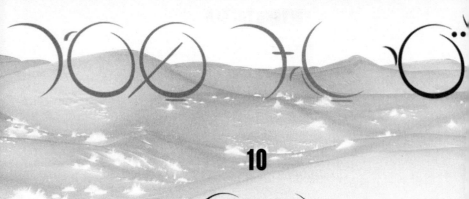

10

Eros

Kora leads me through the winding red pathways—surprisingly empty of guards—out into the desert heat, then back over the cool, stony flooring inside. A flight of stairs up, then another down, and too many turns to count later, she pushes open an elaborate set of enormous red-webbed white stone doors. We enter a large room with a floating desk to the side, four long windows with a view into some kinduv colorful private garden, and a set of double glass doors leading to a sitting area just outside the garden. Built-in bookshelves line the walls and a hovering curtained bed large enough for six people is pressed against the western wall, piled high with red pillows. Across from the bed is a wall-sized mirror, giving the illusion that the room is twice as big.

A bedroom. Her bedroom.

I'm standing in the queen's bedroom.

A flicker of movement on her bed, and my heart jolts. The crimson pillows aren't pillows—it's a ten-foot-long wildcat, watching me with pale blue eyes. A tuft of fur sits between its twitching ears, disappearing down the back of its head in a ridge of longer fur, and two teeth as thick as my fist protrude from its mouth. I've heard about the wildcats before. They roam the desert in perfect camouflage, their sand-colored fur making it all too easy for them to blend—and they've been known to pick off scouts or people stupid enough to wander away from camp alone. Meet a wildcat in the desert, and you better make peace with your maker quick, because it's likely to be the last thing you'll ever see.

And Kora's got one hanging out in her room. Its long tail thumps beside one of its massive paws as it licks its lips and levels its unblinking gaze on me. But if the deadly animal lounging on her hovering bed is a problem, she doesn't show it.

The bed dips slightly as the wildcat rolls over onto its back, swaying back and forth in a slowing rocking motion. Is it normal for the bed to shift like that, or is it just because the cat is so blazing heavy? Does it sway like that during sex, or does it have some kinduv stabilizer? A rocking bed would be kinduv—

Blazing suns. What am I thinking? For stars' sake, focus.

Kora steps to a set of drawers beside her bed and rummages through the contents. After many awkward minutes of silence, she turns around and hands me a small black case, about the length of my pinky finger. "When my medic revealed your eyes to my brother and me, I asked her to make this in secret. I want you to use it."

I glance at the case. Back to the cat. "I take it that's not a reason for concern?" I nod at the ten-foot-long accessory.

Kora glances at the wildcat. "What, Iro? *Naï*, he's harmless." She smiles and sits on her bed, and my face warms slightly as it sways back and forth again. Stars above, I need to stop thinking about floating bed sex. She wraps her arms around the beast's neck and buries her face in his fur, like it's a giant stuffed animal and not a man-eating monster. She's voiding insane. Or suicidal.

But she's smiling. "Isn't that right, Iro? You wouldn't hurt anyone."

A deep rumbling rolls from its throat, and the wildcat licks her cheek, so maybe the cat's just really stupid. She grins and ruffles the tuft between its ears. "See? Harmless."

I'm not convinced, but she's hugging the blazing thing so I guess it's not a concern, at least right now. I open the case. Inside are two small compartments with two tiny droppers— one filled with a swirling silver fluid that looks almost like liquid metal, and the other with a clear liquid.

The clear stuff looks harmless enough, but the silver fluid is roiling on its own. Like it's alive. Cold drips down my chest and into my stomach.

"Is this what I think it is?"

"They'll hide your eyes," Kora says. "Only three people know about them, and I'd like to keep it that way."

I look at her. "These are nanites."

She nods.

"You really think I'm going to use this when the last batch of nanites you used on me nearly *blinded* me?"

"I think you don't have an option. And besides, these are different. You don't inject them—they dissolve onto your iris and change the color superficially. If you want to remove them at any time, you drip the dissolving fluid into your eyes and they'll wash out immediately."

I frown at the case. Bite my lip. "So you're not going to hand me over to the High Royals?"

"I haven't decided yet. But until I do, you'll use that if you want a chance to live."

I close the case. "Why am I here? You didn't have to bring me to your room to change my eye color."

A slight smile slides across her lips and she sits up and crosses her legs. Her skirt slides high on her thighs, and it takes more than a handful of effort to yank my eyes away from the bare spot on her toned upper thigh.

"You're sharp," she says.

"I'm not an idiot, more like."

She taps her fingers on her leg. Maybe she's doing it on purpose. Did she catch me staring? I make a point to look at her eyes and not her breasts or sculpted stomach. Finally, she says, "My personal guard was killed in a recent attempt on my life."

"Sorry to hear that."

If she noticed the sarcasm dripping from my condolences, she doesn't show it. "He wasn't truly loyal to me, but that's besides the point."

I wait for her to continue, but then she doesn't. "What is your point?"

She arches an eyebrow. "Perhaps you're not as sharp as I thought."

"You're not going to ask me to be your personal guard, so I think it's fair I'm confused about where you're going with this."

Kora slides off her bed and steps right up to me again. It takes a lot more concentration to keep my eyes on her face now that I've noticed the rest of her not unattractive body. There must be something seriously wrong with me. She's a fucken murderer for stars' sake,—she burned my home to the ground and killed half my family. No amount of nice curves, round breasts, or gorgeous eyes can change that.

"Why do you say I wouldn't ask you?" she says, watching me. I make a point not to notice her long dark eyelashes and full lips. Wait. Shit.

"You can't be serious. You don't need me to answer that."

"Humor me."

I search her face for a smile, or a hint of a joke or trick, but she looks disturbingly serious. Instead of hidden laughter, her eyes glint with something else—curiosity? "I'm a half-blood. And a slave. And according to your brother, not worth the air I breathe."

"I never said I agreed with my brother."

"You don't have to—it's the one thing humans and Sepharon agree on. Half-bloods are a genetic perversion that shouldn't exist. Humans and Sepharon aren't meant to blend."

"And yet, here you are . . ." She reaches out and traces the thicker line of the light markings on my collarbone. Her touch sends a warm rush into my stomach and a chill over my skin—what is she doing? I suppress a shudder. I hope to the moons that the white powder on my face hides the heat on my cheeks. "You know, the *kara* bath doesn't suit you. You'll be taking normal baths from now on." Her gaze runs over my neck and back up to my face. "And I'll have you grow your hair out. The plucked look is rather odd on you."

I stare. "You're serious."

"As poison, I'm afraid." She steps away from me and sits on the edge of her bed again. It sways. I pretend not to notice. "My guards are no longer loyal to me. It's no secret they would much rather see a man on the throne—they think I cheated Dima of the crown." She shrugs. "You dislike my guard as much as I do, you're trained for combat, and I have little doubt in my mind that anyone else would try to buy your loyalty."

I cross my arms. "And if I decline?"

She grins so sharply it's a wonder she doesn't cut herself. "Well, that'll make my decision much easier then."

My fingers clench into fists. "Decision?"

"Of whether or not to report you to the *Sirae* family, of course. I'm afraid you know too much to be anything less than my personal servant." I scowl, but her smile softens. "Threats aside, you're not going to get a better offer, Eros. As my personal guard, you'll have much more comfortable sleeping quarters, some privacy, and a sense of individuality. I'll keep you well fed and clothed and you won't have to subject yourself to the menial, humiliating work that my brother is sure to assign you. Pledge your loyalty to me, and I will do everything in my power to keep your secret safe."

As much as I want to hate her for cornering me with this bizarre offer, she's right—this is better than anything I could have hoped for. I should be grateful. I should be thanking her.

But despite her *generosity*, she's still the girl who ordered the massacre of my camp. She oversaw the slaughter of hundreds of people. The enslavement of dozens of women and children. And now she wants me to save her. Now she wants me to protect her.

"You killed my people."

She sighs and looks at her feet. Digs her fingers into the blankets. "I am sorry," she says softly, "truly, for the pain I've caused you. My soldiers made decisions I did not consent to, but unfortunately I had little choice."

A rush of heat flares through my center. She's the blazing queen and she didn't have a choice? What does she take me for? "Everyone has a choice."

Kora inhales deeply. Looks up at me. There's something wrong with her eyes—they're kinduv shiny like—no. No voiding way. She is *not* going to sit there and try to make me feel bad for her.

"A group of your rebels tried to kill me. They succeeded in murdering my parents and hundreds of my people."

Her eyes are doing that stupid glistening thing. She believes it, but she's delusional, because that never happened. I shake my head. "We never—"

"Three cycles ago at my coronation, a group of rebels planted several bombs at the Temple d'Elja. It took three cycles to track down the bombers, but we did several sunsets ago—to your encampment."

I clench my fists. "I would know if we'd planned that kind of attack."

"I've done some things I'm not proud of, but I've done it in the name of protecting my people. You would do the same, would you not?" She looks at me again, and it's clear that she knows the answer. She's already seen me do as much. "I'm willing to overlook your transgressions, but I need you to extend me the same courtesy. I need you to pledge to protect me with your life."

I bite my lip. Force the heat down into my stomach. Take a breath. What would my family do? Day would've attacked her the moment he entered her room. He would have ended her life and tracked down Dima while he had the chance. He would have thrown his life away in the name of protecting his loved ones.

But not Nol. Nol would tell me to think clearly, to think with my heart and my mind simultaneously. He would ask me to consider what options I have that don't involve violence. He would ask me to do everything I could to protect my people in the most diplomatic way possible.

I'm not Day, but I'm not Nol, either. And yet, considering their choices helps me make mine.

"I'll agree under two conditions."

Kora nods. "And what are your conditions?"

I straighten my shoulders. "You'll swear to me that you'll stop searching for my people. You'll allow them to recover and live out the rest of their lives in peace."

She pauses. "As long as my life, or my people, are not threatened by yours, I agree. Next?"

This one will be trickier, but I say it as confidently as I can manage. "You'll flush the nanites from the women and children who you enslaved from my camp and release them."

She hesitates. Purses her lips. "I'm not sure I can do that."

"Not sure you can, or not sure you want to?"

"I—"

"You're the queen, aren't you? I was under the impression everyone has to do what you say without question."

"They do, but—"

"Then I don't see what the problem is. Agree to cleanse and release them, and I'll pledge to you right now."

Kora bites the corner of her lip. Taps her fingers on her leg. "The court and council will be very displeased."

"If you'd rather deal with a displeased *Sirae* Court when you tell them I exist and find someone else willing to keep you on the throne and protect you . . ." I shrug and try to look apathetic, but to be honest, if she *did* choose to report me and use someone else, I'd be dead.

She arches an eyebrow. "I wasn't aware you had a preference as to who held the throne."

"I didn't. Until I met your brother."

She smirks. "He's a bit difficult to get along with."

I snort. "That's putting it mildly."

"Fine. I accept your terms."

"You do?"

Kora nods, steps over to her dresser, and rifles through the drawers. After a moment she pulls out a shimmering gold scarf and steps in front of me. "Do you know how to pledge?" My hesitation is all the answer she needs, and she nods again. "Kneel."

I obey, and she takes my right hand in her left and wraps the scarf around her arm, over our clasped hands, and tightly onto my forearm. She does it swiftly, like it's been ingrained in her muscle memory. How many others have pledged their allegiance to her? Finally, when the scarf runs out, she tucks the end beneath a loop and meets my eyes.

"This golden fabric is representative of the holy oath you are making. Just as the cloth binds us, your oath to me binds us together until death. Do you swear this to be true?"

A part of me rebels at those words—*until death*. But what did I expect? I'm a slave now, and will be for the rest of my life—the tattoo on my arm makes that clear enough. Sweat beads the back of my neck and, for a terrifying moment, my hand goes slick against hers. But considering where I am, where I will be for the rest of my life, this is the best I could hope for. I squeeze a little tighter and say, *"Sha."*

If she notices my clammy palm, she doesn't comment. Instead she reaches into her skirt and pulls out a knife from stars know where, spreads the loops of the scarf over the top of my hand, and slices my skin. My breath catches in my throat, and I resist the urge to pull away—not that I could if I wanted to—and she releases the fabric and watches as it soaks up my dark, purple-red blood. She waits until my blood has leaked down the sides of my hand and has dripped onto the edges of hers before speaking.

"Repeat after me: I, Eros of the Eljan Vastlands, swear on my lifeblood and the fate of my afterdeath to serve and protect Kora Mikale Nel d'Elja to the end of my life, or until she freely releases me."

In my mind, Day jerks to the side and crumples in the sand. My parents' clasped hands and the burning tents and tiny bodies littering the sands flash across my eyes and stars alive, I hope I'm doing the right thing. I hope they wouldn't hate me for this and see me as a traitor. Nausea rolls through me and a chill rushes over me, but I repeat her words.

"If I break or fail my oath, I ask that *Kala* dishonor me and my descendants for eight generations, and I submit my afterdeath to the Void."

Maybe I'm a failure for agreeing to this. Maybe I deserve endless nothingness after I die. But I say it word for word, then Kora unwraps her arm and hand and winds the rest of the cloth over mine. "It is done. Wear the fabric until your hand heals, then you may remove it and do with it what you wish. You may rise."

I stand and stare at my stinging hand. She wrapped it pretty tight, so I'm not too worried about the bleeding, but will it leave a scar? A permanent sign of my allegiance to her, etched into my hand?

I suppose it doesn't matter. Scar or not, I've just sworn my life away.

"You'll be given new clothes immediately, and you'll sleep in my chambers." My eyes shoot up at that last bit. She doesn't notice at first—she's examining my blood on her hand—but then she sees my stare and smirks. "You'll have a bedroll. On the floor."

My face goes hot. "I knew that."

"I'm sure you did," she says, sounding vaguely amused. "Now, you need a bath. No guard of mine will wear *kara*."

After scrubbing my skin clean of the waxy white layer stubbornly bleaching my body, I change into the new clothes Kora's servants left folded beside the tub—a weird white pair of pants that looks like a knee-length skirt with pant legs sewn into the bottom and a red stripe along the legs, and a silver metal band to clasp just above my elbow. All of this is better than the white skirt I was wearing before, so I have no complaints.

I step out of the bathroom, feeling more like myself in my bronzed skin—albeit, a pathetically hairless version of myself—and enter Kora's chambers. Iro jumps off the bed and strolls right up to me, pressing against my side as he moves around me, swishing his tail. I stand still and try not to panic, but even on all fours, the blazing cat comes up to my chest, and beneath the soft, thick fur is all muscle. It could kill me in a mo.

"Iro," Kora calls with a slight laugh. "Come here. Don't scare the poor man."

The cat trots over to her side, then flops down beside her. She's waiting at her desk with a woman sitting across from an empty chair holding an inscribed metal band. I recognize the band—it's the same one that burned the tattoo into my skin not twelve hours ago.

Kora's gaze slowly rolls over me, from head to foot, and something about the way she's looking at me almost makes me feel dirty. A hint of a smile curves her lips. "Much better. Now sit."

I take the empty chair, and the woman clasps the band around my marked arm and slides it just under my current tattoo.

"Is this really necessary?" I ask, and Kora raises an eyebrow.

"Your body reads Servant of Elja. You are no longer a lowly servant; you are sworn to me. Now your skin will say as much." She nods at the woman who runs her fingers over the surface of the band and taps a sequence into the surface. The edges glow red and my skin burns.

I grit my teeth and stare at my toes. Iro licks my knee and I grimace—his tongue is like slimy sandrock.

"How do you like your clothes?" Kora asks.

"They're comfortable," I mutter. My fingers squeeze into my knee until my skin stops sizzling and the band cools. The woman then unclasps my arm and Kora nods.

"Thank you, Mijna. Have the servants I specified been gathered?"

"*Sha, el Avra*," the woman says with an airy voice.

"Wonderful. Flush the nanites from their bloodstream immediately and see to it that they are released. I've already informed Jarek and the others of this order."

Mijna bows and steps out of the room. I examine my arm. I still can't read any of it, but the weird black crescent letters follow the contours of light markings swooping over my skin. Which is great, because I really wanted to bring attention to my almost-Sepharon skin.

I force myself to look away and turn to Kora. "Thank you. For keeping your word."

"I expect you to hold me to my words, as I will hold you to yours." Her gaze rolls over me. "I take it you've noticed you are not wearing the uniform of a warrior."

"I hadn't really expected army clothes, all things considered."

She nods. "You must understand it is imperative that all others believe you to be my personal servant, and nothing more. It is essential for your safety, as well as mine."

"That's fine."

"Good. I feared you may be insulted."

I snort. "I'm not that fragile."

She smiles. "I had hoped as much. Thank you, Eros."

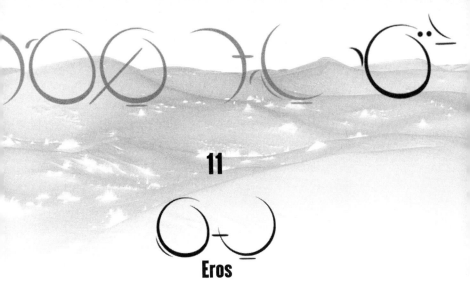

11

Eros

My new job requires shadowing Kora incessantly, and Iro, it seems, feels the need to join us just about everywhere. No one pays him much mind though, so I guess it's a regular thing. When we first left her room, I got more than a couple lingering stares from guards and a few raised eyebrows at the new line inscribed on my arm. But it seems the black text was more necessary than I thought, because no one questions me after looking at my arm.

The first day is mostly uneventful—Kora goes to her personal training room where she works out until I'm exhausted just watching, then returns to her room and eats a quiet lunch of colorful imported fruits and orange meats dripping with a blue glaze. She shares her food with her personal servant Anja, who doesn't wear the uniform servant clothes, either. Instead, she has a long sheer green skirt that's see-through below the knees and a blue top made out of the same kinduv thin material, but wrapped around her body several times and knotted at her waist. It looks nice against her dark skin, I guess, but to be honest, I'm more interested in their food. My mouth waters and my stomach grumbles as I watch them eat. When's the last time I've had a decent meal? It feels like a lifetime ago . . .

They chat idly over their food about her brother and some kinduv celebration over fifty sets—or, a term, as they call it—away. After they've finished, Kora hands me a bowl full of chopped fruit and meat, then walks to the bathroom to bathe and change.

I eat quickly out of habit, but I try to slow down because the food is incredible. I've never had fruit before, and the pink juice is sweet and sour and the pulp is slightly chewy and entirely amazing.

When I pick up the meat with my fingers, Anja wrinkles her nose and hands me two stick-like silver utensils with short twin tines at the end. I have no idea how to use them, so I stab the meat with it and eat it off the end. Anja looks disgusted, but I don't care because the meat is tender, and salty, and sweet, and easily the best thing I've ever eaten.

Maybe I should be insulted that I get the scraps, but these scraps are way too delicious to be blazed about. I suck the blue glaze off my fingers and Anja snatches the bowl out of my hand and shoves a square of fabric at me. I wipe my hands and she takes that, too, shaking her head.

After eating, Anja gives me two metal spheres covered in some sortuv thin, slightly sticky dark blue material. Sephari letters light up under the material at my touch. I have no idea what it says, but after messing with it, I find I can adjust the weight of each ball with a few taps. I use them to work out until Kora emerges. She steps out of the bathroom in a short towel and a scarf tightly wrapped around her left arm and shoulder. That's it. The edge of the towel dangles several inches above her knee and the light markings of her skin swirl around her leg and up into the towel, and there's black text weaving up the inner part of her thigh and into—

Kora clears her throat. Stares at me pointedly. Arches an eyebrow. Suns above, I'm staring. Stop staring! I rip my attention to the window, ignoring the heat of the suns on my face.

There's a garden outside. A ridiculously elaborate garden with more flowers and plants than I've seen my whole life. Who even needs a garden this big? Stars, who has time to take care of a garden this big? How does it even survive in this heat?

And what does she voiding have written on her *inner* thigh?

After she changes, I have the joy of watching her read. For hours. I entertain myself with an extra workout, then inane, pointless tasks, like counting the books on the bookshelves (1,287) and the trees visible from the window (18) and the number of handles in the room (16). I even pet the blazing cat, who seems to have developed a liking to me, and often takes turns rubbing against me, then Kora. I try ignoring him at first, but he nudges my hand incessantly until I give in and rub the base of his ears. Nol would've loved this—he always said if we showed respect to the wild, we would receive respect in return.

Though that advice didn't help the half-dozen people we lost to wildcat attacks over the years.

"Why is he so gentle?" I finally ask. "The only wildcats I've ever heard about were bloodthirsty carnivores."

Kora glances up at me from her book. "What did you call him?"

I hesitate. "We call them wildcats."

She furrows her brow. "Your people are strange."

"Well, what do you call them, then?"

"*Kazim*," she says. "And as a cub, he was injected with nanites that made him docile."

Frowning, I say, "He's brain damaged?"

"*Naï*. He just doesn't have aggressive impulses." She goes back to her book and flips the page, effectively ending the conversation.

But since I'm bored out of my mind, I ask another question that's been nagging at me. "Why do you have all these books when you can use your glass?" I nod at the discarded screen on her desk. "I thought you could read on those."

She doesn't look up from the pages. "*Sha*, but I prefer something a little more tangible."

I frown and turn to the bookshelves lining the walls. I can't read Sephari, and my written English is pretty shaky, but even if I *did* know how to read well, I can't imagine I'd ever have the time to read all these books. "Have you read all of these?"

"Not yet. But I intend to."

Anja knocks on the door and informs us that supper is prepared. Kora thanks her and tucks her book away.

Then she turns to me and sighs. "My brother and Jarek will be present at supper, and they will not be pleased to see you. You are not to say a word unless I instruct you otherwise. Is that understood?"

I nod.

"When I enter the room, you are to pull my cushion out for me—I sit at the apex of the table—and serve me water from the pitcher. Then you will stand against the wall behind me."

"Okay."

She nods. Pauses. "Don't let my brother intimidate you. He has no power over you anymore."

"Your brother doesn't intimidate me."

"Good." She steps out of her room and I follow.

The moment we enter the expansive dining hall, Dima and Jarek stand. But their eyes aren't on Kora as she strides confidently toward her seat—they're on me.

I step in front of Kora and pull out her cushion from under the hovering table for her, like she instructed. She sits on her heels and I take the stone pitcher and fill her glass with purple water, then return the pitcher to the table and step against the wall as Iro lies down beside Kora. Dima and Jarek are still standing when Kora takes a sip and arches an eyebrow at them.

"I take it the two of you will be standing as you eat, then?"

"What is that?" Dima snaps, the full force of his glare leveled on me. I meet his eyes, but keep my face expressionless.

"His name is Eros," she says coolly. "I believe you two have already been acquainted."

Dima scowls, but Jarek kneels at the table. Dima follows suit, kneeling next to him, but he looks like he's just smelled something rancid.

"He's a half-blood," Dima grits out. His hands are squeezed into fists as nearly identical servants flood the room with enough platters of steaming food to feed a couple camps. But while Dima does little to hide his distaste, Jarek sits calmly beside him, his face blank and his posture upright but relaxed. But I know a front of apathy when I see it. I've practiced it myself way too often to miss it.

"He is," Kora says as a servant fills her plate with dark meats, spotted vegetables, and striped fruits—a little from every platter.

"I assume you've reason to keep him," Jarek says smoothly.

"I had need of a second personal servant to take over when Anja is occupied with her side work."

"He's a boy," Dima says.

"Really? I hadn't noticed. That would explain his lack of breasts."

I smirk for just a mo, then force it off my face.

"Don't be disrespectful, Kora," Dima says. "You seem to forget who you're speaking to."

"*Naï,* brother, I think *you* forget who you're speaking to. Last I checked, I was still *Avra* and deserving of your utmost respect."

Dima glares, but Jarek gives him a look and her brother takes a breath. Exhales. Relaxes his hands. "Were there not enough female pureblooded servants to take care of your needs? Surely you could have chosen one of the women from the outpost you recently raided before you decided to release them all."

Kora chews her food slowly. Takes a long drink. "I chose Eros, so I had little use for those slaves."

"*Kala*'s grace, Kora. You're on a first-name basis with the *half-blood*?"

Kora tries to shrug, but the movement is stiff. She cuts a square of meat and keeps her eyes focused on her plate.

"You truly couldn't find a way to use the new servants?" Jarek asks carefully.

"I saw little need to keep extra servants. The effort alone to train the lot of them, assign separate tasks, and feed and clothe them wasn't worth the unnecessary added labor."

"And yet you just claimed to have need of a second personal servant," Dima says.

"I had a need and I filled it. I didn't need hoards of women to fill the position."

"Or perhaps you seek fulfillment of a different need," her brother says with a wicked glint in his eye. "One that a woman could not fill."

Kora chokes on her food as Dima levels his gaze on her. She gulps down water and slams her glass down. "*That* is *disgusting*."

Heat rushes to my face and I resist the urge to scowl.

"I thought it a logical jump, considering your insistence that this particular male half-blood is the only one who could serve your 'needs.'"

Someone's utensil scrapes against their plate, and a grating screech sends chills down my spine. Dima jumps slightly and glances at Jarek with an arched eyebrow, so I guess the bulky soldier is the offender. Jarek glances back at him and lifts a shoulder before he resumes eating.

"Clearly, I don't use my servants the same way you do," Kora says stiffly.

"Well, perhaps if you did, there would be an heir to the throne—albeit an illegitimate one. Or do the council's guidance and the people's demands mean nothing to you?"

Jarek frowns slightly and Kora goes very still. I can't see her face, but I can imagine the look she must be giving him. But her brother jumps in again before she can respond. "Speaking of which, do you know *why* the people were rioting earlier?"

A pause. "I saw the feed."

"They want a man on the throne, Kora," Dima says smugly. "Not that I can blame them. They have little confidence in your ability to rule, or right to do so."

"I was born with the right," Kora snaps. "Had *Kala* wanted you on the throne, you would have been born before me."

I expect Dima to lose all composure at that, but instead he just smiles, cuts into his meat, and brings it to his lips. "Perhaps" is all he says, but the gleam in his eyes echoes something more.

I snap awake, shivering and dripping with sweat. Kicking off the cover of my bedroll, I stand. Cool air calms my heart as I push the echo of screams and crackling flames into the deep recesses of my mind. The moons filter white light through the translucent curtain over the large window, and Iro lays curled up at its base, his tail twitching as he sleeps.

I get up and walk over to the window, leaning against the sill. I try to breathe in outside air—there isn't glass or a screen to block it—but all I get is cold, processed air. Leaning farther out the window, I stick my head outside. As I pass through the opening, warmth surrounds my skin and fills my lungs. It feels a little odd—my shoulders and the rest of my body are cool, while my head takes in the desert air—but the unprocessed oxygen is calming.

When my pulse returns to normal, I lean back inside and inspect the window. The only sign of any kinduv barrier is a thin line of sand running down the center of the sill. I extend my fingers past the line and the outside warmth surrounds my fingertips. So whatever barrier is used to keep the cool air inside also blocks out the sand, but allows larger objects to pass through.

I'm no scientist, but I'm willing to bet it has something to do with nanites.

Mystery solved, I run a hand over my fuzzy scalp and turn back to my bedroll—I should get some sleep while I can.

A soft moan rolls through the night and I squint through the darkness. Kora seems to be asleep, but she's twisted in tossed sheets and hugging her knees to her chest. I take a few hesitant steps forward—she's trembling, and whimpers carry through the quiet. I frown and nudge her shoulder, but she doesn't wake. The light of the moons catches her wet cheeks. Maybe I should let her handle this on her own. We all have personal demons, and we have to face them, one way or another.

But the whimpers and tears don't stop. I can't leave her like that.

I sit on the edge of her bed and ignore the way it dips slightly under my weight. Now is not the time. I gently tap her cheek, then take her shoulder and keep my voice low. "Kora, wake up. You're having a—"

She gasps and sits up, her eyes wide as she pulls the covers to her shoulders. It doesn't cover much—the thin material does nothing to hide the perfect curve of her breasts or the smooth line of her bare shoulder. I hadn't even realized she was sleeping naked. I guess I shouldn't be surprised—I mean, I only kept my pants just in case I had to get up quickly in the middle of the night.

"Sorry," I mutter, ignoring the warmth spreading through my veins. "You were having a nightmare and I just—"

"You're touching me," she whispers, staring at my hand on her shoulder.

I drop my hand to my lap. Take a breath. "Sorry. I was trying to wake you, you seemed like . . . forget it." I stand and turn away, but her fingers clasp around mine. A flash of heat races through me, and my breath catches. I glance back. Tears are streaming down her cheeks as she stares at me.

"Could you . . . stay? For a few minutes?"

My gaze drops to the small twin bumps of her nipples beneath the sheet. I gulp. Stare at her face, not her breasts or the silvery moonlight painting her smooth collarbone and the curve of her neck. She wants me to stay? While she's . . .

Okay, I need to relax. It's not like I've never seen a naked woman before. And besides, she's mostly covered . . . by a ridiculously thin sheet.

Her fingers squeeze mine just slightly. She must really need some company if she's asking me to stay. I can handle it. I'm not fourteen. This isn't a big deal.

I sit on the edge of her bed again.

She pulls her hand away and pulls her knees to her chest, which is good because, between the sheet and her legs, most everything is covered. See? No big deal.

"Did I wake you?"

I shake my head. "I was having nightmares of my own." A pause. I hadn't really meant to admit that. I bite my lip and she nods.

"How do you do it?" she whispers.

"Do what?"

"You say you have the dreams as well, and yet you don't seem bothered."

I smile weakly. "I've been trained to internalize emotion."

"From the military?"

I nod. Kora scoots to the side and glances at the now empty spot on the bed. I take the silent invitation and shift closer to her. Our arms are just barely touching through the sheet and the almost-contact buzzes on my skin. I want to move closer. Without fabric separating us. I want to trace her collarbone and feel her breasts and taste her tattoos. I want our skin together, our—

Stop. She killed my family. I'm not attracted to her—she's Sepharon, and a murderer and the embodiment of everything I've ever fought against and this needs to stop.

"Do you miss it?" she asks. "Your home?"

I hesitate. "I miss my family and the open air and endless sands. But the camp itself?" I shrug.

Kora looks down for several moments, then takes a breath and turns her gaze back to me. "I am truly sorry. About your family. If I could go back I would . . . do things differently."

My eyes sting and I focus on her desk on the other side of the room. I don't say anything. Her apology means nothing because we can't go back, we can't do things differently, we can't return the lives we've taken or take back the pain we've caused. There's nothing to say.

She sighs. "I miss my old life, when Dima and I were children, before the pressure of the throne drove us apart. He was my closest friend, for a time."

When I look at her, her gaze is distant. Caught somewhere in the past, I guess. "What happened?" I'm not sure why I asked that. I don't care. I don't want to get to know her. I don't want her to be anything but a symbol of everything I hate.

And yet, when Kora bites her lip and looks down at her knees, my anger slips away.

For a long moment she's silent, probably because she has no business telling me anything and, honestly, I shouldn't be asking. I shouldn't be giving her the opportunity to explain herself.

But then she says, "No one has ever asked me that before."

I blink. "No one's ever asked you about . . . you?"

She laughs weakly and shakes her head. "This is the Eljan court. It'd be vulgar for someone to ask me personal questions unless they were attempting to interest me."

"Interest?"

She gives me a look. "As a potential suitor."

My eyes widen as my face goes hot. We're sitting on her bed together, and she thinks—no, she can't think that because she wouldn't tolerate that from me for a mo. Right? "I'm not flirting with you," I say quickly. "I was just being . . . nice."

Kora smiles weakly. "I know. It's a pleasant change of pace." We sit in silence for a couple mos before she sighs and continues softly. "To answer your question about my brother and me . . . my coronation happened. I inherited the throne, the explosion took our parents and—" Her voice cracks and she covers her mouth with her hand, fresh tears sliding down her cheeks. Without thinking, I scoot a little closer and put my arm over her shoulders. She stiffens at my touch, but as she cries quietly into her hand, she doesn't pull away. I shouldn't be doing this, I shouldn't be consoling her. I won't feel bad, not for her, not after what she did, and yet I can't fight this fucken ridiculous need to fix this, to hold her until it's okay.

It's not okay. It'll never be okay.

Eventually she quiets, but she doesn't sit back, so I keep her close, waiting for her to tell me to go back to my bedroll.

I hate to admit it, but it feels nice, holding someone like this, and part of me doesn't want to let go.

That part of me needs to take a hike in the desert without water before I do something I'll regret.

But she doesn't tell me to leave. Instead, she says, "Tell me about your people."

"My people?"

She nods. "No one truly seems to know where the red-bloods came from and so I thought . . ." she glances at me. Our faces are closer than I'd realized and, as much as I hate it, the warmth of her body against mine sets my pulse pounding. I should move away. Get off this bed. Get away from her. But instead I hold my breath and look at her lips, which are way too close for comfort.

"I thought maybe you would know," she says.

Know? Know what? Know that I can feel her breathing against me? Know that we're sitting in the dark, nearly naked, on a bed together with only a thin sheet between us? Know that I don't usually lose control so easily, that I should be focusing on her words and not thinking about what her skin might feel like on mine?

Stop. This isn't right. She's Sepharon—hell, she's a Sepharon queen. I can't think this way. I can't be attracted to her. I have to stop, I have to focus. I have to answer her question and breathe. Air.

Her question. Where do redbloods come from?

I'd heard stories about how humans got here—histories passed down from parent to child for generations about another planet galaxies away, about a land where humans are the dominant species and the Sepharon are nothing more than whispers of a tale. A place called Earth where the sky is sometimes blue and sometimes smog, depending on where you are. Where there's only one sun and one moon and one ruling species with many languages.

And they brought their people here, and when the killing and enslavement began, they left us to fend for ourselves.

To be honest, I'd never paid much attention to the stories. What did it matter how humans got here? We were here, and now this was our home, even if the Sepharon weren't keen on sharing it.

"Supposedly the original colony came from another planet called Earth ages ago," I say. "I'm not sure what the point was—I think they wanted to settle here or something. But when they arrived, they found that Safara was already inhabited by a humanoid species. And I guess the Sepharon took over quickly and used us as a slave race. Some got away and started the tribes of the Nomads, and the rest . . ." I shrug and try not to look at the black markings on my arm. Glance at her again. "What do your people say happened?"

"That the redbloods arrived on several ships with intentions to take from our soil. And that we sent a very clear message to the rest of their kind to stay away from our home."

I smile grimly. "Seems they got the message."

Her eyes drift closed and she nods. "So it seems."

We stay like that in the shadows for what feels like a long time. She sinks lower into my side and, as her breathing evens out, my eyelids droop. We breathe together and her hair smells sweet and I expect her to tell me to leave at any moment, but the command never comes.

Everything about this is wrong, and yet I sleep more soundly than I have since that terrible night of fire and smoke.

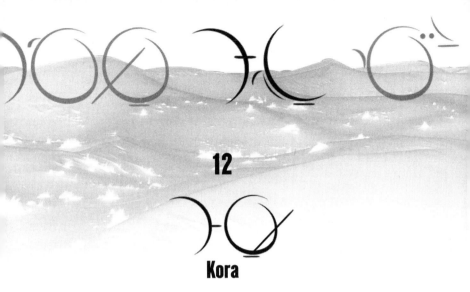

12

Kora

"We're going into Vejla," I say when Eros returns from his morning jog around the grounds.

He stands in the doorway, the sculpted muscles of his chest glistening with sweat as he catches his breath. I have to admit, the uniform suits him. The white fabric makes his tanned light brown skin look rich and smooth, and I certainly don't mind the perfect view of his toned upper body. He's surprisingly well built. Almost handsome, even.

For a half-blood.

I watch him from my spot on the bed, lowering my book as he stares at me. "Did anyone give you trouble?"

"A few glares and I'm pretty sure someone spat at me, but nothing I'm not used to," he says breathlessly.

I scowl, but Eros shakes his head. "It's nothing compared to what I used to get at camp as a kid. Don't worry about it."

His words sink into me one at a time. How is it possible that his own people treated him worse than mine do? "I don't understand. You were a warrior, were you not? Did your people truly not respect you at all?"

"I'm a half-blood, Kora," he says, as though that says it all.

I suppose it does.

Eros wipes sweat off his brow with the back of his hand. "What do you mean we're going to Vejla? We *are* in Vejla."

I sigh and stand. "*Sha*, but we're in the palace complex, which, if you haven't noticed, is kept separate from the city. I want to walk the streets and see my people, and you're coming with me."

Eros frowns and wipes sweat off his brow with the back of his hand. "Are you sure that's a good idea? Eight sets ago, there was that riot—"

"I haven't forgotten the riot, Eros." I turn to my wardrobe. "That's exactly why I need to see Vejla for myself. It's been too long since I've entered the city without the prestige of being *Avra*. I need to see my people up close."

He hesitates. "I'm not sure that's safe."

"Of course it's not safe. That's why you're coming with me." I rifle through the drawers until I find what I'm looking for—a dusty, gray-green hooded tunic with loose, overlapping layers and long sleeves. The back has a large opening with crisscrossing straps, but no one will recognize me by my back. At least, I hope not.

"Besides." I toss the tunic onto my bed. "Dima says he's taken care of the situation, and there haven't been any protests on the guide feed for three sunsets. It seems the people have calmed down, so you have little to worry about."

"Kora . . ." I face Eros and narrow my eyes at him. He grimaces and sighs. "There's no talking you out of this, is there?"

"*Naï,* there isn't." I smile at him and point to a pile of clothes neatly folded at the edge of my bed. "Anja brought those for you. Clean up and put those on so we can go before my brother and Jarek return from their drills. I don't want anyone to know I've gone."

Eros pulls off his black hood as soon as we step outside. I frown and yank the hood back over his head, and he rips it right off again.

"Stop that!" I hiss. "I can't have anyone recognizing us."

Eros scowls. "First off, no one sane wears all black in the middle of the blazing day, especially with long sleeves. I'm going to broil in these ridiculous clothes." He pulls at his thin, sheer black shirt, then glares at his dark pants like they've somehow insulted him.

I frown. "Your shirt's thin enough—it just has to cover your markings."

"*Secondly*," he continues, ignoring me. "You're going to look conspicuous enough in a hood and long sleeves, but *two* people walking around in long-sleeved hoodies is going to attract attention, so I'm not wearing my hood up for your own good. You're welcome."

"Fine." I sigh and step forward. "Let's just go before my brother sees."

Eros moves in front of me, blocking my way.

I roll my eyes. "You aren't going to stop me from going, you know."

"I'm not trying to stop you, I'm trying to keep you from getting killed. Since you've made your mind up, the least I can do is make sure you look the part." He crosses his arms over his chest. "Roll in the sand."

I stare at him. "Excuse me?"

"You're too clean." He gestures to the ground. "Roll around."

I try to step around him, but he stays in front of me. I scowl. "Eros—"

"Do you want to go or not?"

I arch an eyebrow. Did he just interrupt me? "Of course I do."

"Then unless you want everyone to know who you are, do as I say."

Part of me wants to be irritated, but I'm the one who assigned him to protect me. Is it so bad that I actually found someone willing to do the job? His artificially gray eyes are stern as he watches me. If he truly thinks this will somehow help—which he seems to—then I should do as he says.

I sigh and lie in the sand, cover my face with my hands and roll around a couple times. Warm powder coats my skin and gathers in the folds of my tunic, pouring off me in streams as I stand and brush myself off.

"Better?"

"Getting there. Let your hair down."

I scowl. "It's hot. My hair stays up—besides, townspeople wear their hair up. That's not exactly reserved for royals."

He bites the corner of his lip. "I know, but your hair looks too neat. And you're wearing jewelry—that's got to come off."

My hand flashes up to my earring. "I can't take it off."

"You wear it all the time—someone's bound to recognize it."

"I'm wearing a hood for a reason."

"Someone could still see it." He extends a hand, but his face is soft. "I'll keep it safe. Don't worry."

Reluctantly, I pull off the double-stud earring bound together with a light chain—my last gift from Mamae. I squeeze it in my hand for a moment before handing it to Eros, who slips it into his pocket. "Can we go now?" I sigh. "At this rate, it'll be nightfall before you deem me suitable for Vejla."

"Just one more thing." He reaches toward me, then hesitates. "Can I . . .?"

I glance at his hand. "What exactly are you doing?"

"Trust me."

I frown, but nod, and he reaches over and ruffles my long loose bangs and gently pulls some strands of hair out of place. His fingers brush against my ear and the barely there touch warms my cheeks and makes my belly flutter. His fingertips are rough and calloused, but his touch is like a warm whisper of wind against my skin.

I shouldn't be allowing this. No one outside of family is permitted to touch me—and especially not a boy. There are many within the court that would be outraged if they knew I allowed Eros to sleep beside me—the guards, my brother, even Anja would disapprove. Truth be told, I surprised myself the first time I asked—but having his warm presence against me helps to calm me even through the worst of the nightmares. And to be honest, it's not their decision to make.

And now, with his fingers grazing my skin, I can't bring myself to pull away. It's all I can do to resist the impulse to lean into the contact.

"There." He drops his hand to his side; my skin is vacant without his caress. His eyes search mine—what is he thinking as he looks at me? Does he see the monster that destroyed his home and killed his family, or does he see something more?

I want to ask, but I don't. I already know the answer.

I step past him and together we walk beyond the palace gates.

After walking the outskirts of the city, Eros and I slip into an alley between a butcher's shop with long strips of hanging meat displayed in the windows, each cut with flashing blue statistics embedded in the glass, and a fruit and vegetable store displaying new produce flash-grown eight times with nanite technology from sunrise to sunset. A man stands guard at the door with overlapping scars on his thick arms and a bloodstained cleaver in his fist, but he doesn't pay us any mind.

The white-paved streets, I must admit, are emptier than I remember. The once lively chatter of the city has been reduced to whispers as people walk quickly, eyeing us warily as they pass. No one lingers outside—they duck their heads and dart from building to building, as if afraid of being caught unawares on the streets. Even the black orb-guides seem nervous, if that were possible—they zip around heads and chitter quietly, never staying in place for long.

For every four open stores, one or two are shuttered closed, many of them vandalized. We pass a former tailor with broken glass windows, burnt walls, and fabric and rubble strewn inside. A bike shop with two burly men standing outside the entrance, glaring at anyone who comes near. A small temple with the windows boarded up and a handwritten sign posted outside that reads PLEASE SHOW RESPECT with lewd drawings scribbled over it. Armored guards patrol the streets, solar-powered batons and white-rimmed phasers at the ready. Eros and I keep our heads down as they pass.

This is not the Vejla I remember. This is not the city I call home.

"Nice place," Eros mutters, stepping over a wad of rotting trash. "Probably should've worn shoes. I've nearly stepped on broken glass or splintered wood three times already."

"This isn't right," I answer quietly. "Vejla was a place of commerce and wealth, full of visitors from across the territories. Nothing like this."

"When's the last time you've actually visited the city?"

My stomach churns as hot guilt drips down my spine. I remember the occasion exactly—nearly three cycles ago, several terms before my coronation, when Dima and I snuck out to see the Festival of Stars in person. We painted our skin black and drew on ourselves with bioluminescent paint that glowed brightly in the night. We danced with strangers and drank *azuka* mixed with fruit juices until our ears burned and heads spun. A pretty girl tried to kiss Dima, and he barely ducked out of the way, flushed and flustered. Though he didn't find the humor, I laughed endlessly about it until we were both too intoxicated to care.

We danced until the suns rose and Father was furious, but when he yelled at me for being reckless and irresponsible, Dima defended me.

It was the first and last time he stood up for me. It was also the last time I saw my brother truly happy.

"Kora?" Eros frowns at me. "Are you all right?"

My eyes are watering. I rub them quickly and clear my throat, but before I can answer, a *boom* echoes somewhere ahead of us, followed by a flash of blinding green light and—

Eros slams into me, his arms wrapping around me as we hit the ground and a blast of hot wind, sand, and debris crashes into us. My face is buried in his chest as the roar of broiling wind races over us, and Eros presses his forehead against mine and our noses are touching and his lips are so close. I should be terrified, but instead all I feel is the heat of his breath against my face and the tickle of his eyelashes on my skin. All I feel is his strength covering me, the hard planes of his body protecting me.

All I feel is the urge to close the distance between our lips, and it's absurd. He's protecting me from a *bomb blast* for *Kala*'s sake and I'm lying here thinking about how nice his lips must taste. But he protected me—more, he put himself in harm's way to protect me. And it's such a simple thing, to actually have a guard who put himself second to protect me, but I've never had that. No one ever cared.

Eros could let me die to be free of his oath. But instead, he's here, covering my body with his.

"Kora," Eros breathes, and the way he whispers my name sends warmth rippling through my body.

"*Sha?*" I answer softly. The tips of our noses touch but neither of us moves away.

"I think it's safe. Are you hurt?"

"*Naï*," I whisper. "I'm not hurt."

He stares at me for just a moment longer and my heart skips a beat. But he pushes himself up, then extends a hand to help me to my feet. I take it and try not to think about the press of his fingers against mine.

Kafra, what's wrong with me? Eros is not the first attractive boy I've come across—and he's my *guard*. Worse—a half-blood. And in no way someone I can even remotely consider.

I push those thoughts away. "Are you injured?"

"I think my back might be a little cut up, but nothing serious." Eros turns around and cranes his neck, trying to glance back at his shoulders. He's right—a couple cuts and scrapes ooze reddish-purple blood, but it's nothing life threatening.

"You'll survive," I say.

He nods, then looks off in the direction of the blast. "We should probably go. If things are heating up again—"

"I want to see it."

Eros groans. "Kora—"

"I know it's not safe and I understand your hesitation, but I need to see what's happening. We won't get involved. We'll look, then leave. Okay?"

"Are you asking me? Because if you're asking me, then it's not okay."

I smile my sweetest smile. "I'm not asking."

Eros shakes his head and gestures forward. "Then lead the way."

· 🌙 ·

If the smoke and the dust cloud stirred up by the blast hadn't led us right to them, the screaming and angry chanting would have.

We walk quickly through the winding streets, Eros as stiff as a board beside me and clearly unhappy. Not that I can blame him. This isn't exactly my best idea—and *sha*, it could be dangerous, especially for me, but I have to see it. I have to know for sure.

And then I do see it, and despite the heat pouring from the flames and the suns above us, I'm chillingly cold.

My people have set me on fire.

Well, not *me* of course, but my representation. It's highly disrespectful to create idols in anyone's image—even *Kala's*—but every *Avra* and person of influence has some sort of token to represent them. For Alara and Oro d'Inara—the founders of our faith—it's a large sword for Oro, who was a wise warrior, and a *kazim* for Alara, who always had one at her side.

I chose my token a cycle before I took the throne, on the set of my fourteenth lifecycle—a beautiful golden book containing the histories of our nation. It was inscribed by hand by my ancestors and placed outside the history center in a protective glass case the set I took the throne.

Now the whole center is a raging inferno, and all that's left of the case and the golden book is broken glass and burnt black crisps of curled paper.

Hundreds of people are crowded outside the burning center as guides zip around the scene, recording everything. They carry signs that read THIS IS WHAT YOU'VE DONE TO TRADITION and WHERE IS THE ALMIGHTY AVRA NOW? and my stomach churns as the heat of the flames washes over me in an unending wave.

They hate me.

This isn't just dislike—they're burning the history center as some kind of display of how I've destroyed tradition. They're screaming my name and calling for me to step down.

Nothing I can say will help this. I've long passed the point of soothing them with words—I just never realized how bad it was.

"Okay," Eros says softly. "You've seen. Now let's go before the guards get here and see you—or someone recognizes you."

He's right. It's not safe here. If anyone recognized me, I'd be dead. And yet I can't tear my eyes away from the raging orange flames spewing pillars of black smoke into the sky. I can't look away from my people, their anger radiating off them like the heat of the fires.

I'm such a failure.

Eros grabs my arm and pulls me away. I'm too numb to protest.

We leave the burning far behind us as soldiers race to the scene, and we walk until the suns are high above us, their heat soaking into our clothes and broiling our skin. Sweat drips down my temples and between my shoulder blades, and beneath my hood, my hair is plastered to my skin like paint. Eros's black shirt is so soaked it's actually dripping onto the paveway, but he doesn't complain.

I find the brew and spice place where Dima and I binge drank so long ago—it's in a now-depressed part of the city, where all the buildings are boarded up or burnt down and the streets are so littered with trash, sewage, and glass that Eros and I can't enter it without risking injury. But even despite the wreckage and the stink of rotting garbage, people move through the streets and lean against the buildings, leering at us. It's the first time we've seen anyone linger on the streets during our visit, save for the protest outside the burning center.

I rub my arms and inhale deeply through my nose as the echoes of their chants wash over me. Dima said they want me dead, and he's right.

A few children play in the trash; dressed in threadbare clothes, sand coating their skin and gathering in clumps in their hair. A little girl wearing a tattered dress sewn together with random scraps of fabric picks up a discarded twisted mass of metal that may have once been a steering unit, holds it to her chest, and runs. An equally dirty boy chases her, and her giggles fill the air.

I'd known there were problems in the city. I'd known about the riots and unrest, about the violence that drove away commerce and kept visitors down to a trickle. I'd known people were angry since I took the throne, since our city was attacked and our people were killed without retribution. I'd known Eljans were losing confidence in me as a ruler. I'd known they'd always preferred Dima, that nothing I did helped because it would never be as good as what they imagined my brother doing.

I'd known all that, but I never realized just how badly the city was deteriorating. I'd spent all this time bitter that they wouldn't accept me without stopping to think whether it was possible I deserved their judgment.

But I can't blame anyone for allowing Vejla to reach this state. While I was cowering in the palace, trying to get over my grief and fear, my city was falling apart and I did nothing. And if the capital is this bad, what's happened to the rest of the territory?

This is my responsibility. I have to fix this. I will fix this.

"C'mon." Eros touches my arm. "I don't like the way those people are looking at us. We shouldn't be here."

I nod and turn away, but I've barely taken two steps before someone shouts behind us.

"*Avra!*"

The voice is light, like a child's, but loud. It echoes down the street and sends a chill down my back.

"Don't stop." Eros nudges me forward. "Keep walking."

I do as he says, but my heart is clambering into my throat and the voices don't stop.

"*Avra!*"

"It's her! Look, it's *ken Avra!*"

A child runs in front of Eros and me, and I stop quickly to avoid knocking her over. It's the little girl in the tattered dress I saw earlier, though she's no longer carrying that hunk of garbage.

She grabs the edges of her dress and smiles shyly, twisting slightly back and forth, like she might twirl, but keeps changing her mind.

"*Or'jiva, el Avra,*" she greets, giggling.

Eros goes stiff next to me. There are others behind us—I can feel their eyes on my back as I stare at this little girl, unsure of how to respond. I've never really interacted with a child before—what am I supposed to do?

"*Or'jiva,*" I respond carefully. "What's your name?"

My skin is prickling with the pressure of stares. The suns have never been so warm and Eros is frozen next to me. Even though it's just a little girl, I can't help but feel as though I'm walking along the edge of a cliff, and if I say or do the wrong thing, someone will push me into the chasm.

The little girl beams. "*El ljma si* Uljia d'Elja." She says each word carefully, like she practiced them separately when learning how to introduce herself.

I smile softly. "Uljia. That's a very pretty name."

Uljia giggles.

"Kora," Eros says stiffly. "We *really* should go."

I dare a glance back to see what he's looking at, and my breath catches. The street behind us is packed with people. Where they appeared from is beyond me, but most of them don't look pleased to see us.

Uljia runs away, darting into the crowd. Everyone is watching me, expecting me to say something, do something. But what is there for me to say? Words alone can't make this better—what do they expect me to do?

"I'm going to fix this," I say, but my voice sounds weak, even to me. I clear my throat, take a breath, and pull back my shoulders. "I've let this go on for too long, and for that I take responsibility. But I won't let this continue. I'm going to fix this."

Murmurs ripple through the crowd and people turn away, shaking their heads as they return to wherever they came from. The crowd is dissipating and the disappointment in their eyes is a hot brand of failure burning me from the inside out; it's a weight settling on my shoulders, pulling me to the Void.

"I promise you!" I say desperately as they walk away, muttering to themselves. "Vejla won't go on like this—I'll restore this city to the way it was!"

"*Naï*," a wrinkled man with silver hair says, shaking his head as he turns away. "You won't be on the throne long enough."

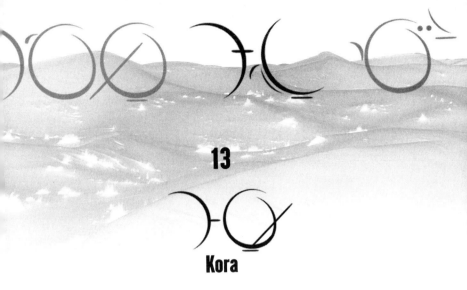

13

Kora

The dust and stench of the city sticks to me like a second skin. Anja's eyes widen when Eros and I enter the palace and stalk past her. She mentions something about preparing a bath and runs off, but I have more important things to do than get clean right now.

I need to speak to my brother.

I never would have chosen Dima to be my second—the person who was supposed to be my most trusted advisor—had it not been the final thing father asked of me before the attack on my coronation killed him and Mamae. My brother is far from the ideal candidate—he's always wanted the throne for himself. He's always resented me for leaving the womb minutes before him ever since he knew what it meant—that I would hold the crown, and he would watch.

My dear, sweet brother has never forgiven me for being born first. But despite the uneasy feeling I had, even as I spoke the words, I couldn't bear to dishonor Father's last request.

So now, with a formulating plan and the echo of Vejla fresh in my mind, I have to depend on the person I trust the least to make sure changes are made immediately to our capital. I march through the twisting hallways, up and down sets of steps, beyond the dining hall and throne room, preparing myself for the argument that is surely awaiting me. Because even if Dima agrees with my plan, he'll argue just for the sake of arguing and not feeling subordinate, pleasant boy that he is.

I reach his bedroom doors and don't bother knocking—he doesn't extend me that courtesy, so why should I extend it to him? I push through the double doors and waltz into his room, inhaling as I prepare for my speech.

And my breath catches in my throat.

Because my brother is tangled in the silky black sheets of his bed, and tangled with him is not a servant or a pretty girl from the city.

It's Jarek.

I choke on absolutely nothing as Dima bolts upright, his eyes wide and his chest heaving. He pushes Jarek off so quickly that the larger man nearly tumbles off the bed, and he jumps to his feet. My brother is flushed, and naked, and there's no question as to what I just walked in on.

"I apologize," I blurt out, stepping back so quickly that I knock into Eros. "I didn't realize—I'll go. It can wait until—"

Dima screams and lunges toward me. The sound is so raw, so angry, it's nearly animalistic, and though I know I should move, my legs are anchored to the tile. Someone rushes into me and spins me around, wrapping their strong arms around me, and it's not Dima.

Eros. Eros has grabbed me. And I can't think. I can't breathe. My brother is screaming behind us and I can't make out what he's saying and it sounds like he might be sobbing, but I don't understand what is happening, I don't understand why I'm so cold or why my brother just tried to attack me or why he hasn't reached us.

I peer over Eros's shoulder and my gut twists; a prickling heat spills over the chill in my bones. Dima has collapsed on the floor and Jarek has him locked in his arms—though whether to comfort him or hold him back, I can't tell.

"Dima," I say, and Eros's grip loosens just enough for me to break free. "Dima, it's okay. It doesn't matter, I won't say anything if you don't want me—"

"GET OUT!" Dima screams.

Two words. Two words rip through me and set my soul on fire. Eros grabs my arm and pulls me out, and I think he's saying something, but all I hear are my brother's sobs as the doors close behind us.

"Dima will never forgive me for this."

Iro hops on the bed next to me, making the bed sway as he curls up around me and rests his head on my lap, purring deep in his throat. Eros sits on the opposite end of my bed, legs crossed beneath him, and rests his arms on his knees.

"Okay, well he obviously didn't want you to find out like that—"

"You mean at all."

"—but as long as you keep their secret, it shouldn't be a problem. Right?"

I shake my head and run my fingers through Iro's soft fur. "It wasn't my secret to keep to begin with. He clearly didn't want *anyone* to know, let alone me."

Eros sighs and runs a hand over his skull. "I don't see what the big deal is. So he likes men, and he and Jarek are apparently together. And?"

I arch an eyebrow. "Is that not a matter of significance with your people?"

He shrugs. "It's not *encouraged*, since we're trying to grow our numbers, but it's not discouraged, either. You can't change who you are, and if it makes you happy . . . why not?"

I sigh and trace patterns into Iro's fur. "It doesn't bother *me*, particularly, but most Eljans won't stand for it. That's not the case everywhere, of course—in Daïvi, Kel'al, and A'Sharo, for example, *lijarae* are completely accepted—but here in Elja, they aren't accepted or respected. If they—or, *Kala* forbid, the council—were to learn of Dima's preferences, he'd likely lose his position."

Eros frowns. "You can't help who you fall in love with."

"I know," I say softly. "And I'm so sorry for Dima that he has to hide it. But try explaining that to Elja."

"Well . . . at least he has you supporting him."

I bite my lip and clench my fingers in Iro's fur. But I don't have to answer, because the truth we both know echoes back at me from Eros's face.

My support for Dima won't be enough for him to forgive this. Nothing will.

It takes me a while to fall asleep, but when I do, I wish I hadn't.

I'm on my bed and *he* is with me. Not Eros. Midos.

His lips are on my neck as he traces the pattern of *Kala*'s mark with his tongue. I grip his long dark hair in my fist and pull him harder against me as his left hand traces my side, slowly sliding lower. My heart races as his kisses work down to my breasts and he sucks softly on the smooth skin there.

"Midos," I gasp as his fingers slide up my skirt and trace the markings on my thigh.

He pauses his kisses to look up at me, his dark eyes glistening. "You're beautiful," he says, but I can't focus on anything except the way his fingers slowly slide higher and lower on my inner thigh, teasing me.

I shudder and press closer to him and he smiles softly. "It's a shame," he murmurs between kisses as he works his way back up until his lips are a breath away from mine.

His hair tickles my cheek as I whisper, "What's a shame?"

Midos's hand moves up to my scarred shoulder and he caresses it softly, running his fingers over the ugly pink skin. "I think we could've been happy."

I frown. "You don't think we'll be happy?"

"Well, it's a little hard to be happy when you're dead."

My heart jolts as ice trickles down my spine. "Dead? Midos, I'm sure you'll live a long and healthy life . . ."

There's something wrong with the smile that splits his face. "Oh, I might," he says. "But you won't."

That's when I see the dagger.

My eyes snap open and my heart is in my throat. I'm shivering and every part of me is frozen, waiting for the knife to come down, searching the shadows for another threat.

But nothing's there, and I'm safe and alive. For now.

I sit up and pull the covers up to my chin, inhaling deeply through my nose as I steady my heart. Eros shifts beside me and twists to face me. His eyes are heavy with sleep as he blinks slowly through the darkness.

"Are you all right?" he mumbles in a low, groggy voice.

I nod, but I'm lying. I shouldn't have to lie; I *should* be fine—it was just a nightmare, albeit a nightmare based off a terrible memory. But I'm not a child—I should be able to handle night terrors on my own, without looking for someone to comfort me.

Especially not Eros. Especially not the half-blood who is here under oath, who even in different circumstances would never be an option. This here—sharing a bed with him, turning to him in the night when the terrors keep me awake—this isn't right. This isn't normal. This is not the way queens behave with their bodyguards, nor guards with their queens. This is not the way Sepharon behave with half-bloods, nor half-bloods with Sepharon.

And yet when Eros extends an arm and nods at me, I don't want to refuse.

So I don't. I slip right into place at his side, his heart beating against my ear. He shifts the blankets to keep me covered, wedging the fabric between us so the only skin-on-skin contact is my cheek on his chest and his arm around my shoulders, but it's enough. Tonight, it's all I need.

His warmth envelops me, and the echo of his steady heart and the smooth scent of his skin lulls me back to sleep.

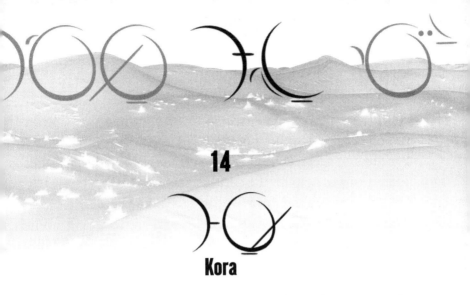

14

Kora

It's been forty-three sunsets since Dima's spoken to me. Or looked at me. Or stood in the same room as me. I tried to apologize, I tried to explain I didn't think any differently of him, that it made no difference to me who he chose to be with, but he didn't want to hear it. And I can't blame him for being angry—it was his secret to share or keep, and I ruined it in a moment of carelessness.

It's been forty-three sunsets in which I've had to use Anja as a messenger to get anything done, because hurt feelings or not, I still have a responsibility to fulfill. Forty-three sunsets in which I've outlined, worried over, and finally began implementing the plan that would hopefully help Vejla recover and stabilize my reign.

Save for the Dima-not-speaking-to-me part, the first two steps were relatively easy. The night after my visit to the city, I instructed Anja to ask Dima to order a nanite sweep through the city to disintegrate the garbage and establish a stronger military presence to discourage the violence. Jarek—who, it seems, would rather pretend I never walked in on them, which is fine by me—informed me three nights later that both had been done, and I corroborated the information with the feed on my glass.

It's not perfect. The streets are cleaner and the vandalism has stopped for now, but the city needs renovation—new buildings to replace the old and new businesses to bring more people in and help lift the depressed areas.

Unfortunately renovation isn't free, and due to the depression of the cities, the territory stores aren't exactly overflowing with wealth. We need wealthy donors, and Anja suggested the perfect way to bring them in—the upcoming lifecycle celebration for Dima and me. She's taken it upon herself to arrange all the details, and in the meantime, I have one more task to focus on.

Father once told me the strongest testament of the stability of a monarch is an heir. He said it was a message to the people that *ken Avra* will continue in history, that their legacy will reign on when they are no longer on the throne.

He said until an *Avra* proves they are there to stay, the people will see them as weak.

I'll admit I didn't believe him at the time—or the council, who echoed his message long after his passing. It seemed to me there'd be more important things to do than find a mate and have children, but the words of the silver-haired man in Vejla have echoed in my head since they were spoken, and I see now Father and the council were right.

I need to find a mate. And soon.

I had Anja devise a list of eligible men, but unfortunately I don't exactly have divine choices.

Out of the eight territory rulers, I am one of two who are unmarried, so most of my options are *ken Avra-kaï* of the other nations and their male relatives. Which seems all well and good until you consider that not only am I the only unmarried female *Avra,* I also happen to be the youngest of the rulers—with exception to newly appointed Kalan d'Inara, who is fifteen, unmarried, and though technically now an adult, still acts like a child.

To be considered, the potential mate must be an unrelated adult—that is, at least fifteen—male of royal lineage, within ten cycles of my age. The blood relation isn't a problem—every one of the nine royalties come from different families—but I can count on two hands the number of eligible men who are within ten cycles of my nearly eighteen.

Dima once said I'm too critical, that I'll die lonely and celibate if I'm not careful. But he seems to forget the first boy I trusted enough to get close to, Midos, nearly put a poisoned blade through my heart on the night we would have been together. Forgive me for not being eager to risk repeating that particular nightmare.

The eligible men Anja has drawn up for consideration are, of course, nothing like Midos. To start, they're not assassins, and even better, they aren't one of my brother's former friends. In hindsight, seeing one of Dima's friends was a horrendous idea to begin with, only worsened when Dima put a blade through his chest when the boy tried to kill me.

Naturally, he blames me for that, too. As if it were my fault Midos turned out to be an assassin.

But these men are royalty, with little reason to hurt me. Unless they support my brother. But I really will die celibate and alone if I fear for my life every time a man comes near me. I can be cautious without being unreasonable.

I glance at Eros, who is standing guard beside the door. Come to think of it, he is the first boy I've allowed close to me since Midos's attempt on my life. And maybe this makes me foolish, but Eros seems so different from the men of the Eljan court I'm so accustomed to tolerating. He agreed to protect me only to save himself and receive a better standard of living in return—but that reasoning alone is more honest than any of those who have lied to me directly in an attempt to circumvent me.

And when we went to Vejla together, he only proved my intuition was right; when the burst bomb exploded, his first instinct was not to save himself, but to protect me.

Eros catches me watching and arches an eyebrow at me. I need to focus.

There are eight men on the list, but four of them I eliminated immediately—*Avra* Kalan d'Inara and *Avra-kaï* Korin da Sekka'l, who are both fifteen and, though technically eligible, I refuse to consider, and *ken Avrae-kjo* from Sekka'l and Ona, who were raised to be extraordinarily chauvinistic. That leaves me with *Avra-kaï* Daven da Daïvi and the three eligible *Avrae-kjo* d'A'Sharo: Sulten, Orik, and Deimos. Unfortunately the royalty of A'Sharo are extremely withdrawn from the rest of the territories, so while I had Anja send a summons to meet them, I'm not entirely surprised I haven't yet heard anything in return.

Which leaves me with Daven.

Unlike A'Sharo's *kjo*, Daven answered the summons yesterday—or rather, his sister *Avra* Riza did, to say she'd be sending her brother for consideration immediately. Immediately, as it turns out, means today. He'll arrive at any moment, and I'm a collection of nerves and nausea and doubts—what if my plan doesn't work? What if nothing I do matters and finding a mate is a waste of time and the people hate me anyway? What if Daven is horrible or something happens and I have to beg the court d'A'Sharo to answer my summons or else consider one of the terrible *kjo* of Sekka'l or Ona?

I close my eyes, inhale deeply, and recite what I know about Daven. Riza is seventeen cycles my senior and has several sisters, as is custom in the only matriarchal territory on Safara.

A man raised in Daïvi might not be so bad to choose as a mate—at least he'd respect me, unlike *ken Avrae-kjo* of Sekka'l or Ona. Daven is the Commander of the Daïvi Division of Arms—which I'll admit doesn't actually soothe me, because if I get stuck mated with a man who is anything like my brother, I may literally die of misery.

I open my eyes, drum my fingers on my desk and look at Eros again. "I hope this isn't a terrible mistake."

He offers me the whisper of a smile. "You don't have to decide today."

Naï, I don't, but I do have to make a decision quickly. If I don't regain the confidence of my people soon, I'll lose the little bit of control I have left. Vejla is on a precipice, and if it tumbles over the edge, I'll have failed. Dima will take my place and violence will be the way of the Eljans.

I can't let that happen. I won't let that happen.

I trace the light chain connecting the ring at the top of my ear with the dark purple gem at the bottom. What would Mamae say, if she were here? Would she have approved of my decision to find a mate so quickly? Would she have thought it necessary?

I suppose it doesn't matter, because she isn't here and I'll never know.

Two knocks on the door, then a voice calls out. "*El Avra*, may I present *Avra-kaï* Daven da Daïvi, responding to your summons."

I stand, pull back my shoulders, and nod at Eros. He pulls open the door. Four men enter the room—one of my guard and three men I don't recognize, dressed in the blue silks of the Daïvi. They all step before my desk and kneel—my guard with his arm pressed against his chest and the Daïvi men with their heads bowed low and their fists held over their stomachs.

I stand. "You may rise." My guard bows out of the room and I'm left with Eros watching from the corner, Iro cleaning his paws beside him, and three colossal men. Though Dima isn't here, they would easily tower over my brother, and I'd always considered him tall. All three wear military-like uniforms—blue with white trim and silver buttons—but the tallest of them has black markings running down his arms, blazoning the creed of Daïvi royals—a creed that I will never place on my arms, even if we are to be united: *with spilled blood comes honor*.

Daven.

As much as I hate to admit it, he's not an unattractive man. He certainly has the body of a soldier, and his eyes have pleasant green centers, a thick ring of hazel, and dark blue borders. It's a combination I haven't seen before, and I catch myself staring.

"Thank you for coming," I say with a smile.

"Thank you for your invitation, *ol Avra*," Daven answers. But I barely hear his words because . . . *his voice*.

The pitch is lighter than mine.

Eros's eyes widen for a breath before he neutralizes his expression. I open my mouth. I need words. "*Sha*," I say stupidly. "Of course. Um. Sit. *Sha*, would you like to take a seat?"

"Thank you," he says airily, and kneels on the embroidered pillows in front of my desk as his guards stand at his attention.

My stomach clenches and roils nauseatingly. This will never do. Even if Daven is absolutely pleasant and suitable otherwise, there isn't a chance in the Void that the stringent Eljan people would respect his authority—which is something that my mate, who would rule beside me as *Avra-ko*, requires. If I don't hear back from the *kjo* d'A'Sharo . . .

Kala, please don't make me choose a mate who would look at me like the sand under his feet.

We talk about meaningless drivel—the journey from the Northern lands, his thoughts of Elja, political nonsense, and the state of his sister's rule. After speaking with him for quite some time, I realize with no small amount of disappointment that it's a shame about his voice, because he seems like a perfectly kind, level-headed, and respectable man otherwise—and certainly no task on the eyes. If he were able to command the necessary respect from the Eljans, he'd be a great candidate.

I tell Daven I'll contact him at the end of twenty-seven sunsets with my decision, but I insist he stay for dinner—it would be rude of me not to offer after he came all this way.

Daven gives Eros a particularly nice smile on his way out, and I very nearly lose my carefully controlled composure right then.

When the doors have long since closed behind the *kaï* and his guards, Eros abandons his formal bodyguard mask and arches an eyebrow. "He *winked* at me!"

I sit on the edge of my desk and groan. "*Kala* hates me."

Eros laughs and steps in front of me. "At least he was nice. It was your first meeting, Kora. You have other options."

I grimace. "Only if they respond. Otherwise I'll have to contact the courts of Sekka'l and Ona."

"It'll work out."

"How can you be so sure?"

"Call it a feeling. You're powerful and not exactly unattractive. Someone will respond."

My face warms at the compliment; Eros must notice because his lips twitch into a smile.

"Well . . ." I smile. "It would seem Daven found you attractive if he winked at you."

"Last I checked, I'm not the one looking for a mate."

"You'd make a great match. Though he stands significantly taller than you. Then again, you know what they say about tall men." I grin, and Eros's face reddens, but his smile still matches mine.

"Actually, I think he might be friendly with one of his guards," he says after a moment. "They stood really close to each other and when the *kaï* winked at me, his guard looked extremely unhappy. I just wonder why he bothered to come if he's already with someone."

"He probably had to, just like I had to see him. I knew I couldn't be the only royal coerced into this marriage nonsense."

"I don't see what the big deal is. It's not like you'll be unable to have kids anytime soon."

"It's not about that at all." I stand and turn to the window. "I'm the first female *Avra* to rule Elja in seven generations, and no one believes I'll last. My people want to see a man on the throne, and if it's not my mate, it'll be my brother."

Unsurprisingly, Dima and Jarek don't make an appearance at supper. One of Dima's men sends his apologies with some message about being caught up with "military matters," so I'm left to enjoy Daven's company alone. Eros and the Daïvi guards watch from the doorways, and now that he's mentioned it, I do notice that the one of the *kaï*'s guards spears Eros with a couple glares.

The conversation itself is uneventful except for one notable difference: Daven actually has me laughing throughout the course.

For that reason alone, I nearly ask the *kaï* to stay an additional night.

Before preparing for the night's rest, I stop by Daven's guest room to wish him a good journey before he leaves in the early morning, as is custom. Usually, this would be Dima's job, but as he couldn't be bothered to attend dinner, I take care of it myself.

Eros's footsteps echo as we walk across the textured floors, through the twisting hallways to the guest suites. As we near the room, the Daïvi warrior standing guard beside the carved white stone door bows low with his fist held over his stomach. One soldier. The other must be inside. We step beside him and I nod at Eros, who knocks twice and moves behind me.

Murmuring voices filter through the heavy door, and a moment later it slides open. To my surprise, Daven, not his friendly guard, stands in the doorway.

"*El Avra*," he says with a bow and a smile. "What an honor. Please, come in."

I blink at his choice of words. When greeting royals from other territories, the customary phrase is *ol Avra*—your majesty. For him to use *el* and call me *his Avra* is a gesture of great respect.

"Thank you," I say softly. The corners of my lips inch northward as he steps out of the way, and I enter with Eros close behind me. The glaring guard from earlier is sitting at a silver desk floating beside the northern wall, his eyes glued to a glass propped up before him, streaming some sort of political broadcast, by the sound of it. He glances over just long enough to bow his head, then returns his attention to the screen.

Both men have removed the upper halves of their uniforms and lounge in silky blue and white pants. Daven's torso is more ink than skin, but his guard doesn't have many more black markings than Eros.

I turn to Daven. "Everything is to your liking, I hope?"

He nods. "*Sha.* Your hospitality has been most welcoming."

He moves behind the inattentive guard and reaches over his shoulder to wave his hand over the screen, turning it off. The guard glances up at him and Daven takes his shoulders firmly and smiles at me. "Please forgive Zek. He was raised beyond the walls of the royal court and has not yet learned all of our customs."

Zek flushes and lowers his eyes.

"Of course." I'm not entirely sure what to make of Daven's undisguised affection. Or is touching not as taboo in

Daïvi culture? I don't remember, but I would think he'd try to be more careful, considering he's visiting Elja under the pretense of being a suitor.

But there's something in the intensity of Daven's gaze. Unspoken words are in his tense fingers and clear eyes. A vulnerability shielded from me upon our initial introduction and dinner.

He doesn't speak, but the message in his gaze is clear enough: he's asking me not to choose him.

I smile softly. "I won't take much of your time. It was wonderful to become acquainted with you, *Avra-kaï*, but you should know that I'll be choosing another suitor."

His shoulders relax and his whole body shifts in a silent exhale. Zek closes his eyes, the echo of a smile washing over his lips. I've made the right decision.

"I understand," Daven says.

I wish him a safe journey and turn to leave as Eros opens the door.

"*Avra*, if I may?"

I glance back at the *kaï*. "*Sha?*"

Daven smiles. "For what it's worth, my sister and the people of Daïvi support you."

My breath hitches in my throat, stealing my words. I can only hope he sees the gratitude in my smile as I bow and leave the room.

I dream, sometimes, of the morning of my coronation, caught somewhere between a memory and a nightmare.

It begins, as always, in the waiting room three stories above the annex of the Temple d'Elja. Pale uniformed servants rush around me endlessly, fixing my makeup, checking my hair, tightening the red ceremonial ribbons around my arms. Despite the activity in the room, they work in near silence, trading only the occasional whispered words. Sitting on a mountain of cushions, I stare at the tiled ceiling and carved stone walls. I focus on breathing and not vomiting. Inhale through my mouth, exhale through my nose. I rub my fingers over the silky fabric of the pillows, tracing the swirling embroidered designs in the red fabric.

Was Father this nervous when he took the throne at the beginning of his fifteenth cycle, so long ago? I can't imagine him as anything less imposing than the disapproving glare he leveled on me this morning. The nerves are another sign of my weakness, I'm sure.

Someone knocks and I spin to the door as Mamae enters, her long brown hair flowing behind her. Tears spring to my eyes at the sight of her, and she rushes over and waves the servants away.

"Leave us," she says. They obey at once. Mamae caresses my cheeks and brushes away the hot tears with her thumbs. As she looks into my eyes, for a breath, it's almost like looking into a mirror—we have the same green to blue to purple eyes, deep golden brown skin, and smooth, curved markings. I'd always been told I looked like a dark-haired version of my mother.

"What is it, my beauty?" Mamae says softly. "Why do you cry in your time of celebration?"

"Dima and Father are angry," I whisper. "They say I don't belong on the throne."

Mamae sighs. "My dear Kora." She kisses my glistening cheeks and smiles. "Do you know what I did when I learned I was carrying twins, not just the son your father promised me?"

I sniffle. "*Naï.*"

"I prayed to *Kala* for a daughter every sunrise until you were born. You are my miracle, Kora, and I thank *Kala* for you every night before my dreams."

I shake my head. "Dima should have been born first. Then Father wouldn't be so angry and Dima wouldn't hate me."

Mamae presses her lips to my forehead. "Your brother's jealousy is fueled by your father, but he doesn't hate you. You'll see, my beauty. Your brother will stand by your side in the end."

I bite my lip and glance out the window. We're too high up to see the street, but the roar of the gathering crowd in and around the temple is an ever-present rumble.

Mamae takes my hands. "Something still troubles you."

"I'm afraid," I admit, turning back to her. "Elja hasn't had a female *Avra* in seven generations. Father says—"

"Forget what your father says. He's been acting like a spoiled child, and his ancestors would be ashamed."

I gasp and Mamae raises a shoulder unapologetically. "Just don't tell him I said so." She stands and takes my shoulders. "You are going to be a blessed *Avra*, Kora. Do you know how I know?"

I shake my head.

"Because *Kala* handpicked you himself the moment he placed you in my womb. You were born for the throne, not your brother. He is far too much like your father."

I frown. "Father is a strong *Avra*. The people respect him."

But Mamae shakes her head. "*Naï*, Kora. The people fear your father. It's time for a new age in Elja, one in which people are ruled by an *Avra* who respects them as much as they do her. One in which the people do not need to be afraid. Do you understand?"

I take a breath and nod. "*Sha*, Mamae. I understand."

She smiles and brushes a tendril of hair behind my ear. "I have a gift for you."

Despite my nerves, a lightness flutters through my gut and pulls the corners of my cheeks northward. "You do?"

She laughs. "Of course, my beauty. Did you believe I'd allow the set my daughter became a woman to pass without a proper gift?"

I shrug. "Father said Elja was my gift and I better appreciate it."

Mamae sighs. "Well you have another gift from me. Close your eyes."

I smile and obey.

Her soft fingers brush my right ear and she pauses. "This is going to sting for a moment." She slides an earring through the piercing at the bottom of my ear, then her fingers travel to just under the notch in the point of my ear. She's so close that the sweet and tangy fragrance of her skin fills my nose. Something cold cradles the tip of my ear as a low humming noise buzzes through the air. A sound like a *koti* sting, the bite of metal through flesh, then the humming stops and Mamae steps away. My ear throbs, but it's not unbearable.

"Open your eyes."

I do as she tells me and then face the nearby mirror, tilting my head to see my new gift. The earring is a deep purple gem connected to a ring at the top of my ear with a light chain made of a blue-tinted metal called *ushara* found only in the Daïvi mountains. A smile tugs at my lips as my fingers run over the chain.

"It was mine," Mamae says. "And my mother's before me, and her mother's before her."

"It's beautiful," I say. "I love it. I'll never take it off."

She smiles. "Just remove the chain while you're sleeping. I'd hate for it to get caught on something."

I start to answer, but a knock at the door interrupts my thoughts.

"*Avra-saï,*" a voice calls. "It's time."

The words are a kick to the stomach. I catch my breath and my eyes widen. "I'm not ready. I can't—"

Mamae takes my hands and pulls me to my feet. "You are ready, my heart. You're not a child anymore, and it is time for you to come into your inheritance. You'll be the best *Avra* Elja has ever seen."

"But—"

"Would I lie to you?" Her eyes glint with pride as she watches me.

I take a breath and shake my head. "*Naï.*"

"*Naï,* of course I wouldn't." She steps behind me and pulls my shoulders back. "Walk with your head held high. If you believe the throne is yours, so will the people."

I do as she says, steeling my face and fixing my posture.

"There," she says with a nod. "Now you are ready."

But she was wrong. Nothing could have prepared me for the screams and ashes of my people.

I wake clutching the knife under my pillow, my heart ramming against my chest. The heat of the unseasonably warm night sticks to my forehead and bakes my skin, but the sweat on my back and temples is cool. I sigh and relax my grip on the knife, chasing away the panic of the always nightmarish ending to that memory.

Breathe.

After calming my heart, I slide out of bed and throw on a loose silk robe. While my feet pad silently against the marble floor, Eros stirs and sits up, rubbing his eyes and squinting into the darkness. "Taking a walk?" he croaks.

"I'm fine," I say softly. "I just need some water. Go back to sleep."

He sways in place for a moment, then falls back onto the bed, dead to the world.

Light from the moons and the glittering stars streams through the open window into my bathroom. I step over to the sink and splash cold water onto my face, drink deeply, then pat my face dry with a towel. Straightening, I catch my reflection in the mirror above the sink. My robe and wrap has slipped over my left shoulder and the ugly pink scar swallowing my shoulder and arm is visible—the ever-present reminder of the violence and death that welcomed me to the throne. A symbol of my inadequacy—a sign, some say, from *Kala* himself that I am unworthy of the throne. That Dima, not his weak-minded sister, should rule.

I am the child who never should have been. My father wanted a son, and he got him, but Father and Mamae never expected me with him. Some call twins *Ul'Inote,* His Act, as my mother did. In Inara, brother and sister twins are revered, considered the highest blessing from *Kala* because they're a reflection of the original prophets of our faith, the twins Alara and Oro d'Inara. But to Father, I was a curse. A punishment. And though I tried, there was nothing I could have done to change his mind.

Now Mamae and Father's spirits have traveled through the veil of this world, and while they aren't here, Father's judgment still sits heavily on my shoulders.

I cover my arm and pull the robe closed. It's late and I should get some rest. I start to turn away from the mirror, but a shadow flickers in my reflection behind me. A streak of black moving—

I throw my arms over my head and duck—the mirror shatters. Broken glass rains over me. I stumble forward and a figure steps out of the darkness, swiping at me. I gasp and jump back—hot pain spears through my foot, streaking up my leg and into my hip. My knee gives out—I hit the tile; my foot throbs. The figure steps toward me, but my vision is blurred with tears and I can barely make out his form. The soles of his shoes crunch on the glass. I pull a shard into my fist, clenching it tightly.

Light floods the room and a guttural scream rips through the air as two men hit the floor: Eros and a shorter, unusually pale man with muscular arms and a scraggly orange beard. Eros holds a knife in the bearded man's shoulder and crimson streaks the floor, the man's torso, and Eros's face. The man grabs a handful of glass and smashes it into Eros's chest, then slams his head into Eros's forehead. Eros loses his grip on the knife and hits the ground hard; the bearded man rushes out of the room.

I try to stand but the pain in my foot is tremendous. Eros jumps to his feet and bolts out the door after the bearded man.

Moments later, my bathroom is flooded with guards and people asking me questions. I demand to see Neja and send the guards after the would-be assassin. Anja helps me to my bed, but blood is everywhere. Purple, red, and somewhere in between—smeared across the tile like a gruesome work of art. Neja arrives minutes later and begins picking glass out of my foot. All the noise and commotion—as well as my shouting—upsets Iro, and he hides under my bed, maybe a little too docile for his own good. Did he even notice there was an intruder in my room? If he did, he probably hid, which I suppose is to be expected considering he's been rendered harmless. Still, I wish he'd made a noise or done *something* to warn me.

Between unpleasant outbursts, I ask about Eros, about the bearded man. Did they catch the assassin? Is Eros alive? How did he get in and how did he get past the guards?

No one has answers and it's infuriating. I ignore the latent nausea twisting my gut, but there's little I can do about my shivering hands or the inexplicable cold chilling me from the inside out. I pray Eros is all right—he's a strong fighter, but if my guards allowed an assassin to sneak into my room . . . is Eros in danger from more than just the assassin?

Neja has sealed and wrapped my foot, and I'm about to demand an update when the door bursts open and a group of three guards drag two men onto my floor. They are both cuffed and painted in blood and one of them is extremely irritated.

"You idiots," I snap, crossing my arms over my chest where my thin-as-a-bedsheet robe obscures little. "Uncuff Eros immediately. I would be dead without his assistance tonight."

One of the guards deactivates and removes Eros's cuffs, and he steps beside me, rubbing his wrists. The bearded man hasn't moved since he was deposited on the floor. A pool of scarlet is forming beneath him and he lies perfectly still. Perfectly dead.

I look at Eros, but he shakes his head. "It wasn't me."

I turn to my guards. "Why is he dead?"

The men glance at each other, then back to me. "I assumed he was killed in the fight," one says.

"Not according to the one who fought him."

They don't say it, but the way they glance at Eros then look at me says it all. "I trust his account, as should you. He wasn't killed in the fight, which means he was killed sometime afterward. Unless someone else was involved in this arrest, I must assume that one of you three delivered the fatal blow. So then? Who was it?"

No one steps forward or speaks. They stand still as stone, their gazes frozen above my head.

I shake my head. "Get him out of here. I want this cleaned up. Eros, with me." I stand—and gasp. Hot pain streaks from my foot to my hip and my knee buckles under me, but a strong arm sweeps around my waist and pulls me up. Eros gently pulls my arm over his shoulder and helps me balance.

We move like that to the sitting area outside, and I'm impossibly aware of his warmth against me. You would think I'd be accustomed to his nearness by now, given that we share a bed, but this is . . . different. Intentional. His body is strong and muscular against my side and yet his fingers are delicate, barely grazing my ribs.

"Are you all right?"

His voice is a splash of cool water on my face. "*Sha*, I'm fine." I lean against the banister and breathe in the clean desert air as Eros closes the doors behind us.

After a pause, he says, "Thank you."

I raise my brows. "I should be thanking you. What are you grateful for?"

He stares over the waves of sand, the light of four moons bathing his face in cool light. "You trust me. Publicly, no less. That's no minor favor coming from . . . someone like you."

"Trust is earned. You earned it tonight."

"It's not going to backfire on you, is it? I mean, politically?"

I sigh and run my fingers through my hair. "Everything backfires on me politically. I've given up trying to please everyone."

"People will always find fault where they want to," Eros says.

I nod. "I don't suppose you know which one of the guards killed the assassin?"

He shakes his head. "I was a little distracted arguing with the guards trying to arrest me. I didn't even notice he wasn't moving until you did."

I groan and press my palms against my eyes. "I've half a mind to remove all three of them from their posts."

"Why don't you?"

I pull my hands away and sigh. "The guards already favor my brother. I don't need to give them further reason to despise me."

"Because you're a woman?"

"Because I'm not a warmongering commander well over six and a half measures tall."

His lips go tight and his fingers clench the banister. "You attacked my people easily enough," he says evenly, but the pain is clear in his eyes. A hot pang strikes my stomach, and I look away.

"It wasn't easy, nor was it a decision I made lightly." I accidentally shift onto my throbbing foot and pain spears through my leg. I grimace. "I know I've said this before, Eros, but—"

A door behind us opens and my brother leans out. "A word?"

Oh, he's speaking to me now, is he? I suppress a glare as Eros helps me off the banister and back into my room. Dima barely looks at me as I hobble back to my bed and sit. The guards salute my brother and a flash of heat sets my hands trembling again—they didn't even acknowledge me when I entered the room.

"*Sha*, I'm doing fine, by the way," I say, reining my temper in—although not by much. "Neja says the cut should complete healing by tomorrow night."

"Good," he says. "I presume you've begun preparations for retaliation?"

I arch an eyebrow. "Excuse me?"

"Surely you won't allow this act of war to go unpunished."

"*Naï,* but—"

"Then you must attack the remaining rebels of the west. Silence them for eternity."

"He wasn't one of us." Eros crosses his arms over his chest. "I know every face from my camp, and I've never seen that man before."

"Then you missed a face," Dima spits. "Know your place, half-blood."

But rather than backing down, Eros steps toward him. "He wasn't even *from* the desert. Didn't you see his skin? He's barely seen a set of sun, let alone cycles baking under two. And our men stay clean-shaven and most keep their hair short. Wherever he came from, it wasn't any of the encampments."

"How dare you address me, you—"

"Step away from him." I stand, shifting the weight onto my good leg. "Eros knows much more about the ways of the rebels than we do, and we would be wise to listen to him."

Some of the guards scowl and I very nearly throw them out, but I hold my tongue.

Dima gapes. "You're defending him?"

"Why shouldn't we listen to him? He was one of them!"

"He's a *half-blood*, Kora! The desert trash doesn't even accept their kind because they know they're a corruption of the races that *shouldn't exist*."

I pull my shoulders back and stand as straight as I can without toppling over. "Regardless of whether he should be here, he is, and he has valuable information we'd be idiots to ignore. If Eros says the man wasn't from the deserts, I believe him."

Dima takes a step back and shakes his head. His lips part and he stares at me as if I've just slapped him across the face. "Unbelievable. You're siding with that waste of air over your own blood."

I don't tell him this so-called *waste of air* has consistently protected me—something my blood can't claim. I don't tell him I'd side with much worse over my backstabbing power-hungry brother. "Get out of my room, Dima. And for the record, I'm not authorizing anything."

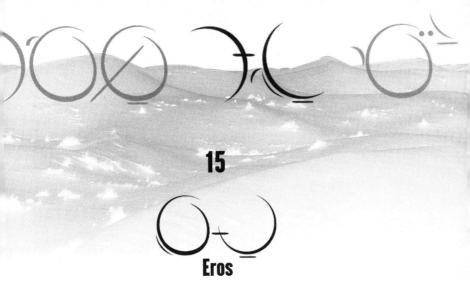

15

Eros

As soon as her foot heals, Kora says we're taking a trip. Whatever that involves.

She tells me to bathe and gives me a new uniform to
wear while she does whatever morning ritual she does with
Anja. I'm not sure how long I've been here, but the cut on
the back of my hand has long faded into a neat pink scar.
And I'm not sure when it happened, but something about
Kora has changed. Or maybe I've changed. Or maybe we've
both changed.

When she first pushed me into that oath, I convinced myself it wouldn't matter. I was doing it for my people—to buy
their freedom back so they could rebuild. I was doing it because it felt like the right thing to do, even if I hated her guts.

And now? Now I don't know. Now she seems to be trying to be a better ruler, even if it might be too late. Now she
seems apologetic for the way she slaughtered my people—
even if she was totally convinced that we were somehow
at fault for what had happened to hers. Now I've seen her
compassionate to that little girl in the slums, vulnerable after
her nightmares, empathetic to a man with a secret lover who

didn't really want to court her, and strong in the face of people who obviously don't want her on the throne. People who she should be able to trust, but can't.

It was so easy to hate her when she was the face of a faraway force we had to run from. When she was one of *them*—the Sepharon who enslaved us. When she didn't make me laugh, and she didn't trust me with her life, and she didn't turn to me when she felt lost.

Now I don't know what to think. But even if I wanted to, I wouldn't be able to hate her anymore.

Kora doesn't just treat me better than I expected as a servant. She treats me better than the Nomads ever did.

Not that any of that makes her *owning* me okay. Not that any of that makes what she did to my home, my family, my people okay. But I can't just ignore it, either.

I take my time washing up mostly so I don't have to watch Kora get her hair done again. When I'm done, I change into the new clothes—a pair of loose white skirt-pants with red cuffs, weird, sandal-like shoes with more straps than I care to figure out how to use, and a loose white jacket made of some kinduv nearly see-through material. The jacket has a silver seal running along the front, but I don't bother. My uniform is usually shirtless, so I doubt she's going to care.

I knock twice, wait for approval, then enter her room. A bag slams into my stomach and I nearly drop it. But not just because I wasn't expecting it—I more wasn't expecting Kora. Or rather, I wasn't expecting such a nice view of her perfectly sculpted and bronzed stomach.

"Good reflexes," Kora says. "Here, you're going to want this." She passes me a white scarf but I'm staring at the smooth skin just beneath her navel, reaching into her low-riding pants. She looks so soft and toned and—

"Something you'd like to say?" she asks, her eyes glinting.

I rip my gaze up to her face. She's smirking. Of course she's smirking. Could I be any more obvious?

I clear my throat and take her in, fighting the heat spreading across my body. She's wearing a tight white top—some kinduv stretchy material covering her breasts, left arm, shoulder and little else—and loose white pants, which sit just above her hips. I've never seen so much of Kora and, to be honest, it's hard to find anything to say at all.

Thank the stars the bag is keeping my dignity covered.

"Are we leaving the grounds?" I manage, focusing my eyes on hers.

"Like I said, we're taking a trip." She slides a scarf identical to mine out of her dresser and wraps it around her nose and mouth. "I wasn't kidding about the scarf. Put it on."

"You know people will recognize you even with the mask." I wrap the fabric around my head with my free hand.

"It's not meant to be a disguise, desert boy. I thought you'd have figured that much out."

I take a sharp breath. Grin. "We're going into the desert?"

She laughs, and though I can't see her lips, her smile reaches up to her eyes. "Well, I didn't dress us for heat and sand to play costume."

I swing the bag over my shoulder. Bounce on my toes. "What are we waiting for?"

"Hold on. We're riding Iro?"

Kora sits on the giant cat like this is a perfectly normal method of transportation and grins at me. "What—don't tell me you've never ridden a *kazim* before."

"Sure." I eye the cat. "We Nomads ride *kazim* every set before breakfast."

She laughs and offers me a hand. "It's entirely safe. I promise."

I grumble and take her hand as I swing my leg over the cat and hoist myself onto his back. The muscle and fur between my legs is uncomfortable, to say the least, and there's nothing to grab. What am I supposed to do—grip with my legs?

Kora snickers and leans forward, holding onto Iro's neck. "You can take my waist, Eros."

Well. Maybe this won't be so bad after all.

I scoot forward and gently place my hands on her waist. Her skin is just as soft as it looks.

Kora's hand clasps over mine, and she drags my hand over to her navel. Warmth fills me and my breath catches in my throat as she twists back to look at me. She's smirking again. She knows exactly what she's doing.

"You don't have to be delicate, Eros."

My lips part before I can stop them and heat attacks my face. "What?"

Her smirk widens. "You're going to fall off if you don't hold on."

Oh. Right. Obviously. I shut my mouth, lean forward, and wrap my arms around her stomach. She smells slightly sweet, like the fruity body wash I accidentally used the first time I bathed. It smells way better on her.

"Ready?" she asks, and I nod. I'm starting to wish I'd sealed my jacket now, because my bare stomach is pressed tightly against her bare lower back, and the skin-on-skin contact is a thousand miniature lightning bolts jumping between us. We are way too close for her not to notice a slip in control.

The almost-incident back in her room was humiliating enough. I am *not* going to embarrass myself.

We bolt out of the gates faster than I thought possible, and not embarrassing myself isn't a top priority anymore—holding on for dear life is. For a terrifying fifteen breaths, as the world races past us, I'm sure I'm going to fall. But then I get used to the rhythm of Iro's movements over the ground, and I start to relax. Even enjoy it, somewhat. I'm riding a *kazim*. Day never would have believed this.

Soon the tall white walls are a line in the distance, and we skirt around the edge of the city with its gleaming white buildings for what feels like moments, then the air is hot and dry and the world is an ocean of endless red sand. We don't ride for long, but at Iro's shocking speed, we don't really need to. He slows down by a patch of thick, tube-like prickleplants and after we climb off, slices one in two with his claws. I guess the poison on the prickly blue skin that can kill a human in less than an hour doesn't affect him, because he digs right in to the hollow center, lapping up the cool water stored inside.

I kick my sandals off and bury my toes in the soft desert. Not enough. I strip off the jacket and fall back into the sand. Kora laughs as the powder poofs around my head and coats my face, but I don't mind. The smooth warm sand on my skin, the suns on my chest, the baked air on my tongue—I close my eyes and, for a mo, it's almost like home. Iro seems to like it, too—once he's finished drinking, he buries his face in the sand and presses against the powder, his tail swishing happily.

"I can bury you two here, if you'd like," Kora teases, nudging my side with her foot.

"Don't tempt me." I sit up and unwrap the scarf. Sand pours off my shoulders and I resist the urge to lie down again. "So why are we here?"

"It's the only place I can get away from prying eyes. Last thing I needed was some guard witnessing you and me sparring."

"Sparring?" I hesitate. "For whose benefit?"

Kora unwraps her mask and stretches her arms over her head. "Don't worry, desert boy, I'll go easy on you, being that it's your first time and all."

I stand and dust myself off. "I think we both know this isn't my first time."

She smiles devilishly. "*That* first time doesn't count—I wasn't trying."

"Oh sure," I say with a laugh, but she trains her smile on me.

Kora bounces. Stretches her legs. Steps back into a comfortable stance and raises her fists. "Well, let's see what you've got."

"I don't want to hit you."

"You're not going to."

"A little overconfident, are we?" I shift into a basic stance. "Last chance to change your mind."

"What's wrong, Eros? Afraid you're going to be beaten by a woman?"

I feign right and kick at her head—she ducks under my leg and her foot slams into my spine. I stumble a step forward and spin back in time to narrowly miss her heel to my nose. I lean back to duck out of the way and she slams into my midsection. Sand explodes around us as we wrestle for the top position, but she's stronger than she looks and it takes more effort than I expected to pin her down. Sweat drips between my shoulder blades and my muscles burn as I press her neck into the sand—not hard enough to cut off any air, but enough to show I could.

"Okay." I gasp for air. "You're better than I thou—"

She thrusts her right hip up, slams her hand into the crook of my elbow, and throws her whole weight against me. I tumble into the sand and her hand grabs the back of my head as her weight settles on my back. Hot breath rolls over the side of my face as she brings her lips to my ear.

"What were you saying?" she says with a breathy laugh. "I think it started with 'Kora just made me look like an amateur.'"

I try to shift into a better position, but she's got my arms pinned beneath my body so it's not as easy as it sounds. I'm actually stuck. I dig my fingers into the sand and push some into my palms. Sigh and relax my shoulders. "Blazing suns, Kora. Do you even need me for protection?"

She laughs. Her weight shifts just slightly back and the pressure on my neck lessens. It's all I need. I twist hard, throwing her off, and jump to my feet. She recovers quickly and snaps to her feet, but the moment she faces me, I throw the sand in her face and tackle her down. This time I'm careful—I pin down her ankles and wrists. She squirms and spits muddy sand, then laughs. "That was cheating. You pretended to give up and threw sand."

"No such thing as cheating in a real fight. No rules, either."

"Fair enough." She smiles at me, and . . . we are . . . really close. The tips of our noses are inches apart and I'm on top of her. In the sand. Half-naked.

Heat floods my system and every skin-to-skin point of contact hums—her bare stomach on mine, her fingers on my palms, our ankles, feet, and wrists pressed together in the sand. My heart is racing and our lips are so close I can taste her warm breath. The spice of some kinduv perfume wafts through my nose, mixed with the sweet scent of her skin. Her soft breasts are pressed against my chest and, if I leaned forward, just a little, our lips would meet and—

Fuck. There's no hiding my body's response to her—not when we're so close. I sit up and lean away, my face flaming. Gulp. "We're um . . . we're done, right?"

Her smile fades and she nods. She must've noticed my slip-up—I mean, I was on top of her for stars' sake—but she doesn't mention it, thank the sands. "*Sha.* Thank you, Eros."

There's a mob of those floating black orbs—which I'm realizing might be cameras, as well as annoying talking things—and a sea of ports outside of the palace gates when we arrive. It takes no small amount of maneuvering and no less than fifty guards to let us in without a reporter or an orb slipping in. I'm glad the jacket covers some of my skin and the scarf covers my ears as well as most of my face, because I can only imagine what a picture of Kora with a half-blood on Iro's back would do to her image.

Then again, there isn't much we can do about the faded markings on my bare skin. I guess we'll just have to hope no one notices.

Kora leads Iro right up to the front of the palace and slides off at the bottom of the steps. She pulls the scarf off her nose and mouth and turns on the nearest guard.

"What in *Kala*'s name is going on and why wasn't I alerted?"

Despite standing heads and shoulders above her, the guard looks terrified. His eyes dart to me, then back to her. "*E-el Avra*, I believe *ken Kaï* said he had notified you of—"

Kora marches up the steps and I follow in silence. She throws open the front doors, rips the scarf off her head, and throws it at me. "I'm going to kill him! He purposely failed to notify me of whatever—I'll wring his neck, I swear to *Kala*—" She spins on her heel and starts down the hallway toward the dining room, where voices and laughter slide under the doorway. Four guards in strange black and gold long-skirt uniforms I've never seen before stand on either side of the doors. I consider stopping her—I mean, we just came out of the desert and we smell just as sweaty as we look, and stars and suns know who's in there or who these black-clad guards are. But then I see her clenched fists and the murder in her eyes. I keep my mouth shut.

I'd rather take on the entire army than get in Kora's way right now.

Despite their somewhat intimidating presence, they must recognize Kora because they say nothing when she throws the doors open and marches into the room. The chatter cuts off, leaving only the slight scrape of utensils against plates, as two men look up at us from their overflowing plates. The first is Dima, but the second . . . He wears a similar black uniform with golden trim, but his is sleeveless and show his heavily tattooed arms. None of that tells me who he is or why he's here.

His eyes do, though.

Because the centers of his irises are a thick ring of gold.

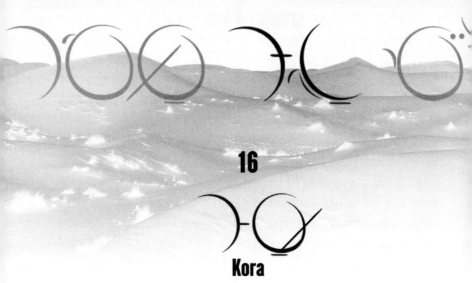

16

Kora

My breath catches when I see his eyes. The golden centers can only mean one thing—someone has betrayed me and revealed Eros to the *Sirae* Court. And I know just the bastard.

But I can't react, not here, not now in front Serek, *ken Sira-kaï*.

"Well," Dima says, "look who decided to join us."

My face burns, but I'm not sure if it's anger or embarrassment that sets my blood boiling. I bow low and clench my fists. "*Sira-kaï*, I apologize for my tardiness. I was not informed of your arrival." I shoot a quick glare at Dima, but he just smiles pleasantly back at me. How I want to rip those lips off his handsome face.

Serek stands and smiles, and something about him disarms me. Black wavy hair curls around his ears and *Kala*'s mark runs in an unusual pattern on his deep suns-bronzed skin—parallel and intersecting perpendicular lines race across his body, all at heavily slanted angles. From what I can see, nearly all of his markings are filled in with black text—from the splitting lines meeting at a point at the center of his neck, to the long lines reaching over his toned arms and down to his fingertips. But what catches me most is his smile. His grin echoes in his magnetic eyes and lights up his whole face. "Miscommunications are common in my brother's court as well, *ol Avra*. Truly, it is I who should be apologizing—I should have given fair warning before arriving."

Somehow I doubt the message would have reached me with or without warning, but I don't say that. "Not to worry. I'll . . ." I'm dressed in sweaty desert clothes. Coated in sand. Standing in front of *ken Sira-kaï*, who hasn't looked at Eros yet, who is still smiling at me like I'm not a sweaty, disgusting, embarrassing mess of an *Avra*. I clear my throat. "I should wash up. I will return, *Sira-kaï*. I do apologize . . ."

"Take your time," the *kaï* says. He's still smiling, though it's a softer, patient kind of smile. "And please, call me Serek."

"He's going to kill me," Eros says the moment my bedroom door closes behind us. "Your brother's told him about me and he's going to execute me."

I shake my head. "I won't let that happen. I'll talk to him—we'll work something out. I gave you my word—"

"You have to let me—"

I grab his shoulders and Eros stutters. His gaze dips to my fingertips on his skin, then back to me. The bump in his throat bobs as he swallows and I can see his pulse racing in his neck. He's scared and I'm to blame. I never should have allowed Dima to enter the room when Neja revealed his eyes. I've endangered him with carelessness, and if he dies now . . .

Naï. I won't let him die.

"Kora . . ." he begins softly, but I cut him off.

"I swear to you, Eros, I will do everything in my power to keep you safe. If the time comes and there is no other way, I will release you, but doing so early will bring extra attention to you and your people, especially considering I just released sixty redbloods last term. If I release you, as well, people will ask questions." I force a thin smile. "Besides, we don't know for sure that's why he's here. I haven't spoken to him yet . . . maybe this is about something else."

He takes a breath, pulls his shoulders back, and clears his throat. "We both know this isn't a coincidence."

I can't argue with him; not two nights ago I had that argument with Dima after the attack—worse, Eros humiliated him—and now Serek is here. On the off chance Dima hasn't told Serek about Eros, the threat is clear.

"I've shown you that I trust you. Now I need you to do the same. Can you trust me, Eros?"

He bites his lip and watches me for a long moment. I hold my breath—will he not answer, or worse, refuse?—but then he nods.

"Thank you," I say. "Now we have to distract a *kaï*."

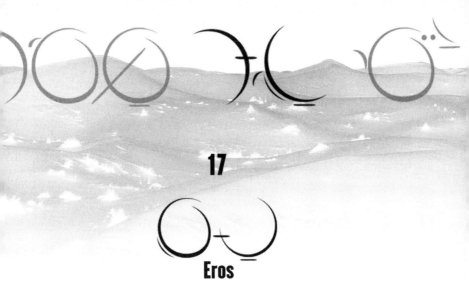

17

Eros

I stare at the stone-tiled ceiling as Anja—who ignores me like everyone else—dresses Kora. I don't know what under the suns could be taking them so blazing long, but I don't really care.

Kora asked me to trust her, and I do. I trust she'll try to keep my head on my shoulders. I also trust she'll let me know if my only chance is to run. But if I get the chance early, I may have to take it. Anything if it means breathing a little longer.

The thought of leaving bothers me more than I ever thought it would. I miss the desert—no amount of nice food and cooled air will make me forget the endless sands, open air, and heat of the suns on my skin. But the past few weeks have been more than bearable, and today in the desert with Kora . . . I almost forgot I'm not supposed to be enjoying my-self. That I'm just a slave and she's the queen of pureblooded Eljan Sepharon. She'll always be the symbol of everything I cannot be, of everything I don't want to be.

And yet, part of me wants to stay. Because sure, people still hate me here, but sometimes I think Kora doesn't. Some-times I think maybe she sees me, maybe she can look past my ears, almost-markings, and weirdly colored blood. Maybe she doesn't care that I shouldn't be here, that I shouldn't exist, that no one like me should exist. No one outside of my family has ever looked at me like that. Not the people I grew up with, not the women whose freedom I negotiated. They'll never see me that way, and yet sometimes I think Kora does.

And I'm not sure why or how. But with half my family gone, it's something I'll never have again if I leave.

Then again, do I really have it now? It's not like I can have Kora—she's going to up and marry some Sepharon royal. I can never have Kora—I can never have anyone, because who would want to be with a dirty half-blood like me? The humans and Sepharon hate me equally, and worse, now I'm a slave. Half-bloods don't get happy endings, and half-blood slaves don't even get to think about a future.

Maybe Kora sees me as more than a slave now, but that's not going to last as soon as she has someone else. Someone she can actually be with.

Someone she actually cares about.

"Eros."

Kora's voice snaps me back to the present and I pull my gaze away from the ceiling. She's wearing a shimmering black dress cut in all the right places. It hugs her curves like a second skin, dips low on her back to a point that meets at the base of her spine, and glimmers under the light as she twirls in front of me and smiles. Stars. She looks incredible.

"What do you think? Sufficiently distracting?"

My mouth has gone dry. I nod once. Lick my lips. "What are you distracting from?"

She arches an eyebrow and gives me a meaningful look: *What do you think?*

Right. She's distracting from me. Of course.

"I think if he looks anywhere except you, he might as well meet up with Daven."

She smiles. "Good. Now, are you going to escort me to the dining hall or not?"

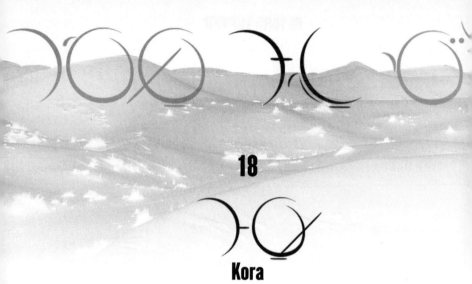

18

Kora

Dinner passes without incident, thank *Kala*. I pull out all the stops and throw every smile and batted eye I can manage without being obvious, and truth be told, it's easier than I thought it'd be. Unlike my brother, Serek is a pleasant conversationalist, and I find, much to my relief, that I rarely have to force a laugh.

We eat fruit-glazed fish imported from the southern coast served with crisp blue and purple Inaran vegetables, and we spend a considerable amount of time exchanging stories and smiles as the frozen desserts melt into white stone bowls. Afterward, Serek asks if I'd like to accompany him outside. I, of course, oblige and tell Eros to take Iro to my room and ensure my chambers remain undisturbed—mostly to get him away from Serek.

The night warmth is wonderful on my skin after sitting in the overly cooled dining hall. Although I don't think he's been here before, Serek leads me to the gardens, and soon we're surrounded by the glowing moonflowers and miniature night birds hopping from flower to flower, branch to leaf. Serek sits in front of our grandest fountain—a white stone structure with eight tall spires of violet bottom-lit water. The glowing water fills the garden with a warm golden light that accentuates Serek's eyes.

After a pause, he turns to me and smiles; his eyes glitter with the stars. "As wonderful as your company has been, I imagine you are well aware that I haven't traveled here just to visit."

So here it is. I review the arguments I practiced in my head—no one has to know about Eros, he saved my life and I owe him a debt, he seems perfectly content to stay here, away from the watchful eye of the *Sirae* court.

He pulls his shoulders back. "I've come to offer you a marriage contract."

I open my mouth and snap it shut, then run his words through my head again. What?

What's the right thing to say? It's so hard to think with the way he's analyzing, *naï*, searching me with his gold-ringed eyes. His pupils are dilated and his fingers flex, then press flat against his lap. He pulls his lips together and keeps a soft, careful smile. Oh.

Oh wow. He's nervous. *Ken Sira-kaï* has come here to offer me a marriage contract and he's actually afraid I might turn him down.

Does Dima know about this?

"I . . . don't know what to say. I didn't expect . . ."

He arches an eyebrow and his lips quirk into a small smile. "You didn't? I understand Daven da Daïvi visited recently for a similar purpose."

"Well, *sha*, but that was Daven and you're *ken Sira-kaï* and I didn't think . . ."

Serek grins. "I would be honored to stand by your side here in Elja and father your children, *ol Avra*." He has the most gorgeous smile and it's all I can do to focus on his words. He would be honored? He's *ken Sira-kaï*, brother of the most powerful man on the planet and second in line to the throne in Safara's capital, Asheron. And he would be honored to marry *me?* And . . . father my children?

My stomach swoops at the thought, and I look him over more carefully. Serek, to put things plainly, is a beautiful man. Tall, strong body rippling with toned muscles. Gorgeous blue to gold to green eyes. Perfectly bronzed skin, thick dark eyebrows, and that smile . . .

Naï, sharing a bed with him would not be a chore.

I see it in flashes—holding his hand as the priest wraps our hands together with the golden bonding ribbon and we swear ourselves to each other. Lying in bed next to him, with his gentle fingers in my hair and his lips brushing over my skin. Playing with our beautiful, golden-eyed children . . . I could have a life with him.

I could make my people happy and even find happiness myself with him.

"You don't have to answer now, of course." He offers me a gentle smile and my belly flutters. "Take all the time you need to consider my offer." Serek leans forward, takes my hand in his, and presses his lips against my knuckles. His lips are as smooth and soft as pillows and his grip is so very gentle. He helps me stand and I'm glad for the extra support. My legs are numb and my head is buzzing and did *ken Sira-kaï* just propose?

"You seem shocked," Serek says with a slight laugh, releasing my hand. "You're tormenting me with your silence, *ol Avra.*"

"Kora." I look up at him. "Please, call me Kora. And I apologize. I must admit your proposal caught me by surprise."

"I can't imagine why. Even without your status, I imagine your beauty alone would bring suitors from around the territories."

Warmth fills my cheeks and settles in my stomach. "I'm afraid my people don't see it that way. They think Dima better suited for the throne."

"Truly? I would think him a belligerent ruler, if given the opportunity."

My eyes widen and my heart skips a beat. Hearing what I've feared from someone else—from *Serek*, no less—is like a new breath. The danger is clear to him, too. It's not just me.

He hesitates, then adds, "May I ask you a personal query?"

I nod. "*Sha.*"

"If your people wish to see Dima on the throne, why not allow them to have what they seek? Give the throne to your brother and live your life as you wish?"

I twist my fingers together and watch the fountain in silence as the lights tint the water deep red.

"The people don't understand what they're asking for," I finally say. "They see Dima as a beacon of strength, as a military leader deserving of the highest respect—which he is, but they don't know him like I do. They haven't seen his rages, they haven't seen how quickly he uses violence." My fingers trail over the chain in my earring and I lower my hand to my lap. "My mother told me once that Dima wouldn't be good for Elja, that he's too much like my father and would reign with fear rather than respect. I understand now she was right."

After a pause, he nods. "But you don't strike me as someone so eager to spill blood."

I glance at him, unsure of how to respond. It's well known that his older brother, *Sira* Roma, has a violent streak, as did his father before he passed the throne down to Roma and Serek's eldest brother, Asha, and retired to Shura Kan, where all monarchs live their final cycles after their reign has ended. Asha, however, wasn't *Sira* long before he was murdered, and Roma has been on the throne in Asheron ever since. But now that I think about it, I don't know very much about Serek, except that he's twenty-one and supposedly very skilled with technology. Some call him a technical genius. He's always remained quiet, out of the eye of the media. The people of the capital seem to like him well enough, but I know very little about his political views.

I take a chance. "I'm not. But not everyone sees that as an advantage."

"Hmm." Serek's hand rests on my waist and we walk aimlessly through the garden. "And do you see it as an advantage?"

"I'm not sure," I admit. "I've made military decisions with his counsel, but now I wonder if they were ill-conceived."

"Decisions made under pressure are the ones we often question the most." He smiles at me. "Which is why I would like you to take your time with the decision I present to you. It's one I would like you to be secure with."

"Thank you," I say as he faces me.

He has the sweetest smile, this man, and he looks at me like he never wants to look away. A thrill shoots through my stomach as I hold his gaze, and he takes my hand again. His skin on mine sends a shaft of warmth through my core as I step closer to him. He's bold, touching me here where anyone could see, but he doesn't seem concerned. He pulls my hand to his lips and kisses the same spot on my knuckles. His lips are warm and soft against my skin. I've never seen a man smile so much through his eyes, and when he whispers, "Good night, Kora," I know.

I've already made my decision.

19

Eros

"I'm going to marry Serek," Kora says as she enters her room.

I keep my face blank. Frozen air drips down my throat. Something in my chest tightens, a vice squeezing the air from my lungs. Marriage? He's been here for all of a day and now they're getting married? "Well that's . . . unexpected."

She sits on her bed and pulls off her shoes. Shakes her head. "I still can't believe he offered."

So it's just like that. Mr. High and Mighty Prince of the World waltzes in here with his gold-ringed eyes and stupid white smile and offers to marry her and she throws herself at him. I can just imagine how that conversation went—*Sha, of course I'll marry you, my gorgeous Serek. We'll make beautiful babies together.*

Ugh.

"So that's why he's here?" I cross my arms. "To offer you a marriage contract?"

She blinks. "You don't think he knows?"

"I'm not the one who spoke to him. Or agreed to marry him."

"I didn't agree, not officially. But I will. At my upcoming lifecycle celebration, I think." Kora pulls her hair down and sighs. She says it so easily, like there's not even a consideration, and it hits me—there isn't. She has to choose a mate, and it's not going to be Daven.

What did I think was going to happen? That because we sleep better next to each other, we have some kinduv bond? Serek is the blazing High Royal Prince. There isn't an option. And besides, what do I care? She's a Sepharon queen, and she destroyed my life. She means nothing to me.

"As for you," she continues, "I'm not sure. He didn't say anything and he barely looked at you, so . . . maybe not?"

"And he just happened to show up today of all sets to propose to you." I clench my fists. "Seems convenient."

She shrugs. "He said he'd heard about Daven, and it's common knowledge that I'm looking for a mate, so it's not out of the question."

She reaches for her dress and I face the wall while she undresses. And see my reflection. Fuck. I completely forgot about the wall-sized mirror she has across from her bed, which—blazing suns—shows more than just my reflection. "Uh, Kora—"

Her dress falls around her feet, leaving only the scarf wrapped around her shoulder and left arm. Heat awakens inside me and sinks to my groin. Suns and stars alive. I thought I'd seen most of her before, but she's . . . wow. From the perfect curve of her neck to the gorgeous curves of her waist and ass, to her strong, toned legs, she's beautiful from head to toe. Tattoos blacken the paths of her tanned back, partially covered by the dark arm wrap she always has on. Her skin looks so soft, and for a mo I remember her slightly sweet scent. I stare for longer than I should, then close my eyes and take a deep breath I'm dangerously close to embarrassing myself again. And she may have a gorgeous body, but she's still an alien queen, and a murderer, and everything I don't want to be.

Dammital. She'd be a lot easier to hate if she wasn't so fucken stunning.

"Kora," I bite out. "I'm facing a mirror."

"*Kafra!*" She gasps and fumbles with something. "Not a word. Not one word from you."

I smile and keep my eyes closed. The glimpse I got was quick—well, sortuv—but it hangs in my mind.

"Okay. I'm dressed."

I turn again and try not to stare too hard at the thin, silky black robe hugging her body. Force my gaze up to her face.

"Pervert," she mumbles, sitting on her bed.

My face is warm, but I still can't hold back my grin. "I did try to warn you."

She bites back a smile. "Besides the point."

"If it's any consolation, I only saw everything from behind."

"Don't make me blind you again."

I snicker. "At least my last sight will be one to remember." The words are out before I can stop them—my eyes widen as her face flushes purple. Shit. I'm flirting. Why the fuck am I flirting? She's practically *engaged*.

I take a steadying breath. "Right. Well. If you don't need me, I'm going to wash up."

She nods. I step quickly toward the bathroom, but then she says, "Wait." I close my eyes. Inhale deeply. Glance back, and a sortuv softness in her face makes me pause.

"Am I making the right choice?" she whispers.

The right choice? The wedding. I hesitate. "You're asking me?"

"I don't see anyone else here."

She's right, of course—we're the only ones in the room—but I'm not sure when my opinion started to matter. Or why. I'm not sure why any of this matters to me, why the tightness around my heart hasn't eased since she announced her pre-engagement, why the thought of her marrying Serek fills me with a twisting emptiness I don't understand. But none of that matters, because as much as I hate it, there's only one answer.

"Do you have a choice?"

Her gaze falls to her lap. She presses her lips together. Shakes her head. "*Naï*," she sighs. "I suppose I don't."

I step out of the room before the tightness in my chest spreads to the rest of my body.

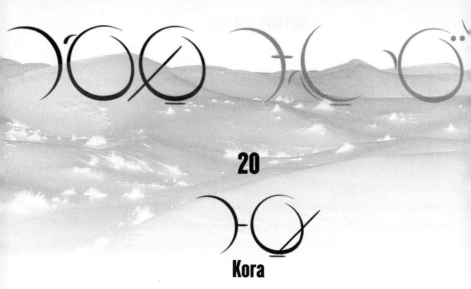

20

Kora

I've never been nervous for a party—let alone my lifecycle celebration—but tonight I am terrified. The chatter builds downstairs, mixing with the rush of servants slipping through the halls and the clatter of plates and low hum of music as the guests arrive. None of it bothers me—I've never been intimidated by crowds or busyness.

But tonight isn't just the celebration of my eighteenth cycle. Tonight is the night I tell Serek I will be his mate.

My stomach churns and I take a breath through my nose. How things have changed in four sunsets. A term ago, no one had expected anything out of the ordinary of me this celebration; now, with Serek lingering in Vejla, the rumors have spread quickly. The glances and whispers trail me like a shadow. Even Dima, who refuses to speak to me except for cordial remarks in Serek's presence, must know.

Tonight, everyone expects a formal announcement to be made. And they won't be disappointed.

Anja smiles at me through the mirror as she weaves and braids my hair on top of my head. "Nervous?" she asks.

"Not at all." I twist my hands in my lap. "I always feel like I'm going to vomit before a party."

Anja slides a golden bead into my hair and twirls it with her expert fingers. "Is it *ken Sira-kaï* who makes you nervous?"

I bite my lip and glance at Eros through the mirror. He watches, stone-faced, and I direct my attention back to Anja. "Not exactly. I enjoy his company . . . I'm more nervous about the conversation we're going to have. About . . ." I interlace my fingers and press them into my lap. "You know."

Anja nods, weaving her fingers through my hair. "He will make a good mate."

"*Sha,* I think so." Eros catches my eye through the mirror again, and I offer him a small smile. He meets my eyes, but doesn't offer one in return. "The dress uniform suits you well, Eros." I force a larger smile. He glances down at his clothes—a sleeveless top made of a silky red fabric with silver buttons, smooth white pants, and silver cuffs on his upper arms, just above the black markings.

He pulls at the shirt. "I look like a performer."

I laugh and roll my eyes. "Never happy."

"I'm perfectly happy with my normal uniform, thanks."

I am too, I almost say, but I catch myself. Those kinds of jokes may be acceptable in private, but not in front of Anja. Not that I don't trust her—she and Eros are the only two people in my court I *do* trust—but they aren't the sort of remarks I should be making with company. Thankfully, Anja saves me from a response, finishing with my hair and turning my chair around to face her.

"Close your eyes, please," she says, and I obey. A cold, slick brush runs along the edges of my eyelids, followed by several layers of powder, a dry brush, then another coat of cold makeup. I open my eyes and stare at the ceiling as she paints my eyelashes, then shapes my brow, then dusts my cheeks with some kind of shimmery golden powder. She then reaches into her pocket and hands me a wrapped sweet of some sort. It's soft and white, almost like a chewy mint.

"It'll calm your stomach," she says. I pop it in my mouth— it tastes vaguely of tangy *ljuma* fruit and some kind of slightly bitter berry, but it's not bad.

Finally she pulls out a deep purple bottle, almost the color of blood, and holds it up to the light. It shimmers like liquid gems.

"That's pretty," I say.

She shakes it and smiles at me. "It's new. It'll complement your dress, I think." She's right—it matches the color of my dress and earring almost perfectly. I keep still as she applies it to my lips, then blows gently as the gloss dries. "There. You look beautiful."

I stand and face the wall-length mirror beside my door. With my hair piled high on my head and my shimmering, form-fitting dress angled so it cuts off high on my right thigh but reaches down to my left ankle, I am radiant. Like a glittering bloodgem. "Thank you, Anja." I smile.

"If I may, I think *ken Sira-kaï* will be very pleased."

I take a shaky breath and distract myself from the blush by smiling at Eros. His eyes are glued to mine, and he pulls his lips together as he stands stiff as a board against the wall. "What do you think?" I ask. "Too much?"

He clears his throat and shakes his head. "Not at all. You look . . ." He glances at Anja, then back to me. "Serek will be happy."

I smile and step into my heels. Anja adjusts the clasps, sprays me with a flowery fragrance, and steps back. "You will be the most beautiful woman in the room, *el Avra*. As always."

I swallow the last of the sweet. My stomach still feels like it's tied in knots three times over, so I hope it kicks in soon. Preferably before I see Serek. No amount of lipstain and shimmery fabric will help if I vomit the moment I see him.

"Are you ready, *el Avra*?" Anja asks.

"*Naï.*" I close my eyes and inhale deeply. After holding it in for a pause, I exhale and open my eyes.

Eros is staring at me, and this time he actually offers a weak smile when our eyes meet. "You'll do great, Kora," he says. Anja elbows his side and he rolls his eyes. "*El Avra.*"

I smile and step toward them. "Okay," I say. "I'm as ready as I ever will be."

And so Eros opens the door.

Just before I step into the ballroom, Jarek opens the door and announces my arrival. I barely hear my name over the pounding of my pulse in my ears, and the drumming of my heart in my throat.

The ballroom looks beautiful. A pair of long crescent-shaped stone tables are on either side of the large landing area of the ballroom—those on the left hovering waist-high, packed with bowls and plates of fruits, vegetables, pastries, breads, snacks, and drinks of all shapes and sizes, those on the right lower to the ground and twice the size of the food-covered tables with a red setting for each guest. Behind the dining area is a curved triangular partition brimming with colorful dried herbs and leaves for brewing or smoking, as well as beautiful flowers and plants from across Elja.

Beyond the partition is a set of steps, leading down into the lowered section of the room where dancing and performances take place. On the far side across, a gigantic-sized Eljan crest is carved into the white stone wall, glistening with water that runs endlessly over the entirety of the far wall. But my favorite part is, and always has been, above. Fist-sized white lights fly above our heads, rotating ever so slowly around the room, like the stars have come down just to join the celebration. And beyond that, the largest glass ceiling in the palace reveals an expanse of true glittering stars and the regal moons of the night skies of Safara. Each one is visible from the ballroom tonight—a rarity I haven't seen since my seventh celebration. Mamae always used to say that when the four moons of Safara came close together, it was because they were gathering to watch what was happening below.

How nice it must be, to sit on the moon and gaze down at the world below. Away from responsibilities and assassination attempts and marriage proposals. Surrounded with silence and the beautiful array of *Kala*'s eternal canvas.

But that's not my reality.

I move slowly. My head is light, and my feet are numb, and I'm terrified I'm going to fall over before I even step inside. I'm walking, somehow, and people are staring and I haven't even seen Serek yet and I don't know if I can do it. I don't know if I can tell him I'll be his mate. I don't know if I can agree to be anyone's mate, agree to bear anyone's children.

Kala, I'm going to pass out.

A strong arm slips around mine and a warmth passes through my skin and spreads to my stomach. "You look beautiful," Serek says.

I smile so widely that my cheeks hurt. "Thank you."

I look at him for the first time and my breath catches. He's wearing his customary black and gold, but the dress uniform could not fit him better and the gold accents, buttons, and cuffs mirror the golden rings in his eyes, and his smile. . . His smile steals the air from my lungs and blows it down my back.

The lights dim, and my brother strolls across the far side of the room, where a large, circular tracking light follows his movements and brings the crowd's attention to him. He's dressed in deep red traditional-style pants bound up to his waist, and crimson ceremonial patterns are painted across his chest and face, swirling around the light markings of his skin and the black text on his arms and chest, accentuating his status.

I've never been one for performance, and today, one isn't expected of neither me nor Dima—our role of host in tonight's celebration is enough. But every cycle, my brother has opted to be in the center of the spectacle that is the opening ceremony, and tonight is no different.

A red streak of light bursts through the darkness for the briefest of moments, splitting the lowered section of the floor in two. The stone platform beneath Dima rises, slowly floating higher off the ground as he bows low and sinks into *Enjo*, the stance of power. He centers his weight and brings his fists together over his abdomen, and the crowd falls quiet as the floor silently rises until it's level with the first half of the room. Serek's lips brush my ear and I suppress a shudder.

"It would appear the opening ceremony is about to begin," he whispers. "I will return."

"*Kala*'s blessings," I whisper, and he smiles at me before disappearing into the gathering.

My brother stands before the crowd with his eyes closed, in a perfect demonstration of focus. The room is so quiet you could hear the wings of an insect—not a whisper breaks the hush.

A hand touches the small of my back and I jump, but it's just Eros. He drops his hand before anyone sees and nods toward the front of the crowd, then guides me through them, making way so I stand at the front, just before the banister that divides the room into the lower section. I almost invite him to stay there with me, but the moment I'm in place, he melts back into the mass.

Then Dima shouts and pounds his chest, and a line of men step beside my brother together. These are Dima's best warriors—I recognize a couple faces, Jarek among them—and they wear the same ceremonial warrior garb of the time of old Elja. Traditionally, *kazim* blood was used to paint their torsos and dye their pants, but that custom was banned and replaced with dyes many cycles ago, thank *Kala*.

Together, they change stance in perfect choreographed synchronization, pounding their feet and chests and chanting in Ancient Eljan—a tongue long ago discarded upon the unification of the eight territories. They move with power and grace, eventually picking up long carved *huni* staffs, slamming them against the ground and twirling them in complicated combinations around their bodies. I was never particularly adept with the *huni* staff, but Dima was born for it. He moves with it like an extension of himself, completing complicated kicks, flips, and turns with the staff.

Then most of the men step back, falling away into the darkness, leaving Dima and Jarek. They face each other and bow deeply. Along the right wall, drummers set the pace with a powerful beat that rumbles through the room like thunder, and the men begin to spar.

My brother is the best fighter in the entirety of our guard, but Jarek is a close second. They move around each other with ease, dodging spinning kicks and twirling staffs. This isn't a true sparring match, per se, as ceremonial matches aren't about injuring the opponent, but showing off their expertise—and I don't doubt for a breath that Dima and Jarek are the two most skilled fighters in all of Elja.

The ceremonial match ends all too soon, and I join in as the crowd cheers and my brother and his second bow and step back into the shadow.

As is custom across the territories, when royalty hosts a royal guest from another territory for an extended period of time, the guest must show his gratitude in some grand gesture. Oftentimes in celebratory situations such as this one, the gesture is some kind of performance.

So when Serek steps out of the darkness next, I am not surprised. He has stripped off his shirt and shoes and now wears just his black and gold pants. He reaches into the shadow at his feet and picks up two long chains with metal cage-like spiked spheres at the end. At first I don't recognize the strange contraption, but when the lights fade, plunging the room into total darkness and the two spheres burst into flame, understanding hits me in the gut.

They're *shi*, instruments of fire dancing, occasionally used as weapons.

Serek begins slowly, twirling the balls of flame in large, lazy circles, spinning carefully as he moves across the floor, and the *shi* begin to accelerate. Then, as the drums grow louder and beat faster, Serek picks up speed, whipping the fireballs around his body in smooth revolutions of deadly light. As the fire dances around him and he spins through the air with a powerful and unquestionable grace, I stop watching the *shi* trace orange paths of light in the darkness and focus on him instead. The way he moves with such precision, the way the bronze light catches the angles and valleys of his perfectly sculpted arms and torso . . . he has never looked more beautiful to me. And by the end of the night, I will be engaged to marry him.

The *shi* go out, and the lights turn on, and everyone cheers as Serek bows and the platform lowers into the floor. Chatter fills the room and music plays as people migrate down to the dance floor. I stand awkwardly by the tables full of assorted pastries, frozen candies, creams and juices, and flutes of powerful drinks as passersby bow and wish me a blessed lifecycle, and my brother converges with his warrior friends, deep in conversation. They occasionally smile or wink at attractive women, particularly Dima, who is already partaking in a carafe filled to the brim of clear blue *azuka*. The women bombard them with flirtatious glances, and the only one of my brother's crew who doesn't seem to be enjoying the attention is Jarek, though it's hard to say whether Dima's really relishing their advances, or just pretending to. Jarek stands stiffly at my brother's side, his arms crossed and his lips pressed into a thin line. Dima nudges him with his shoulder and says, "*Naïjera.*" Relax.

Jarek grunts and takes a carafe of *azuka*.

"Would you honor me with a dance?" Serek asks, stepping in front of me. He's back in his dress uniform—though how he changed so quickly is beyond me—and he offers me his hand.

"Of course." I take his outstretched hand, and though I feel silly grinning like a giddy child, I can't help it. A dance is the only time it's acceptable to publicly touch anyone outside the family, and his brilliant grin is contagious as he leads me down the steps and twirls me to the center of the floor. I swear I'm floating a measure off the ground.

The beat of the drums twisting with stringed *alaja* and *nejdo* plays somewhere in the back of my mind, but all I know is the strength of Serek's hand on the small of my back, his grip on my hand, and the way his eyes pull me in and hold me in his gaze. I'm swimming in his eyes, in his smile, in the strength of his arms and the smoothness of his hands. We drift apart, then together, weaving back and forth through the steps of the dance with the rest of the crowd. We shout and stomp at all the right times, and when we come together, his warm breath rolls over my neck, my cheek. We twirl apart, connected by the tips of our fingers—we twist together, our hips moving in sync. His lips just brush my skin as he tells me how beautiful I am, as he asks me if I'm enjoying myself, as he wishes me a wonderful lifecycle and a blessed eighteenth cycle.

I think I speak. I think I answer his questions, but maybe I'm just smiling a lot. Maybe I'm just melting in his arms and moving when he moves, and smiling when he smiles, and maybe my heart is beating in tune with his, or maybe it's beating so loud that I can't hear the music. I don't know, I don't care, it doesn't matter.

Right now, the only thing that matters is the way Serek is holding me, and the way his eyes sparkle every time I meet them.

"Your brother is watching," Serek murmurs in my ear. "He seems to be in good spirits tonight."

"Does he? That's a surprise." The music slows and I rest my cheek against his chest as our bodies slow and sway. The heat of his skin warms the side of my face and his heartbeat echoes strong and deep.

"How so?" Serek's low voice rumbles in his chest against my ear.

"Our courtship isn't something he wanted," I say.

"And you?"

I pull away enough to look up at him. I'm so close I can make out the markings on his chin—they're in Old Inaran, a language I'm not quite so well versed in, but I can work out enough to know they're lines from the sacred texts, written in their original language.

My gaze rises to his, and his eyes are stunning and focused solely on me. A thrill shoots through my stomach as I process his question. "What about me?"

"Is this what you want?" he asks.

I blink. "You have to ask?"

His gaze travels somewhere above my head—to Dima, I would guess—then back to me. "You say it's not what your brother wants, but what about you? What do you want?"

This is the moment—the one I've been terrified of since he first asked me that night in the garden. But now, somehow, with his gaze swallowing me and our bodies swaying together, I'm not afraid. Not anymore.

I close the gap between us, stretch onto my toes, and bring my lips close enough to his to taste his breath. "I want this," I whisper. "I want to be your mate."

His lips touch mine and his tongue swoops across my bottom lip. My mouth opens and he deepens the kiss slowly, taking his time, like every breath is ours and we have eternity. His hand slides to the back of my head and he pulls me close, our bodies pressed tightly together, his fingers caressing my hair. My heart skips a beat and drums faster as our breaths mingle together. He breaks for just a moment, then kisses me again, harder, with an eagerness that warms my belly. My fingers brush through his hair and he tastes like spice and sugar and his scent fills my nose—the faintest hint of firewood and herbs.

Serek pulls away first and, when he smiles at me, my heart forgets to beat. "We have an audience." He smiles softly, and heat creeps into my cheeks and the back of my neck.

I almost forgot where we were.

Someone starts clapping and the applause spreads like wildfire. Serek offers the crowd a warm smile and I do the same, although I wish more than anything the crowd wasn't here and Serek and I were alone.

We could be alone. Tonight. After the celebration is over, I could invite him to my room, where our kisses wouldn't be judged by hundreds of eyes. Where we could be together, for the first time, as a pair. A flutter rushes through my belly. My heart stutters at the thought, and Serek is watching me with the most incredible look, and we could do it.

The night that Midos stole from me, Serek could return to me.

He spins me to the music and I am certain more than ever that I'm going to do it. This is how I'll move beyond my past and embrace the future—this is how my life with Serek will begin—and I'm twirling and I catch a glimpse of smiles and winks and Eros.

Eros, watching stiffly from the edge of the room, his arms at his sides and his lips pressed tightly together. My stomach falls out from under me. I don't understand. Why does one look from my servant suck the smile and heat from my core and replace them with this heavy, cold air?

But then I complete my turn and lose his gaze and Serek presses his lips to my ear again. "I think your brother would like to dance," he mutters.

The last thing I want is to dance with Dima, and I can't imagine why he'd have any interest in dancing with me, but I sigh and nod. "If I must."

He kisses my cheek. His lips are smooth and soft against my skin. "Don't worry, *el Avra*. I will rescue you before the end of the next song."

I smile as he twirls me away and into my brother's arms. I try to force the smile to stay, but Dima didn't choose to dance with me just to be near me. Is he trying to get me away from Serek? Or perhaps he intends to lecture me about bold displays of affection or remind me, somehow, of my inadequacy? I take his hand and follow the steps and stare over his shoulder.

I don't see Serek. Or Eros.

"Happy lifecycle, sister," Dima says. "May this cycle be your best one yet."

I blink. He's wishing me well? He ignores me for nearly a term, argues with me, and now wants to wish me well? "Happy lifecycle, Dima," I say cautiously. "Although we both know you hate this celebration." He smiles and shrugs and I arch an eyebrow—when's the last time I've seen him smile? Not since before the incident with Jarek. Well before that, even. "*Kala*," I say. "You're actually in a good mood."

His smile widens just slightly and he twirls me once. "Why shouldn't I be? It's a special occasion, Kora. The celebration of our birth, and, I imagine, a happy announcement later on?"

"Perhaps." I watch him carefully. "You've been drinking. And smoking?" Dima laughs. He has to be intoxicated. I literally haven't heard him laugh in two cycles. "You have been, haven't you?"

"Does it matter if I have? This celebration is for us, remember?"

"It doesn't matter," I answer. "*Kala* knows it's good to see you smile."

"It's good to have a reason to smile." He twirls me again and I'm almost enjoying myself, which feels unnatural considering my company.

"I'm glad to hear it," I say when we face each other again. "I would have thought the possible news would have you . . . in considerably less agreeable spirits."

"My sister's possible engagement to *ken Sira-kaï* is a reason to celebrate, I would think."

"I would think so, too, but then again I rarely understand the motivation behind your moods."

He shrugs. "I am a complicated man." I snort and he raises an eyebrow. "I do hope you've been more attractive in front of your would-be mate."

I slap his arm and he laughs again and, for a moment, it's almost like we're young again and he doesn't know to be angry at me, he doesn't know to resent me for being born first and stealing his place on the throne. Had I known all it took to bring him to this state was a couple of drinks or a long smoke, I would have flooded him with *azuka* and *zeïli* leaf eons ago.

"Dima, while you're here . . ." I hesitate. Will he be angry if I bring it up? I suppose it doesn't matter—he refused my apology before, but maybe now, when he's in a significantly better mood, he'll be willing to listen. "I apologize for invading your privacy. It was your secret to keep, and I understand why you were upset with me."

Dima stiffens and his smile fades, but he doesn't push me away or interrupt me, so I rush into the rest before he tries to stop me.

"I just want you to know it's okay, and I won't say anything to anyone, but you don't have to hide it from me."

His eyes harden and he shakes his head. "I don't want to talk about it, Kora. I'd rather we both pretended it didn't happen."

I frown. "It doesn't have to be that way—"

"I *want* it that way. Do you understand? I won't discuss this any further." His grip on my arms is stiff as he stares hard over my shoulder.

"Okay." I bite the corner of my lip. "Just know if you ever need someone to talk—"

"I don't."

"I know, but—"

Someone screams behind me, and the sound is a bucket of ice water down my spine. Dima stops in mid-step and I spin around to see who screamed. The crowd is surrounding someone and they're looking at the floor. Someone collapsed?

Black-coated guards rush forward and start pushing through the crowd. My breath freezes in my lungs. I quickly maneuver through everyone—they move out of the way as soon as they see I'm the one shoving them to the side—and my guards are moving toward me, but I have to see before I'm pulled away, I have to know what's happening. I push through the final ring of the crowd and people are screaming for a medic and I can't breathe. I'm going to be sick.

Serek is convulsing on the floor.

"Neja!" I spin around and search the crowd for my doctor—then I spot her, struggling to move through the thick mass. My guards have almost reached me but I point to Neja. "*Naï!* Get her through now!" They spin around to reach her and Serek's guards form a circle around him, pushing the crowd back. My eyes sting. I might be sick. How could this be happening?

"Kora," Eros whispers in my ear. "We have to go. You can't be here."

"Wait," I say, but I can't see Serek anymore through the wall of black-clad bodies. Neja has slipped into the circle and my guards are pulling me away and Eros keeps saying *he'll be all right, we have to go, you're not safe* and I'm not safe but I don't care.

Hands grab my arms and pull me out of the room. I'm too numb to struggle.

My cheeks are hot with streaks of tears and I'm in my room hugging Iro and I don't know how I got here or how long I've been sitting on my bed or when I took off my shoes or if I've been crying all this time.

Eros is watching me from across the way. My guards are nowhere in sight—probably standing in the hall.

"I don't understand what happened," I whisper.

"I'm not sure, either," he says. "He was dancing with an ambassador and he collapsed."

"He was fine," I hear myself say. "He was fine before. I was just with him . . ."

Eros takes my hands. I'm not sure when he got so close to me. He's not allowed to be this close to me, not here where anyone could enter at a moment's notice.

I'm not sure I care.

His hands are courser than Serek's, but equally strong as he kneels in front of me and rubs his thumbs over the back of my hand, sending sparks of heat skittering over my skin. "He's being well taken care of. Neja saved my life. She'll help Serek, too."

I nod repeatedly. Although I stare at Eros, I focus on nothing.

Kala, if he doesn't recover . . . nausea surges through me and I press my hand over my lips. I can't think that way. Eros is right—Neja is extraordinarily skilled. She'll help him. He'll be fine.

Please be fine.

How could this be happening again? Have I displeased *Kala* so much that He would allow not one, not two, but *three* of my lifecycle celebrations to be ruined with some sort of tragedy? My coronation and Midos a cycle later were awful enough, but now this?

Please please please be fine.

Eros leans toward me and looks deeply into my gaze. He passes me a washcloth and offers me a small smile. I crumple the cloth in my hand, and stare at the cloudy gray filtering of his eyes. I hadn't noticed it before, but now that his hair has grown back, Eros has very long dark eyelashes.

"Kora," he says. "I'm going to let go now. You should wash up and prepare to see visitors. You'll probably be getting updates on Serek's condition very soon."

I nod and his hands slide out of mine. I move numbly to the bathroom and splash cold water on my face, blinking until my reflection comes into focus. I submerge my face until my eyes stop stinging, rub the makeup off my eyelashes and eyelids, and clean the dark streaks off my cheeks. I try to wash the stain off my lips, but it sticks stubbornly to my skin. It'll fade in the night. When I emerge from the bathroom, I am still alone, and Eros is standing beside the door. I glance at him, but he shakes his head. No word yet.

I sit on my bed and twist my fingers in the fabric of my dress. "What if it was meant for me?" I whisper.

"I was thinking the same," Eros says, "but we still don't know this is an attack."

I shake my head and squeeze the fabric into my hand. "It has to be. Serek wasn't ill."

"I know, but—"

"Eros, please. We both know this was an attack." I pull my shoulders back. "And I will see to it that whoever is behind it is punished severely."

We wait in near-silence for several segments. Anja is conspicuously absent, but I don't summon her—I wouldn't want her here, anyway. Eros stands in place beside the door, but I pace incessantly across the room, to my window, to the glass doors leading to the garden, to the bathroom, onto my bed, back over the carpet. My pacing makes Iro anxious, and he moves back and forth across the room with me. I drum my fingers and try to read, but I can't focus on the words. I can't focus on anything but memories of Serek's convulsing body on the stone floor.

Kala, I hope he's okay.

My stomach turns endlessly and tides of heat, then cold, overwhelm me as I imagine the worst—Serek's dead, or comatose, or in severe, permanent pain, or something equally awful. My fingers shake and I grip the windowsill. I close my eyes and force myself to breathe. One lungful of air after another.

"Would you like some water?" Eros asks, and I shake my head and spin around.

He's standing right in front of me, and he places his hands on my shoulders. Even though I want more than anything to collapse in his arms, I almost tell him to step away—it won't be long before someone comes with news of Serek's condition. But there's a softness in his eyes, a deep-set worry trapping the words in my throat, and I can't bring myself to speak them.

"It's going to be okay," he says. "Everything will be fine. I promise."

I know I shouldn't—it's dangerous and I need to get away from him before someone sees—but I melt. He pulls me into his arms and caresses my hair and says everything I need to hear. We sit on the edge of my bed and he watches me and there's a strength there, in his face, in the intensity of his gaze that I need.

But the comfort isn't just in his eyes, it's in his body against mine. It's in the way his muscular form holds mine upright, the way his strong arms hold me together and his breath blows smooth and slow onto my hair. It's the spicy scent of his skin, the rumble of his voice, the way my head fits perfectly in the space beneath his chin.

This feels right, somehow. This feels perfect. This feels like we were molded together and separated for so long, until now. This embrace, this beating of his heart against my ear and rhythmic inhale-exhale of his chest, this is everything I could want wrapped up in a single moment, were it not for the undertone of waiting for bad news.

But if this is perfect, then there must be something wrong with me, because there's nothing perfect about an Eljan queen getting close to her half-blood servant.

I close my eyes and push away the thought. I don't want or need to think of politics right now. This night has been terrible enough without my ruining a much-needed moment of peace.

"Thank you," I whisper.

"Sure," he says. Then, after a pause, he touches the wrap on my disfigured arm and a chill washes over me, turning my muscles to stone. "Why do you keep your arm covered all the time?"

No one has ever asked me that before, but it's because most everyone knows. It's hard to forget a coronation that ends in a ball of raging fire. I shudder and pull my arm across my chest and stare out the window. "I mentioned to you the assassination attempt at my coronation that killed hundreds of people."

He hesitates, then nods.

I bite my lip. "Well, I didn't escape unscathed."

He frowns and opens his mouth—just as the doors slam open. We leap away from each other and I gasp as guards flood my room—both black and gold guards of the *Sirae* palace and the red and white-clad guards sworn to protect me. I step toward them and open my mouth—they can't just barge in here—but then Dima and Jarek step into the room and I clamp down on my irritation.

"Thank you for knocking," I say. "How is Serek? Is he hurt?" Stupid question. There must have been some repercussions to whatever happened to him. At the very least a bump to the back of the head when he fell.

I can only hope that's the extent of the damage.

"He will live." Dima crosses his arms over his chest. "Neja was able to detoxify his system before any permanent damage set in."

His words are a cool blanket soothing my stomach. I sigh and sit on the edge of my bed feeling as though I've run for sets without rest. "Thank *Kala*," I whisper, and someone steps next to me. I glance up at Eros, who stands beside me, his hands stiffly at his side. Something's wrong.

I look at Dima, Jarek, and the guards, and ice drips down my back. They watch my every move, and there's something strange about the way Serek's guards are eyeing me, at the malice hardening their gazes and the stiffness of their posture.

Dima and Jarek do not move or speak. They are waiting on me, it seems.

I stand. "Do we know what happened? Was he attacked?"

"*Sha*," Jarek says. "He was poisoned."

Heat chases the chill from my limbs, replacing the fatigue with a fire that curls my fingers into fists. "Poison," I repeat, and my voice doesn't sound like my own. It's a cold, hard thing I barely recognize.

"Administered orally," Dima says. "Moments before he fell."

The fire lessens. At the ball, he was dancing with me moments before he fell, and as far as I could tell, he hadn't eaten or had anything to drink just before taking my hand. "I don't understand. Did he eat before the celebration?"

"Neja doesn't believe it originated from food." My brother steps toward me. "She says the traces originated from lipstain left from a kiss."

I blink. "Lipstain?"

Everyone is staring at me and I don't understand. Poisoned lipstain? Who else was Serek kissing before he danced with me? Or was it after? My stomach twists and sinks at the thought, but *naï*. I would have noticed, wouldn't I? If there had been traces of another woman's makeup on his lips, wouldn't I have seen it? I was close enough that it should have been obvious, and I don't remember there being anything on his lips.

And even if there was something there, wouldn't it have affected me as well?

Dima steps past me and picks up a dark purple tube resting on my dresser. He holds it up to the light and it glimmers like crushed gems.

The lipstain Anja gave me.

Dima extends his hand to the guards, and one of them passes him a smaller version of the glass I have on my desk. I recognize the strange fist-sized octagonal shape instantly—it's a medical unit, like the kind Neja uses. He lays it flat on my dresser, opens the lipstain, and pours a droplet onto the glass.

"Substance identified," it chirps, but Dima waves his hand over it twice, silencing it. He's grimacing when he passes the glass and my lipstain to Jarek, who looks at the screen and shakes his head.

"I'll give this to Neja," Jarek says, and he bows and steps out of the room. Eros is standing so close to me that his heat radiates against my arm. I nearly step away, but his hand is held just slightly in front of me, almost as if to tell me to stay back. Almost as if he's trying to protect me, but from what?

"Kora," Eros whispers, just loud enough for me to hear. "When I say so, take the garden entrance behind us with Iro and run as far as you can into the setting suns. They'll find you."

I stare at him. What in *Kala*'s name is he talking about? Take the garden entrance with Iro and run to the suns? What does that even mean?

"Take them," Dima says. He turns away and steps toward the door; understanding slams into my stomach like a well-placed kick.

Everything happens at once.

Eros leaps in front of me and shoves me back as the guards converge. There's a knife in his hand and they're pointing phasers at him and he screams, "Kora, now!" My feet are rooted to the floor. How is this happening? How can they believe I would do this, that I would try to kill the man I was going to marry?

Eros screams and something warm slaps my cheek—blood. One of my guards lunges around him and reaches toward me. My heart slams against my ribcage and instinct snaps me awake. I have to move. I have to move or I'm going to die.

My hand slides under my pillow to grab the knife, and I throw it with all of my might. It slams home in the guard's chest and he slumps to the ground. Somehow Eros got an unlocked phaser and he's backing toward me and shooting at the guards. He shouts "Run, you idiot!" and he means me.

I lunge for the glass doors, scream for Iro, and burst into the warm night air, jumping over the banister and skidding to a stop just outside the sitting area. I can go right into the garden or left around the palace and into the city.

There isn't really an option.

Iro leaps out behind me, and Eros takes half a step outside, but arms wrap around his waist. He's screaming something and he's saying *run*. He's saying *move* but all I see are guards yanking him back inside and he's going to die.

He's going to die.

But I'm going to die if I don't run.

I want to go after him—I do. I want to rush back inside and free him, but I don't even have my knife anymore and I'll be arrested on the spot. And then what?

So I climb onto Iro and urge him to run as shame burns tears down my cheeks.

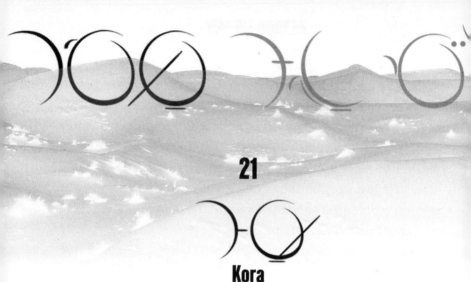

21

Kora

Iro and I slip through the shadows of the night, and I'm grateful for my dark dress, which helps me blend significantly better than my normal bright clothing would have. Most of the patrolling guards have been diverted to the uproar inside, so I'm able to direct Iro past the long training wing, the warrior sleeping quarters, and the animal pens without incident. My heart pounds manically in my chest and I keep crouched low over Iro's back, clinging to the fur on either side of his neck for support. He moves through the sand as smoothly and silently as a shadow, and I focus on calming my panicked breaths and listening as carefully as I can.

There are distant voices behind me and shouting inside. They're still looking for me, no doubt, but I'll encounter the large majority of guards as I reach the gate. I'll have to move quickly and pray I'll be able to break through the barrage of guards undoubtedly waiting for me.

We sprint along the edge of the wall, pausing behind every building to wait for footsteps to pass or voices to fall away. My heart drops with every murmur carried in the wind, but soon we reach the north end of the wall and the gate is within sight.

It's open—and surrounded by white and red-dressed guards. I count sixteen standing sentry with their phasers ready. Would they shoot me? Iro could handle the blast of a phaser easily, but my skin isn't so tough. I'm terrified of finding out just how far my guards have turned against me, but I can think of no other way to get past them. There's only one way out of the complex, and they know it all too well.

Sweat drips down my back as I look for another exit. The walls are sleek and far too tall to climb. The building hiding me from sight is a small, vacant temple. It was once the main temple of the complex, when the palace was first built, but has since been replaced with one ten times its size located on the west side. The roof is steeply pitched, then cut off at the top. The edge of the roof is so low that it is even with my shoulders—an architectural aesthetic lost many generations ago—and the walls are a thick, course stone. I rest my forehead against the ridge of thick fur on the back of Iro's neck and close my eyes. He grumbles softly and I run my fingers through his fur, soothing him.

I have to get across. I have to break through these men, or I might as well turn myself in.

And then what? There is only one punishment for a crime as vile as the one I am accused of—death. And of a most vicious, public kind. Considering the severity of the crime, I'd be lucky to be granted a beheading. *Naï*, my execution would be something much slower—like being hung by the arms in the center of Vejla and eaten from the inside out by specially programmed nanites.

My heart bleeds for Eros, who is at their mercy at this very moment. *Kala* knows what my brother will do to him. Every step away from my most loyal friend is a shard of glass tearing through my core. But if I turn around now, his sacrifice will be for nothing.

And Serek, who is fighting for his life—dear *Kala*, please spare him. If he survives, he will think me a traitor, a girl who would kiss him and kill him simultaneously, but I don't care as long as he lives. Tears prick my eyes but I rub them clean. I can't get emotional. Not when the guards stand just two hundred paces away. I open my eyes and take a deep pull of warm air.

If this doesn't work, I'm going to die.

I have to move before I scare myself out of it.

"Iro," I whisper, combing my fingers through his fur. "We have to get through that gate."

I don't know how much he understands, if any of it. *Kazim* are highly intelligent creatures, but there's debate whether the domesticated creatures understand much more than their names and a few simple commands. I like to think he understands, but I mostly speak to him for my own benefit. No matter what happens, at least I'm not entirely alone.

A low growl rumbles through his body. I wince and hope the guards don't hear. Iro backs up against the wall and crouches low. I groan. Is he truly taking *now* of all times to nap? But then he races forward, leaping onto the roof and a gasp hitches in my throat. He doesn't stop there, though— two quick steps on the plateau of the roof, and I squeeze my fingers into his fur as he unleashes a roar that turns my blood cold and leaps over the guards.

I see some faces. Wide eyes. Open mouths. We're half-way over the guards before they drop to the ground with their arms over their heads or scatter, panicked. Someone shouts out as we sail over them and hit the sand behind them, leaving a crimson cloud in our wake. The phaser blasts begin almost immediately, but nothing navigates the desert as well as a *kazim*. I press myself against his back as we zig-zag through the night, racing around the edge of the city, flashing past curved stone buildings and parked transport of all shapes and sizes. My heart is a drum in my ears and I'm not sure if he's been hit, but every time I peer up, a sizzling flash of red whizzes past my ear, so I keep low and let Iro's instincts carry us away from the chaos and screaming phasers.

I don't look back until the blasts have long since faded away, Vejla is a smatter of darkness behind us, and the rising suns stain the horizon a violent shade of purple and red. All I see are endless oceans of scarlet, but I don't dare ask Iro to stop. I press my face against the back of his neck, hold on tight, and try not to think about all I am leaving behind.

The suns are well over our heads by the time I accept that we've lost any potential pursuers. Iro has slowed considerably and his breaths come labored and heavy as we move through the forever sands. The heat is unbearable; my hair is plastered to my face like soggy adhesives and sweat dampens my skin, stings my eyes, and soaks large swaths of my dress. I'm tempted to peel the cursed thing off—the dark color that worked perfectly to conceal me at night drinks up the heat of the suns and magnifies it onto my blistering skin—but wandering naked in the desert is probably not my best idea.

Despite my discomfort, I'm more concerned about Iro. He ran nonstop for hours and now his steps are uncertain. He's exhausted.

I pat the side of his neck. "It's okay. We can stop now, Iro."

A sound like a groan rolls through him and I smile weakly as he slows to a stop. I slide off him and wrap my arms around his neck. He nuzzles against me, then drops to the sand. I almost laugh—I'm so tired I'm tempted to nap in the sand beside him, but—wait—there's blood on my leg. Have I been injured? *Naï*, the blood is the wrong color—not purple, but red.

My gaze flashes to Iro and finds a patch of matted, bloody fur on his side. I drop beside him and my stomach twists and sinks. The wound is deep and has penetrated his rib cage—maybe even his lung—and a swath of fur as long as my arm is drenched in blood. This isn't the burn wound of a phaser; Iro was stabbed, probably as we were trying to escape from my room. And I ran him for half the night and much of the morning as he lost blood and exacerbated the wound. Now, alone in the middle of the desert, there's nothing I can do to help him. I can't even ease his pain.

The sobs come suddenly as I cling to his neck and weep into his fur. He looks up and licks my cheek a couple times before resting his head in the sand.

"I'm so sorry," I whisper into his neck. "I love you, my friend. Thank you for saving me. Thank you for everything."

I run my fingers through his fur, scratch behind his ears, and pet under his chin as his eyes droop closed. I listen to his slowing heart and run my fingers through his fur, matting his coat with my tears. And I hold him, whispering the gentlest lies and singing to him softly until his breaths come slowly, then not at all.

I stay like that with Iro long after his spirit has faded and crossed the veil, until I manage to push onto my shaking legs and rub the tears from my eyes. If I'm going to survive, I have to orient myself, then keep moving. Alone. As much as I want to stay with my only remaining friend, lying here with Iro will make me prey for vicious scavengers.

I spin in a slow circle, and something hot gnaws at the back of my throat. I am surrounded on all sides by waves of beautiful red sand. By a cloudless violet sky, and blazing orange and red suns, four ghostly moons, and not a single differentiating marker in any direction—not even a patch of rocks or a group of plants. I have no idea where I am, or how far I rode, or where the nearest city is. How far from Vejla did we travel? In which direction was I even riding?

I panicked and rode without thinking and now I'm lost.

Kala help me, I don't have anything on hand. With the surge of adrenaline gone, the emptiness in my stomach and dryness of my tongue has never been more apparent. The average Sepharon can last nearly a term and a half without food—or about eighty sunsets—but we won't live to see eight sunrises without water.

I don't have water. I don't have anything but my ripped dress and the pins barely holding up my hair.

I close my eyes. I need to clear my head and think. I can't panic; I can't make careless decisions, not when any decision could be my last. Not when I'm alone, with only the company of my twin shadows, in a desert I don't know. But something

Eros said before I ran echoes in my mind: *Run toward the setting suns. They'll find you.*

The suns set in the west. We rode for half the set at maximum speed, so we must have covered well over a thousand leagues. The suns are directly above my head, but they were rising behind me, so I suppose all this time I've been running where he told me to. But there's nothing here, not even the smallest of settlements, and certainly no one ready to find me. Where am I supposed to be running to?

I'm going to die. And I don't even have a knife to ease my passage.

So I do the only thing I can—I walk true west. I take step after step, and my toes sink into the sand, and I try not to think about my chances of survival. I try not to think about Eros, or Serek, or Iro, or about the untamed *kazim* and poisonous creatures that wander these lands, or how I'll likely be dead in eight sunsets.

I walk through the scarlet sands with my head held high and my eyes facing west.

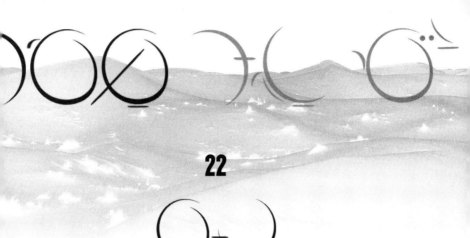

22

Eros

Ice-cold water.

My body starts and I jerk against the restraints that bind me to the cold metal wall in this blinding white bare bones room. My eyelids flutter open, then close. I just need some rest. I just need to close my eyes and—

The wall is burning. My eyes wrench open and I arch off the searing metal, but my wrists, my ankles—something is burning and it's my skin and I'm gasping for air—

Cold water drips off my eyelashes. Down my cheeks. Frozen air blasts over me and my teeth chatter and my whole body shudders uncontrollably. I'm staring into horrible white lights. Not a sound interrupts the silence—I cough just to break the quiet. Stare into the lights. As long as I keep my eyes open, as long as I don't sleep, I am safe.

I don't know how long I've been down here. No one has visited me since they stripped off my clothes, bound me to this wall, and slammed the door shut.

At first I thought myself lucky. I'd expected some kinduv torture, questions, demands. I'd expected knives and blood and something horrific, something out of the stories we heard as kids about the bloodthirsty Sepharon. I was ready for that. I was ready to sew my mouth shut and take whatever they put me through.

But nothing happened. I stood naked against this metal wall with my arms outstretched and stared into the cold white lights and waited. Sure, I was freezing, but I could manage that. I could withstand cold air. I counted the seconds, the strips of light on the ceiling. I counted the polished stone tiles of the floor—sixteen long by fourteen across. I searched for cracks in the walls and floor, and I tapped my fingers against the wall, and I thought if they intended to kill me with boredom, they may very well succeed. Then my eyes drifted closed and pain shot through my wrists and ankles so quickly, for a split second I thought they were broken. Burning energy raced through my arms, slamming into my chest and jolting my entire body. My eyes raced open—it stopped.

The second time I closed my eyes, a scream shattered my eardrums and slammed my heart against my ribcage.

Their intent is clear: I can't sleep. I'm not sure what the end purpose is, to break me I guess, and I wish I could say it's not working. My legs ache with a dull fire, my shoulders and wrists burn, and a persistent throb has spread behind my eyes, wrapping around my skull with vice-like fingers. Every second that passes feels like ages. I keep my eyes moving and try to keep my mind alert—try to distract myself with meaningless trivia, with stupid stories I remember from childhood about disobedient children and bloodthirsty *kazim*, with facts about bikes and how much pressure it takes to crack Sepharon bone—something I can do that no one else at camp ever could. Half-blood.

I don't allow myself to think about Kora. I won't fill my mind with statistics about how long you can survive in the desert without food or water, or think about the poisonous animals that can kill you with a single bite, or the scavengers that travel in packs to rip you apart, and criminals that search the sands for lost travelers to take advantage of. Not her, not her, I won't think of her.

I shift my weight from left to right and push onto my toes to try to take the pressure off my shoulders. I whisper songs and hum tunes I don't even like and bounce on my toes when I can manage it.

Anything to keep my eyes open. Anything to stay awake.

The scream sounds like my mother: *Open your eyes*. I don't remember closing them, but my ears are ringing and the following vacuum of silence weighs on my shoulders like a blanket: *Keep your eyes open*. Small commands are easy to follow. Stare at the floor. Count your toes. Wiggle your fingers until you can feel them again. Stare at the ceiling, into the lights until tears blur your vision. My stomach aches, my mouth is sand.

Keep your eyes open.

How long have I stood here?

I can't feel my legs anymore. I can't feel my arms either, or my fingers or my toes. I can't feel anything, which is good, probably. Feeling hurts. Feeling rages through my body and makes me want to sleep. Feeling rips me in two when Kora and Serek kiss and Day and Nol and Esta die, over and over, and Day's eyes are leaking blood and Aren asks me where his father is.

Numb. Numb is good. Empty is good.

Darkness is good—ice water jerks me to white and I lick my lips. Try to lick the water off my shoulder, but I can't reach. Next will be the heat. The burning skin. Then the screaming, then the pain. Or maybe the pain, then the screaming? I don't remember. I don't remember.

Where am I? Why am I here? Why am I fucken naked and why is it so blazing cold? My eyes start drifting closed, but I force them open. Not sure why. What's so wrong with sleep? Stars, sleep sounds wonderful. I'm so heavy. My brain is a boulder and my neck is too tired to support it. Just a quick nap. Just a second, less than a second, just a mo to close my eyes—

The door slams open. I jerk up and blink and blink. Two guys are stepping toward me. One of them I know. Maybe. They're very tall, very muscular, very dressed in white and red and they don't seem happy to see me. I'm not sure if I'm happy to see them, either. But I haven't seen anyone in a very long time, I think, so maybe this is good.

Or maybe this is very bad.

A third guy enters the room and I should recognize him. It's his eyes, maybe, that part of me remembers—the endlessly dark centers and piercing cold edges. I know him. I know him.

I don't know how I know him.

"I'm going to make this very easy, half-blood," the guy with the strange eyes says. He calls me half-blood, but I don't think that's my name. Eros. Eros is my name. I have more than half of my blood, but people call me half-blood, I remember that. I remember people.

The guy pulls out a knife. Its edge is sharp and uneven, like metal teeth. There's a name for that kinduv edge and I know it, but I can't think of it right now. I can't think of anything right now.

I think I'm tired. I think if I had some sleep, I would remember more.

"You're going to tell me where my sister fled, or I'm going to make this even more uncomfortable for you. Then these men will make sure you don't bleed to death, and we will inject you with accelerated healing nanites and start over. And you will not sleep. And you will not eat. And I will keep you down here and cause you a great deal of pain until you tell me what I want to know. Do you understand?"

I blink. He expects an answer. I'm supposed to tell him yes or no or maybe something else, maybe something he wants to hear. That would be good, because he has a knife. But I'm not sure what he wants to hear. Maybe I would know what he wanted after some rest. Maybe if I just close my eyes . . .

"I need to sleep," I breathe.

He smiles. Pats my cheek. "Tell me what I want, and you will sleep for a very long time. Forever, in fact. How does that sound?"

Amazing. That sounds fucken amazing. I think I say, "*Sha*." Because he's Sepharon and they don't speak English. He smiles and says he knew I'd be cooperative, but he doesn't put the knife away.

"Now tell me," he says. "Where is my sister?"

I blink hard. Stare at the knife. It's strange, because a mo ago there was just one knife, but now there are three. Or two. They fade in and out and merge into each other and split again.

The man takes my chin and lifts my head. Bores into me with his strangely colored eyes. "My sister, half-blood. Where is the traitorous *Avra*, hmm?"

Sister. He has a sister. I know his sister. At least, he seems to think I do, so I must, but my head is swimming and my body is numb and burning and painless and agony.

"Sister . . ." I say.

He scowls. Squeezes my chin. Maybe it should hurt, but it doesn't, not really. That's good, probably. "*Sha,* you brainless idiot. My sister. Kora. The former *Avra d'Elja*, remember?"

"It may be the sleep deprivation," the familiar-looking white and red man says. "It's been known to cause short-term memory loss."

"I know that, Jarek," the brother snaps. His breath smells like salt and some kinduv spiced meat. He slaps my cheek and brings the tip of the knife to my cheek. "Think. You re-member Kora, don't you? You were her personal servant until she attempted to kill *ken Sira-kaï*. You attacked my men. Do you remember this?"

Kora. Her name fills me with something hot that eats away at the numbness and I try to shove it back, but it opens like a flood within me. It breaks over my chest and seeps into my arms and legs and I'm shivering again and my teeth are clattering and there's an ache inside me I can't place. A pain I don't recognize sits between my lungs and drips into my stomach.

Kora.

I'm drowning in images, memories I don't want to see. Kora and Serek, twisted in each other's arms in the crowd of dancers. Screaming and the prince convulsing on the floor and Kora crying. I think I pulled her away. I think I brought her to her room. I think I was holding her and we were so close and there were things I wanted to do. Things I couldn't do.

Waiting. The guards. Running.

Here.

I take a shaky breath. "I remember . . ." I whisper, but my mouth is so dry all I can manage is a hoarse wheeze.

"*Sha?*" Dima steps toward me, his nose just inches from mine. "Tell me. Where is she?"

I switch to English and whisper nonsense words, blending vowels together until he leans closer to try to pull out my words.

"*El Avra—*" Jarek begins, but Dima holds his hand up to silence him.

I switch back to Sephari. "Kora . . ." I say softly. "She . . ."

He tilts his head closer. Closer.

"*Ve,* I truly don't—"

I chomp down on his ear. My teeth rip through skin and cartilage easier than I thought they would, and a horrible scream explodes from Dima's lips. Blood and saliva floods my mouth and something breaks off in my teeth. I gag and spit the long chunk of pointed and notched flesh onto the floor. Dima is doubled over cradling his ear and purple blood coats his fingers and I'm going to vomit, but at least my mouth isn't dry anymore. Jarek and the other guard raise their phasers to my skull, but Dima throws his free hand out and shouts, "Don't kill him!" My lips and chin are warm and wet. I spit at Jarek and his friend flinches half a step back.

Dima slowly straightens, his body shaking as he presses his slick hand over what's left of his ear. "Leave him," he hisses, breathing hard through his nose. "We'll see what a few more sets on the wall does to his resolve."

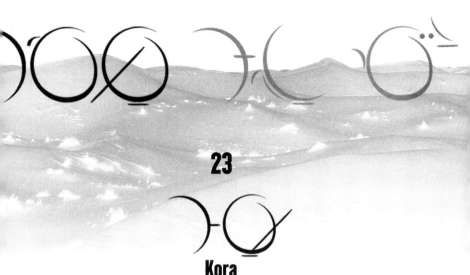

23

Kora

Someone is poking my cheek.

"I think she's dead," a child's voice says.

"You think? Someone should tell Gray."

"Tell him what? There's a dead alien lady lying here in a dress?"

"It's a pretty dress," a girl says quietly.

"*Naï* it's not—it's all ripped and sandy."

"*Sha,* but it was pretty. You can tell because it's sparkly, see?"

"Lucky she didn't get eated."

My eyes flutter open. There are three fuzzy figures standing over me, but they must not be looking at me because they haven't noticed my eyes are half open. My lips feel like they're glued together and my entire body aches down to my bones. I try to clear my throat, but all I manage is a slight hiss through my nose, followed by a gravelly groan.

The blobs jump back and I blink hard. They come into focus as the tallest of the three—a young boy with light brown skin and strange orangey hair standing straight up on his head—leans toward me. He has a long stick in his hand and he wears loose, layered clothing, like scraps of fabric sewn together like a quilt. Not unlike the little girl Eros and I saw in Vejla—Uljia.

Rebel children. Clothed like people from my own city. Speaking Sephari.

"She's alive!" the smallest exclaims. His hair is pale, and he seems too small for his age, but then again, I haven't seen many rebel children before. He jumps beside me and red sand flies into the air. I squeeze my eyes shut and cover my face with my arms—the quick movement sends hot pain across my shoulders and into my fingers.

"Aren!" the girl exclaims. "Stop it! You're going to hurt her!"

"*Naï,* look! She's awake, see?"

"*Sha,* I think we got that," the oldest says. I open my eyes again and slowly sit up. Sand slips off my face; I'm coated in the stuff—dusted red from head to toe. The boy with the strange hair squints at me and points the stick at my chest. "Who are you?"

I open my mouth to answer and my lips crack. Pain and warmth blossoms over my lips and slides onto my tongue.

The girl wrinkles her nose. "Ew. I think she needs water, Mal."

"We can't just give a stranger—"

"Her lips are all bloody! She can't talk like that, stupid!" The girl snatches a leather flask from the boy's hip and offers it to me. I take it without hesitation, washing my lips off first, then drinking deeply. Warm water has never tasted so sweet, so perfectly wonderful. I drink until my pull comes empty and lick my lips when I'm done.

The children are staring at me with a sort of wide-eyed horror. I must seem like an animal to them, covered in sand, barely able to speak, and drinking their water like . . . well, like someone lost in the desert without water.

I sigh and offer the flask back. "Thank you."

The red-headed boy frowns. "You're not supposed to do that. Mamae says if we get really thirsty, we have to drink slowly or it'll make us sick." I glance at the flask. Back at them. I try to return it, but they step back and the tallest boy shakes his head. "Keep it. I don't want it anymore."

I stand, slowly, carefully. For a moment, I'm sure my legs won't hold, but then the shaking in my knees subsides. These children are smaller than I anticipated. The tallest of them barely reaches my chest, but he doesn't seem intimidated by my height. He holds the stick out like a sword, keeping his distance, his free hand held out in front of the younger children.

"Hi," the smallest boy says. "What's your name?"

"We're not supposed to talk to strangers, Aren," the girl says.

"You're also not supposed to say each other's names in front of strangers," the tallest boy says, frowning at the girl.

"Oops."

"Kora," I say. "My name is Kora."

The girl looks up at me. "I like your dress."

I glance down at what's left of my gown. It's a miracle it covers me anymore, considering how tattered and torn it is. It's ruined. "Thank you," I say. "How do you speak Sephari?"

"Our Uncle Eros and Daddy taught us," the girl says, standing up straight. "We were practicing, that way we can—"

The tallest boy covers her mouth and frowns at me. "What are you doing in the middle of the desert . . . in a dress?"

I hesitate. But I can't think of a good reason not to be honest to them, so I open my mouth just as something warm and hard presses into the back of my head. The dull hum of a phaser buzzes in my ears. A woman speaks to the children, but I don't understand what she's saying. They do, however, and they nod and scamper off somewhere behind me.

I don't move. Someone whispers behind me, then the pressure of the phaser disappears.

"Turn around," a man says. "Slowly, with your hands where we can see them."

I do as he says, and face three rebels—two women and a man, all dressed in similar layered, loose clothing. The women are armed with phasers and the man carries a knife as long as my forearm.

"Who are you?" the man says in fluent Sephari. Before Eros, I was under the impression that rebels didn't speak our language, but that's clearly not the case. How many of them speak Sephari so fluently? Furthermore, how did they learn our language to begin with? As we don't speak their tongue, it would seem, as far as languages go, the rebels hold a distinct advantage.

The only advantage, as far as I know.

"I am Kora Mikale Nel d'Elja," I say, holding my hands out. "*Avra d'Elja*. Or . . . I was." The three narrow their eyes; maybe sharing that bit of information was not my most intelligent move, but it's too late now. I clear my throat. "Do you have water? I don't know how long I've been wandering, but I'm very thirsty."

The man says something to one of the women, and she tosses me another flask. I drop the one the child gave me and just manage to close my fingers in time around the new flask. I empty that one as well.

"Eros sent me," I add, and the man frowns.

"*Avra.*" His gaze runs from my eyes down to my toes. "As in, the ruler who ordered the slaughter of our people."

My stomach twists. I can't very well deny it, though— the truth is mirrored in the sharpness of his gaze and the tightness of his lips. "I was led to believe your people attacked me first. It would seem I was mistaken." I'm not sure he'll believe it, but it's the best defense I have. I can only hope that if Eros was able to accept it, his people will, too.

"A convenient story," he says. "But not a believable one. Our people have never entered the city, let alone started any violence."

The scarred skin on my arm prickles like miniature pins pressing into me. I picture the pale man with his knife and wild beard, but it's hard to reconcile the assassin next to these people. Eros was right—his people are deeply bronzed by the sun, and the man's face is clean and his hair kept trim, not unlike our military.

But then where did the assassin come from?

I nod. "It would seem I was deceived, and for that I am truly sorry. If the decisions I made were based on false information—"

"If?" The man steps toward me and quirks an eyebrow. "If you thought for a second we'd waste precious lives trying to start a war that could only end in the destruction of my people, then I promise your information was off."

Eros's disapproving gaze echoes in this man's eyes, and my heart sinks. I try not to think of Eros, who I left behind. Of the bloodstained sand and tears streaking paths down his ash-coated cheeks when I pulled him from Jarek's grasp so many moons ago.

I was so wrong, but there's nothing I can do to give back the innocent lives I've taken.

"I can't make this right with words," I say softly. My knees hit the sand and I pull my shoulders back and meet the man's eyes. My voice shakes and my whole body trembles—I don't want to do this, but I pray *Kala* will honor it nonetheless. "If taking my life will help to right my wrong, I will not fight."

This is the right thing to do. This is what *Kala* would want; this is what honor demands. Blood for blood.

But none of that calms the panicked sea rising inside me.

He watches me for a long moment, his dark eyes searching mine. The redblood influence in Eros is more obvious than ever—in the wideness of his eyes, the single true color of his irises, the silent strength in his face and posture.

In his hesitation, when most Sepharon men would have executed me on the spot.

Finally the man turns and says something to the women I don't understand. It must be an execution order—I'm going to die—but then they holster their phasers and step toward me. One offers me a hand and helps me to my feet. The other passes me a black hood, presumably so I don't see where I'm going. They nod at the hood. I must put it on and go with them, but the thought of wearing it and being at their mercy steals the heat from my blood. And yet, I don't have a choice. I'm already at their mercy.

I just wish I'd been able to apologize to Serek and see Eros one more time before the end.

24

Eros

My body shudders with every breath. Every beat of my heart. My pulse. I try not to blink—when I blink, my eyelids fill with liquid weight and stay closed.

The pain—
screaming—
cold—
burning—

My throat is raw. Every muscle burns with strain. My skull is filled with acid, the space behind my eyes inhabited with miniature red-hot nails. I stopped feeling cold forever ago—I stopped feeling anything but agony forever ago.

I think they're just going to let me die here. I think I'm going to blink and I won't be able to open my eyes again, not even when the chaos begins, not even when the pain becomes unbearable and rips me to pieces. I don't know why I'm hanging on. I don't know why I'm still fighting, why I stand slumped against this wall, why I try to take a breath, take a breath, keep my eyes. Open.

My legs are wet with sweat and urine and the room reeks of me. Of things I don't want to think about. Of Dima's dry blood on my face.

I close my eyes—open them again. Quickly. The room is white and the floor is slick and clean except for the spot around my feet, where it's stained purple and yellow. I'm too tired to be embarrassed. Too tired to care that, at any moment, they could come back and kill me. Use the knife, this time, when I won't have the energy to try to fight back.

I want to forget. I want to be empty again, to feel the numbness that kept me floating through the first few days of this torture. But now that I've remembered Kora and Serek and everything that brought me to this dungeon, it's like my brain has decided to punish me for not sleeping and, while my nerves tear apart my body, the memories riot in my mind.

Why am I protecting her? I am protecting her, I think. I told her how to find the Nomads, I told her where to go to find the ones who live and breathe sand. But I'll never admit it to Dima, I'll never betray her. Or my people. I don't even know if she made it, so maybe I have nothing to protect her against anyway. Maybe she's already dead in the desert. You won't survive long out there without food and water and a sense of navigation. And Kora didn't have any of those.

She's dead. She must be.

But I still won't say. Because Kora may be dead, but my people and what's left of my family—Jessa, Mal, Nia, Aren, and the unborn baby—are not, and I won't betray them even now. Because maybe, just maybe, Kora isn't dead. Because maybe every second I buy her is a second more she has, because maybe, even though I don't want to care, even though I shouldn't care, even though she doesn't care, I do.

I care about her, and it's stupid, and I hate it, but I do.

Maybe I'm an idiot and maybe I'm protecting someone who couldn't care less what happened to me, but I will not break because I won't be the reason that Kora or Jessa or Mal or Nia or Aren or that kid dies. I'll protect them with my last breath.

I hold on to that determination with everything I have left, which isn't much. But it's something. It's something to cling to, while the rest of me falls away.

Someone is in my tomb.

I didn't hear the door open, I didn't see the guards enter, I didn't even notice Dima come in through the door with a thick bandage on the side of his head and murder in his eyes. He has the knife again, but this time he means to use it. This time it'll be my blood staining the floor.

"Disgusting," he spits. "You're no better than an animal."

I keep waiting for the kick of adrenaline, the burst of hot energy that at least for a few mos keeps my eyes open, but this time it doesn't come. The world slides slowly to the left and my focus swims in and out. Dima seems to sway back and forth as he steps toward me, like his body is made of jelly and every step makes him wobble. I focus on keeping my eyelids open.

He steps around the stains at my feet. Wrinkles his nose and brings the knife behind my ear. I should have expected this, I guess. I bit off half his ear, now he'll cut off mine.

Maybe I'll bleed out and this nightmare will finally be over.

Dima grabs my jaw and presses my head against the wall with his free hand. "My patience has worn thin. You'll tell me where my sister is, or I'll begin with your ears."

"Hard to answer questions when you can't hear," I rasp. My voice sounds like sandrock coated with desert. The tip of the knife stings my scalp. Digs into the skin behind my ear.

Warmth drips down the side of my neck and onto my shoulder, but the pain isn't as intense as I'd expected.

"The location, half-blood. Now."

I want to spit at him, but my mouth is dry. A lifetime ago, I would have had another witty response ready. A whole arsenal to choose from, ready on my tongue. Or an insult, something just to make him angry.

But now. Now I'm staring at the spittle around Dima's lips and the sharpness of his canines. Now I'm thinking it's strange we have the same teeth, humans and Sepharon.

He slams my head against the wall. My eyes flutter, vision sputters in and out like a dying engine. Something hot and prickly creeps across my skull. I think it's pain. I think it barely matters, because my body turned to liquid agony ages ago.

I laugh. Or try to—the sound comes out dry and cough-like and I taste rust as I smile. Dima's eyes narrow and he squeezes my jaw harder.

"I don't see the humor, half-blood."

"This must infuriate you," I choke out. "You know if you kill me, you'll never find Kora. But there's nothing you can do to me that will make me tell you."

His fingers are shaking. His face flushes and his eyes narrow, sharp as daggers. I'm sure he's going to do it. He's going to take that knife and plunge it into my heart.

Maybe he just needs a little more convincing.

"This half-blood has beaten you." I'm grinning. Or at least, I think I am. "You will never break me."

He screams. The knife slices along the side of my neck, leaving a burning trail in its wake. The tip jabs into the soft part beneath my chin and something slams behind him.

"Stop!"

Dima is shaking from head to toe, but he doesn't move. The knife bites my skin and somehow I am still smiling. If I have the power to do anything, it's die with a smile on my face and infuriate Dima for the rest of his life. That thought alone is enough to seal my lips with a northward turn.

"Release him," someone says. Someone else is here. Someone other than his guards, who would never order him around. "As betrothed to the former *Avra*, I take ownership of this servant."

I don't remember passing out. I don't remember sleeping, or dreaming, but I must have done both, because I wake.

I'm lying on a seat more comfortable than any bedroll I've ever used, and I'm wearing my uniform pants again. The air is cool, but pleasant, unlike the refrigerator of the white room. The distinct hum of an engine and something else— soft music, with lyrics spoken so quickly I don't bother trying to understand them—drifts around me.

I open my eyes. Blink again and again, until my tears clear away the blurriness. Someone says, "He's awake, *el Kaï*."

"Is he? How are his vitals?"

Someone dressed in black and gold leans over me and holds a semi-transparent octagonal screen over my face. "Stable. He took well to the nanite serum—his brain function and cell energy levels are nearly restored back to normal, and his body's nutrients and sustenance needs have been replenished. He'll need more rest and nutrient-enhanced meals, but he's recovering well."

I'm in a port of some kind. A port with several rows of bench-like seats with backrests facing each other in pairs, tinted windows with a digital readout flashing down the glass in gold unreadable letters, and a smooth, synthetic black leather interior. The man with the screen is sitting beside me, and his hip brushes against my hair.

Some kinduv blurry privacy force field thing—like the one I saw in the infirmary forever ago—separates our cabin from the driver up front, and there's a large digital map on it, with a blinking gold dot moving slowly across it. I can't read any of the labels, so I have no idea what it says, but my guess is it must be our surrounding area. I squint at it, but I'm not even sure what to look for—I've never seen a map of Safara, or even Elja, for that matter. We always navigated with the stars, landmarks, and knowledge of the area, but it was too dangerous to write it down, in case we were ever caught. Last thing we needed was the Sepharon getting their hands on a drawn map of all of our locations.

Serek is watching me from the row facing mine. His gold-ringed eyes seem soft. Almost concerned. But he wouldn't be concerned about me—he barely knows me—so I must be reading him wrong.

I start to sit up, but the man with the screen holds a hand on my forehead, pressing me to the seat. "Best if you don't—" he starts, but I shove his hand off my face and sit up. The rows twirl around me and I grab the door for support. Blink slowly as the world stops spinning.

Serek looks amused. "Welcome to the world of the living. You've been asleep for quite some time."

"Which is to be expected," the man beside me says. "Considering you hadn't slept in six sunsets."

Six sets? It felt like six cycles. I glance out the window to oceans of scarlet sand. Home. The man sitting beside me, who I guess is a sortuv doctor, hands me a black water bottle. I drink without asking, and nearly groan when cool, slightly sweet water hits my parched tongue. There isn't very much—just enough for two long pulls, but I feel instantly better after drinking it. I hand back the bottle and face Serek, who is still twisted in his seat, watching me.

"Where are you taking me?"

"I was hoping you would tell me," Serek says.

I raise an eyebrow. "Aren't you supposed to be the prince of Safara or something?"

He chuckles. "Being *Sira-kaï* doesn't equate to expert of the southern deserts. I believe you are far better acquainted with these lands than I am."

That's probably true. "Where are you trying to get to?"

He pauses. "Dima seemed to strongly believe that you know of the former *Avra*'s location."

I glance out the window and grimace. If I was in Dima's dungeon for six sets and slept for suns know how long after that . . . surviving in the desert that long takes training and resources she didn't have. I didn't even give her halfway decent directions.

"You know as well as I do she's probably dead," I mutter.

"Perhaps. Unless someone with knowledge of these sands told her of a safe place before she escaped, as some seem to believe."

I school my expression. Keep focused on the waves of red sand passing us by. "And what do you believe?"

"That she's alive. And that you know where to find her."

I lick my lips and turn back to him. "I nearly died protecting that information. I hope you don't think just because you saved my life, I'm going to give up whatever I know freely."

Serek nods. "I'm not going to threaten you. I don't believe in unnecessary shedding of blood, but I do believe you care for her—perhaps as much as I do—and you do not wish to see her harmed."

I snort and turn my gaze to the window again. Heat crawls up the side of my neck and my stomach is doing flips and I've never been so grateful for my training. Whatever I feel for Kora is none of his business. I keep my arms loose and my breathing even and I smirk at Serek and meet his eyes again. "If you really believe that, you're even more delusional than Dima."

A sharp glare prickles the side of my face, but it's not from Serek—it's the doctor. I don't pay him any mind, and neither does the High Prince. He watches me with a soft, calm gaze that reminds me way too much of the way Nol would look at me when I told him I didn't care what the others said. That their leers, jokes, and beatings didn't matter.

A patient sadness.

"You knew full well what Dima's men would do to you if you were taken, and yet you sacrificed yourself to allow Kora to escape. I don't believe that to be the loyalty of obligation."

I lean back in my seat. "It would have been a waste if we were both taken. It only made sense that at least one of us escaped."

Serek tilts his head slightly and raises his eyebrows. "Then why not save yourself? Your odds of survival were much higher than hers, I would think. If we're looking at this logically."

The High Prince, apparently, isn't as dense as Dima. "They would've caught me."

"*Naï*," he says softly. "You could have left at any time. My man checked, and you aren't being tracked—and likely haven't been in well over a term. You're clearly a fighter—perhaps even a warrior, and you know how to survive these lands. You've been free to go since the moment they removed the tracking nanites from your system, and yet you stayed. Willingly."

Something inside me twists—a tight energy constricting my lungs and sinking into my stomach. I don't know how he sees right through me, how he can read me so easily, but my defenses are crumbling and I'm not sure how to keep up this front. Because he's right. About everything.

I turn to the window again.

"I'm not trying to disarm you, Eros—I just don't believe you want to see Kora dead any more than I do. And I believe in your heart, you know she's out there, alive, and you can find her."

Inhale. Exhale. I don't look at him. I don't move.

"You're the only one who can find her. If you refuse, I won't punish you, but I don't believe she will last much longer in the desert without assistance."

He's right, of course. And if he's serious about caring about her, about wanting to see her safe . . .

I analyze his reflection in the glass. Everything about him is eager, but in an earnest, worried kinduv way—not the manic rage that kept Dima obsessed. But even if he's fooling me, even if he doesn't have her best intentions in mind, if this conversation is going where I think it is, it might be exactly what I need. If I'm careful about this, I might just get the chance to go find Kora myself.

Dead or alive, I have to know.

"She won't last," I say. "If she hasn't found them, she's dead already."

Serek sits up and his eyes widen. "So you did tell her where to go."

I face him and cross my arms. "I can find her, but I'm not taking you with me. I'll go on my own, on my terms, and I'll bring her back to safety."

He hesitates. "How do I know that you will return her to me?"

"How do I know that I should? I don't know you. As far as I'm concerned, you're just as much a danger to her as Dima is."

He frowns. "I would never harm her."

"Why not? She supposedly tried to kill you. Most would seek revenge."

"She didn't try to kill me."

My brows lift, but Serek continues before I can speak. "I'll admit that I initially believed it, but it didn't make any sense. Why would she make an attempt on my life just before a possible engagement? If she didn't want to marry me—which was entirely her decision—she could have said so and sent me home without an issue. My death wouldn't have benefited anyone, and certainly not her, considering the wrath it would have brought upon Elja and her rule. But if Kora was the murderer, then it would benefit one man: the one who would inherit the throne when she was abdicated and put to death for her crime."

"Dima," I say.

He nods. "It's the only scenario that makes sense. I don't believe Kora was aware of the poison she was carrying."

I watch him for a moment. Nod. "Maybe you're not as delusional as I thought."

"Thank you."

"Wasn't a compliment," I say without thinking. Not that I really care if I insult the high and mighty prince. He needs me too much to do anything about it.

He arches an eyebrow and smirks. "You're very bold."

The doctor beside me looks about ready to stab me. *Bold* probably isn't the word he'd use to describe me. "I'll find and return her if that's what she wants," I say. "But you won't come with me, you won't follow me, and if I think for a second you're a threat to either Kora or myself, I'll slit your throat."

The doctor's face is flushed and he's shaking with what I assume is rage when he opens his mouth, but Serek holds up a hand to silence him. "I agree to your terms to a point, but understand mine: I will give you three sunsets to find and return her safely. If you fail, I have the largest army on the planet at my disposal, and I will not hesitate to use it to find you." The port slows to a stop and the door beside me opens. Serek hands me a small black and gold bag with straps. "Everything you will need to survive for three sunsets is in that bag. Bring her to safety, Eros, and I will owe you a debt."

I glance at the bag. "I don't suppose you have a sand bike on hand."

"You'll find a black cube inside the bag. Hold it in your fist until it glows, and toss it in the sand. When you're ready to be found, activate the tracking unit on the bike."

"A cube?"

Serek smiles. "Trust me."

"I wasn't aware that kind of technology existed."

His smile turns to something more smug. Proud, even. "It didn't. Until I programmed it."

Until he—what? I must look as bewildered as I feel, because Serek chuckles and adds, "I'll explain it to you another time, perhaps. For now, I believe we have more pressing priorities?"

I nod and step into the warm, soft sand. Close my eyes as the heat of the suns bathes over my skin and my lungs fill with clean, free air.

"I pray *Kala* will show you great favor," he says with a soft smile. "I'll see you in three sunsets."

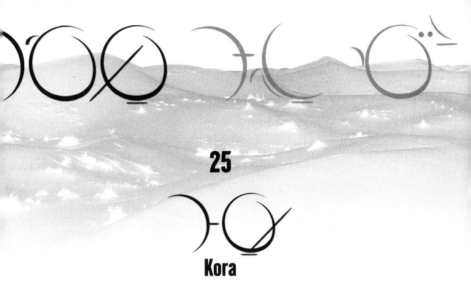

25

Kora

After removing my hood, they left me in a tent with the assurance that someone would stun me should I attempt to escape. I didn't test them—I sat cross-legged in the sand, inhaling deeply through my nose and fighting nausea as I drew pictures with my fingers in the soft, red powder.

My poor attempt at a distraction didn't help, but there was very little I could do to combat the cold terror raging through my system, setting a tremor to my fingers, and twisting through my stomach. How long did I have before they killed me? And why hadn't they done so already?

I'm not sure how long I've been here. Time is deceptive when you're bored, and even more so when you're bored and waiting to die, a combination that leaves me pacing in the small confines of the tent. Voices drift through the air around me—children laughing, the patter of feet, the mumble of layered conversations I do not understand. There are two men standing on either end of the tent—their shadows paint the sand-colored fabric surrounding me, and their voices are loudest of all. I was an idiot not to ask Eros to teach me his language, particularly after learning he spoke mine fluently.

I suppose I never thought I'd need to know it. How wrong I was.

A third silhouette steps before the entrance of the tent, then ducks inside. This is a man I don't recognize, and though I stand taller than him, he holds himself like one used to respect. Silver speckles his trim black hair and his eyes are hard, dark, and strangely small and angled. He is also clean-shaven and his skin is well-colored from the suns. How ridiculous it must have seemed to Eros that we would think the pale, bearded man was one from his camp.

"My name is Gray," he says in fluent Sephari. "I am to understand that you are *ken Avra* Kora d'Elja."

I swallow my fear and hold myself upright. "And you are the leader of the rebels?"

"I'm an authority figure here." He crosses his arms as his gaze rolls over me like a soldier sizing up an opponent. I've seen Eros do this several times—to every guard or stranger who looked at me for more than a couple breaths. "You're younger than I expected."

I scowl. "And you're shorter than I expected."

He makes a noise that sounds almost like a grunt, then lowers his arms to his sides. "I've been informed that a certain half-blood made you aware of our location?"

"Eros told me you would find me if I traveled west."

"And where is the kid?"

I bite my lip and look away, a sharp pang striking my chest. "He was taken prisoner just before I escaped. Without his help I . . . I wouldn't be alive."

"Hmm." He watches me for a mo, then nods. "We've decided not to kill you, although there were many calling for your head all a-splatter."

I grimace slightly. "Thank you."

"We've decided not to help you, either. Whatever circumstances brought you to our lands unprepared are yours to handle. My men will bring you a single meal and water bottle, then we'll return you to where we found you. The Big Guy will decide what to do with you."

"Who?"

Gray arches an eyebrow. "You lot believe in a higher power, don't you?"

"*Kala*, of course."

"Right. That's what I said." He turns away and steps toward the tent entrance. "Enjoy your last meal."

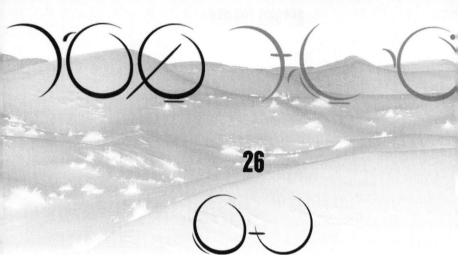

26

Eros

I wait until Serek's port is a dark speck on the horizon before pulling the black cube out of the bag, holding it until it glows gold, and tossing it in the sand, as instructed. The glowing square—which is less than half the size of my fist—bursts into a cloud of what looks like silvery-black dust as soon as it touches the ground. The dust molds and forms in the air into bits of polished black metal that come together and morph, creating a sleek black and gold bike that rises from the sand. I don't get exactly how it works, but Serek said he *programmed* it, so it must have something to do with nanites.

I touch the steering unit and the thing wakes like a living creature. Golden light shoots across the slick black metal and it rises silently off the sand. I arch an eyebrow and lean closer, but the engine is a whisper, impressively quiet. I smile—Day would've flipped sand over this. It makes his treasured old girl look like a wheezy junker.

I climb onto it and grip the handles as it rises a little higher. The controls are all in Sephari, so I can't read anything, but Kora will know which button engages the tracking unit when I find her.

And if I don't find her, it won't matter, because I won't want it on anyway.

I do look for the tracker just in case, but I don't see the telltale blinking light anywhere, so it must be some sortuv internalized unit. But considering there's no way I'll be able to find Kora on foot, I'm going to have to take it.

Plus I'd be lying if I said I wasn't at least a little eager to ride this blazing amazing sand bike.

Judging by the position of the four moons, I'm a little southeast off course to camp, but not so far off that it'll take me days to readjust—in fact, if I hurry, I should be able to make it well before nightfall.

The thing about Nomads is we never stay in the same place. We're as still as the sand—we move with the wind and travel in bursts, not leaving a trace behind.

The idea is never to settle in one place for long, so our location may never be compromised—not even the people know the route, just in case anyone is taken. But I know exactly where my former camp is headed, because Day was the one who planned the route for the next decade, and I was at his side when he did it.

I'm counting on Gray not knowing I was present during the planning. Day never told him just how involved I was, because Gray would never approve. Gray never trusted me—no one ever trusted me except for the Kits. To everyone else, I was a soldier not because I was stronger, faster, and more equipped for the desert than anyone else, but because I had nowhere else to go. Nothing else to do. Gray believed it too—he never thought for a second Day would trust me with anything more than grunt work. Why would he? I'm not human, so why would they ever trust me?

They never will. Nothing can change that I am, and always will be, half-Sepharon. I'm not one of them. I'm not one of anyone.

I speed across the desert, my eyes on the northern horizon. After an hour, I recognize telltale landmarks—an outcrop of tall, weathered rocks that form a crooked finger pointing dead east; patches of bulbous, water-filled desert flowers essential for survival and waving blue prickleplants; a dried up oasis that was the center of camp two hundred years ago. Another five hundred leagues after the oasis, I turn off the bike and park it in the sand beside a striped, white flower and rock patch. Although Serek said the tracker wouldn't be activated until I wanted it to, I refuse to risk taking it any farther. Camp should be about a ninety-minute jog from here—far enough that if I'm being tracked, they'd have trouble locating it without assistance, but close enough that I can return when I'm ready.

I drink from the bottle in my pack, wrap a scarf around my head to protect me from the suns, and start running.

It feels good to be moving again. My muscles ache as I run—I guess I'm not entirely recovered despite whatever serum they gave me—but they loosen over time and I'm soon moving like I did months ago in training. The suns are hot against my skin, sweat drips over my nose and runs between my shoulder blades, and hot air fills my lungs and makes me feel clean. Alive.

I could run like this forever.

I stop only to take water breaks and stretch out my sore limbs. My toes dig into the sand and the endless waves of desert have never looked so incredible. Something bubbles inside me—a latent excitement, the sense of being home—and

I resist the urge to throw myself in the sand and bake in the suns' rays.

When the setting suns have painted the sky red and orange, I slow to a walk. The camp is about a league away—I know because the wind carries whispers now. Day could never hear the chatter in the air—he was convinced I was making it up until the blind test before my official promotion to soldier. Before being initiated into the army, every would-be soldier is blindfolded, taken to a random location within two leagues of camp, and left to find his way back. Those who returned were initiated. Those who didn't were buried in waves of red, their bones picked clean by scavengers.

I returned in less than an hour—the fastest any soldier had passed. I may not be fully Sepharon, but I guess I inherited enough of their enhanced senses anyway.

But being a league away from camp means more than a short journey—it means I've passed into the surveillance border, where the soldiers lay hidden in the sand for hours, ready to shoot anyone who enters unauthorized.

I may be one of them, but with the markings of a royal servant on my arms and the uniform of a slave, they won't know it.

I scoop sand into my palm and mix it with water until it forms a cold, muddy substance and paint a long vertical line on my chest, with two short horizontal lines near the top— the symbol of surrender. I draw it the best I can on my back, using my spine as a guide, though it probably looks terrible. With any luck, I won't get shot from behind.

I walk another half-league without interruption, which is unusual. I would've expected a visit from several soldiers by now, or at the very least a warning shot. The sands slide around me in silence until, finally, the hiss of sand slipping off shoulders and gear whistles through the air behind me. I spin around and meet the barrel of a phaser. But something's wrong. The soldier looks barely older than Mal—and definitely not old enough to be carrying a phaser and patrolling the border alone.

And he looks terrified.

"Hello," I say carefully. "My name is Eros. I used to live in camp with the Kit family."

"I remember you." The phaser shivers in his grip and he holds it with both hands and sinks into a wide stance. The poor kid wouldn't stand a chance against an actual intruder.

"Great. I need to speak to Gray."

He hesitates. Looks at the markings on my arms. "You can't if you're tracked."

"I'm not tracked."

"All slaves are tracked." I crouch to meet him at eye level. He jumps back, shaking from head to toe. "Don't move!"

"It's okay," I say, keeping my voice calm. "I just want to talk to Gray. I promise you, if I was tracked I wouldn't have come here. I'm clean."

He hesitates. Squints at me. Bites his lip. "How do I know you're not lying? Gray says all the slaves are tracked."

"They usually are, but the tracker didn't work with me. Don't worry about it. Do you have a com? I need to see Gray."

He shakes his head. "I don't think you're allowed in."

I take a deep breath. Try not to get impatient. "I'm part of the camp. Of course I'm allowed in—take me at phaserpoint if you want to, but I have to talk to Gray. Or give me your com, if you have one."

The boy hesitates, then takes a hand off the phaser and touches his ear. "Perimeter zone, sir. Eros is here and wants to talk to Gray." Long pause. I rub my gritty fingers on my pants and hold my breath. "He says he's not tracked." A nod. Then he reaches into his pack and tosses me a black hood. "Put it on."

I catch it and arch an eyebrow at him. "I know where camp is."

"They said put it on or I can't take you."

I roll my eyes and put the thing on. I don't have the time to waste arguing with some kid who can't even grow face-fuzz. He shifts behind me and nudges me with the phaser. And so we walk.

They bring me to the center of camp, to Gray's tent. It's too quiet, here. Wrong. There was always noise before, constant talking and laughing, grunting hodges and chittering fetchers in the livestock pen, shouting from the training grounds and the pop and crackle of people cooking over fires—but today all I hear are footsteps and muted conversations. The emptiness roils through my stomach like spoiled hodge milk.

Supposedly I don't know where I am, but the whole hood-over-my-head thing is for show because I was taught by the man in charge of security. I helped enforce the rules and train other soldiers. And considering who I am and what I've demanded, they'd take me straight to Gray.

So I'm not the least bit surprised when he pulls off my hood and takes two steps back. Two soldiers who are actually of age stand at his side, which is still less than half of what his guard used to consist of.

And then I realize. The raid that killed my family did more than burn a couple tents and take prisoners.

"Have to say, I didn't expect to see your face again after the raid," Gray says, crossing his arms over his chest. "Nice tats."

It's not a compliment. I scowl and pull my shoulders back. "I'm looking for someone."

"I know."

I raise an eyebrow.

"As the old ones would say, doesn't take a rocking scientist to guess why you're here, not after our guest the other day."

I close my eyes. Sigh a breath of relief. She managed to survive. "So you have her."

"Didn't say that."

"You just said—"

"She stopped by, but she sure as the shining suns couldn't stay."

I frown. Did they let her stay at all before kicking her out? My people aren't exactly fond of the Sepharon—especially Sepharon royalty—but I would have thought they'd at least help her along so she didn't die out there.

Then again, maybe not. We let our own trainee soldiers die in the desert—why not exiled alien royalty?

"Did she have a cat with her, by chance?" I ask.

Gray arches an eyebrow. "A cat?"

"Yeah, like a . . ." He stares at me and I sigh. He would've known what I was talking about if Iro had made it to camp, which means she's wandering out there, somewhere, alone. "Forget it."

Gray shakes his head. "You can't stay either. As far as I'm concerned, you're one of them."

His words are a kick to the gut. They shouldn't be—I've always known everyone felt that way, that nothing I could do would ever convince them to trust me—and yet I can't help the angry heat that rises inside me.

I scowl. "I grew up here. I'm just as much a Nomad as you are."

But he doesn't back down. "We tolerated you because the Kits are good people. Nol, Esta, and Day were my friends, but they're gone and so is your immunity." He steps toward me and shoves a small pouch into my hand. "Nol asked me to give that to you if anything happened to him, so I've let you into camp one last time because I promised the old man I'd keep it safe. Now my promise is fulfilled, and you have to leave." He steps away and the guards move toward me.

He's kicking me out. He's actually kicking me out of the only place I've ever called home, like some fucken traitor. Like I don't belong.

Fire races across my chest and into my skull. I bled for these people—I would *still* bleed for these people, and he's banishing me from ever returning to the last bit of family I have left. I'll never see Jessa or Mal or Nia or Aren, I'll never know if Day's youngest kid is a son or a daughter, I'll never live in the desert with my people again.

But I knew that, didn't I? I've known that ever since Kora's people marked me a slave. So why does this hurt so fucken bad?

I shove the pouch into my bag and take a calming breath. Exiled or not, I still need to find Kora. That's why I came, after all—not for some fantasy reunion. "Gray, hold on. I'll leave, but I just need to know what happened to—"

"We knocked her out and dropped her off four leagues southwest from here last night. If she's still alive, you'll find her near Devil's Eye." He faces me again, and this time his eyes are cold and hard. "I'm letting you go, so consider this your last free pass. If I ever see you again—or I hear that you gave away our location to someone else—I'll stop your heart, and I don't mean that figuratively. Clear?"

I grit my teeth. Swallow fire. Clench my fists. "As glass."

"Good. Get him out of here."

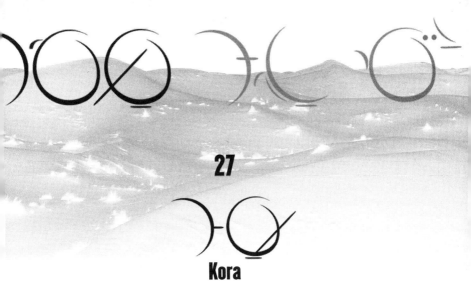

27

Kora

They threw me out of the back of a van, like a sack of rotten vegetables. I hit the sand and rolled several times before skidding to a stop. Powder stung my eyes and became cold mud on my tongue. I spit sand, rubbed the dirt from my eyes, and turned in a small circle. Identical waves of the purest red sand surrounded me with only two landmarks—a tall cluster of rocks towering over every dune, with a plateau in the front and a wall of weathered, spike-like rocks behind it, and at its base, a grouping of dark shapes, scattered half a league across.

Kala's Throne and the abandoned city of Enjos.

I'd never seen the formation or the ruins myself, but it was once a sight of pilgrimage for the more devotionally inclined. Enjos was a rich city then—full of merchants selling religious trinkets to those passing through—and the grandest temples in all of Elja, save for Vejla. The histories say the city became so popular that some sought to make it the new capital.

That is, until the Great War began and the pagan armies of Sekka'l swept through Ona and into Elja, razing many of our cities, including the once-great Enjos. The darkness that followed lasted sixteen cycles—a time of bloodshed and child sacrifices to the gods of Sekka'l, until the golden-eyed Jol d'Asheron united the armies across Safara for the first time in history to crush the darkness and begin a new rule. One in which we are all united under a single crown—a line made up of Jol's descendants.

But Enjos was never rebuilt, and as a way to respect the dead, it never will be. And now Kala's Throne is a cluster of rocks deep in the desert, forgotten by most.

I walked toward them. At least with Enjos and Kala's Throne on the horizon, I knew I was headed in a straight line rather than wandering in large, aimless circles. At least I had a destination, even if it was likely I would die once I reached it.

My mind wanders. Alone, at the mercy of the twin suns, I have far too much time to think. To ask questions I'm terrified to answer—like whether Serek survived the attack, or Anja knew what she was doing when she gave me the poisoned lipgloss, or if Dima's happiness was caused by something other than *azuka* and *zeïli*. An ache blossoms deep inside me at the thought of it, and I push the questions away.

There must be another answer. An explanation that doesn't involve a betrayal from those closest to me.

At least I don't have Dima and his guard breathing down my back, demanding war with the rebels. I'm free of the whispers trailing me like a spirit, the uncomfortable silences when I address the people, and the mutterings of my council advisors about my weaknesses.

Because as much as I fought it, they were right—all of them. I failed as *Avra*, and although this realization should be a crushing weight, I've never been so free. Granted, that freedom will only last until I die in this cursed desert, but from here until my final breath, every decision will be my own. And no one will ever take that from me again.

Focusing on that, rather than the failed legacy I've left behind, is how I choose to spend my final thoughts.

The suns travel through the sky, changing the shape of my shadow doubles. The arid, unending heat bakes the sweat from my pores and saps my energy. Small, round lizards skitter past my feet, burrowing into the sand. But I keep moving. I must keep moving.

Halfway through the set, I begin to wonder if perhaps I'd made a mistake, eating and drinking in the rebel camp. Perhaps I should have continued with a dry mouth and an empty stomach—it would have ended the torment much faster than having to wait for my body to dehydrate all over again.

Despite having walked nonstop, the suns dip way below the horizon before I even begin to near the formation. It's larger than I expected, and regardless of how far I walk, I never seem to near it. It remains a stubborn shadow on the horizon, taunting me with its distance.

Maybe I was wrong. Maybe I'll die before I reach it.

But Enjos. Enjos seems close. I can make out the crumbled buildings half-buried in waves of sand. It can't be more than two leagues away, and if I just keep moving, maybe with Kala's grace I can reach it. Maybe He will allow me to die in the sacred city, on the bones of a people lost long ago.

Another step.

Another step.

Just one more.

This is how I stumble through the sands. This is how I fight the aching of my bones. This is how I take a breath and keep moving because I'm close, so close, so close to the ruins where I can rest at last.

I don't count my steps. I barely register my feet dragging through the soft crimson sand. But my hands meet the rough surface of a red sandstone wall laced with black, rope-like vine and somehow, incredibly, I've done it.

I made it to Enjos.

I don't stop as much as I sink—lower and lower into the sand until exhaustion overtakes me and I can't bring myself to take another step. Kala's Throne is still a silhouette somewhere beyond the ruins—one I will never reach, but it doesn't matter. I'm here. I collapse, and I've barely closed my eyes before my consciousness drifts and drops me into sleep.

Something hums in my dreams, an incessant buzzing like a stubborn insect, determined to whiz around my mind despite my attempts to smother it into shadow. Louder and louder it becomes until I can fight it no longer and my eyes snap awake.

But the buzzing doesn't stop. *Naï*, not buzzing—humming. The low, steady hum of engines.

I sit up and fist-shaped orange lizards skitter away from me, chittering as they race into their burrows. Headlights—six spots of light—swerve and wave toward me. Six sand bikes steadily growing larger, coming closer. I don't know if they've seen me—*naï*, they probably haven't. They're still far enough away that their light is nowhere near me. Lying in the sand like this, at the base of an abandoned building, I must blend into the night with relative ease.

Truth be told, I'm not sure if it's good or bad that I've remained unnoticed. It's not likely to be anyone I want to see: my people don't roam these lands in the middle of the night, and even if they did, they would likely want me dead now that they believe I've attempted to kill Serek. I doubt it's the rebels who abandoned me in the desert this morning, because it would make little sense to leave me to die only to come pick me up again.

Could it be Eros? A jolt of excitement races through me at the thought, but I dismiss the notion entirely: Eros has been captured by my brother and his guard. Assuming he's still alive, he's probably locked up in one of Dima's dungeons. And even if he did somehow manage to escape, he would be traveling alone.

So then who are these six?

Maybe they're a band of thieves. Criminals have been known to wander these lands—both Sepharon and rebel—out where the reach of the guard is thin. And it isn't unlikely that they might travel in small packs, like scavengers, to protect themselves from wandering wild *kazim*.

If that's the case, I can't lie here. It's only a matter of time before they come across me—their current path will bring them right to me—and then what?

I crouch and move as quickly as I can, backing into the ruins while keeping low to the ground. If I can just manage to move out of their path unnoticed, I can bury myself in the sand or duck into a building until they pass. I can hide and pray they don't see me, pray they drive right past me and I live another night. Their outlines are clearly visible now—six burly men on bikes. I can't tell if they're Sepharon or rebels. I'm not sure which I'd prefer.

Four steps back and the worn edge of a crumbling flat roof is even with my shoulder. My heart slams against my chest, once, hard as my blood goes cold. *Kafra*! I'm on the peak of an uphill slope—they'll see me if I don't move!

I scramble over the ridge and tumble over the other side, kicking up sand as I slide and roll to the bottom. Scattered half-buried buildings surround me, some leaning so far to the side, it's a wonder they're still standing at all. A crumbling white totem carved into *Kala*'s name sticks haphazardly out of the sand, towering over me.

A whoop of laughter breaks the quiet of the night, followed by echoing cries and shouts. The lights swerve and shine over the sand dune I just spilled over.

I've been spotted.

My initial instinct is to run. To race across these sands as quickly as my legs will take me and duck into a partially destroyed building. But they are on sand bikes, and it would be all too easy to trap me in these ruins. Inevitably, they would catch me and I would be too exhausted to defend myself. Not to mention running and hiding would only excite them, and *Kala* knows that's the last thing I need. So instead I stand, swallow my galloping heart, and wait. I clench my fingers into fists behind my back, I keep my eyes high and school my face. Whoever these people are, I will not allow them to see my terror. I am—was—*Avra* of these lands. It's not the first time I've swallowed my fear.

They catch up quickly—they must have been closer than I'd anticipated. Their lights blare in my eyes as they cut over the crest and blaze down the dune. They form a tight circle around me as they slow to a stop and step off their bikes. I can't make out their faces because of the blinding lights, but their excessive height tells me all I need—they're Sepharon. And they're not in any uniform, which makes my non-guard theory likely.

I keep my eyes on the man closest to me. He steps in front of his bike, blocking the light and temporarily revealing his face. He's much older than me, perhaps forty or so, with a trim black beard, dark hair pulled back into a knot at the base of his skull, and a sharp smile like a bloody knife.

His gaze rolls over the markings on my bare arm, and a slow realization dawns behind his eyes like a sputtering torch. "What a nice surprise. *Ken Avra* herself, wandering the deserts . . . alone?" He glances around and smiles. "*Sha*, it would seem alone."

"Former *Avra*," the man to his left—a shorter man wearing a headscarf—says. "They say Dima is *Avra* now."

"About time," someone behind me says. "Women don't belong on the throne." The others mutter in agreement.

The bearded man steps toward me, flashing me with his menacing smile. "In most circumstances, I would consider returning you to the capital, *Avra*, but as I understand it, they're not interested in you as much as they're interested in your corpse." His fingers reach for my cheek and I duck out of the way. The others snicker and his smile widens. "You know, I've never had royalty before. None of us have, isn't that right men?"

Whoops and fits of laughter. I keep my racing heart in check with a quick burst of air and smother the hot panic clambering up my throat. His gaze rolls over me like I'm naked in front of them—truth be told, my skin-tight shredded dress isn't covering much. Maybe it would have been better if the rebels had just killed me. I'd take a phaser to the chest or a beheading over this.

I clench my fists. *Naï.* I'll die before letting anyone overpower me and use my body for their pleasure.

The urge to run is overwhelming—I dig my toes into the sand and steel myself into a strong stance, ignoring the tremor in my hands.

"What do you think, *Avra?*" The bearded man moves closer to me. This time when he reaches for my cheek, I bite down bile and stand still. His coarse fingers brush against my skin and coldness washes down my back. "A little generosity only seems fair, all things considered. And perhaps, if you're any good, we'll even reward you with your life. A good trade, I think."

His fingers trail down the side of my neck and finger the cloth wrapped tightly over my scarred shoulder as he licks his lips. Nausea broils inside me and my nails dig into my palm. I must keep focused. I can't panic; I can't allow fear to overtake me. If I'm going to survive this, I have to be logical. I have to be calculating. I have to be ready.

And so I don't move.

The man takes another step, closing the distance between us. His waist brushes against my stomach and his eyes are fixated on the spot where my neck meets my shoulder. He brings his lips to my ear and his salty breath washes hot over the side of my face. "I've been told I'm quite a good lover, although I can't promise the same for the others." His slimy lips touch the side of my neck and I step into him, pressing my body against his. He gasps in surprise as my arms slide around his waist and I train my eyes on his face. His lips are parted just slightly, the shock widening his eyes.

He reacts exactly as I expected him to—with a hunger I do not share.

A hunger that distracts him from my fingers wrapping around the hilt of his phaser, tucked away at the back of his pants. His lips close over mine and I slam the phaser against his temple with all of my strength. He crumples like a discarded doll.

I aim at the man with the headscarf and pull the trigger.

Nothing. The phaser doesn't even charge up. It's fingerprint-locked.

The lost moment is a lifetime—and twice the time the others need to pull out their phasers and aim at my skull. The man with the headscarf seems to be in charge now, stepping toward me with his phaser outstretched. "Drop your weapon," he says. His hands are steady and a fire rages behind his eyes that I understand all too well—he won't hesitate to kill me on the spot.

I slowly crouch and place the phaser in the sand. Draw a handful of red powder into my fist and stand.

"Check him." He nods to the bearded man lying in the sand.

Someone off to my right rushes over to check his pulse. "Alive," he announces. "Just unconscious."

"Good." He takes another step toward me, then stops, keeping distance between us. Apparently he's not as impulsive as his friend. Which is good, because I might throw up if one of them touches me again, but it's also very bad. I can fight a man who comes close enough to feel the impact of my knee against his groin. Much more difficult to fight an opponent at this distance without a weapon to throw in his direction.

Will the sand reach? I need to get closer.

The bearded man I knocked out has a knife strapped to his left leg—the silver handle glints in the soft moonlight. If I can somehow manage to get over there and grab the knife . . .

"On your knees," the man says.

I step closer to him and he matches my movement with a step back.

"Don't move any closer. I said *on your knees*."

I'm going to have to do something undignified if I'm going to get close enough for this to work. I allow my facade to melt away—my lips tremble and my eyes swim with tears. "Please," I whisper, taking a baby step toward him. "I'll do anything, I'm not ready t-to . . ." I stifle a sob with my free hand as hot tears splash down my cheeks and I slide another step closer.

The man doesn't move. His dark eyes are glued to my gaze, and a tremor has developed in his hand.

"Be careful, Kel," a man calls out behind me. "You saw what she did to Rodin."

But another off to my right laughs. "Please, Rodin wasn't paying attention and he let the whore grab his phaser. She had a moment of fortune—nothing more."

"Just kill her and get it over with."

"Don't kill her—Rodin will want to restore his honor when he wakes. Let him decide what to do with her."

Someone laughs. "Restore his honor or have his way with her?"

"Same thing, is it not?"

They snicker, but Kel doesn't seem amused by the conversation. "Quiet!" he snaps, glaring at them. "Don't you see I'm trying to—"

I dive toward Rodin's leg, grab the dagger, and twist hard as I let the knife fly. The blade slams home at the base of Kel's throat and he drops, choking on metal and blood. Curses batter the air as I lunge over the new corpse, rip the knife through his jugular, and scramble to my feet in front of a third man. My footwork is terrible and I stumble. It nearly costs me, but the man's shot races over my shoulder. I throw sand in his eyes and hammer the blade into his wrist. He screams—I duck—a red phaser burst rams his chest and silences him, but when I sit up, a crimson phaser glows breaths away from my nose.

My gaze darts around to find the other men standing—I can't lose track of them, not now—but they're gone. Did they run? Why would they run?

"That's enough," my attacker hisses through crooked yellow teeth, his finger ready on the trigger. "Did you enjoy yourself? Because it's the last—"

"Where are your friends?" I frown. "I thought there were six of you?"

His eyes narrow, but he keeps his gaze on me. "There were. Until you killed three of them."

"Two. The third is unconscious. And there should be two others, standing at your side."

He hesitates, then glances back just as two hands grab either side of his head and twist sharply to the left. I gasp—a loud crack twists my stomach as he collapses into the sand.

Eros wipes his palms on his white pants and offers me a grim smile. "Maybe you do need me, after all."

I slam into him, throwing my arms around his neck and crushing him to me. He gasps and stumbles into place as my lips press into his, parting slightly as our tongues meet and my fingers slide into his bristly hair. His shoulders relax and his hands slide around my waist, pulling me tight against him. I deepen the kiss, pressing against him until my lips hurt. His breath is my breath and he smells like sweat and endless oceans of sand. We press closer—we are not close enough.

We break for just a moment, but he pulls me in again, sliding his hands under my thighs and lifting me against him. My legs wrap around his waist and he takes several steps forward until my back hits a rough wall. His calloused fingers slide up the sides of my stomach, tracing fiery paths on my skin. The kiss becomes desperate, hungry, like he's dying and I am his final drink, his final breath, his final thought. His fingers are in my hair, his taste is on my tongue, and I want more. I want his lips to taste every part of my skin, I want to trace the hills and valleys of his body. Heat blossoms in my stomach, tingles at the base of my spine, and spreads across my torso.

Eros pulls away, his face flushed and his voice breathy as he speaks, "Tell me if you want me to stop."

I bring my lips to his collarbone and taste his skin, running my tongue over the light line of *Kala*'s mark. He shudders as I trace the path up his neck, kissing the underside of his chin, the stubble on his jaw, the corner of his mouth.

My lips are on his when I whisper, "Don't stop."

His mouth closes hard over mine, and our tongues slide together. My hands slip down his neck, down his back, and over his sculpted abs. I trace the angled cuts of muscle until my fingers find the hem of his pants. The air is sweltering and he breaks away and grabs my hands, pressing them against the wall over my head as he buries his head against my neck, sucking on my skin, setting me on fire. The stubble on his cheeks scratches against the underside of my jaw—I gasp and arch against him as he presses into me—our fingers twined tightly together. He works his way across my neck and up my jaw and a soft groan escapes my lips. His hips grind against me and my whole body shudders, my every breath desperate. There's no hiding his body's response, twisted together like this. He rubs hard against me and I grip tighter with my legs.

I've wanted this for so long. I just didn't realize it until now.

Our mouths meet and I'm floating. He releases my hands and I pull him closer, brushing my fingers through his hair, then pressing his head harder against me. His fingers find a rip in the right side of my dress at the top of my ribcage and his hand slides inside, working its way up to my breast, massaging it gently. I am fire. I am the suns. I want to rip my cursed dress off so there's nothing between us and we can become one, because his skin on mine, his taste on my tongue, the salty scent of his body making me dizzy—everything is perfect. Everything is so much better than anything I'd ever imagined.

He's perfect.

He takes my lower lip into his mouth and gently sucks on it. My fingers dig into his back and his moan sets the base of my spine tingling. Closer. We need to be closer and I don't know where this desperation is coming from—when this need to have him, all of him, began. I've never felt this way before—not for Midos, not for Serek—but this feels right.

His left hand slides down to my shoulders.

His fingers slip beneath the wrap on my arm.

My blood is frozen—everyone is screaming—ash fills my lungs—I can't see, I can't breathe; my arm is a beacon of exquisite, burning pain. Where is everyone?

I'm on my bed and Midos is caressing my shoulder and his long dark hair tickles my cheek and there's a dagger in his hand.

I gasp and break away, pushing him back. I gulp in the cool night air and catch my breath. My heart is racing, my mind is on fire, and I'm not in the temple, I'm not in my bedroom, I'm in Enjos, pressed against a wall of an abandoned building and my legs are wrapped around Eros's waist.

Eros. Eros, the half-blood. Eros, my *servant*. What in *Kala*'s name am I doing?

"Put me down," I breathe. "Now. Please."

He stares at me, wide-eyed, his face flushed, his lips swollen, and his breaths coming in loud, heavy pulls. But he lowers me, gently, so gently, and my toes touch the sand and he doesn't move. So I move. I step around him and swallow the night and press my palms against my eyes until the phantom images are long gone.

Eros touches my shoulder and my body goes rigid. He pulls away quickly, and I wait a breath before turning around to face him.

His gaze slides over me in a way I never would have allowed not so long ago, but there's something behind his eyes—hurt? He takes a step forward, then back. "I—" he begins, but I shake my head.

"I shouldn't have done that. I apologize. I don't know what I . . ." I take a breath, straighten the tatters of my dress, and pull my shoulders back. "Thank you. For helping me."

He frowns, then looks at my lips, my breasts, my eyes. After a pause, he closes his mouth and nods. "You're welcome . . ."

I close my eyes for just a moment, just long enough to focus, calm my racing heart, and smother the part of me that wants to pull him close again. I can't do this. I can't allow myself, even for a moment, to entertain thoughts of what can never be.

Even if I wasn't royalty, even if Eros wasn't a slave, even if my life wasn't forever a public display, I could never risk a relationship with a half-blood. I couldn't live knowing that, at any moment, soldiers may come knocking on my door to take any forbidden children we had away—to execute him for spreading his tainted mixed blood. For living.

I won't do that to myself—*naï,* I won't do that to either of us. The law is the law, and I am no longer in the position to try to change it. There is no chance of a future with Eros.

When I open my eyes, he is watching me, and I steel my expression. "I'm assuming you didn't walk here." I step over the corpse with the broken neck and walk past him and the building we just defiled. It has a low, sharply peaked roof and the stone has a faded metallic shine to it, like it was painted to be reflective.

It was a temple. We just did *that* against a temple in Enjos, of all places.

I'm going to the Void.

I dare a glance back at Eros, but he hasn't moved from his spot several measures back, turned away from me.

I sigh and bite the corner of my lip. "Eros, we shouldn't stay here."

He turns, frowning, and shakes his head. His mouth is painted with wet sand, which almost looks like rebel blood, and his hands are stained purple—from *actual* blood. I'm covered in both—from the fight, and from . . . well.

"Sorry," he says. "I thought I saw—never mind. What did you say?"

"That I'm assuming you didn't walk here."

Eros moves into place at my side and wipes his mouth with the back of his arm, smearing wet sand over his skin. "Serek gave me a bike. I've been told to activate the tracking unit once I find you."

I stop. "Serek sent you after me? You're working with them?"

"He knows you're innocent. He thinks Dima's behind the attack."

Something inside me sinks, pulling the air from my lungs and crushing the latent flutter in my stomach. I'd suspected as much all along—seen it even, when Dima ordered my arrest and turned away from me as the guards came forward—but hearing it hurts all the same.

My brother has always wanted the throne, but part of me wanted to believe he would never hurt me to get it.

"Serek said that?" I whisper.

Eros nods. "He said Dima is the only one who would have benefited from what happened—it wouldn't make sense for you to kill Serek because you'd get nothing out of it."

Relief washes over me like a much-needed rain. "And you trust him?"

He glances down and digs his toes into the sand, his bloodstained hands hanging loosely at his sides. "For now."

"Good enough." I climb onto a dead man's bike and start the engine. Eros does the same to a black and gold bike discarded between two lopsided buildings leaning precariously against each other several steps away. "We'll stop a couple leagues from this mess and turn on the unit there." I don't wait for a response—Eros will follow me. I slam down the accelerator and drive as quickly as I can away from the blood and bodies.

Away from the memory of a kiss I can never repeat.

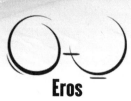

28

Eros

Kora refuses to look at me after she activates the tracker and we wait for Serek to find us. Sitting beside the stolen bike, she keeps her eyes low and sifts sand through her fingers, then turns to the stars or stares off across the desert waves. When I sit next to her, she gets up and moves away, careful to keep her gaze off me, as if I've got some infectious disease and she's afraid of catching it with a single glance.

I don't bother trying to fight for her attention. If she wants to kiss me and run her hands all over me while obviously enjoying it, then fucken pretend I don't exist, that's her choice. It doesn't matter. It never mattered—*she* never mattered. I should be used to this. Stars above, it's not even the first time it's happened—Aryana never spoke to me again after we had that night together. Apparently I'm good enough to fuck around with, but too disgusting to stick with afterward.

It doesn't matter. None of this matters. I've been alone since the moment of my birth—my own mother didn't even want me. I'll never have a future with anyone—I won't have a mate and I'll definitely never have kids because I'm a half-blood. And half-bloods are worth less than dirt.

I know that. I just wish this didn't hurt. I wish I didn't let myself hope, even for just a mo, that this time might be different. Because I never expected anything from Aryana—that was just sex and we were both drunk and I knew even then that it didn't mean a blazing thing.

But this didn't feel like a meaningless kiss. This didn't feel like trading tongues for the sake of it. This felt real. This felt like the moons had aligned and the stars were shining in our favor and every breath was ours, every touch was right. This felt like eternity in a blink, like our lives unraveled and spun together, like the convergence of always and never and every step I've ever taken and every pain I've ever endured lead to that moment. So how can something that felt so perfect be worth nothing at all?

Stupid. I was stupid and now I have to deal with the fallout. Now I have to deal with the cold pain festering deep between my lungs, freezing me over from the inside out.

I sit in the sand and open up the pack Serek gave me. There's an extra bottle of water still unopened, and I toss it beside Kora. She doesn't look at me, but she takes it and downs half the bottle without pausing to breathe. I finish off my bottle and find two strips of dried meat wrapped in foil. Again, I throw one to Kora before chewing on one myself. Again, she takes it without acknowledging me.

Girls.

I chew absently on the salty meat and pull out the remaining contents of the bag—a switchblade I used to cut the first thug's throat, a dozen more packs of dried meat, and some sortuv powder that I think you're supposed to mix with the water to replenish nutrients or something. I throw that at Kora, too. It smacks her arm and slides to the sand—she still doesn't look at me as she takes it.

Then there's the pouch Gray gave me, from Nol. To be honest, I'd been so focused on finding Kora that I'd forgotten about it altogether, but here it is. It doesn't look all that special—the pouch is made of some kinduv thick, rough black fabric tied with a leather drawstring and engraved with a large gold Sephari letter that looks like the sliver of a moon. When I open it up and dump the contents into my palm, a black ring rolls out. It's hard to see in the darkness, but I hold it up and catch the light of the moons and stars. It's a simple ring made of some kinduv smooth, near-black metal, with a semi-translucent gold band running through the center. Some kinduv polished gem, it looks like, cut into a circle and embedded into the ring.

I slide it onto my ring finger—it fits perfectly.

"Eros."

My eyes snap up at my name. Kora still isn't looking at me, but she's standing and pointing to a small group of headlights on the horizon. Serek's procession. "That's him," I confirm, closing my pack again. And so we wait in silence until they arrive.

The doctor hovers around Kora like a child clinging to his mother. He takes blood samples, cleans every tiny little scratch, and gives her all sorts of nutrients in the form of stick-on gel patches. He gives her about a half-dozen bottles of freshly chilled water and bowls of fruit before Serek dismisses him and he joins another car in the caravan. But none of that compares to the way Serek looks at her—to the warmth in his face and eyes every time she glances at him, to the way he gently touches her hand and caresses her palm and smiles at the smallest thing.

He's in love with her. Completely and utterly.

I thought she shared his feelings—at least, I was convinced of it at the party before everything went to the Void. But now I'm not so sure—now her responses seem hesitant, like she's forgotten how to smile or share his secret glances. And even now, as he holds her hand and kisses her knuckles, she watches him with this stiff little smile.

But she doesn't look at me. Not once. And the cold in my chest spreads a little farther.

It doesn't matter, I remind myself. *It doesn't matter, it doesn't matter, it doesn't matter.*

Maybe if I think it enough, it'll be true.

I stare out the window as the sand races by. We can't return to Vejla, so we're headed to the capital of Safara, Asheron, but I'm not sure why I'm still here. I'd expected Serek to leave me to fend for myself in the desert after returning Kora, but instead his guards demanded I get in the port beside him, and so here I sit, the observer of this awkward courting. If you can call it that.

I tap my fingers against the door, then finally lean back on the seat and close my eyes. It doesn't take long before exhaustion washes over me and I start to drift . . .

Someone is holding my wrist in the air. I startle awake and try to rip my hand away, but Serek's grip is firm. His glare slides from my hand to my face, and I blink the sleep from my eyes and yawn. "I'm assuming there's a reason you're cutting off the circulation in my wrist."

His grip shifts and he squeezes my ring finger with his thumb and forefinger. "What is this?"

"A finger," I say.

"Don't play games with me, Eros. You know very well I'm not referring to your finger."

I glance at my hand. Back to Serek. "A ring."

He scowls. "I know what it is, boy. What I don't know is how you came to acquire it."

His insistence on calling me *boy* sends a twinge of irritation through my gut. "I can't feel my fingers."

"Answer the question."

"Release me, and I will."

His glare is sharp enough to shred bone, but he throws my hand back at me. I rub my wrist and sit up. Glance at Kora. She shifts her eyes to the blurry divider with the digital map cutting off the front seat from the passenger's cabin. My chest throbs.

"It was a gift," I finally say. "From my father." Kora's eyes snap to mine—oh, she must think I mean—"My adoptive father," I correct. "The man who raised me, Nol."

She nods once and glances at Serek. But he doesn't look satisfied—his glare deepens and a hint of a snarl wrinkles his nose. "And where did this 'Nol' acquire it?"

"I don't know. I just got this the other set. I was told he asked someone to make sure I got it if anything happened to him." Serek is fuming and I don't know why. I don't get what's wrong—what does the ring mean? I hesitate. Raise my hand to the light. "Does it mean something?"

"You truly don't recognize it?" he snaps.

I raise an eyebrow and lower my hand. "Should I?"

"It's the Ring of *Sirae*," Kora says softly, turning to me again. "It was *Sira* Asha's, for a short time, before he . . ." Her voice falters and she bites her lip.

"Before he was murdered by rebels," Serek spits. "Eighteen cycles ago."

My blood chills and the ring is cold against my finger. I run my thumb over the cool band and dare to glance at Serek. For a man who doesn't like unnecessary killing, he looks disturbingly like he wants to rip my throat out with his teeth.

"So I ask again, boy: how did a rebel come to acquire the ring missing from my dead brother's finger?"

I shake my head. Clench my fingers into fists. "I don't know."

"I think you know very well." Serek leans toward me. "It doesn't take a great leap of logic to come to a conclusion."

"Nol wasn't a murderer," I say. "He wouldn't do that. He didn't even like my training to become a soldier because he was against spilling blood."

"A likely story, considering the gem you dare put on your finger."

I fight the urge to lean away from him and match his glare with my own. "I don't know why he wanted me to have it, and I don't know how he got it, but I know he wasn't a murderer and he must have had a reason to hold on to it until now."

Serek snorts. "To hide his involvement in Asha's killing, I am sure."

"Nol had nothing to do with that."

He shakes his head. "I can't say if it's naïveté or stupidity that blinds you to the truth."

"MY FATHER WASN'T A MURDERER!" Every muscle in my body is tense and my heart slams in my ears as Serek's glare shifts from angry to downright murderous. He opens his mouth to speak, but a smaller voice interrupts him.

"Eros," Kora whispers. "I think we should tell him."

The hot energy setting my blood to a boil evaporates with those words. I shake my head. "I don't think—"

"Do you want to die? Because if you don't explain, that ring is going to get you killed."

"But—"

"You are aware"—Serek crosses his arms over his chest—"that I am sitting between you two."

"Show him, or I will," Kora says. "Now."

Something builds inside me at her tone—that she'd resort to ordering me around like her pet, like her slave. I thought we left that pretense behind at the palace, but it's clear I'm nothing more to her.

I glare at her. "I can't. I lost that dissolver stuff you gave me when your brother stripped me naked and tortured me for six sets."

If my jab affected her, she doesn't show it. Not that I should expect it to affect her, since she apparently doesn't give a blazing thought about me.

She turns to her precious Serek instead. "Do you have a medical glass?"

Serek reaches behind his seat and hands Kora a palm-sized octagonal glass. She taps on the surface a couple times, her fingers sliding and swirling across it doing stars knows what, then she lifts it up, leans forward, and holds it over my right eye. It's see-through, and it doesn't look like it's doing anything special from my end, but judging by Serek's reaction, I have a pretty good guess what it's doing on his.

The prince has gone rigid—his eyes widen and his lips part like he's frozen in mid-breath. Then his body relaxes, one muscle after another, and the tension slides off him like a heavy blanket falling off his shoulders.

"He never knew his father." Kora hands the glass back to Serek and turns to him. "I assumed it was someone further down the line, but what if your brother's ring wasn't stolen? It's passed down from firstborn to firstborn, isn't it?"

Serek doesn't speak. He's looking at me in a whole new way—analyzing the planes of my face. It's a little uncomfortable to be watched this closely, and it's all I can do to maintain eye contact. I shift in place and try not to fidget.

Then Kora's words sink into my mind. "Wait. You mean Asha's firstborn?"

She nods and glances at Serek, but he's too busy staring me down to say anything.

I laugh. I haven't laughed in a while, but I full-out shake-the-stars laugh. Me. Asha's son. Some half-blood half-royal joke of the universe. That's the stupidest thing I've ever heard—like a royal, *especially* the world-blazing-ruler, would *choose* to have a half-blood kid. Sure.

"I don't understand what you find so funny about this," Kora says.

"I'm not Asha's son. There isn't a blazing chance in the Void."

"It's more likely than you might think." Kora stares out the window. "Asha frequented the outskirts while he was *Sira*. The night he was killed, he slipped past his own guards and went out into the deserts in the middle of the night. No one ever knew why, but they found his body alongside the path back to the city. He was returning to the palace when he was attacked—and he was missing his ring."

I shake my head. "That doesn't mean a blazing thing. He could have been doing anything."

She turns to me. "He could have been witnessing the birth of his son. He would have given your mother the ring for safekeeping until you came of age, which would explain why you didn't have it and why your adoptive family was holding on to it until now."

"Or he could have gone out for an entirely different reason and lost his ring when he died. That's ridiculous, Kora, you can't assume just because—"

"What is the set of your birth?" Serek asks, and his tone makes me pause. He almost sounds . . . concerned? Is he actually considering this?

I glance at him. "It doesn't matter. I'm not Asha's son."

"Don't be stubborn, Eros. Just tell him."

I shake my head, but answer anyway. "The thirty-sixth of Summer, eighteen cycles ago." I pause. "On the full lunar eclipse."

The cabin falls quiet. Serek leans back in his seat and runs a hand through his hair. Kora is biting her lip and nodding, staring at the ring on my finger. My stomach twists—humans and Sepharon may be on different calendars, but the eclipse that marked my birth is an event that only happens once every twenty cycles. And if they're taking this seriously . . .

"That's when Asha died, isn't it?"

Kora nods. "They found him the next morning."

Heat drips down the back of my throat and slips around my lungs, squeezing slowly. This all has to be some weird coincidence, right? I mean, I thought the gold-eyes thing was weird, but I figured some distant barely royal relative did something thoughtless. But the *Sira*? If Asha is really my father . . .

"Roma will kill you," Serek says, finishing my thought.

My stomach turns and this port is broiling. I can't get air. My breaths aren't enough and my head is spinning and sweat drips down my spine and I'm going to throw up that dried meat I ate all over Serek's polished shoes.

I gulp down sweltering air. "Stop the port."

Serek arches an eyebrow. "Excuse me?"

"Stop the port. Now." Air air air. I don't have enough air. This isn't happening. This isn't right. This isn't real.

"Eros—"

I can't be Asha's son, because if I am, it means I'm a royal. No, worse than a royal, I'm a *high* royal—I'm one of the very people I'd grown up despising, one of the rulers of all who sees no problem with an enslaved race and the murder of innocent people.

If I'm Asha's son, then all along, everyone back at camp was right—I'm one of *them*.

My fingers are clenching my hair and I can barely breathe and they're both staring at me like I've lost my mind and I'm going to lose it. I'm going to fucken *lose* it if I don't get out of this blazing port *now*.

I throw the door open and Kora screams and Serek pounds on the privacy barrier behind them and the port slows to a stop and I'm on my knees, in the sand, with the heat of the suns on my back.

Breathe.

My heart is pounding out of control.

Breathe.

The world is spinning around me and my fingers are digging into the sand and I need to get myself together. I need to take a deep breath and slow down and think.

What would Esta and Nol think? Did they know? Would they even be surprised? But they wouldn't keep something like this from me, would they?

I have to believe that if this is true, they didn't know. Because the alternative means even after I came of age, they kept this life altering secret from me. They kept a truth that could *kill* me to themselves.

Then again, maybe that's exactly why they wouldn't say anything at all.

Soft fingers touch my back and I'm back in the dungeon with frigid water slamming over my skin. I jump up and take a long step away from her. Spin back, heaving in air, my fists shaking at my sides.

"*Don't* touch me," I hiss. "Don't you *ever* touch me again."

Kora's eyes widen for just a breath, just long enough for me to see before she plasters on that nothing-fazes-me face. She nods. Gestures to the port. "Let's sit down and talk this through."

Sit down and talk this through. Right. Like this is a problem you can wash away with fancy words and batted eyelashes.

"If what you're saying is true, I'll be dead the moment I step into the capital."

Kora bites her lip. "Not if he doesn't know who you are."

"Roma will know the moment he sees him." Serek steps onto the sand. He looks at me again, but this time his eyes are soft. Almost sad. "You look like Asha."

I scowl. "You didn't think so twenty minutes ago."

"I didn't know Asha as well as Roma did—I was very young when he was killed. And I wasn't looking for the similarities. But your eyes, the way you hold yourself, even the set of your jaw right now mirrors him entirely. Roma will know."

But Kora's shaking her head. "He won't as long as Eros doesn't dissolve the nanites and no one says anything. You said it yourself—Roma won't be looking for similarities."

Serek stares at me for a long mo, then nods and turns to Kora. "He will need to be genetically matched before we can be certain. I will administer the test myself, so we can keep this between us. And until then . . ." He sighs and glances back at me. "Until then you are Kora's servant. And nothing more."

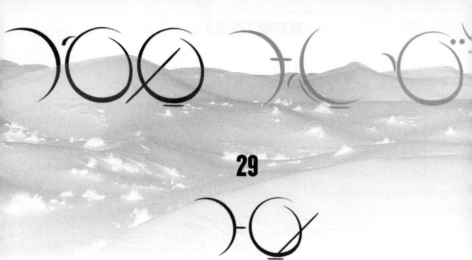

29

Kora

After riding in silence for hours, Eros eventually falls asleep with his cheek pressed against the glass window. I try to get some rest—my body is certainly exhausted enough—but nervousness claws through my stomach and keeps my mind awake. So I sit in silence, staring out the window instead.

Serek's gaze wanders over to me several times. His presence is always there—a warmth against my side, the occasional touch of his fingers on my hand. And I want more than anything to hold his hand and feel the same affection and careful excitement I felt on the ballroom floor so many nights ago. But instead his touch turns my stomach and stabs my heart with sharp heat. Because when I close my eyes, when I try to remember what we had that night, the echo of Eros's lips are on mine instead. His hands igniting my body, his taste filling me with heady sensations.

And I am ashamed.

I don't know what I was thinking when I kissed him—*naï,* I wasn't thinking at all. I was reacting, releasing an emotion I didn't realize I'd buried. Doing exactly what I wanted at that moment, even though I can't fathom why I wanted it in the first place. I'd never looked at Eros romantically in the past, at least, not seriously—why now?

And why do I want his hand—not Serek's—in mine?

Don't you ever *touch me again.* His words are a burning ache behind my lungs, a frozen emptiness stealing the glow from my cells. And I can't even be angry at him for his hurtful words, because I hurt him first.

"If he is truly Asha's son, we may face a serious problem," Serek whispers, so as to not wake Eros. His words pull me out of my thoughts as his fingers gently squeeze my hand. I push the painful memory of Eros's anger away as I face Serek.

"It's only a problem if you alert your brother," I say. "If Roma doesn't know, we have nothing to worry about."

But Serek shakes his head. "It's not a matter of Roma knowing, it's a matter of inheritance. As Asha's son, Eros would have right to the throne—not Roma. And my brother will not give up his place so easily."

Serek is looking at me, but my gaze drifts to Eros. He seems younger as he rests—cycles of hardship, abuse, and more recent trauma wiped clean from his face. He seems softer, like his skin is smoother, like his embrace would be perfect.

Like his lips would be clouds on my skin.

I take a breath and close my eyes—I need to focus. I can't allow myself to be so distracted every time I look at Eros. I open my eyes and turn to Serek. "I don't think he'll want the throne. He doesn't relish attention."

"Regardless of whether he would want it, his birthright would demand it. Denying him his inheritance would dishonor Asha's memory."

"You truly think he could ever take the throne? The people would never accept him—not in his court and not in the public eye." *Kala* knows that's not an experience I would wish on anyone. I catch myself watching him again and look away. "He may deserve the honor, but you know as well as I do that a coup wouldn't go over smoothly."

"I know." Serek sighs and runs his hands down his face. "*Kala* knows what my brother was thinking. Taking a red-blood as a lover is controversial enough, but fathering a child with one? And a son, no less?"

"Is it possible he intended to announce Eros's birth himself? Even take them to the capital?"

"If he passed down the ring, as it seems he has, I'd imagine that was his plan. But as he never reached the capital, I doubt we will ever know."

Serek's hand slides over my palm again, and his fingers interlace with mine. He sighs and offers me a tight smile. "To be truthful, I'm still praying this is a misunderstanding and he's not who we suspect he is." He runs his thumb back and forth over the back of my hand, and my gut twists with guilt again. "For now, I think it best we pretend he's your personal servant. It will take some convincing because of his obvious half-blood heritage, but I should be able to convince Roma to overlook it."

"Thank you," I whisper.

He nods, then takes a breath. "There is another matter we must speak about."

I already know what it is, but I nod anyway. "Go on."

He leans forward, takes both of my hands in his, and kisses my knuckles. My heart catches in my throat and I pray he doesn't notice my skin going cold. After planting another kiss on my wrist, he looks up at me. "I proposed a contract to you once. Much has happened since then, but my offer still stands. I don't believe that you harmed me intentionally, and I will fight any and all accusations that state otherwise."

The memory of Eros's fingers flutters through my hair when I whisper, "I know."

"I hate to pressure you into making a decision, but I must know where we stand when I bring you before my brother. He will have heard about the attempt on my life and, if I arrive with you, he may assume it is to assist in your execution." He pauses. "I'm not sure how well I will be able to defend you without an established relationship between us."

The echo of Eros's lips is on my lips, on my neck, on my jaw. His scent surrounds me, and his touch—the cabin is sweltering and my stomach roils with nauseating waves. "You still want me to marry you?"

He nods. "As your betrothed, I will be in a better position to protect you."

His lips, his hands, his taste. *Kala*, what have I done?

Serek's gaze pierces mine. "If you accept, Kora, I promise to be a good mate to you. I will protect you and care for you until the end of my time, this I swear."

His sincerity rolls off him, attacking me with a truth I can no longer deny: Serek loves me. He may even be falling *in* love with me.

"Why?" I whisper. He frowns, not understanding, and I bite my lip. "Why do you want to be my mate?"

He sighs. "Do you remember that night in the garden? The night I first asked you to be my betrothed?"

"Always," I breathe.

"I asked you why you didn't give the throne to your brother, if that's what your people wanted, and you said it was to protect them from what they believed they sought. Instead of stepping down, which would have been the easier choice, you dealt with their disdain and disrespect to protect the very people who didn't accept you." He touches my chin and smiles. "I realized in that moment, Kora, that your spirit is just as beautiful as your exterior, and I knew I'd be lucky to have you."

My eyes sting. Tears blur my vision and I pull my hand out of his grasp to wipe my eyes with the back of my hand. "I was going to accept that night. Before . . . I'm so sorry—" My voice cracks—I can't continue. Serek pulls me against him and I can't contain the pent-up tears any longer. He caresses my hair; his embrace is strong and gentle and warm, but despite his best intentions, it makes me feel worse.

Because even now, as I breathe in his smooth, clean scent and his heart beats against my ear, I think of Eros. I'll never be able to undo that kiss. I'll never be able to forget the explosion of emotion and want that I unleashed.

But I can't have Eros. I can never have Eros—he's a slave, a *half-blood* slave, and I need to accept Serek for everyone's sake. Because not only would it give Serek more grounds to defend me, but a marriage would distract Roma from Eros, and I will do everything in my power to keep him safe.

So I accept.

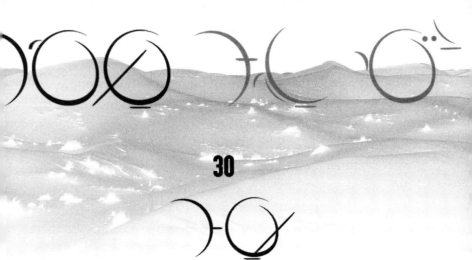

30

Kora

I do eventually fall asleep, and I wake to someone gently nudging my shoulder. I open my mouth to tell Eros to leave me alone and let me sleep, but—*naï*, I'm not in my bed. This isn't Vejla. I open my eyes, blinking away the grogginess.

Serek smiles at me and nods to the window. "Look."

I yawn, turn my gaze outside, and sit up.

The world is white. Or at least, the ground is, all traces of red desert lost somewhere behind us. Tall trees with long golden leaves and purple flowers the size of my head tower over us, lining the packed white road. The buildings here are large, beautiful homes made of white stone that sparkles with color under the light of the suns, with slightly peaked roofs of blues and purples. In the distance, the famous mountains of Ona, Denae D'Aravel, reach into the sky, and although I can't see it from here, the sacred city of Shura Kan lies somewhere in their midst—the city where all retired *Avrae* and *Sirae* go to live.

Mirror-like hovercraft race through the sky above us, and people mill about in the streets as we move slowly through the crowd. Children smile and point, and men nod respectfully to the caravan as dozens of reflective orb-guides zip through the air and bob around the ports, trying to get the best viewing angle for recording.

Everything is newer here—the whole city is brimming with the most up-to-date technology in all of Safara, from the orb-guides several models newer than the ones we have in Vejla, to the hovercraft, which are a rarity in Elja, to Serek's impressively updated transport—down to the embedded digital display in the windows—and countless other luxuries I've yet to see.

We pass through the city and the road begins to climb. That's when I see it—the Palace of *Sirae*, sitting majestically at the top of a natural overlook. The walls shimmer and reflect the suns' rays in bursts of color, giving the entire complex the appearance of semi-transparency, as if it isn't actually there. Like a desert mirage. Tall spires tower high into the sky and elaborate fountains dot the complex.

This may very well be the most beautiful city I've ever seen.

"What do you think?" Serek asks softly; his lips are a breath away from my ear. Heat rushes to my cheeks—Eros is watching us from the other side of the row—and I'm glad my face is turned to the window.

"It's incredible," I say.

His smile moves against my cheek. "I've grown up here, and it still leaves me breathless upon returning. *Asheron or'jeve.*"

"*Sha*," I breathe. Asheron's greeting is one I won't soon forget.

We glide to a stop in front of the largest building in the complex—the one I was able to see from the bottom of the hill. Black and gold-clad soldiers open the door and I step out. The guards wear black sleeveless shirts with high collars, gold trim running down the off-center left seal, and long ankle-length black matte cloth tied tightly around their waists called *ulae*——a traditional uniform worn by Ona's military men since before the Great War.

Serek and Eros stay back in the transport for a few moments, muttering something I can't hear, until Serek steps out, tucks something into his pocket and flashes me a smile. Eros moves silently in place at my side, but when I catch a flash of his fingers as he clasps his hands tightly together at his back, I understand the holdup in the car—Serek took his ring for safekeeping. Eros glances at me, and presses his lips tightly together, but his stiff posture and the set of his jaw says everything I need to know. He's nervous. And rightfully so.

He has stepped from a court that despised him for his blood, to a court that would kill him in an instant for his birthright. And I have put him here.

"Come," Serek says. "I must explain your innocence to my brother before he makes assumptions about why I have brought you here."

I've taken all of two steps into the polished halls of the palace before a group of guards shift toward me with the steel of orders in their eyes. Eros takes half a step in front of me and Serek moves in front of us both.

"I would have an audience with my brother before you carry out your orders," he says confidently. "I will escort these two myself."

The guards don't hesitate—they bow their heads, step back in unison, and Serek passes, motioning us to follow. My gut twists as we move deeper into the halls. I'm tempted to be distracted by the elaborate display inside—by the inscribed statues and weapons hung ceremoniously upon the walls, by the flags of the territories and the beautifully polished floors. But for every moment I appreciate the beauty, I'm overwhelmed with ten beats of terror.

Every guard here watches me like I'm a prisoner with a pardon. Like I'm someone who doesn't—and never will— belong.

This is how Eros must feel everywhere he goes. This is how people look at him, from territory to territory, and even, according to Eros, among the people he was raised with. I take in their sharp glances and the tightness of their posture and I store it away. If Eros can move through life freely, dealing with this all the time, I can suppress my discomfort for a few moments.

I miss a step when we enter the throne room. For a split second, I forget why we're here—my sense of awe leaves me speechless. The room is at least ten times the size of the one at home, both in length and width. This singular room is larger than most of the common homes, I would imagine, with black and gold flags draped on the walls, beautifully carved stone statues of kazim or rippling polished bands with the histories carved into them, and enough guards lining the wall to populate a small city. Eros nudges me and I fall back into step with Serek. We cross the lengthy procession up to a beautiful, intricately carved throne made of some kind of thick glass, where a man dressed in silky black is watching us.

We stop just five measures from the foot of his throne, and I'm surprised by how little Roma looks like Serek. Where Serek is tall and lean, Roma is a mountain of muscle. Serek's eyes are warm with a thin band of gold; Roma's are nearly black with thick golden centers. Serek wears his status with the humility of one who sees his birthright as a blessing; Roma wears it like my brother—like he was born with it all along and the throne never belonged to anyone else. He wears it like a badge, like a crown, like an elaborate robe gilded in gold. And he analyzes us with a calculating curiosity that reminds me far too much of my father.

Serek drops to one knee at the foot of the throne, his head bowed low and his right arm balanced like a board on his knee. Eros and I mimic him, and I suppress a chill as Roma's dark eyes take me in. But he glances at me for only a moment before turning to his brother.

"I'm assuming there's a reason these two were not immediately escorted underground."

"*Sha, el Sira*," Serek says, but he still doesn't look up.

"Then rise, brother, and speak." Serek stands and explains everything—from the attempts on my life, to the incident at the ball, to having to run, Eros's capture, and Dima taking my place. He says Eros was tortured for six sunsets, but didn't give up my location. He says Eros protected me and even gave himself up so I could escape.

My cheeks burn with shame remembering the look in Eros's eyes as he'd said the same in the desert. I'd suspected what Dima had done to Eros before, but I'd been too afraid to ask. How will I ever be able to face him again?

Why did he protect me? He could have so easily given me up—stronger men than he have crumbled under the horrors of interrogation. He could have let them take me from the start and escaped. And yet he stayed behind for my sake, and I thanked him by kissing him in the desert and then pretending he didn't exist.

My stomach churns.

Serek ends with our engagement, and my gut sinks lower. He says he's certain of my innocence, that it was all a ploy to get Dima on the throne, and he wishes to take me as his mate and keep me safe here, at the capital, far from Dima's reach.

Silence follows Serek's final words. I dare a glance up at *ken Sira*, but to my surprise, his eyes aren't set on Serek or me.

They're on Eros.

"Interesting," he finally says. He taps his fingers on the arm of the throne and watches Eros in silence for a long moment. "Eros, they call you?"

Eros looks up. Nods once and lowers his eyes to the floor. "*Sha, el Sira.*"

"Rise, Eros."

He does, and stands at his full height. I am now the only one kneeling, and it's difficult to keep my eyes lowered and see what is happening at the same time.

"Have you been a servant of Elja's court for long?" Roma asks.

Eros shakes his head. "A little over a term, *el Sira.*"

"And yet you devote yourself so wholly to a ruler you barely know?"

Eros glances at me, then back to Roma. "She's been kind to me, and I believe in her innocence. It would've been dishonorable to let her suffer for a false accusation."

Roma nods. "This is true, but honor is not the way of your people. Am I incorrect?"

He hesitates. "I'm not sure I understand."

"I know the look of a boy bred into servitude. You say you have been a servant of Elja's court for just over a term, but judging by your physique and the way you hold yourself, I'm assuming you were not a servant before entering Elja's court. In fact, I see a warrior in you. Am I incorrect?"

If Roma's disturbingly accurate assumption bothers Eros, he doesn't show it. He nods once and says, "You speak the truth, *el Sira*."

"Then you would not identify yourself as Sepharon, but as human. Correct?"

Eros inhales deeply through his nose, then steels his gaze. "I am neither, *el Sira*."

Roma arches an eyebrow. *"Naï?* Your blood is not purely human, that much is clear, but I'm speaking in manners of loyalty, not genetics."

"Nevertheless, I am neither. The people of the deserts don't accept me as their own, and I expect equal treatment from the Sepharon courts. I am no one." He's standing stiff as a board, but it isn't strength holding his posture. His voice trembles slightly. He blinks several times and my heart breaks for him. I want to tell him it's not true. I want to take his hands and assure him he is so much more than rebel or Sepharon.

But I keep my eyes low and my mouth closed.

"I see." Roma sits back and turns his gaze on me. "Rise," he says, and I finally stand.

"What do you think of this half-blood?" he asks.

I fight the urge to look at Eros. "He saved my life, and I would be honored to have him continue to serve me. In the short time he has been in my service, he has shown me more loyalty and strength than the entirety of my former guard, *el Sira*."

"Then you trust him?"

"Entirely."

Roma nods and stands. He's not as tall as Serek, but he seems more imposing. Confidence and absolute power rolls off him like thunder before a storm. "I don't usually allow humans or half-bloods within my court, but I will make an exception. He is to remain your servant, and you are to monitor him. Is that understood?"

Eros and I nod, and Serek smiles softly.

"As for your innocence . . ." Roma's eyes trail back to his brother. "You are certain the new *Avra d'Elja* is behind this attack?"

"Absolutely," Serek says, and I close my eyes. *Oh, Dima.* Even now, after his betrayal seems undeniable, I wish there was another explanation. An answer that didn't make my brother a traitor.

"You realize this would mean breaking the peace of the territories for the first time in generations. Such an act could not go unpunished, and unless he gives himself up willingly, it would mean war."

"I understand, *el Sira*," Serek says.

I bite my lip. Elja has always been well known for its exceptionally trained army, but Asheron's sheer numbers alone would decimate them. How many will die because of my brother's ambition?

And Dima. He will be executed when the war is over. The back of my throat stings and my vision blurs—I focus on my reflection in the polished black stone at my feet.

"So be it. I bless this union and expect further news of this engagement to be made public shortly." He pauses. "After her innocence is established, that is."

Serek nods and bows low. Eros and I follow suit. "Thank you, brother," he says. "I am certain *Kala* will bless your wisdom."

Roma nods curtly and Serek turns and motions for us to follow. And so we leave the halls of *ken Sira*, with his eyes on our backs and his words ringing in my ears.

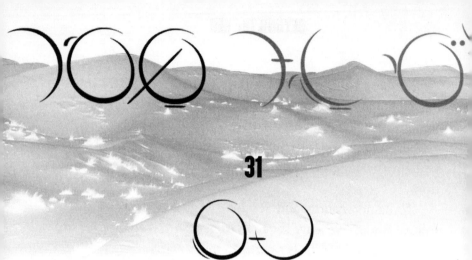

31

Eros

Serek wastes no time. He brings us straight to Kora's new room—a room three times the size of her old enormous bedroom, with flowers, silks, miniature golden or gem-carved statues, intricately carved walls, and more pillows than an orgy house would need strewn over every inch of the place. She falls back on a hovering bed large enough for six or seven people and Serek asks her if the room is to her liking. They laugh about something and I move beside the door and watch the sheer curtains around the bed blow in the gentle breeze.

They act like everything is fine. Like a war isn't looming on the horizon and all that matters is their ill-timed marriage and whether the fucken bed is comfortable.

"I'm glad to hear it." Serek kisses her cheek. "I have to get something, but I'll return shortly. Just stay here."

"Okay," Kora says with a stupid little smile. It's all I can do not to roll my eyes. Serek kisses her again—this time on the lips—and leaves the room. The door closes behind him and silence follows—a heavy, uncomfortable air like the un-conversation in the desert. Once again, Kora avoids my gaze and turns away from me. Once again, she intends to pretend that I don't exist, that I'm not here, that nothing happened between us in the ruins.

I'm sick of being treated like her toy. Like someone not worthy of any sortuv explanation.

"Are we not going to talk about what happened?" I finally say.

She doesn't turn to face me. "There isn't anything to talk about."

I snort. "*Naï,* of course not. Nothing at all."

She sighs and runs a hand through her hair. After a long beat of silence, she stands and faces me. "I'm sorry, Eros. For everything."

I scowl. "I don't want or need your apology."

"I've hurt you."

I clench my fists. Stare at the wall above her head. "You must think me weak if you believe you've unraveled me with a single kiss. Or maybe you think yourself miraculously special."

She frowns. "I didn't say that. I just . . . it shouldn't have happened. I'm sorry for initiating it—I don't know what I was thinking."

"Me neither." My words sound sharp. I hope they cut.

Kora looks at me for a long moment. "I'm marrying Serek."

"So I've gathered."

She bites her lip. Starts to step toward me, then steps back. "Thank you for protecting me. It was very brave of you, and you didn't have to—"

"It wasn't for you." I lower the full force of my gaze on her. "Telling your brother where you were meant betraying the location of my people. Unlike you, I don't want the blood of hundreds on my hands."

Her gaze falls. "Nevertheless, thank you," she whispers. "Regardless of your motivation, I am in your debt."

It's a lie and we both know it. She'll never be in my debt—she's royalty and I'm a half-blood slave. She'll marry the second most powerful man on the planet, and I'll live forever in their shadow, serving the very people who slaughtered mine, the very people who would kill me given any opportunity.

I would leave at first light, but I don't have a people anymore. I have nowhere to run to, nowhere to go. If I came across humans in the desert, they would kill me. If I ran into guards in the city, they would stop my heart with a phaser pulse. Sepharon in the streets would beat me to death, or watch me starve, or parade my broken body through the streets.

I have nothing. I am nothing. If I want to live, it'll have to be here, serving a royalty I'd love to see burn to the ground.

The back of my hand itches and I rub the tiny light scar etched into my skin. Yet another reason I'll never be in her debt. Her gaze follows my hand and she purses her lips.

A knock at the door, and Serek enters, carrying a wrapped square of some kind and a small octagonal glass. He pulls out a chair from the desk set to the side of the room and motions to it. "Please sit, Eros."

I sit, like a good little pet.

Serek unwraps the package—it's a clear, circular gel with tiny points like dull teeth on one side. He motions for my arm, and I consider questioning him, but what's the point? He'll get what he wants either way, and I don't have the right to say a word about it because I'm a slave. Captured and marked like an animal.

I was stupid to think one kiss might have changed that.

I give him my arm. He flips it wrist-up and wipes the crook of my elbow with the inside of the wrapping—some kinduv sanitizer, I guess—and presses the patch into place. It stings, but the pain is nothing. Like several bug bites at once in a concentrated area. Serek turns to the glass and begins tapping on the surface. He grimaces and sighs.

"Well?" Kora moves toward him.

"It matches up. Eros is Asha's son."

The air in my lungs goes cold. *It doesn't matter*, I repeat over and over again until I can breathe.

Kora's eyes are wide and she stares at me like the news should mean something. As if it matters that my father should be sitting on the throne. As if my birthright would somehow mean something in a Sepharon court. No, I take that back—it *would* mean something—that I would have to be executed immediately, before word leaked to the public. Because suns and stars forbid a fucken half-blood would have right to the throne. I shouldn't even be alive—I'm diluting their *perfect* race with my disgusting human blood. To have me on a throne would be blasphemous.

Good thing I have no interest in going anywhere near that ridiculous throne of glass.

They're still waiting for a reaction, so I stand and rip the patch off my arm. Pinpricks of blood rise to the surface, and I press down with my free hand. "It doesn't matter," I repeat, aloud this time. "No one can ever know, and I'm not about to ask to be executed, so you can guarantee I'll never tell anyone." I look at them. "I'm assuming you won't, either."

Serek sits and slides the glass on the table. Scrubs his face with his hands. "This isn't right. The laws of birthright stand for a reason."

I roll my eyes. "Laws of birthright don't matter when you're a half-blood. We don't have rights to anything. We don't even have the right to live."

Serek winces. Looks up at me. "You don't believe that."

"What I believe doesn't matter. I'm a half-blood slave."

Kora sighs. "Eros, you know you're more than that."

I arch an eyebrow. "Really? Tell me then, what am I? I can never leave this place—I'd be killed on the spot. I can't claim my birthright even if I wanted to—I'd be executed before the words left my lips. This is all I have left, whether I like it or not. It's all I've had since someone razed my camp and murdered my family."

Kora bites her lip, but at least she doesn't have the nerve to apologize again. Because she knows full well this is her fault, and no amount of words can undo what's already been set into motion. Nothing she says will make an ounce of difference, so I don't want to hear it.

I turn away and face the window. Stare out into the foreign white streets and golden trees, into a land that will never be my home. "This is who I am. I've accepted it, and it's time you do as well."

Serek leaves when some female servants enter the room to help Kora get cleaned up and dressed for dinner. I wait in the bedroom while she bathes, and face the wall as she gets dressed. They put her in a long black and gold dress—because apparently no one's allowed to wear any other colors here—and I'm handed a new set of clothes and told to bathe while they continue to prepare her hair or whatever it is they do.

The bathroom looks nearly the same as the one back in Elja, except it's bigger, of course. The tub isn't really a tub—it's a pool in the center of the floor, filled to the brim with steaming hot water. I strip and climb in, scrub the sand out of my hair and the dirt and blood off my skin. I'll admit it's nice to be clean again after sitting in my dirt and sweat for far too long, but I don't linger. It's strange enough being here without sitting in a luxurious bath meant for royalty.

My new clothes—or, skirt-pants, I should say—are pretty similar to the uniform I wore in Elja, except it's black and gold, of course, and the cloth is made of some kinduv shiny silky material that slips through my fingers as easily as water. No shoes again, which works for me because I'm used to walking around barefoot anyway.

I knock twice before entering the bedroom and step inside. Stare at the wall and try not to die of boredom waiting for them to finish coating Kora's face in emphasis she doesn't need. When she turns around, her eyes are lined in thick, smoky black, her eyelashes look twice as long, and her lips shimmer with a dark gloss. She smiles at me and I pull open the door and stare straight ahead.

Serek is waiting in the hallway, and he takes her arm in his when she steps out. They smile at each other and Serek says she looks beautiful. Maybe I should have drowned myself in that tub to save a lifetime of this ridiculous posturing. Suns and stars, I don't even want to think about what'll happen after they marry. And start having heirs.

I follow them to the dining hall. Like everything else, it's too large and too extravagant and too shiny and black and gold and covered with banners. The crescent-shaped floating table is barely visible beneath the mountains of meat and drink and colorful fruit and vegetables and soups and desserts. Kora and Serek kneel across from Roma, and I step against the wall, a foot or so away from the line of guards.

"Good," Roma says. "You're all here."

Serek smiles. "Did you expect anything less?"

Roma takes a long drink and slams his goblet down so loudly that it echoes. Kora jumps and the room falls silent. My heart thumps in my ears and the hair on the back of my neck stands on end.

Serek isn't smiling anymore. "Is something wrong, brother?"

"Wrong? *Naï*, not at all. Not anymore." Roma looks up at me—no, not at me, at his guards standing just beside me. "Arrest the half-blood and bring him underground immediately."

My heart stops and my blood goes cold as someone grabs my arm. My instinct screams *fight*, but there are literally hundreds of soldiers in this room alone. I don't stand a chance, so I let them yank my arms behind my back and cuff my wrists together. Serek and Roma are arguing, and Kora keeps shouting, "He's my servant, I need him!" but I've already missed half of the conversation and she whips around to face me and she's crying. Gray tears streak down her face.

She's not in any danger, so why is she crying?

"And you believe him?" Serek exclaims. "Dima is not to be trusted!"

The guards yank me out of the room and the door slams behind us, cutting off the mounting voices. They push me down a long hallway, jostling my steps and walking deliberately fast. But I keep on my feet to the end of the hall and out into the cool night air. Through a courtyard with nine fountains, past half a dozen buildings, into a small black building with a sleek exterior and a thick metal door.

One of the guards places his hand on the metal, and a small screen above the doorframe blinks green before it slides open. They lead me through several thick doors, each with a security check that requires touching the door or entering a code or speaking a command. Down a long set of steps that seem to go on into the core of the planet itself.

The deeper we go, the cooler and wetter the air gets, until my skin is sticky and cold. Finally we reach the bottom level, where the floors are black and so cold it burns the pads of my feet as I walk. The only light here comes from dim strips above each thick door, and the hall is so silent, every step sounds like an explosion. They lead me to the very end of the hall, where a guard presses his hand against the door, waits for the telltale green light, and opens it.

They shove me inside and the door hisses closed behind me.

32

Eros

I sit in darkness with my eyes closed and my head against the wall. I've lost all sensation in my feet from the cold, but I still squeeze my toes together and rub them in a failed attempt to keep them warm. I'm not sure what will happen if I don't get feeling back in them soon, but it can't be good.

The problem with isolation is it gives you way too much time to think. And when I have endless time to my thoughts, I remember things I've worked so hard to bury, memories I never wanted to unearth from the darkest places in my mind. Sitting here in absolute silence, the shadows call them from the corners of my mind like a beacon to a lost wanderer in the desert.

I think of Day, lying in the sand, drenched in red from sand and blood. I think of Nol and Esta—of sharing tea with them the morning before the raid. Of rolling my eyes at the kisses Esta pressed to my cheeks while balanced on the tips of her toes. Of hurrying the embraces from Nol so I could make it to my shift on time. I think of my brother, clasping my shoulder and telling me I'm an uncle, long before I understood what it meant.

I think of Kora, wrapping her legs around my waist, digging her fingers into my back, and kissing me like her life depended on it. Of the sounds she made as I felt her soft breast and the way she shuddered against me as my lips traced the markings on her neck and our bodies pressed tightly together.

I think of the way she went rigid when I touched her shoulder afterward, like she actually thought I might hurt her. Of the way she turned away from me and completely shut me out, like what we felt together didn't mean a blazing thing.

I stare up at the pitch-black ceiling, wishing I could see the night sky. Wishing I could look up into the glittering expanse of the universe and feel Day and Esta and Nol watching over me. *We'll be with you wherever the stars reach,* Esta said, but all I see is empty shadow.

I'm in the place where the stars don't reach, far from home and family and everything I ever loved. And now, I'm going to die alone.

Emptiness feels like a living thing. A parasite growing in the center of your chest, somewhere behind your heart, taking every ounce of warmth and light and happiness and consuming it until there's nothing left. Emptiness feels like exhaustion, like there's no reason to fight, no reason to take another breath, no reason to try to survive.

But emptiness also feels like freedom. Because it doesn't just take the good, it takes the bad, too—the anger, the bitterness, the pain—and when it's done, it leaves you with just you. A cold, shell-like echo of yourself, but still you.

After hours of staring into nothing, the echo is all I have left.

Footsteps. The sound is muffled, like dripping water several yards away. I open my eyes and stare into empty space as a low, buzzing noise slices through the silence. My door slides open with a quiet hiss and I stand, squinting through the dim light flooding my cell.

Roma enters and nods at someone behind him. The ceiling flickers to life and cold white light surrounds me. I squint harder and peer through the white as the door glides closed and Roma steps toward me. He told his guards to wait outside, which doesn't seem right. Why would he come in here by himself? I'm obviously cuffed, but do I seem that unimposing that he feels it's safe to enter my cell without a single guard for protection?

Maybe there is protection—protection I can't see. Or maybe he's an opponent I shouldn't underestimate, especially with my hands tied.

Roma walks right up to me and pushes me against the wall. He leans in so close that the tip of his nose nearly touches mine. He peers into my eyes. His grip slides from my shoulder to my jaw and he presses my head against the wall and reaches toward my left eye.

I squeeze my eyes shut and try to lean away from him, but his fingers force my eyelids open and he squeezes a liquid from a little dropper onto my eyeball. He repeats the process on my right eye, and my eyes sting and flood with tears as he releases my jaw and steps back. Roma glares, clenching his fingers into fists, crushing the dropper in his hand. Shakes his head.

"You're a fool if you truly believed cosmetic surface nanites could disguise you, half-blood." He steps back and crosses his arms, his heavy glare softening into a sortuv curiosity I wouldn't have expected from him. "So tell me, then. Which one of my weak relatives dishonored my family? Hmm?"

He doesn't know. I blink away the tears from my stinging eyes. "I don't know."

Roma snorts. "You don't know, and yet you have the audacity to come to this place? It'll take much more than a golden gaze to take me from my rightful place on the throne, boy."

Blazing suns, is every royal so paranoid? I roll my eyes and lean against the wall. "I'm not here for your throne."

"If you expect me to believe—"

"I'm here for Kora," I say. "I'm here because I have nowhere left to go. Because I've been assigned to protect her, and I made an oath, and it's the only choice I have."

He raises his eyebrows. Cocks his head slightly to the left. "So the desert trash have rejected you entirely. Interesting."

I just shrug and look away. "I have no ambition to take your throne, and anyone who tells you otherwise is just trying to make you paranoid." I pause and add, "I doubt I even have the right to take your place, anyway. I imagine not all of your golden-eyed relatives have the right to rule."

"Not all do," he says, eyeing me. "But you aren't the least bit curious to see if you're one of them?"

"You say you're not a fool, but neither am I. I know full well a half-blood will never sit on the Sepharon throne. Who fathered me doesn't matter—I've been disqualified since before I was born."

"True."

I face him again. "So you can release me."

Roma laughs. "Release you? And I thought you said you weren't a fool."

I grimace.

"Your ancestry doesn't matter. The fact is, you are living proof of a great dishonor that has befallen my family. You may not be a threat to the throne, but you are a threat to my family's name, and that cannot stand. You should have been eliminated at the moment of your unfortunate birth."

I steel my expression. Pull my lips together and clench my fists.

"You'll be executed tomorrow morning in Jol's Arena. Pray to *Kala* while you can, for your hours are numbered."

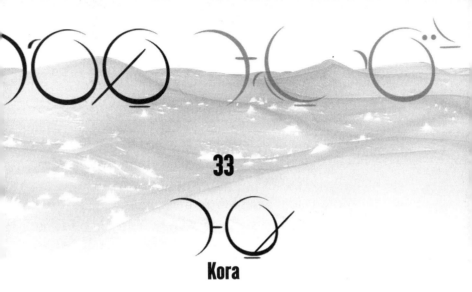

33

Kora

Serek and Roma argued for several moments before a guard came to my side and suggested I wait upstairs for the dispute to cease.

Serek didn't even notice when I left.

I paced in my room for what felt like an eternity. Washed my face of tears and makeup and sat on the floor, tracing shapes on the stone. Eros was a prisoner, again, and it was my fault, again. I owed him so much and yet it seemed all I ever managed to do was get him arrested, hurt, or tortured.

He saved my life and I couldn't even manage to keep him decently safe. What use am I, if I can't even accomplish that much?

Two knocks and the door opens behind me. I spin around and face Serek, but the sight of him sends my stomach plummeting—his eyes are hard and sad.

Whatever was said, it clearly didn't go well.

He straightens his shoulders and clasps his hands behind his back. "Kora . . ." he begins, but I don't want to hear it.

I rush toward him and clasp his arms. "You have to convince him. You know Eros doesn't deserve this—he saved my life twice, Serek! I can't just let this happen!"

"Is that all?" he asks.

I frown. "Is what all?"

"Is that the sole reason you wish to save him? Because you owe him a debt?"

My hands slide off his arms and hang useless at my sides. I can't meet his eyes. "What are you asking me?"

"You know exactly what I'm asking, Kora."

I do, but I'm too terrified to answer. Because I know what the answer should be, and yet I can't seem to speak it.

"I see." Serek sighs heavily and looks away. He steps to the desk and sits in one of the chairs. My stomach churns and guilt nags at the back of my mind, but then he speaks. "He cares for you as well."

My gaze shoots up to his and his shoulders slump—a defeated exhale. He readjusts his posture and the hurt in his eyes twists a guilty knife in my core, but I can't deny what he seems to already know.

"I can't be with him," I whisper. "It'll never work."

"Because he's a half-blood?"

I can't meet his eyes to answer. "And a slave. With my authority over him . . . it wouldn't be right."

"Kora . . ." Serek sighs, stands, and steps toward me. He rests his hands on my shoulders and when I dare to look up at him, his expression surprises me. He should be angry, or disgusted, but instead he looks at me with a soft understanding that I don't deserve. "One way or another, I believe Eros's status will change. As for his blood . . . has his mixed heritage made him a lesser man in any way?"

I shake my head.

"Then what is it? If you care for him, what stops you?"

"I don't know," I admit, and he smiles sadly.

"I told you once our union was a decision I wanted you to be secure with. What I didn't say, and I should have, is I don't want you to choose me for the wrong reason. I care very much for you, Kora, but having you and seeing you regret choosing me would be much more painful than letting you go. Just give that some thought." He releases me and sits at the desk again, inhaling deeply as he rubs his face with his hands. Something inside me aches seeing him like this, knowing how much I've hurt him.

But he's right. As much as I care for Serek . . . I'm falling in love with Eros.

"Roma spoke to your brother," Serek says.

My brother. I bury the emotions welling up inside me and glance up at him. "And?"

He sighs. "Roma says Dima provided compelling evidence against Eros. He wouldn't say what, but he said it proved to him without a doubt that Eros replaced your lipstain with poison and gave your hand servant the antidote in the form of a sweet to give to you, so that you wouldn't poison yourself."

I clench my fists at my sides. "Eros never even looked at my accessories, let alone switched some of it with . . . that's ridiculous, Serek."

"Furthermore, he said Dima showed him proof that Eros was taking orders from the rebels. That they intended to strike your brother and you next." Serek looks at me and shakes his head. "Roma has made up his mind."

My whole body is shaking. "You can't believe this. That doesn't even make sense—if they supposedly wanted me dead, they wouldn't have bothered with an antidote. Tell me you don't believe this nonsense—"

"I don't, Kora, but what I believe doesn't make a difference. I am not *ken Sira*, Roma is, and he has already made a decision. There's no talking sense to him. Eros is to be executed tomorrow morning."

Something like a knife rips through me, filling my lungs with fire. Eros is going to die. Eros is going to be executed and it's my fault. I brought him here. I destroyed his home, cut the only ties he had to his people, and dragged him across the sands to this place.

His blood is on my hands. But this time, I won't sit idly by. "We have to release him." I step toward the door, but Serek grabs my arm.

"There's more."

I try to pull out of his grasp, but his grip is strong. "I don't care about anything else—I'm going to release Eros before—"

"He's ordering the immediate execution of every untracked redblood."

The fire within me dies and is replaced with the coldest of winds. "What?" My voice is a breath.

"He said they're more trouble than they're worth. That Safara must be cleaned of their . . . infection."

I can't breathe. "But Serek, that's . . ."

"Genocide. I told him as much, but he wouldn't listen. He's already begun preparations." Serek's hand slips off my arm and he covers his mouth, then stares at the floor.

My legs go numb, so I sit beside him. "He can't just . . . that's tens of thousands of lives!"

"Kora, he can do whatever he wants. There isn't a spirit on Safara that can overrule *ken Sira*."

He's right, of course—everyone answers to *ken Sira*. His word is law. But how could he order something so horrible?

How is it even possible? "And he intends to send his armies across the planet to somehow track them down and slaughter them all?"

"Not an army, *naï*."

"Then?"

He bites his lip. "Nanites. He's programming nanites to target and kill all who share their genetic code and aren't tracked."

Nanites? "Can that even be done? I didn't think they could seek out a genetic code."

"I didn't either, but Roma has assured me it can be done." He frowns and stares out the window. "I'm not the only programmer working for my brother. There are brilliant men and women on the team, and if he believes it possible, then he must have something ready."

Bile rises in the back of my throat. I close my eyes and see the blond boy from the camp. The children playing in the sands. Even the man who left me for dead in the desert.

Entire generations decimated by a force they cannot fight. An invisible killer impossible to avoid.

"When?" I whisper.

"Tomorrow night."

My breath catches in my throat and ice trickles down my spine. "We have to release Eros so he can warn them. It's their only chance."

"Kora, even if he warns them, they can't fight it. And he can't warn his entire species—"

"It doesn't matter—he won't stay here while his people are dying. We'll release him and we'll stop Roma ourselves." Serek hesitates, and I take his hands before he can speak. "You told me once you didn't believe in the unnecessary shedding of blood. I know you don't believe this is right—you know *Kala* would never honor this. It's genocide. It's up to us to save countless lives. No one else will do it, Serek, and no one else can."

Serek takes my hand and squeezes it gently. "Kora, believe me when I say I will do everything in my power to try to stop this. But there's nothing I can do for Eros. Roma suspects us. We've been specifically forbidden from setting foot in the underground for two nights, and Eros will enter Jol's Arena tomorrow morning. We've been ordered to attend."

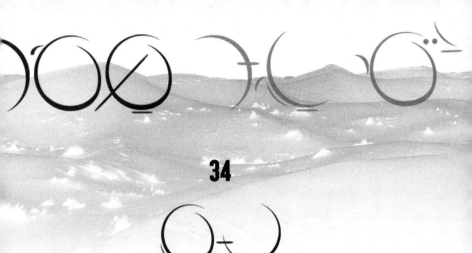

34

Eros

I don't really sleep much, so when the door to my cell opens and six guards in black and gold step inside, I'm already awake. One of them comes forward and pulls me to my feet. I don't bother fighting. They're armed with phasers, whips, and knives, and I'd rather not give them an excuse to use them.

They move into formation around me and lead me through a series of tunnels I don't recognize or waste energy trying to remember. As we move closer to the surface, the eerie silence of the underground is replaced with a distant rumbling, like thunder. The closer we get, the louder the sound, until the walls shake with the ever-present roar.

We stop before a black metal door. I'm not sure what we're waiting for, but the door doesn't open and I'm about to ask what the hold up is when the guard behind me speaks.

"If *Kala* shows you favor and interferes, you will be granted immunity," the guard says. "May he have mercy on your afterdeath."

I snort. I've heard of the Sepharon so-called system of justice. Supposedly, if you're innocent of the accused crime, their god will save you. Evidently he's not the saving type, because I've never heard of anyone surviving the Arena.

The door opens and bright hot light blinds me. Someone gives me a hard shove, and I stumble onto the coarse white sand, straining to regain my balance as we move steadily forward. The door slams shut behind us and the roar of the crowd surrounds me. They're chanting one word, over and over again, and it takes me a mo to pull out what it is.

Then I get it and my stomach twists. They're shouting *ikrat*. Death.

The Arena is enormous—at least half a league across—and the walls trapping me inside are fifteen feet of slick black rock. A curved screen as large as a hovercraft floats high above the wall, and I am on it, walking forward, my hands cuffed behind my back, staring at the screen with guards following me. They've got this whole thing recorded and blown up so everyone can see every last gritty detail. The surrounding stadium is packed, and hovering above the crowd is the dark glass viewing box where Roma undoubtedly sits. Although I can't see the *Sira* hiding behind his tinted glass, I hope he's watching and sees I won't let him defeat me.

I straighten my shoulders and walk confidently forward, toward two large, dark men with arms as thick as my thighs, dressed in nothing but those long black skirts they have all the guards wearing here. The one on the left stands next to a long, crescent-shaped blade attached to a thick, wrapped hilt sticking up straight in the sand. Between the guards is a black stone block.

In a way, I'm relieved. Decapitation isn't so bad—I was kinduv expecting something long and painful, like flesh-eating nanites or shooting out my joints, stabbing me repeatedly, and leaving me to hang by my wrists until I bleed out. But I guess Roma wanted something quick and efficient, so there wouldn't be any chance of escaping.

Knowing how I'm going to die fills me with a surge of energy. I take careful breaths and steady steps and look up at Roma's glass box and smile. I'm going to die today, but I'm not defeated. Not even the ruler of Safara can take that from me.

We step right up to the executioners. They have long black hair tied back into knots and unexpectedly warm orange and green eyes. They must be twins, because they look like copies of each other, but the weird part is they're not glaring at me. They don't even look angry. They just nod at me, and I nod back, then the guards holding my cuffs turn me around and I'm facing the block.

I'm on my knees. This white sand isn't like the soft powder of the deserts I love—it's hard and gritty and digs into my skin. I close my eyes. Inhale deeply. Tilt my face back to the sky and feel the warmth of the suns on my face. The clamor of the crowd fades away, and I imagine Esta and Nol and Day looking down at me, smiling softly, welcoming me home.

The only stars in the sky may be the suns right now, but I know they're with me.

A hand grabs the back of my head and forces it down. The illusion shatters—the crowd is roaring—and I open my eyes in time to see the block and turn my head before they smash my face into it. The hand releases me, but I don't move.

The stone is cool against my cheek. There are grooves in the otherwise smooth surface—scars from where the blade has hit it before. My whole body is shaking and I'm sure I have a couple breaths, maybe less, before the blade comes down on my neck and my blood stains the sand.

Despite the crazed crowd, I make out a hiss. The shift of sand. Someone has lifted the blade and I'm holding on to my last breath. This is it. This is what oxygen tastes like in my lungs, this is how the suns feel on my back.

This is the sweat on my brow, the slamming of my heart, the trickle of cold dread in my gut.

A thousand claps of thunder rock the stadium and the ground trembles beneath me. The shouts of the crowd morph to bloodcurdling screams as thick black smoke swirls into the air, dotting out the suns.

I'm standing. I don't know when I got to my feet but the guards that cuffed me are on their faces, in the sand, and I don't know if they're dead or stunned, but I'm not about to wait around to find out. The smoke is curling closer, a blanket moving in from all sides, and the executioners—where are the executioners? Too late. The smoke overwhelms me and everything is gray.

My eyes burn and fill with tears, but my hands are still cuffed and I have no idea how to deactivate the blazing things, so I do the only thing I can—I run.

I run forward, choking on poison and following the sounds of agony, the endless screams and the chaos and crying and it's all too real, it's all too much—

It's like I'm back at camp and everyone is dying and I can't do a blazing thing to help. It's like I'm racing through the smoke with a useless phaser and I'm not fast enough and Day jerks sideways and he's dead.

It's like I'll trip over Nol and Esta any second, like my feet are moving forward and my lungs are choking on smoke, but my mind is trapped in that nightmare and it's happening again and the screaming is making me sick.

A soft breeze clears a patch of smoke ahead of me and I stumble forward, gulping in the clearer air, spitting black from my lungs. Focus. I need to focus and get out while I can. The gray is closing in again, but just ahead is a pile of rubble where the wall used to be, and above that is a landing where the crowd is streaming out into the city, covered in tears and ash and blood.

That's my exit. That's how I escape.

I take one last breath of barely clean air and move forward—something heavy slams into my back. I'm falling—my head cracks against a slab of rubble and the world blacks out for just a breath. There are hands on my arms and someone shoves my face into the sand, but before I can try to fight back, the pressure releases.

I stagger to my feet. Spin around. Multicolored stars dot my vision and everything is smoke and whatever attacked me is gone. Something hits my toe and I jump, but it's just a rounded piece of smooth metal.

Cuffs.

My hands are free.

I have no explanation for what the blazing suns just happened, but I can't stay here. I turn until I can make out the broken bit of wall through the smoke and move quickly. I lean forward to keep my balance as I climb, digging my toes into the broken slabs of rock. It's slow, tedious work—I slip three different times, cut my knees and palms on the sharp rubble, and nearly step on a bloody, fleshy mass that I think was once a hand. But I don't stop until my feet have reached the smooth, cool landing before the first row of burnt, bloody stands, littered with purple-coated chunks of people and body parts.

I slip into the crowd. We run together. No one seems to notice or care that I've escaped—something horrible happened and it doesn't matter if a few minutes ago they were cheering for my head. All everyone can think is to get out, all everyone can think is to find their loved ones.

All I'm thinking is run. Into the suns, into the sands, away from here and alone and run.

I run with the crowd into the tunnel between the stands. I bolt out of the exit and into the crowded city streets, breaking through the mass of panicked people and stopping for no one. I tear through the streets, past gaping merchants and swerving ports, panicked cries trailing behind me. Silver orbs zip over my head and toward the flaming stadium and I don't look back—I zig-zag between people and run as straight as I can manage and pray I'm headed for the open desert.

And then I see it—endless oceans of white sand, just a quarter league away. My lungs are burning and my heart is careening out of control, but if I can just get to the desert, if I can just make it away from this place—

Pain rams into my side and a force like a cannon blast rips me off the ground. My shoulder slams into the polished stone street and I roll several times before sliding to a throbbing stop. Everything hurts like I've been hit by a phaser cannon, but I stumble to my feet.

Something strikes the side of my head and I drop to my knees. A soldier steps around me and shoves a red-ringed phaser in my face. My ear is ringing. My body pulses with pain.

"Don't move," the guard says, and I don't. I gasp for air and spit up black gunk and I don't move.

Then he jerks and his eyes roll to the back of his head as he crumples to the ground in front of me.

Serek yanks me to my feet, throws a black and gold helmet over my head, takes off his shirt and tosses it to me. "Put it on and don't ask questions." There's a sand bike hovering behind him and he pushes me toward it. I stumble—I'm shaking uncontrollably—but I manage to throw on his shirt. I don't bother with the seal on the front and I climb onto his bike.

"What was—" I start, but Serek cuts me off.

"Roma intends to use nanites to target and kill every untracked redblood on the surface of the planet. He will launch the attack at sunset—"

"What?" My heart punches my chest. "He wants to kill . . . everyone?"

"Anyone who shares the redblood genetic code and doesn't have tracking nanites."

A heat fills me, burning through the pain and terror shaking my limbs. "He can't—"

"He can do whatever he wants—he's *ken Sira* and we're wasting time talking about what he can and can't do. He's already set things in motion, and now with this attack on the Arena, he'll be determined more than ever to get it done. We need your help to stop him."

Part of me wants to turn around and find Roma so I can rip him apart myself, but when Serek starts to turn away, I grab his arm. "I can't go with you. I need to warn my people."

He shakes his head. "Eros, warning them won't help—"

"I don't care. I need to be there, I need to—" My voice breaks and I close my eyes and take a breath. Ignore my stinging throat and look at him again. "Roma and his guards are looking for me anyway, so you'll never get anywhere if you take me with you. They might even blame me for whatever voiding happened back there. If I leave the capital, Roma won't have any reason to keep you under watch and you and Kora can do whatever you need to to stop this in secret."

Serek hesitates. "We could disguise you so Roma doesn't get to you."

I snort. "What, with your shirt, bike, and a fancy helmet? Yeah, that's going to be inconspicuous."

He sighs and hands me an empty vial about the length and width of my pinky finger. "That vial is filled with nanites. When they are activated, they will glow, and from there you'll have moments at most."

I rev the engine and nod. "Thank you, Serek."

He grimaces. "Don't thank me until your people are safe."

I slam down the accelerator and race into the desert with the suns bleeding over the sky above me.

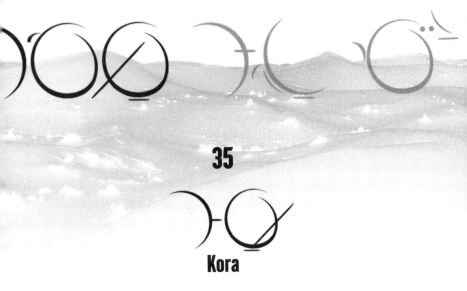

35

Kora

"He's out." Serek closes the door behind him, sits at the desk, and rubs his soot-coated face with his palms. "He insisted on warning his people, like you said he would. If Roma hears that I attacked that guard and helped him escape, he'll have my head."

I want to be relieved at the news, but the explosions at the Arena have left my stomach churning and the echo of screams playing endlessly in my ears. My fingers are shaking as I sit next to him and take his hand. "Even if he hears something, he won't have any proof."

"He doesn't need proof—you saw what happened in the Arena. He could very easily blame us for that atrocity and say we did it to save Eros."

I take a shuddering breath. "Suspicions aren't enough to merit the execution of *ken Sira-kaï*. And he won't want to blame you, he'll want to blame the rebels to bolster support for the nanite attack tonight."

Serek sits back in his seat and nods. "He'd be right, you know. The rebels must have set off those explosives. I can't imagine anyone else would be responsible."

I close my eyes and try to block out the screams and the acrid odor of blood and smoke, but no matter how hard I try, I can't stop seeing the burnt corpses, blood-splattered children, and disembodied limbs. The attack was almost an exact replica of the one that took my parents' lives. But if Eros's people weren't responsible for these attacks, then who was?

I squeeze his hand and release his fingers. "Are you still willing to do this?"

Serek sighs. "Roma's plan will murder more innocents than it will criminals. What happened was horrific, but . . . it doesn't justify such a wide-scale slaughter."

"I agree. But how are we going to stop it?"

He sits back in his seat and shakes his head. "I don't know."

I bite my lip. I hate to admit it, but Roma's plan, if he's truly figured out how to track by genetic code, is genius. The nanites are already in the air, as they have been for well over a generation—they're used to eradicate disease, encourage stronger, faster-growing crops and animals, and even to cause rains during severe droughts and heal soldiers on the battlefield. With the right programming, they can do just about anything.

But they need a source of command.

"All Roma has to do is program them to execute redbloods and send out the order," I say, thinking aloud.

Serek nods. "Correct."

Standing, I step to the window and find it immediately—a gold and glass winding spire reaching far above even the tallest buildings, high into the heavens. The control unit, from which every nanite command originates, known as the Spire.

"We need to get into the Spire and stop them from sending out the order."

He sighs and steps beside me. "It's not that simple."

"How isn't it simple? We have to stop this, Serek, we can't just let them—"

The door slams open behind me and we jump. Serek moves in front of me as Roma enters the room, his eyes livid. He grabs Serek's shirt and slams him into the wall. "Where is he?"

I start toward them, but a guard grabs my arm and yanks me back. My shoulder burns as I stumble into him. I spin around and slap his face. "How dare you?" I hiss. "Release me."

The guard doesn't budge.

"Kora," Serek says firmly. "Relax. I'm sure this is all a misunderstan—"

Roma laughs and releases Serek. "Oh, *sha*. I'm sure this is an enormous misunderstanding, brother. Evidently you misunderstood me when I told you the boy would be arrested and executed and that my order was final. You also seem to have misunderstood that my word is law, and not even you are above it."

Serek arches an eyebrow. "I understand those things perfectly, brother."

"Do you? Then tell me: where is the boy?"

"I'm assuming you mean the half-blood."

Roma takes an impatient breath, then forces a sharp smile. "*Sha*, Serek. The half-blood. Where is he?"

"Far away from here, I would think. Unless your men caught him?"

Roma licks his lips and maintains the twisted smile. "Do you think this a joke?"

"Not at all."

"Then you think me a fool."

"Of course not, brother. You gave an order and I respected it, as I always have. I don't always agree with your decisions, but that doesn't mean I don't honor your word."

Something changes behind Roma's eyes—the anger shifts to something else, something uncertain. His gaze slides to me, then back to Serek, and his smile fades. "One of my men claims to have almost detained him, but someone attacked him from behind and the half-blood escaped."

Serek nods. "As I understand it, he was a trained warrior. Perhaps he defeated your man."

"He insists there was someone else involved."

"After what happened in the Arena, I don't doubt there are some on the streets that might think *Kala* interfered to make way for his escape, thus earning him his freedom. Considering the laws of justice, I'm tempted to agree with them."

Roma scowls. "You mean to tell me that you have no idea where he is, or how he managed to escape?"

"We all saw how he escaped clearly enough. Certainly you don't think me involved in such a horrific attack."

Roma turns away from him and paces back and forth across my room. He twists back to Serek. "My sources say it was an attack from the redbloods, but if I come to learn that either of you were involved in this, I will have you both executed on the spot. Understood?"

"Naturally," Serek says calmly. "I would expect nothing less."

Roma turns away and motions for his guards to follow as he storms out the door. The guard releases me and closes the door behind him.

And leaves us in silence.

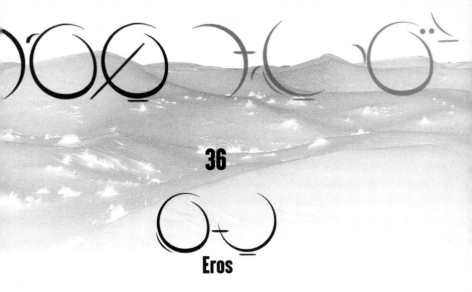

36

Eros

I cross the sands at full speed. The white ground turns pink and powdery, then blood red as I race across the deserts. Without a helmet, I would never be able to travel this quickly—the sands kicked up by the thrusters below the bike would blind me. But with the visor over my face and a computerized system outlining the land in front of me, I could move at full speed through a sandstorm. And if I want to reach camp before nightfall, I'll need to maintain this pace all day.

The suns rise above me and heat pours over my shoulders and back, soaking my skin, shirt, and pants in sweat. The kicked-up sand coats me like an extra layer, turning my skin red and creating sickly crimson trails down my arms. I monitor the directional units tracking my position and the distance I've traveled in the corner of the visor. In most circumstances, I'd abandon the helmet to avoid being traced, but keeping the location of the camp a secret isn't a priority anymore.

It doesn't matter whether they know where the humans are. The nanites will find them without directions.

I still don't know how we're going to fight them. I don't know if we can. I don't know if it's even possible. But I have to do something. I have to believe that someone might have an idea, that somehow we'll pull something together and survive the attack.

Bram—the man I watched shot down along with his wife and son the night of the raid—would have thought of something. He always had the craziest ideas Gray called "fucken miracles"—without his insight, we never would have developed the coms or hacked the locked phasers stolen from soldiers. He would have known what to do. Not that he can help us now.

By the time I near the location, the suns are descending in the sky and it's far too near sunset. If I blast through the security border like this, I'll definitely be shot at, but even if I slow down and trace the symbol of surrender on my chest, I'll be shot at anyway. At least speeding on a bike, I stand a chance of outmaneuvering them and, with any luck, making them miss.

When I'm twenty leagues from the boundary, I begin to swerve left and right. I twist through the sand without a pattern—a long left, a short right, another sharp right, then left. It slows me down, but it also makes it much more difficult for snipers to land a shot, and I'll be of no use if I get shot. For the first hundred leagues past the boundary, I move without incident. Maybe I'm wasting my time. Gray did mention they'd lost most of their guard—what if I'm nowhere near one of the posts?

Then a flash of hot red light races past my shoulder and I swerve faster. Five hundred leagues from camp and the shots increase, racing past my skin, several times way too close for comfort. I move more erratically, speed up and slow down, all the while moving toward camp.

Then I crest the final dune and face a line of soldiers, armed with long- and short-range phasers. They don't hesitate—a wall of red and white lights races toward me and I slam the bike down into the sand. I skid several hundred feet and my left side burns. I release the bike—it crashes into a couple soldiers too slow to get out of the way, knocking them over—and I jump to my feet, rip off my helmet, and throw my hands up. "Wait!"

Miraculously, no one shoots me.

Sweat and sand cover every inch of my exposed skin. The knocked-over soldiers stand, glaring at me and raising their phasers. I turn to the closest soldier and nod to the com placed in his ear. "My name is Eros. Gray will tell you to shoot me, but I need to speak with him now. The Sepharon are launching a nanite attack that will kill every one of you at sunset. I need to speak with him."

The soldier hesitates and presses his hand to his ear. An amateur mistake, but someone is speaking to him and that's all the news I need. It has to be Gray.

I just hope he doesn't order my execution without hearing me out.

The soldier pulls the silver com out of his ear and tosses it in the sand at my feet. "Put it on."

I pick up the blinking earpiece and shove it into place.

"You've got a lot of nerf, you know that?" Gray's voice says in my ear. "I don't know how you found us, but give me one good reason I shouldn't order them to shoot you right now."

"I already gave you a reason. Do you want to die tonight?"

"I don't know that you're telling the truth. As far as I'm concerned, this could all be some hodgeshit to trick me into letting you into camp again."

I roll my eyes. "Why would I bother breaking into camp when I know you and everyone else wants me dead?"

"Blazing Void if I know. Revenge. Maybe you've got yourself hooked up with bombs. Maybe letting you in will be the reason people die tonight."

"I'll strip down naked to prove I'm clean if I have to, Gray, but you have to let me in."

Gray makes a noise like choking on something disgusting. "I swear to the suns, kid, if you start stripping I'll come out there and shoot you myself."

I restrain a smile. "So you'll let me in?"

"You have five moments to convince me not to shoot you, starting the mo you enter my quarters."

"Thank you."

"Don't thank me. You better have a helluva speech ready."

The camp falls quiet as I enter the borders. Whispers and glances surround me as I search their faces for ones I recognize. Ones I care about.

I don't blame them for staring—I was an anomaly to begin with, and now I'm back with gold eyes, wearing a shirt off the High Prince's back. I'm covered in sweat and sand, with my hands cuffed behind my back, phasers pressed to my spine, and an escort of men that I helped train. I would stare, too, if I were one of them.

"Uncle Eros!" Something tiny slips between the guards and slams against my leg. Aren looks up at me, his eyes glinting between strands of sweaty blond hair with a grin wider than a crescent moon. "You're back! I told Mal you would come back, but he said you got taken away and you were in the desert and not allowed to come back, but I told him—"

I crouch in front of him and he wraps his arms around my neck, hugging me tightly. I wish I could hug him, but I settle for leaning my head against his, then sitting back on my heels and grinning right back at him. "I missed you, little guy."

"I know." He smiles and buries his face in the sweaty crook of my neck. "Don't go away again, okay? A lot of people went away and everyone was crying. Daddy went away, too, and Gamma and Gampa."

I wince and glance at Gray's tent with the white Le crest sewn onto it and guards standing outside his station, just fifteen feet away. "Aren, buddy, I need you to go find your mom, okay?"

He looks up at me with wide blue eyes. The tears glistening in his gaze are a kick to the stomach. "I don't want you to go away," he whispers.

I sigh. "I know, I don't want to go away either. But Mal's right; I'm not allowed here anymore. I'm just visiting, and then I have to go."

He starts crying. Stars and suns, this kid. I hate seeing kids cry.

"Will you visit again?" he croaks.

I want to say yes. I want to say yes in the worst way, just to see him smile. Just to make him happy, if only for a few more minutes.

But I can't promise him something that'll never happen. I won't do that to him.

"Half-blood," a guard says, nodding to the sky. "You're out of time."

He's right. The suns are moments away from setting. I slip out of Aren's grip and kiss the top of his head. "I love you, buddy. Don't ever forget that. But I gotta go now, and I won't be allowed to come back anymore, so you be good and take care of your mom and siblings, okay?"

Aren rubs his eyes with the back of his hand. Sniffles. "Okay."

I start to stand, but he grabs my arm and shows me a twine bracelet. "Nia made me make it. It's a protection bracelet, so nothing bad can happen to you when you wear it. I made it for when Daddy comes back, but I want you to have it."

"Aren—"

"Keep it? Please?" His lips tremble and he blinks several times and stares at me with those eyes, which are way too big for his head, and I can't say no. Not to him.

I sigh and twist around to show him my hands. "You'll have to put it on for me."

"Okay," he whispers, and his little fingers work the bracelet onto my wrist. It's tight as it slips over my hand, but once it's on my wrist, it fits okay. "I'll never take it off." I stand and face Gray's tent. "Be good, buddy."

Someone nudges my back with a warm phaser and we step inside. Gray's tent is the largest in the compound, but it's clear they haven't been here very long because he doesn't have much set up. A simple bedroll, a pile of bags, and several cases of weapons lined up in the sand. That's it.

"Took you long enough." Gray steps toward me. "Now let's hear it. Doer die."

And so I tell him everything Serek told me. It doesn't take long—the plan isn't that complicated. With a few lines of code and the flip of a button, millions of people will die.

Gray is silent for a full mo after I finish. His face is pale and his fingers are slack. Finally, he turns to a guard standing by the exit. "Uncuff him."

The guard steps behind me and removes the cuffs as Gray pinches the bridge of his nose. "You're sure about this?"

I nod and dig through my pocket. Hold up the tube Serek gave me. "I've been told this will glow when the order is executed."

"That's not helpful."

I grimace. "I know."

"You're sure it's nanites? You're absolutely positive."

"I believe Serek. He'd have no reason to lie to me—at least, not about this."

Gray scowls. Runs his hand over his lips. Glares at the ceiling. "We can't fight nanites."

No one answers. There's nothing to say, because he's right—we don't have a single defense against nanites. How can you fight something you can't see? Something so small that a single breath of air could transport hundreds of thousands into your lungs? It'd be like trying to fight your own cells or the oxygen in your blood.

Impossible.

"I don't know why you bothered even coming here to tell us," Gray says. "There's literally nothing we can do."

I sigh. "I was hoping maybe someone here would have an idea. And I wasn't going to stay there while you . . ." I can't say it. I won't say it. I take a breath and start over. "I figured a warning was better than nothing."

"I don't know about that." Gray turns and crosses his arms. "As the old ones would say—ignorances blessed."

I clench the vial in my hand. Stare at the sand.

Gray faces me again. "What happened to your eyes?"

I look up. "What?"

"Your eyes. They used to be green, but now they're gold." He squints at me. "What, you get some bizarre alien eye infection or something?"

"No. There were nanites in my system that made my eyes look green, but when they injected me with tracking nanites, they interfered with the ones already in my body and nearly killed me."

He frowns. "Why? What's your eye color matter?"

I shift. The truth isn't going to help me right now, and it's a long story we don't have time for anyway. So I say, "It doesn't."

Gray paces back and forth, his hands clasped behind his back. "But you got them out of your system."

I hesitate. I might know where he's going with this, but the answer isn't going to be what we need. "With help."

"How?"

"I'm not sure. A doctor was in charge—she said something about cleansing my system. Some kinduv filter or transfusion or something. I don't know."

"And I don't suppose they were kind enough to provide you with one of those filter things when they sent you over here."

I bite my lip. Shake my head.

"Of course not." He stops and faces me. "Step back a mo—you said they *nearly* killed you."

"Right. But the doctor stopped it before it caused permanent damage."

"With the machine?"

I start to say yes, but then I think back to the incident. I wasn't really coherent for most of it—all I remember is pain and blackness, but there was something else Kora said, after the fact. Something about the doctor shooting me . . .

My breath catches. "The phasers."

Gray arches an eyebrow. "Phasers?"

"Kora said the doctor stunned me to short out the nanites, then used the filter to clean them out of my system afterward. But they were shut down first."

"With the phaser," Gray says.

A burst of energy rushes through me, quickening my pulse. The phasers—how didn't I think of it before? "She stunned me, which shorted out the nanites. I think."

"You think? This is a little important—"

"I was barely conscious when it happened, so no, I'm not sure. But that's what Kora told me."

Gray hesitates. Turns to his men. "Spread word to everyone with a phaser to set them to stun. Anyone who shows symptoms of—" Gray gasps and drops to his knees, clutching his skull. Screams slice through the air as the soldiers drop, one by one—some immediately and others writhing in the sand, clutching their heads.

The vial in my hand grows hot and glows red.

It's too late.

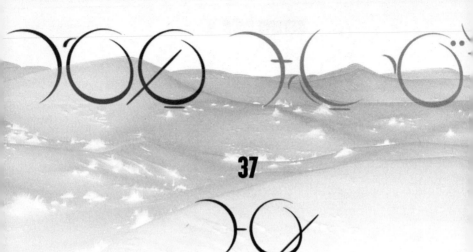

37

Kora

As soon as the door shuts behind Roma, Serek leaps to the desk and grabs the rectangular glass sitting beside the medical unit, his fingers dancing across the screen. I step beside him and peer over his shoulder. He's writing *some*thing, but the words are cut off and mixed with symbols and numbers and the text is flying across the screen so rapidly it's a wonder he can read it at all.

"What is that?" I ask.

"I'm writing a program to shut down the nanites. It might take some time—I'll need to write a stable enough entry point to get through the security checks installed—but I know it's possible."

Evidently, those rumors about Serek's technical prowess were true. "How do you know how to get through the security?"

He stops typing and glances up. His eyes are soft and sad when he says, "I wrote the security program. I'll be able to get in, but rendering the nanites useless is an entirely different battle—one that we won't be able to test."

I nod. "Is there anything I can do to help?"

He hesitates. "It will be faster if I do this on my own . . . but it might be a good idea to listen by the door for any further unexpected interruptions."

"That I can do."

He smiles grimly, nods once, and resumes his work on the screen.

I'm not sure how long we stay there, with Serek typing manically through the code while I lean against the door and listen for any potential interruptions—but the hall beyond the room is silent. The few times he pauses, his fingers twitch, as if eager to continue their work. My body hums with an eagerness to move, to do something, anything, but without Serek's code, there's nothing we can do. I close my eyes and pray for Eros. I can only hope he reached his people and figured out some sort of way to defend against the impossible.

When I open my eyes, Serek's vial is glowing bright red, and a strange silence has fallen over the grounds. It's as if the air itself knows what is happening—as if the whole planet is mourning this atrocious act.

And then the howling begins.

At first it sounds like a low whistle, or a groan carried on a breeze. I step toward the open window and a chill washes over me as the sound grows, building in intensity like a woman's cries during a birthing. Serek looks up from the screen, his body rigid and his eyes wide.

"Is that . . .?" he whispers.

"Screaming," I say. "From the city."

It's the most haunting sound I've ever heard—the echo of a cry, repeated and layered over and over again. Pain I cannot imagine, the horror of watching your loved ones die before your very eyes. I didn't realize there were untracked redbloods in Asheron, but the sound of anguish is unmistakable.

I spin away from the window and step beside him. "We have to go. Now."

He pulls a flat disc the size of my thumbnail out of his pocket and places it on the screen. A blue line slowly traces the edge of the disc, then finally, when it makes a full circle, Serek picks it up, slides it into his pocket, and passes me a phaser.

We don't waste time with words.

He shoves open the door and we race through the hallway, down the steps, and into the screaming outside air. The Spire towers over the center of the complex, a circle of guards spaced evenly around its base. We race toward them without a plan, without anything but instinct and the push of agonized voices carried in the wind.

The soldiers notice us when we're two hundred paces away. Out of the eight standing guard, two lift their phasers, but others are hesitant—they can't very well shoot *ken Sira-kaï* and his betrothed, can they?

Serek shoots first—firing a burst of five shots, three of which hit their mark as the remaining guards dive out of the way. I take down two others and don't stop running until we're on top of the soldiers. A guard levels his phaser at Serek and screams "Stop!"—I shoot him in the chest with a white burst just as someone tackles me from behind. We hit the sand hard, the brunt of the impact on my forearms. Two high-pitched whines cut through the air and the guard on my back slumps over. His weight slides off me moments later as Serek helps me up.

"Are you all right?"

"I'm fine." I nod to the heavy metal door in the sparkling gold tower just three measures away. "Let's go."

Serek presses his palm into the door and a blue light flashes above it before sliding open. I glance down at the men at my feet—they're breathing, but unconscious. Serek set the phasers to stun.

"C'mon," he says, and we slip inside.

Two guards stand by the door, apparently in mid-conversation as they break off and stare at us. Serek stuns them both without hesitation and drags one of the unconscious men to the door. He scans the guard's hand, then his own. Two flashes of blue light, and that door opens as well.

Stairwell. A tall, curving set of stairs with seemingly no end, spiraling to the very top. I don't have to ask Serek what level we need to get to—the control unit is on the top floor.

We start climbing.

38

Eros

I stun Gray first, then fire off bursts at the guards still moving in the sand. The ones who have fallen still I can only assume are dead, and I don't have time to check. I duck out of the tent and start shooting anything that moves. The screams are awful—grating on my ears and heart and stomach. There are too many who have already fallen still in the sand, too many that are too late to save.

And as far as I can tell, I'm the only one left unaffected.

I can't save everyone. The realization pulls me lower with every shot, stings my eyes and twists my gut. People are dying around me and I'm stunning as swiftly as I can, running as fast as my legs will take me, trying to find those still with fight left in their bodies. But it's not enough. With every person I stun, two fall and stop breathing.

I need to find Aren, Jessa, Mal, and Nia. I need to find what's left of my family and save them before it's too late.

I race toward their tent, stunning everyone I see on the way, praying it's not too late, blinking the sweat from my eyes and ignoring the burning in my lungs and legs and twisting through the rows of tents to reach the outskirts, where Jessa will be with the kids. There are too many bodies. Too many children who have fallen in mid-stride, too many mothers forever holding their babies in the sand. There isn't any blood. The dead almost appear to be sleeping, but they're too still for that. They're empty shells of their former selves.

The tent with the Kit family crest is a hundred paces away, placed at the edge of camp. Cries and screams surround me and I can't tell if it's coming from the tent. I stun a teenager dressed in army fatigues and his little sister. A mother and her child. Three girls, scarcely breathing.

Something heavy and cold weighs on my gut. Even set to stun, the pulses have been known to cause heart attacks—how many am I killing with the stunning blow? But I can't think about that. Not now.

I duck into Jessa's tent. There's crying here, but only one of them is moving. They're huddled in the center of the tent, Jessa holding the children, a hand over her swollen stomach. Aren, Nia, and Jessa are perfectly still, perfectly silent. Mal is whimpering in his mother's arms, still holding Aren close to his chest. Mal's eyes are squeezed closed and his face is streaked with tears.

I pull the trigger. My eyes sting and I'm going to be sick. I can barely breathe but there are still cries out in the sand. There are more I can save.

But it will never be enough.

39

Kora

Serek bursts through the door and stuns the four men at the controls. They drop like sacks of muscle and bone. Roma is nowhere to be seen.

Serek drops the phaser and races to the controls, typing frantically through the low hum of the running computers. Tears stream down his cheeks as he inputs commands I don't understand, then places the disc on the screen. His fingers fly across the surface of the computer and finally he slams his hand over the screen and silence falls. He stands, gasping for air, shaking from head to toe, staring out at the overlook.

"Did it work?" I ask. "Is it off?"

"I've disabled all functioning nanites," he whispers. "Permanently."

Cool air blows through me. "All of them?"

"I didn't have time to finish a differentiating program, Kora. A mass kill command was the only option."

This doesn't feel like a victory. People's lives, fields of crops, doctors and the domesticization of animals like *kazim*—not to mention the foundation of Safara's technological advancements—all depend on nanites. This solution will cause a host of chaos on its own.

I step beside him and look out over the clusters of buildings, over a city that has fallen eerily still. "How many do you think are dead?"

He shakes his head. "Impossible to say until the coming sets."

I step next to him and he slides his fingers between mine, then squeezes my hand. "I hope Eros's family is okay."

He sighs. "Eros—"

The door crashes open behind us. We spin around and Roma takes two long strides, raises a large, gleaming black cylinder with a glowing red barrel strapped across his shoulder, and squeezes the thick trigger. Something hot splatters on my face and Serek gasps, stumbles back a couple steps, and sinks to the ground. But he isn't stunned.

There's a hole in his chest the size of a fist. Roma isn't holding an ordinary phaser—it's a cannon. I start toward him, but Roma releases the cannon, letting it hang off his shoulder, grabs my throat, and shoves me against the wall. "I told you I would have your head for this," he hisses. He glances at Serek, bleeding and gasping on the floor, and for a moment his face softens. "I warned you not to get in the way."

Roma turns back to me and his eyes harden. He squeezes my neck and stars dot my vision. But I am not helpless yet.

I grab the knife in my belt and ram it into the crook of his elbow. He screams and his fingers slip—I rip the knife out of his arm and crash into him. He shoots, but it bursts into the floor. The knife is slick and warm in my hand and I bring it down over his heart with a scream. Roma catches my wrist with his uninjured arm before the blade reaches him, shaking with effort. I push down with all of my weight, but it's not enough—he's much stronger than anyone I've ever sparred with.

He twists my wrist hard and the knife clatters from my hand. Pain shoots up my arm, but I ignore it and lunge for the knife with my free arm. He yanks me back and my shoulder burns as my head slams into the ground.

Roma is on top of me, pinning my arms to the metal floor, blood dripping out of his arm and onto my chest. He laughs, and with the blood on his face and the wideness of his eyes, he looks crazed. Maybe he is. "Very good," he says. "You know how to defend yourself. How refreshing."

I spit at him and he presses down on my flaming wrist. Pain burns through my arm and a cloud of darkness floods my eyes. I stop struggling and let the tears fall. Blinking back the darkness, I stare up at him. "*Kala* will never honor this. You'll spend your afterdeath in the Void."

"You think so, do you?" Roma smiles. He knows he's won, and now he'll take his time enjoying his victory. "I suppose you'll find out before I do. Now, where's that knife, hmm?"

"Please," I whisper. He laughs and reaches for the knife, looking away for just a moment.

But a moment is all I need.

I strike his groin with my knee and twist hard, throwing him off me. Rolling on top of him, I stab my fingers into the soft spot at the base of his throat, then slam my hands over his ears, poke his eyes, and lunge. The knife is out of my reach, but his phaser cannon isn't. He's too busy blinking away tears and fighting off the onslaught of pain to see me grab it. Which is a shame, because I would have liked to see his face when he realized he lost.

I smash the barrel of the cannon against his temple, and he slumps, still.

Climbing off him, I race over to Serek. With the adrenaline fading from my veins, the pain in my wrist is unbearable, but I ignore it until I reach him.

My heart sinks as I crouch next to him. His face is pale and drenched in sweat, and he's bleeding out far too quickly. I rip off a portion of my shirt and tie it around his chest. The cannon hit him close to his abdomen, and while it doesn't seem to have sliced all the way through, he must have damaged organs. He needs a doctor immediately.

Serek hands me a syringe with a glowing blue vial inserted in the tube. "Inject this into Roma," he rasps. "Hurry."

I take the syringe with shivering fingers and move back to Roma, inserting it into his arm. Serek nods his approval, so I press the plunger and hurry back to his side. "What was that?"

"The last of the live nanites," he whispers. "It'll keep him comatose indefinitely."

My stomach sinks. "Nanites? But you could have programmed those to heal—"

"We don't have time. It's done. There's a broadcasting unit in the cabinet on the left wall. I need you to get a guide and begin streaming. I can tell you how, but you must hurry."

"Serek, you need a doc—"

"Do this. Now." Despite the pain he must be experiencing, his eyes are fierce. I can't waste time, not now. I rush to the cabinet and rip it open. There are rows of identical mirror-like orb-guides about the size of my fist. I grab the nearest one and run back to Serek. Crouching next to him, I tap twice on the orb-guide, waking it, then open my hand, releasing it. It bobs in the air just above my palm several times, then steadies and spins slowly in the air.

"Do you require assistance?" it chirps.

I look at Serek. "Now what?"

"Help me to the control panel. I'll activate it and you'll do the rest."

I slide my arms under his and pull him as gently as possible toward the panel. Sharp pain rips up my arm, but I grit my teeth and ignore it. Serek groans and pushes with his legs to help the best he can, then finally shouts "Enough!" and reaches for the screen. He presses his bloody hand over the panel until the screen lights up.

"You are in need of medical assistance," the orb says, whizzing over Serek's head. "Shall I call for a medic?"

"*Naï*," Serek gasps. He closes his eyes and shudders, squeezing my hand. "Touch *voice activation*."

I find the icon and press it.

"Command?" a computerized voice says.

"Inter-territory streaming," Serek says. "Immediate emergency override. Begin."

"Record from nearest guide?" the computer asks.

Serek nods at me and I release his hand and step away. "*Sha,*" he says. "Begin."

The computer makes three long beeps, then the guide spins quickly, bobs at eye-level in front of Serek, then says, "Streaming live."

Serek trembles and looks at the guide. "People of Safara, this is *Sira-kaï* Serek d'Asheron. My brother Roma, the former *Sira*, has committed an atrocious act, ending countless lives. As such, I have acted as I must and removed him from his position." Serek closes his eyes, inhales deeply, and opens them again. "I have been fatally injured by the former ruler, and as such will be unable to take his place on the throne. But there is a man with royalty in his veins, a man whose birthright outweighs Roma's."

My hand clasps over my mouth, stifling a gasp as tears spring to my eyes.

Serek takes a shaky breath and looks at the camera again. "His name is Eros, and he is the firstborn son of former *Sira* Asha. His genetics have been tested, and I personally verified his birthright to the throne is legitimate. He is a half-blood with golden eyes, somewhere in the desert, and he is the only rightful heir to the throne."

Serek gasps and grimaces, then opens his eyes again and shivers. "Eros, please return to Asheron. The territories—and your people—need you." He nods at me and I tap the guide twice, turning it off and catching it as it drops to the floor.

Serek closes his eyes and slides lower to the ground. I put the guide down and kneel beside him. My fingers find his and Serek struggles to open his eyes. He smiles ever so softly, and when he touches my cheek, his fingers are a light breeze. My chest aches and everything slows—I take his hand and press it against my tear-stained cheek and every breath is an eternity.

Blood dribbles from his lips and he watches me with smiling eyes. His pain is a heavy blanket smothering my lungs. I'm choking on tears, trying to smile, holding his hands as he struggles to breathe. I want to call for help, I want to get him the best emergency care possible, but there's nothing to be done. Serek destroyed the nanites and our best medical care with it. He used the last of the functioning nanites to keep his monster of a brother comatose, rather than killing him like he deserves and using them to heal.

Serek, who refuses violence even in his final moments, even if it means an untimely death. And there's nothing I can do but hold his hand and wait.

My vision blurs and I blink the hot tears away—I don't want to miss a moment, not one breath of the beautiful peace smoothing over the pain in his face. His fingers gently stroke my cheek and he doesn't say it, he doesn't say anything more, but I see it in his eyes, more powerful than any words could ever express.

"I love you too," I whisper.

Serek's eyes flutter closed. He sighs, and all at once, becomes perfectly still.

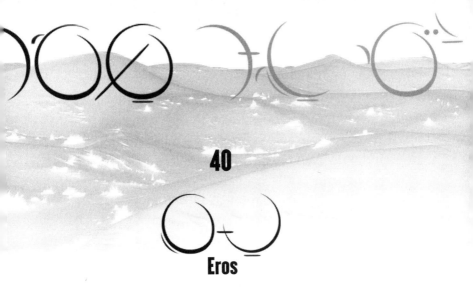

40

Eros

The screaming stops like the flip of a switch. Like *Kala* pressed the mute button on the world, or maybe I've gone deaf, maybe I've heard too much.

The camp is horrifically still. I sink into the sand, surrounded by the unconscious and dead, sweat on my back and tears in my eyes. The suns are low in the sky, painting the dusk with deep shades of blood red and purple, and not even a breeze disturbs the perfect, chilling quiet. This is a gravesite. A battlefield, with only casualties and not a single victor.

I don't know how long I stay there, kneeling in the sand and shivering in the silence. Eventually, my legs move and I find myself in Jessa's tent again. I check pulses even though I know what I'll find. Only Mal's heart is still beating.

I carefully lift Aren from his arms. Holding his tiny body sends a pain through my center like I've never experienced. He's too still, and he'll never wake. I'll never see him smile again and it fills me with an empty rage that blinds me with a sickly black tar spreading through my veins like acid. I scream to the sky, to the suns, to this unfair and cruel place, this life that has allowed me to live and stolen the air from the purest life I know. Why? How could anyone even try to justify this? How could anyone end a life—countless lives— with the press of a button?

I wrap Aren in silks from Jessa's pack and place him in the sand. I do the same for Nia, then Jessa herself, careful to cover her permanently swollen stomach. When they're fully wrapped, I pick Mal up and duck out of the tent.

I won't have him waking next to his dead family.

Some are stirring around me as I step through camp. A few are already awake and watch me with wide eyes as I walk. I don't know if they heard me scream, I don't know why they look at me with something like wonder. Whispers slip around me, and still I keep walking. I don't know where I'm going. I don't know where I can put Mal that'll allow him to wake without the horror of death around him.

Death is everywhere.

"Eros."

I don't stop at the sound of my name. I don't care what Gray has to say to me.

"Eros, wait." He takes my shoulder and I shrug out of his grip. But I stop walking. My shoulders burn from carrying Mal—I'm exhausted in every sense of the word—but nothing compares to the agony inside me.

Gray steps in front of me and hands me a com. "You should listen to this."

I can't believe him. After everything that's happened, after all this death, after the silence and the screams, he's giving me a blazing com to listen to?

"It's important," he says, and something about his gaze stops me. It's the way the others are looking at me. With a sortuv respect and gratitude that doesn't make sense. I shift Mal's weight onto my left arm and slide the com into place.

Serek's voice comes over the speaker. ". . . and he is the only rightful heir to the throne. . . . Eros, please return to Asheron. The territories—and your people—need you." A pause, then the message begins again. "People of Safara, this is *Sira-kaï* Serek d'Asheron . . ."

And then something happens that I can't explain. Something I don't want, something I don't need, something I don't deserve.

Gray drops to one knee and bows his head. "Thank you," he whispers. "You saved our lives."

Murmurs of agreement ripple around me, and one by one, all who are awake follow his lead and kneel in the sand.

"Uncle Eros?" Mal whispers. "Why are you crying? Why is everyone bowing?"

But I don't answer. My voice is caught in my throat, and I can never reconcile what's happening here today or Serek's words playing endlessly in my ear.

The territories—and your people—need you.

Acknowledgments

For years, I've loved reading the acknowledgments at the back of my favorite books, both because it shows how much work goes into publishing a novel, and because I'd imagine writing my own. Now I get to.

First thanks go to the Big Guy upstairs, as Gray would say. While I never imagined it'd take me a decade to get here, You put this dream in my heart to begin with. I couldn't be happier.

All the squishy hugs, cuddles, and gratitude to Astasia, who's been my supporter and #1 bestie for longer than she hasn't and was there when the very first version of Eros and the Sepharon were imagined. I'm glad I hogged you in second grade.

So much gratitude will forever go to my amazing agent, Louise Fury, and to Rachel Brooks, both of whom believed in my weird alien book first. Your unfailing enthusiasm has literally changed my life.

Stars, hugs, and high-fives to my lovely editor, Nicole Frail, with your helpful, warm, fuzzy-making, and hashtag genius-making A+ notes (#TeamEros!). And a big thank-you to the rest of the Sky Pony team, especially Sarah Brody for the gorgeous cover I still can't stop looking at, Kerri Frail for that perfectly amazing map, and Joshua Barnaby for making my nerdiest dreams come true with that incredibly awesome interior design.

Beyond the Red's fabulous CP team, Laura, Caitlin, and others: you guys saw *Red* first and your insights and encouragement were instrumental in how it developed. Extra-special shout out to Laura, who came up with the title that was later tweaked into *Beyond the Red,* and to Team Fury, whose editorial notes never fail to inspire.

To Vicki and Kate, my lovely CP/support team, you may not have read the early drafts, but I hope you both know you've helped me grow so much as a writer. *Red* wouldn't be here without you two, either.

To my freshman year English teacher who helped me write my first ever query letter: that book wasn't meant to be, but you helped me get here first. And to Mr. C, I kept those notes tacked onto my final senior AP Lit project for years and looked to them for encouragement more times than I can count. Thank you.

Hugs to my mom, for never saying wanting to be an author is a ridiculous dream, to Richard, for always enthusiastically asking about book news, even when you don't entirely know what it means, and Cristina, for being the first to listen to many of my stories, *Red* included, even though you fell asleep half the time.

To my Twitter lovelies and friends who are too many to name, but mean so very much to me—I can't thank you enough for the DMs, emails, hugs, and unwavering support. To Team Rogue YA, the Sweet Sixteeners, enthusiastic book bloggers, and the Community of Awesome, thank you all for reminding me how blazing amazing the bookish community can be.

And finally, to you, reading this book. You guys make my dream possible every day. Thank you, thank you. Your kind words will stay with me wherever the stars reach.

Glossary/Pronunciation Guide

Note: /r/ is rolled (similar to a Spanish /r/) and /j/ is closer to an English /y/.

a/al (ah/ahl): the (places, objects, etc.)

alaja (ah-LAH-yah) and nejdo (NEY-doh): stringed instruments

Avrae/Sirae (AH-vray/SEE-ray): plural forms of Avra and Sira

el/ol Avra (el/ohl AH-vrah): my/your majesty; Avrae are rulers of the eight territories

azuka (AH-zoo-kah): a powerful drink, somewhat equivalent to alcohol

el ljma si . . .(el LYEH-mah see): my name is . . .

ikrat (EE-kraht): death

kaï (KAH-ee): prince

Kala (kah-lah): God

kazim (KAH-zeem): wildcat

ken (kehn): the (people and living beings)

kjo/sjo (kyoh/syoh): plural forms of kaï and saï

ko (koh): a ruler's spouse; ranks directly under the ruler

lijarae (lee-YAH-ray): umbrella term equivalent to LGBTQUIAP+ people

ljuma (LYOO-mah): a tangy fruit

naïjera (nah-EE-yeh-rah): relax

naï (NAH-ee): no

orenjo (oh-REN-yoh): honor that is earned

[City] **ora'jeve**: (oh-RAH-yeh-veh): [City] greets you (all)—the equivalent to "Welcome to [city]."

or'jiva (ohr-YEE-vah): greetings (to one person)

saï (SAH-ee): princess

Safara (SAH-fah-rah): the planet the Sepharon and nomads live on; in a separate solar system from Earth

Sephari (SEH-fah-ree, as pronounced by Sepharon; SEH-fur-ee, as pronounced by nomads): the language all Sepharon speak

Sepharon (SEH-fah-rohn, as pronounced by Sepharon; SEH-fur-on, as pronounced by nomads): the native species of Safara

sha (shah): yes

shi (SHEE): instruments of fire dancing, occasionally used as weapons

(sun)sets: equivalent to a day

el/ol Sira (el/ohl SEE-rah): my/your high majesty; the Sira is the high ruler who all Avrae must submit to

term: month (50 sets)

ulae (OO-lay): a traditional uniform worn by Ona's military men since before the Great War

ve (veh): sir

zeïli (zeh-EE-lee): a leaf that's dried and smoked for a relaxing and mood-boosting effect

31901059283079